John Bowring

A Visit To the Philippine Islands

outlook

John Bowring

A Visit To the Philippine Islands

1st Edition | ISBN: 978-3-75234-225-3

Place of Publication: Frankfurt am Main, Germany

Year of Publication: 2020

Outlook Verlag GmbH, Germany.

A VISIT

TO

THE PHILIPPINE ISLANDS.

BY

SIR JOHN BOWRING

PREFACE.

The Philippine Islands are but imperfectly known. Though my visit was a short one, I enjoyed many advantages, from immediate and constant intercourse with the various authorities and the most friendly reception by the natives of every class.

The information I sought was invariably communicated with courtesy and readiness; and by this publication something will, I hope, be contributed to the store of useful knowledge.

The mighty "tide of tendency" is giving more and more importance to the Oriental world. Its resources, as they become better known, will be more rapidly developed. They are promising fields, which will encourage and reward adventure; inviting receptacles for the superfluities of European wealth, activity, and intelligence, whose streams will flow back upon their sources with ever-augmenting contributions. Commerce will complete the work in peace and prosperity, which conquest began in perturbation and peril. Whatever clouds may hang over portions of the globe, there is a brighter dawning, a wider sunrise, over the whole; and the flights of time, and the explorings of space, are alike helping the "infinite progression" of good.

    J. B.

CHAPTER I.

MANILA AND NEIGHBOURHOOD.

Three hundred and forty years ago, the Portuguese navigator Fernando de Magalhães, more generally known by his Spanish designation Magellanes, proposed to Carlos I. an expedition of discovery in the Eastern seas. The conditions of the contract were signed at Zaragoza, and, with a fleet of six vessels, the largest of which was only 130 tons burden, and the whole number of the crews two hundred and thirty-four men, Magalhães passed the straits which bear his name in November, 1520; in the middle of March of the following year he discovered the Mariana Islands, and a few days afterwards landed on the eastern coast of the island of Mindanao, where he was well received by the native population. He afterwards visited the island of Zebu, where, notwithstanding a menaced resistance from more than two thousand armed men, he succeeded in conciliating the king and his court, who were not only baptized into the Catholic faith, but recognised the supreme sovereignty of the crown of Spain, and took the oaths of subjection and vassalage. The king being engaged in hostilities with his neighbours, Magalhães took part therein, and died in Mactan, on the 26th April, 1521, in consequence of the wounds he received. This disaster was followed by the murder of all the leading persons of the expedition, who, being invited to a feast by their new ally, were treacherously assassinated. Guillen de Porceleto alone escaped of the twenty-six guests who formed the company. Three of the fleet had been lost before they reached the Philippines; one only returned to Spain—the *Vitoria*—the first that had ever made the voyage round the world, and the Spanish king conferred on her commander, Elcano, a Biscayan, an escutcheon bearing a globe, with the inscription, "Primus circumdedit me." A second expedition, also composed of six vessels and a trader, left Spain in 1524. The whole fleet miserably perished in storms and contests with the Portuguese in the Moluccas, and the trader alone returned to the Spanish possessions in New Spain.

About one hundred and twenty of the expedition landed in Tidore, where they built themselves a fortress, and were relieved by a third fleet sent by Hernan Cortes, in 1528, to prosecute the discoveries of which Magalhães had had the initiative. This third adventure was as disastrous as those which had preceded it. It consisted of three ships and one hundred and ten men, bearing large supplies and costly presents. They took possession of the Marianas (Ladrone Islands) in the name of the king of Spain, reached Mindanao and other of the southern islands, failed twice in the attempt to reach New Spain, and finally

3

were all victims of the climate and of the hostility of the Portuguese.

But the Spanish court determined to persevere, and the Viceroy (Mendoza) of New Spain was ordered to prepare a fourth expedition, which was to avoid the Molucca Islands, where so many misfortunes had attended the Spaniards. The fleet consisted of three ships and two traders, and the commander was Villalobos. He reached the Archipelago, and gave to the islands the name of the Philippines, in honour of the Prince of Asturias, afterwards Philip the Second. Contrary winds (in spite of the royal prohibition) drove them into the Moluccas, where they were ill received by the Portuguese, and ordered to return to Spain. Villalobos died in Amboyna, where he was attended by the famous missionary, St. Francisco Xavier. Death swept away many of the Spaniards, and the few who remained were removed from the Moluccas in Portuguese vessels.

A fifth expedition on a larger scale was ordered by Philip the Second to "conquer, pacify, and people" the islands which bore his name. They consisted of five ships and four hundred seamen and soldiers, and sailed from La Natividad (Mexico) in 1564, under the orders of Legaspi, who was nominated Governor of the Philippines, with ample powers. He reached Tandaya in February, 1565, proceeded to Cabalian, where the heir of the native king aided his views. In Bojol, he secured the aid and allegiance of the petty sovereigns of the island, and afterwards fixed himself on the island of Zebu, which for some time was the central seat of Spanish authority.[1]

Manila was founded in 1581.

Illness and the despotism of the doctors, who ordered me to throw off the cares of my colonial government and to undertake a sea voyage of six or seven weeks' duration, induced me to avail myself of one of the many courtesies and kindnesses for which I am indebted to the naval commander-in-chief, Sir Michael Seymour, and to accept his friendly offer of a steamer to convey me whither I might desire. The relations of China with the Eastern Spanish Archipelago are not unimportant, and were likely to be extended in consequence of the stipulations of Lord Elgin's Tientsin Treaty. Moreover, the slowly advancing commercial liberalism of the Spaniards has opened three additional ports to foreign trade, of which, till lately, Manila had the monopoly. I decided, therefore, after calling at the capital in order to obtain the facilities with which I doubted not the courtesy of my friend Don Francisco Norzagaray, the Captain-General of the Philippines, would favour me, to visit Zamboanga, Iloilo, and Sual. I had already experienced many attentions from him in connection with the government of Hong Kong. It will be seen that my anticipations were more than responded to by the Governor, and as I enjoyed rare advantages in obtaining the information I sought, I feel encouraged to record the impressions I received, and to give publicity to those facts which I gathered together in the course of my inquiries, assisted by such publications as have been accessible to me.

Sir Michael Seymour placed her Majesty's ship *Magicienne* at my disposal. The selection was in all respects admirable. Nothing that foresight could suggest or care provide was wanting to my comfort, and I owe a great deal to Captain Vansittart, whose urbanities and attentions were followed up by all his officers and men. We left Hong Kong on the 29th of November, 1858. The China seas are, perhaps, the most tempestuous in the world, and the voyage to Manila is frequently a very disagreeable one. So it proved to us. The wild cross waves, breaking upon the bows, tossed us about with great violence; and damage to furniture, destruction of glass and earthenware, and much personal inconvenience, were among the varieties which accompanied us.

But on the fifth day we sighted the lighthouse at the entrance of the magnificent harbour of Manila, and some hours' steaming brought us to an anchorage at about a mile distant from the city. There began the attentions which were associated with the whole of our visit to these beautiful regions. The *Magicienne* was visited by the various authorities, and arrangements were made for my landing and conveyance to the palace of the Governor-General. Through the capital runs a river (the Pasig), up which we rowed, till we reached, on the left bank, a handsome flight of steps, near the fortifications and close to the column which has been erected to the memory of Magellanes, the discoverer of, or, at all events, the founder of Spanish authority in, these islands. This illustrious name arrested our attention. The memorial is not worthy of that great reputation. It is a somewhat rude column of stone, crowned with a bronze armillary sphere, and decorated midway with golden dolphins and anchors wreathed in laurels: it stands upon a pedestal of marble, bearing the name of the honoured navigator, and is surrounded by an iron railing. It was originally intended to be erected in the island of Zebu, but, after a correspondence of several years with the Court of Madrid, the present site was chosen by royal authority in 1847. There was a very handsome display of cavalry and infantry, and a fine band of music played "God save the Queen." Several carriages and four were in waiting to escort our party to the government palace, where I was most cordially received by the captain-general and the ladies of his family. A fine suite of apartments had been prepared for my occupation, and servants, under the orders of a major-domo, were ordered to attend to our requirements, while one of the Governor's aides-de-camp was constantly at hand to aid us.

Though the name of *Manila* is given to the capital of the Philippine Islands, it is only the fort and garrison occupied by the authorities to which the designation was originally applied. Manila is on the left bank of the river, while, on the right, the district of Binondo is the site inhabited by almost all the merchants, and in which their business is conducted and their warehouses built. The palace fills one side of a public *plaza* in the fortress, the cathedral another of the same locality, resembling the squares of London, but with the advantage of having its centre adorned by the glorious vegetation of the tropics, whose leaves present all varieties of colour, from the brightest yellow to the deepest green, and whose flowers are remarkable for their splendour and beauty. There is a statue of Charles the Fourth in the centre of the garden.

The most populous and prosperous province of the Philippines takes its name from the fortification[2] of Manila; and the port of Manila is among the best known and most frequented of the harbours of the Eastern world. The capital is renowned for the splendour of its religious processions; for the excellence of its cheroots, which, to the east of the Cape of Good Hope, are generally preferred to the cigars of the Havana; while the less honourable characteristics of the people are known to be a universal love of gambling, which is exhibited among the Indian races by a passion for cock-fighting, an amusement made a productive source of revenue to the State. Artists usually introduce a Philippine Indian with a game-cock under his arm, to which he seems as much attached as a Bedouin Arab to his horse. It is said that many a time an Indian has allowed his wife and children to perish in the flames when his house has taken fire, but never was known to fail in securing his favourite *gallo* from danger.

On anchoring off the city, Captain Vansittart despatched one of his lieutenants, accompanied by my private secretary, to the British consulate, in order to announce our arrival, and to offer any facilities for consular communication with the *Magicienne*. They had some difficulty in discovering the consulate, which has no flag-staff, nor flag, nor other designation. The Consul was gone to his *ferme modèle*, where he principally passes his time among outcast Indians, in an almost inaccessible place, at some distance from Manila. The Vice-Consul said it was too hot for him to come on board, though during a great part of the day we were receiving the representatives of the highest authorities of Manila. The Consul wrote (I am bound to do him this justice) that it would "put him out" of his routine of habit and economy if he were expected to fête and entertain with formality "his Excellency the Plenipotentiary and Governor of Hong Kong." I hastened to assure the Consul that my presence should cause him no expense, but that the absence of anything which becomingly represented consular authority on the arrival of one of Her Majesty's large ships of war could hardly be passed unnoticed by the commander of that vessel.

Crowds of visitors honoured our arrival; among them the archbishop and the principal ecclesiastical dignitaries; deputations from the civilians, army and navy, and the various heads of departments, who invited us to visit their establishments, exhibited in their personal attentions the characteristics of ancient Castilian courtesy. A report had spread among the officers that I was a veteran warrior who had served in the Peninsular campaign, and helped to liberate Spain from the yoke of the French invaders. I had to explain that, though witness to many of the events of that exciting time, and in that romantic land, I was a peaceful spectator, and not a busy actor there. The bay of Manila, one of the finest in the world, and the river Pasig which flows into it, were, no doubt, the great recommendations of the position chosen for the capital of the Philippines. During the four months of March, April, May, and June, the heat and dust are very oppressive, and the mosquitos a fearful annoyance. To these months succeed heavy rains, but on the whole the climate is good, and the general mortality not great. The average temperature through the year is $81° 97'$ Fahrenheit.

The quarantine station is at Cavite, a town of considerable importance on the southern side of the harbour. It has a large manufacturing establishment of cigars, and gives its name to the surrounding province, which has about 57,000 inhabitants, among whom are about 7,000 *mestizos* (mixed race). From its adjacency to the capital, the numerical proportion of persons paying tribute is larger than in any other province.

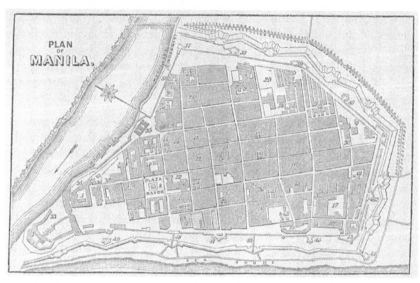

PLAN OF MANILA.

1 Artillery
2 Hall of Arms
3 Hall of Audience
4 Military Hospital
5 Custom House
6 Univ. of S. Thomas
7 Cabildo
8 Palace & Treasury
9 Archbishop's Palace
10 Principal Accountancy
11 Intendance
12 Consulado
13 Bakery
14 Artillery Quarters
15 S. Potenciano's College
16 Fortification Department
17 Barracks (Ligoros)
18 Barracks (Asia)
19 Nunnery of S. Clara
20 S. Domingo
21 Establishment of S. Rosa
22 Cathedral

26 S. Juan de Dios
27 S. Augustine
28 Orden Tercera
29 S. Francisco
30 Ricolets
31 S. Ignatius
32 Establishment of the Jesuits
33 Santiago Troops
34 Bulwark of the Torricos
35 Gate of S. Domingo
36 Custom-house Bulwark
37 S. Gabriel's Bulwark
38 Parien Gate
39 Devil's Bulwark
40 Postern of the Ricolets
41 S. Andrew's Bulwark
42 Royal Gate
43 S. James's Bulwark
44 S. Gregory's Battery
45 S. Peter's Redoubt
46 S. Luis Gate
47 Plane Bulwark

8

The city, which is surrounded by ramparts, consists of seventeen streets, spacious and crossing at right angles. As there is little business in this part of the capital (the trade being carried on on the other side of the river), few people are seen in the streets, and the general character of the place is dull and monotonous, and forms a remarkable contrast to the activity and crowding of the commercial quarters. The cathedral, begun in 1654, and completed in 1672, is 240 feet in length and 60 in breadth. It boasts of its fourteen bells, which have little repose; and of the carvings of the fifty-two seats which are set apart for the aristocracy. The archiepiscopal palace, though sufficiently large, did not appear to me to have any architectural beauty. The apartments are furnished with simplicity, and though the archbishop is privileged, like the governor, to appear in some state, it was only on the occasion of religious ceremonies that I observed anything like display. His reception of me was that of a courteous old gentleman. He was dressed with great simplicity, and our conversation was confined to inquiries connected with ecclesiastical administration. He had been a barefooted Augustin friar (Recoleto), and was raised to the archiepiscopal dignity in 1846.

The palacio in which I was so kindly accommodated was originally built by an opulent but unfortunate *protégé* of one of the captains-general; it was reconstructed in 1690 by Governor Gongora. It fills a considerable space, and on the south-west side has a beautiful view of the bay and the surrounding headlands. There is a handsome Hall of Audience, and many of the departments of the government have their principal offices within its walls. The *patio* forms a pretty garden, and is crowded with tropical plants. It has two principal stone staircases, one leading to the private apartments, and the other to the public offices. Like all the houses at Manila, it has for windows sliding frames fitted with *concha*, or plates of semi-transparent oysters, which admit an imperfect light, but are impervious to the sunbeams. I do not recollect to have seen any glass windows in the Philippines. Many of the apartments are large and well furnished, but not, as often in England, over-crowded with superfluities. The courtesy of the Governor provided every day at his table seats for two officers of the *Magicienne* at dinner, after retiring from which there was a *tertulia*, or evening reception, where the notabilities of the capital afforded me many opportunities for enjoying that agreeable and lively conversation in which Spanish ladies excel. A few mestizos are among the visitors. Nothing, however, is seen but the Parisian costume; no vestiges of the recollections of my youth—the *velo*, the *saya*, and the *basquiña*; nor the tortoiseshell combs, high towering over the beautiful black *cabellera*; the fan alone remains, then, as now, the dexterously displayed weapon of womanhood. After a few complimentary salutations, most of the gentlemen gather round the card-tables.

The *Calzada*, a broad road a little beyond the walls of the fortress, is to Manila what Hyde Park is to London, the Champs Elysées to Paris, and the Meidan to Calcutta. It is the gathering place of the opulent classes, and from five o'clock P.M. to the nightfall is crowded with carriages, equestrians and pedestrians, whose mutual salutations seem principally to occupy their attention: the taking off hats and the responses to greetings and recognitions are sufficiently wearisome. Twice a week a band of music plays on a raised way near the extremity of the *patio*. Soon after sunset there is a sudden and general stoppage. Every one uncovers his head; it is the time of the *oracion* announced by the church bells: universal silence prevails for a few minutes, after which the promenades are resumed. There is a good deal of solemnity in the instant and accordant suspension of all locomotion, and it reminded me of the prostration of the Mussulmans when the voice of the Muezzim calls, "To prayer, to prayer." A fine evening walk which is found on the esplanade of the fortifications, is only frequented on Sundays. It has an extensive view of the harbour and the river, and its freedom from the dust and dirt of the Calzada gives it an additional recommendation; but fashion despotically decides all such matters, and the crowds will assemble where everybody expects to meet with everybody. In visiting the fine scenery of the rivers, roads, and villages in the neighbourhood of Manila, we seldom met with a carriage, or a traveller seeking to enjoy these beauties. And in a harbour so magnificent as that of Manila one would expect to see skiffs and pleasure-boats without number, and yachts and other craft ministering to the enjoyment and adding to the variety of life; but there are none. Nobody seems to like sporting with the elements. There are no yacht regattas on the sea, as there are no horseraces on the shore. I have heard the life of Manila called intolerably monotonous; in my short stay it appeared to me full of interest and animation, but I was perhaps privileged. The city is certainly not lively, and the Spaniard is generally grave, but he is warm-hearted and hospitable, and must not be studied at a distance, nor condemned with precipitancy. He is, no doubt, susceptible and *pundonoroso*, but is rich in noble qualities. Confined as is the population of Manila within the fortification walls, the neighbouring country is full of attractions. To me the villages, the beautiful tropical vegetation, the banks of the rivers, and the streams adorned with scenery so picturesque and pleasing, were more inviting than the gaiety of the public parade. Every day afforded some variety, and most of the pueblos have their characteristic distinctions. Malate is filled with public offices, and women employed in ornamenting slippers with gold and silver embroidery. Santa Ana is a favourite *Villagiatura* for the merchants and opulent inhabitants. Near Paco is the cemetery, "where dwell the multitude," in which are interred the remains of many of the once distinguished who have ceased to be. Guadalupe is illustrious for its miraculous image, and Paco for that of the Saviour. The Lake of Arroceros (as its name implies) is one of the principal gathering places for boats loaded with rice; near it, too, are large manufactories of paper cigars. Sampaloc is the paradise of washermen and washerwomen. La Ermita and other villages are remarkable for their *bordadoras*, who produce those exquisite piña handkerchiefs for which such large sums are paid. Pasay is renowned for its cultivation of the betel. Almost every house has a garden with its bamboos, plantains and cocoa-nut trees, and some with a greater variety of fruits. Nature has decorated them with spontaneous flowers, which hang from the branches or the fences, or creep up around the simple dwellings of the Indians. Edifices of superior construction are generally the abodes of the mestizos, or of the gobernadorcillos belonging to the different pueblos.

Philip the Third gave armorial bearings to the capital, and conferred on it the title of the "Very Noble City of Manila" (*La mui noble Ciudad*), and attached the dignity of Excellency to the *Ayuntamiento* (municipality).

During my stay at Manila, every afternoon, at five or six o'clock, the Governor-General called for me in my apartments, and escorted by cavalry lancers we were conveyed in a carriage and four to different parts of the neighbourhood, the rides lasting from one to two hours. We seldom took the same road, and thus visited not only nearly all the villages in the vicinity, but passed through much beautiful country in which the attention was constantly arrested by the groups of graceful bamboos, the tall cocoa-nut trees, the large-leafed plantains, the sugar-cane, the papaya, the green paddy fields (in which many people were fishing—and who knows, when the fields are dry, what becomes of the fish, for they never fail to appear again when irrigation has taken place?), and that wonderful variety and magnificence of tropical vegetation,—leaves and flowers so rich and gorgeous, on which one is never tired to gaze. Much of the river scenery is such as a Claude would revel in, and high indeed would be the artist's merit who could give perpetuity to such colouring. And then the sunset skies—such as are never seen in temperate zones,—so grand, so glowing, and at times so awful! Almost every pueblo has some dwellings larger and better than the rest, occupied by the native

11

authorities or the mixed races (mostly, however, of Chinese descent), who link the Indian to the European population. The first floor of the house is generally raised from the ground and reached by a ladder. Bamboos form the scaffolding, the floors, and principal wood-work; the nipa palm makes the walls and covers the roof. A few mats, a table, a rude chair or two, some pots and crockery, pictures of saints, a lamp, and some trifling utensils, comprise the domestic belongings, and while the children are crawling about the house or garden, and the women engaged in household cares, the master will most probably be seen with his game-cock under his arm, or meditating on the prowess of the *gallo* while in attendance on the *gallinas*.

VIEW FROM MY WINDOW SAN MIGUEL.

The better class of houses in Manila are usually rectangular, having a court in the centre, round which are shops, warehouses, stables and other offices, the families occupying the first floor. Towards the street there is a corridor which communicates with the various apartments, and generally a gallery in the interior looking into the *patio* (court). The rooms have all sliding windows, whose small panes admit the light of day through semi-transparent oyster-shells: there are also Venetians, to help the ventilation and to exclude the sun. The kitchen is generally separated from the dwelling. A large cistern in the patio holds the water which is conveyed from the roofs in the rainy season, and the platform of the cistern is generally covered with jars of flowering plants or fruits. The first and only floor is built on piles, as the fear of earthquakes prevents the erection of elevated houses. The roofing is ordinarily of red tiles.

The apartments, as suited to a tropical climate, are large, and many European fashions have been introduced: the walls covered with painted paper, many lamps hung from the ceiling, Chinese screens, porcelain jars with natural or artificial flowers, mirrors, tables, sofas, chairs, such as are seen in European capitals; but the large rooms have not the appearance of being crowded with superfluous furniture. Carpets are rare—fire-places rarer.

Among Europeans the habits of European life are slightly modified by the climate; but it appeared to me among the Spaniards there were more of the characteristics of old Spain than would now be found in the Peninsula itself. In my youth I often heard it said—and it was said with truth—that neither Don Quixote nor Gil Blas were pictures of the past alone, but that they were faithful portraits of the Spain which I saw around me. Spain had then assuredly not been Europeanized; but fifty years—fifty years of increased and increasing intercourse with the rest of the world—have blotted out the ancient nationality, and European modes, usages and opinions, have pervaded and permeated all the upper and middling classes of Spanish society—nay, have descended deep and spread far among the people, except those of the remote and rural districts. There is little now to distinguish the aristocratical and high-bred Spaniard from his equals in other lands. In the somewhat lower grades, however, and among the whole body of clergy, the impress of the past is preserved with little change. Strangers of foreign nations, principally English and Americans, have brought with them conveniences and luxuries which have been to some extent adopted by the opulent Spaniards of Manila; and the honourable, hospitable and liberal spirit which is found among the great merchants of the East, has given them "name and fame" among Spanish colonists and native cultivators. Generally speaking, I found a kind and generous urbanity prevailing,—friendly intercourse where that intercourse had been sought,—the lines of demarcation and separation between ranks and classes less marked and impassable than in most Oriental countries. I have seen at the same table Spaniard, mestizo and Indian—priest, civilian and soldier. No doubt a common religion forms a common bond; but to him who has observed the alienations and repulsions of *caste* in many parts of the Eastern world—caste, the great social curse—the blending and free intercourse of man with man in the Philippines is a contrast well worth admiring. M. Mallat's enthusiasm is unbounded in speaking of Manila. "Enchanting city!" he exclaims; "in thee are goodness, cordiality, a sweet, open, noble hospitality,—the generosity which makes our neighbour's house our own;—in thee the difference of fortune and hierarchy disappears.

Unknown to thee is etiquette. O Manila! a warm heart can never forget thy inhabitants, whose memory will be eternal for those who have known them."

De Mas' description of the Manila mode of life is this:—"They rise early, and take chocolate and tea (which is here called *cha*); breakfast composed of two or three dishes and a dessert at ten; dinner at from two to three; *siesta* (sleep) till five to six; horses harnessed, and an hour's ride to the *pasco*; returning from which, tea, with bread and biscuits and sweets, sometimes homewards, sometimes in visit to a neighbour; the evening passes as it may (cards frequently); homewards for bed at 11 P.M.; the bed a fine mat, with mosquito curtains drawn around; one narrow and one long pillow, called an *abrazador* (embracer), which serves as a resting-place for the arms or the legs. It is a Chinese and a convenient appliance. No sheets—men sleep in their stockings, shirts, and loose trousers (*pajamas*); the ladies in garments something similar. They say 'people must always be ready to escape into the street in case of an earthquake.'" I certainly know of an instance where a European lady was awfully perplexed when summoned to a sudden flight in the darkness, and felt that her toilette required adjustment before she could hurry forth.

Many of the pueblos which form the suburbs of Manila are very populous. Passing through Binondo we reach Tondo, which gives its name to the district, and has 31,000 inhabitants. These pueblos have their Indian gobernadorcillos. Their best houses are of European construction, occupied by Spaniards or mestizos, but these form a small proportion of the whole compared with the Indian *Cabánas*. Tondo is one of the principal sources for the supply of milk, butter, and cheese to the capital; it has a small manufacturing industry of silk and cotton tissues, but most of the women are engaged in the manipulation of cigars in the great establishments of Binondo. Santa Cruz has a population of about 11,000 inhabitants, many of them merchants, and there are a great number of mechanics in the pueblo. Near it is the burying-place of the Chinese, or, as they are called by the Spaniards, the *Sangleyes infieles*.

Santa Cruz is a favourite name in the Philippines. There are in the island of Luzon no less than four pueblos, each with a large population, called Santa Cruz, and several besides in others of the Philippines. It is the name of one of the islands, of several headlands, and of various other localities, and has been carried by the Spaniards into every region where they have established their dominion. So fond are they of the titles they find in their Calendar, that in the Philippines there are no less than sixteen places called St. John and twelve which bear the name of St. Joseph; Jesus, Santa Maria, Santa Ana, Santa Caterina, Santa Barbara, and many other saints, have given their titles to various localities, often superseding the ancient Indian names. Santa Ana is a pretty village, with about 5,500 souls. It is surrounded with cultivated lands, which, being irrigated by fertilizing streams, are productive, and give their wonted charm to the landscape—palms, mangoes, bamboos, sugar plantations, and various fruit and forest trees on every side. The district is principally devoted to agriculture. A few European houses, with their pretty gardens, contrast well with the huts of the Indian. Its climate has the reputation of salubrity.

There is a considerable demand for horses in the capital. The importation of the larger races from Australia has not been successful. They were less suited to the climate than the ponies which are now almost universally employed. The Filipinos never give pure water to their horses, but invariably mix it with *miel* (honey), the saccharine matter of the *caña dulce*, and I was informed that no horse would drink water unless it was so sweetened. This, of course, is the result of "education." The value of horses, as compared with their cost in the remoter islands, is double or treble in the capital. In fact, nothing more distinctly proves the disadvantages of imperfect communication than the extraordinary difference of prices for the same articles in various parts of the Archipelago, even in parts which trade with one another. There have been examples of famine in a maritime district while there has been a superfluity of food in adjacent islands. No doubt the monsoons are a great impediment to regular intercourse, as they cannot be mastered by ordinary shipping; but steam has come to our aid, when commercial necessities demanded new powers and appliances, and no regions are likely to benefit by it more than those of the tropics.

The associations and recollections of my youth were revived in the hospitable entertainment of my most excellent host and the courteous and graceful ladies of his family. Nearly fifty years before I had been well acquainted with the Spanish peninsula—in the time of its sufferings for fidelity, and its struggles for freedom, and I found in Manila some of the veterans of the past, to whom the "Guerra de Independencia" was of all topics the dearest; and it was pleasant to compare the tablets of our various memories, as to persons, places and events. Of the actors we had known in those interesting scenes, scarcely any now remain—none, perhaps, of those who occupied the highest position, and played the most prominent parts; but their names still served as links to unite us in sympathizing thoughts and feelings, and having had the advantage of an early acquaintance with Spanish, all that I had forgotten was again remembered, and I found myself nearly as much at home as in former times when wandering among the mountains of Biscay, dancing on the banks of the

Guadalquivir, or turning over the dusty tomes at Alcalá de Henares.[3]

There was a village festival at Sampaloc (the Indian name for tamarinds), to which we were invited. Bright illuminations adorned the houses, triumphal arches the streets; everywhere music and gaiety and bright faces. There were several balls at the houses of the more opulent mestizos or Indians, and we joined the joyous assemblies. The rooms were crowded with Indian youths and maidens. Parisian fashions have not invaded these villages—there were no crinolines—these are confined to the capital; but in their native garments there was no small variety—the many-coloured gowns of home manufacture —the richly embroidered kerchiefs of piña—earrings and necklaces, and other adornings; and then a vivacity strongly contrasted with the characteristic indolence of the Indian races. Tables were covered with refreshments— coffee, tea, wines, fruits, cakes and sweetmeats; and there seemed just as much of flirting and coquetry as ever marked the scenes of higher civilization. To the Europeans great attentions were paid, and their presence was deemed a great honour. Our young midshipmen were among the busiest and liveliest of the throng, and even made their way, without the aid of language, to the good graces of the *Zagalas*. Sampaloc, inhabited principally by Indians employed as washermen and women, is sometimes called the *Pueblo de los Lavanderos*. The festivities continued to the matinal hours.

LAVANDEROS OR WASHERWOMEN

In 1855 the Captain-General (Crespo) caused sundry statistical returns to be

16

published, which throw much light upon the social condition of the Philippine Islands, and afford such valuable materials for comparison with the official *data* of other countries, that I shall extract from them various results which appear worthy of attention.

The city of Manila contains 11 churches, with 3 convents, 363 private houses; and the other edifices, amounting in all to 88, consist of public buildings and premises appropriated to various objects. Of the private houses, 57 are occupied by their owners, and 189 are let to private tenants, while 117 are rented for corporate or public purposes. The population of the city in 1855 was 8,618 souls, as follows:—

——	Males.	Females.	Total.
European Spaniards	503	87	590
Native ditto	575	798	1,373
Indians and Mestizos	3,830	2,493	6,323
Chinese	525	7⁴	532
Total	5,433	3,385	8,818

Far different are the proportions in another part of the capital, the Binondo district, on the other side of the river:—

——	Males.	Females.	Total.
European Spaniards	67	52	219
Native ditto	569	608	1,177
Foreigners	85	11	96
Indians and Mestizos	10,317	10,685	21,002
Chinese	5,055	8⁵	5,063
Total	16,193	11,364	27,557

Of these, one male and two females (Indian) were more than 100 years old.

The proportion of births and deaths in Manila is thus given:—

——	Spaniards.	Natives.	Total.
Births	4·38 per ct.	4·96 per ct.	4·83 per ct.
Deaths	1·68 ,, ,,	2·72 ,, ,,	2·48 ,, ,,
Excess of Births over Deaths	2·70 per ct.	2·24 per ct.	2·35 per ct.

In Binondo the returns are much less favourable:—

Births 5·12

Deaths 4·77

The statistical commissioners state these discrepancies to be inexplicable; but attribute it in part to the stationary character of the population of the city, and the many fluctuations which take place in the commercial movements of Binondo.

Binondo is really the most important and most opulent pueblo of the Philippines, and is the real commercial capital: two-thirds of the houses are substantially built of stone, brick and tiles, and about one-third are Indian wooden houses covered with the nipa palm. The place is full of business and activity. An average was lately taken of the carriages daily passing the principal thoroughfares. Over the *Puente Grande* (great bridge) their number was 1,256; through the largest square, Plaza de S. Gabriel, 979; and through the main street, 915. On the Calzada, which is the great promenade of the capital, 499 carriages were counted—these represent the aristocracy of Manila. There are eight public bridges, and a suspension bridge has lately been constructed as a private speculation, on which a fee is levied for all passengers.

Binondo has some tolerably good wharfage on the bank of the Pasig, and is well supplied with warehouses for foreign commerce. That for the reception of tobacco is very extensive, and the size of the edifice where the state cigars are manufactured may be judged of from the fact that nine thousand females are therein habitually employed.

The Puente Grande (which unites Manila with Binondo) was originally built of wood upon foundations of masonry, with seven arches of different sizes, at various distances. Two of the arches were destroyed by the earthquake of 1824, since which period it has been repaired and restored. It is 457 feet in length and 24 feet in width. The views on all sides from the bridge are fine, whether of the wharves, warehouses, and busy population on the right bank of the river, or the fortifications, churches, convents, and public walks on the left.

The population of Manila and its suburbs is about 150,000.

The tobacco manufactories of Manila, being the most remarkable of the "public shows," have been frequently described. The chattering and bustling of the thousands of women, which the constantly exerted authority of the female superintendents wholly failed to control, would have been distracting enough from the manipulation of the tobacco leaf, even had their tongues been tied, but their tongues were not tied, and they filled the place with noise.

This was strangely contrasted with the absolute silence which prevailed in the rooms solely occupied by men. Most of the girls, whose numbers fluctuate from eight to ten thousand, are unmarried, and many seemed to be only ten or eleven years old. Some of them inhabit pueblos at a considerable distance from Manila, and form quite a procession either in proceeding to or returning from their employment. As we passed through the different apartments specimens were given us of the results of their labours, and on leaving the establishment beautiful bouquets of flowers were placed in our hands. We were accompanied throughout by the superior officers of the administration, explaining to us all the details with the most perfect Castilian courtesy. Of the working people I do not believe one in a hundred understood Spanish.

The river Pasig is the principal channel of communication with the interior. It passes between the commercial districts and the fortress of Manila. Its average breadth is about 350 feet, and it is navigable for about ten miles, with various depths of from 3 to 25 feet. It is crossed by three bridges, one of which is a suspension bridge. The daily average movement of boats, barges, and rafts passing with cargo under the principal bridge, was 277, escorted by 487 men and 121 women (not including passengers). The whole number of vessels belonging to the Philippines was, in 1852 (the last return I possess), 4,053, representing 81,752 tons, and navigated by 30,485 seamen. Of these, 1,532 vessels, of 74,148 tons, having 17,133 seamen, belong to the province of Manila alone, representing three-eighths of the ships, seven-eighths of the tonnage, and seventeen-thirtieths of the mercantile marine. The value of the coasting trade in 1852 is stated to have been about four and a-half millions of dollars, half this value being in abacá (Manila hemp), sugar and rice being the next articles in importance. The province of Albay, the most southern of Luzon, is represented by the largest money value, being about one-fourth of the whole. On an average of five years, from 1850 to 1854, the coasting trade is stated to have been of the value of 4,156,459 dollars, but the returns are very imperfect, and do not include all the provinces. The statistical commission reports that on an examination of all the documents and facts accessible to them, in 1855, the coasting trade might be fairly estimated at 7,200,459 dollars.

At a distance of about three miles from Binondo, on the right bank of the Pasig, is the country house of the captain-general, where he is accustomed to pass some weeks of the most oppressive season of the year: it has a nice garden, a convenient moveable bath, which is lowered into the river, an aviary, and a small collection of quadrupeds, among which I made acquaintance with a chimpanzee, who, soon after, died of a pulmonary complaint.

1

A recent History of the Conquest of the Islands, and of the Spanish rule, is given by Buzeta, vol. i., pp. 57–98.

2

I visited some Cochin Chinese prisoners in the fortification. They had been taken at Turon, and one of them was a mandarin, who had exercised some authority there,—said to have been the commandant of the place. They wrote the Chinese characters, but were unable to understand the spoken language.

3

Among my early literary efforts was an essay by which the strange story was utterly disproved of the destruction of the MSS. which had served Cardinal Ximenes in preparing his Polyglot Bible.

4

One woman, six children.

5

All children.

CHAPTER II.

VISIT TO LA LAGUNA AND TAYABAS.

WATERFALL OF THE BOTOCAN.

Having arranged for a visit to the Laguna and the surrounding hills, whose beautiful scenery has given to the island of Luzon a widely-spread celebrity, we started accompanied by the Alcalde Mayor, De la Herran, Colonel Trasierra, an aide-de-camp of the Governor, appointed to be my special guide and guardian, my kind friend and gentlemanly companion Captain Vansittart, and some other gentlemen. The inhabitants of the Laguna are called by the Indians of Manila *Tagasilañgan*, or Orientals. As we reached the various villages, the *Principalia*, or native authorities, came out to meet us, and musical bands escorted us into and out of all the pueblos. We found the Indian villages decorated with coloured flags and embroidered kerchiefs, and the firing of guns announced our arrival. The roads were prettily decorated with bamboos and flowers, and everything proclaimed a hearty, however simple welcome. The thick and many-tinted foliage of the mango—the tall bamboos shaking their feathery heads aloft—the cocoa-nut loftier still—the areca and the nipa palms—the plantains, whose huge green leaves give such richness to a tropical landscape—the bread-fruit, the papaya, and the bright-coloured wild-flowers, which stray at will over banks and branches—the river every now and then visible, with its canoes and cottages, and Indian men, women, and children scattered along its banks. Over an excellent road, we passed through Santa Ana to Taguig, where a bamboo bridge had been somewhat precipitately erected to facilitate our passage over the stream: the first carriage got over in safety; with the second the bridge broke down, and some delay was experienced in repairing the disaster, and enabling the other carriages to come forward. Taguig is a pretty village, with thermal baths, and about 4,000 inhabitants; its fish is said to be particularly fine. Near it is Pateros, which no doubt takes its name from the enormous quantity of artificially hatched ducks (*patos*) which are bred there, and which are seen in incredible numbers on the banks of the river. They are fed by small shell-fish found abundantly in the neighbouring lake, and which are brought in boats to the *paterias* on the banks of the Pasig. This duck-raising is called *Itig* by the Indians. Each pateria is separated from its neighbour by a bamboo enclosure on the river, and at sunset the ducks withdraw from the water to adjacent buildings, where they deposit their eggs during the night, and in the morning return in long procession to the river. The eggs being collected are placed in large receptacles containing warm paddy husks, which are kept at the same temperature; the whole is covered with cloth, and they are removed by their owners as fast as they are hatched. We saw hundreds of the ducklings running about in shallow bamboo baskets, waiting to be transferred to the banks of the river. The friar at Pasig came out from his convent to receive us. It is a populous pueblo, containing more than 22,000 souls. There is a school for Indian women. It has stone quarries worked for consumption in Manila, but the stone is soft and brittle. The neighbourhood is adorned with gardens. Our host the friar had prepared for us in the convent a collation, which was served with much neatness and attention, and with cordial hospitality. Having reached the limits of his *alcadia*, the kind magistrate and his attendants left us, and we entered a *falua* (felucca) provided for us by the Intendente de Marina, with a goodly number of rowers, and furnished with a carpet, cushions, curtains, and other comfortable appliances. In this we started for the Laguna, heralded by a band of musicians. The rowers stand erect, and at every stroke of the oar fling themselves back upon their seats; they thus give a great impulse to the boat; the exertion appears very laborious, yet their work was done with admirable good-humour, and when they were drenched with rain there was not a murmur. In the lake (which is called *Bay*) is an island, between which and the main land is a deep and dangerous channel named Quinabatasan, through which we passed. The stream rushes by with great rapidity, and vessels are often lost in the passage. The banks are covered with fine fruit trees, and the hills rise grandly on all sides. Our destination was Santa Cruz, and long before we arrived a pilot boat had been despatched in order to herald our coming. The sun had set, but we perceived, as we approached, that the streets were illuminated, and we heard the wonted Indian music in the distance. Reaching the river, we were conducted to a gaily-lighted and decorated raft, which landed us,—and a suite of carriages, in one of which was the Alcalde, who had come from his *Cabacera*, or head quarters, to take charge of us,—conducted the party to a handsome house belonging to an opulent Indian, where we found, in the course of preparation, a very handsome dinner or supper, and all the notables of the locality, the priest, as a matter of course, among them, assembled to welcome the strangers. We passed a theatre, which appeared hastily erected and grotesquely adorned, where, as we were informed, it was intended to exhibit an Indian play in the Tagál language, for our edification and amusement. I was too unwell to attend, but I heard there was much talk on the stage (unintelligible, of course, to our party), and brandishing of swords, and frowns and fierce fighting, and genii hunting women into wild forests, and kings and queens gaily dressed. The stage was open from the street to the multitude, of whom many thousands were reported to be present, showing great interest and excitement. I was told that some of the actors had been imported from Manila. The hospitality of our host was super-abundant, and his table crowded not only with native but with many European luxuries. He was dressed as an Indian, and exhibited his wardrobe with some pride. He himself served us at his own table, and looked and moved about as if he were greatly honoured by the service. His name, which I gratefully record, is Valentin Valenzuela, and his brother has reached the distinction of being an ordained priest.

Santa Cruz has a population of about 10,000 souls. Many of its inhabitants are said to be opulent. The church is handsome; the roads in the neighbourhood broad and in good repair. There is much game in the adjacent forests, but there is not much devotion to the chase. Almost every variety of tropical produce grows in the vicinity. Wild honey is collected by the natives of the interior, and stuffs of cotton and abacá are woven for domestic use. The house to which we were invited was well furnished, but with the usual adornings of saints' images and vessels for holy water. In the evening the Tagála ladies of the town and neighbourhood were invited to a ball, and the day was closed with the accustomed light-heartedness and festivity: the *bolero* and the *jota* seemed the favourite attractions. Dance and music are the Indians' delight, and very many of the evenings we passed in the Philippines were devoted to these enjoyments. Next morning the carriages of the Alcalde, drawn by the pretty little ponies of Luzon, conducted us to the *casa real* at Pagsanjan, the seat of the government, or *Cabacera*, of the province, where we met with the usual warm reception from our escort Señor Tafalla, the Alcalde. Pagsanjan has about 5,000 inhabitants, being less populous than Biñan and other pueblos in the province. Hospitality was here, as everywhere, the order of the day and of the night, all the more to be valued as there are no inns out of the capital, and no places of reception for travellers; but he who is recommended to the authorities and patronized by the friars will find nothing wanting for his accommodation and comfort, and will rather be surprised at the superfluities of good living than struck with the absence of anything necessary. I have been sometimes amazed when the stores of the convent furnished wines which had been kept from twenty to twenty-five years; and to say that the cigars and chocolate provided by the good friars would satisfy the most critical of critics, is only to do justice to the gifts and the givers.

We made an excursion to the pretty village of Lumbang, having, as customary, been escorted to the banks of the river, which forms the limit of the pueblo, by the mounted principalia of Pagsanjan. The current was strong, but a barge awaited us and conveyed us to the front of the convent on the other side, where the principal ecclesiastic, a friar, conducted us to the reception rooms. We walked through the pueblo, whose inhabitants amount to 5,000 Indians, occupying one long broad street, where many coloured handkerchiefs and garments were hung out as flags from the windows, which were crowded with spectators. We returned to the Cabacera, where we slept. Early in the morning we took our departure from Pagsanjan.

VILLAGE OF MAJAJAY

We next advanced into the more elevated regions, growing more wild and wonderful in their beauties. As we proceeded the roads became worse and worse, and our horses had some difficulty in dragging the carriages through the deep mud. We had often to ask for assistance from the Indians to extricate us from the ruts, and they came to our aid with patient and persevering cheerfulness. When the main road was absolutely impassable, we deviated into the forest, and the Indians, with large knives—their constant companions —chopped down the impeding bushes and branches, and made for us a practicable way. After some hours' journey we arrived at Majayjay, and between files of Indians, with their flags and music, were escorted to the convent, whence the good Franciscan friar Maximo Rico came to meet us, and led us up the wide staircase to the vast apartments above. The pueblo has about 8,500 inhabitants; the climate is humid, and its effects are seen in the magnificent vegetation which surrounds the place. The church and convent are by far the most remarkable of its edifices. Here we are surrounded by mountain scenery, and the forest trees present beautiful and various pictures. In addition to leaves, flowers and fruits of novel shapes and colours, the grotesque forms which the trunks and branches of tropical trees assume, as if encouraged to indulge in a thousand odd caprices, are among the characteristics of these regions. The native population availed themselves of the rude and rugged character of the region to offer a long resistance to the Spaniards on their first invasion, and its traditional means of defence were reported to be so great that the treasures of Manila were ordered to be transported thither on the landing of the English in 1762. Fortunately, say the Spanish historians, the arrangement was not carried out, as the English had taken their measures for the seizure of the spoils, and it was found the locality could not have been defended against them.

We were now about to ascend the mountains, and were obliged to abandon our carriages. Palanquins, in which we had to stretch ourselves at full length, borne each by eight bearers, and relays of an equal number, were provided for our accommodation. The Alcalde of the adjacent province of Tayabas had come down to Majayjay to invite us into his district, where, he said, the people were on the tiptoe of expectation, had made arrangements for our reception, and would be sadly disappointed if we failed to visit Lucban. We could not resist the kind urgency of his representations, and deposited ourselves in the palanquins, which had been got ready for us, and were indeed well rewarded. The paths through the mountains are such as have been made by the torrents, and are frequently almost impassable from the masses of rock brought down by the rushing waters. Sometimes we had to turn back from the selected road, and choose another less impracticable. In some places the mud was so deep that our bearers were immersed far above their knees, and nothing but long practice and the assistance of their companions could have enabled them to extricate themselves or us from so disagreeable a condition. But cheerfulness and buoyancy of spirits, exclamations of encouragement, loud laughter, and a general and brotherly co-operation surmounted every difficulty. Around us all was solitude, all silence, but the hum of the bees and the shrieks of the birds; deep ravines below, covered with forest trees, which no axe of the woodman would ever disturb; heights above still more difficult to explore, crowned with arboreous glories; brooks and rivulets noisily descending to larger streams, and then making their quiet way to the ocean receptacle. At last we reached a plain on the top of a mountain, where two grandly adorned litters, with a great number of bearers, were waiting, and we were welcomed by a gathering of graceful young women, all on ponies, which they managed with admirable agility. They were clad in the gayest dresses. The Alcalde called them his *Amazonas*; and a pretty spokeswoman informed us, in very pure Castilian, that they were come to escort us to Lucban, which was about a league distant. The welcome was as novel as it was unexpected. I observed the *Tagálas* mounted indifferently on the off or near side of their horses. Excellent equestrians were they; and they galloped and caracolled to the right and the left, and flirted with their embellished whips. A band of music headed us; and the Indian houses which we passed bore the accustomed demonstrations of welcome. The roads had even a greater number of decorations—arches of ornamented bamboos on both sides of the way, and firing of guns announcing our approach. The Amazonas wore bonnets adorned with ribands and flowers,—all had kerchiefs of embroidered piña on their shoulders, and variously coloured skirts and gowns of native manufacture added to the picturesque effect. So they gambolled along—before, behind, or at our sides where the roads permitted it—and seemed quite at ease in all their movements. The convent was, as usual, our destination; the presiding friar—quite a man of the world—cordial, amusing, even witty in his colloquies. He had most hospitably provided for our advent. All the principal people were invited to dinner. Many a joke went round, to which the friar contributed more than his share. Talking of the fair (if Indian girls can be so called), Captain Vansittart said he had thirty unmarried officers on board the *Magicienne*.

TRAVELLING BY PALKEE.

"A bargain," exclaimed the friar; "send them hither,—I will find pretty wives for all of them."

"But you must convert them first."

"Ay! that is my part of the bargain."

"And you will get the marriage fees."

"Do you think I forgot that?"

After dinner, or supper, as it was called, the Amazonas who had escorted us in the morning, accompanied by many more, were introduced; the tables were cleared away; and when I left the hall for my bedroom, the dancing was going on in full energy.

Newspapers and books were lying about the rooms of the convent. The friar had more curiosity than most of his order: conversation with him was not without interest and instruction.

We returned by a different road to Majayjay, for the purpose of visiting a splendid waterfall, where the descent of the river is reported to be 300 feet. We approached on a ledge of rock as near as we could to the cataract, the roar of which was awful; but the quantity of mist and steam, which soon soaked our garments, obscured the vision and made it impossible for us to form any estimate of the depth of the fall. It is surrounded by characteristic scenery—mountains and woods—which we had no time to explore, and of which the natives could give us only an imperfect account: they knew there were deer, wild boars, buffaloes, and other game, but none had penetrated the wilder regions. A traveller now and then had scrambled over the rocks from the foot to the top of the waterfall

We returned to Majayjay again to be welcomed and entertained by our hosts at the convent with the wonted hospitality; and taking leave of our Alcalde, we proceeded to Santa Cruz, where, embarking in our felucca, we coasted along the lake and landed at Calamba, a pueblo of about 4,000 inhabitants; carriages were waiting to convey us to Biñan, stopping a short time at Santa Rosa, where the Dominican friars, who are the proprietors of large estates in the neighbourhood, invited us as usual to their convent. We tarried there but a short time. The roads are generally good on the borders of the Laguna, and we reached Biñan before sunset, the Indians having in the main street formed themselves in procession as we passed along. Flags, branches of flowering forest trees, and other devices, were displayed. First we passed between files of youths, then of maidens; and through a triumphal arch we reached the handsome dwelling of a rich mestizo, whom we found decorated with a Spanish order, which had been granted to his father before him. He spoke English, having been educated at Calcutta, and his house—a very large one—gave abundant evidence that he had not studied in vain the arts of domestic civilization. The furniture, the beds, the tables, the cookery, were all in good taste, and the obvious sincerity of the kind reception added to its agreeableness. Great crowds were gathered together in the square which fronts the house of Don José Alberto. Indians brought their game-cocks to be admired, but we did not encourage the display of their warlike virtues. There was much firing of guns, and a pyrotechnic display when the sun had gone down, and a large fire balloon, bearing the inscription, "The people of Biñan to their illustrious visitors," was successfully inflated, and soaring aloft, was lost sight of in the distance, but was expected to tell the tale of our arrival to the *Magicienne* in Manila Bay. Biñan is a place of some importance. In it many rich mestizos and Indians dwell. It has more than 10,000 inhabitants. Large estates there are possessed by the Dominican friars, and the principal of them was among our earliest visitors. There, as elsewhere, the principalia, having conducted us to our head-quarters, came in a body to present their respects, the gobernadorcillo, who usually speaks Spanish, being the organ of the rest. Inquiries about the locality, thanks for the honours done us, were the commonplaces of our intercourse, but the natives were always pleased when "the strangers from afar" seemed to take an interest in their concerns. Nowhere did we see any marks of poverty; nowhere was there any crowding, or rudeness, or annoyance, in any shape. Actors and spectators seemed equally pleased; in fact, our presence only gave them another holiday, making but a small addition to their regular and appointed festivals. Biñan is divided by a river, and is about a mile from the Laguna. Its streets are of considerable width, and the neighbouring roads excellent. Generally the houses have gardens attached to them; some on a large scale. They are abundant in fruits of great variety. Rice is largely cultivated, as the river with its confluents affords ample means of irrigation. The lands are usually rented from the Dominicans, and the large extent of some of the properties assists economical cultivation. Until the lands are brought into productiveness, little rent is demanded, and when they become productive the friars have the reputation of being liberal landlords and allowing their tenants to reap large profits. It is said they are satisfied with one-tenth of the gross produce. A tenant is seldom disturbed in possession if his rent be regularly paid. Much land is held by associations or companies known by the title of *Casamahanes*. There is an active trade between Biñan and Manila.

Greatly gratified with all we had seen, we again embarked and crossed the Laguna to Pasig. Descending by that charming river, we reached Manila in the afternoon.

CHAPTER III.

HISTORY.

A few sketches of the personal history of some of the captains-general of Manila will be an apt illustration of the general character of the government, which, with some remarkable exceptions, appears to have been of a mild and paternal character; while the Indians exhibit, when not severely dealt with, much meekness and docility, and a generally willing obedience. The subjugation of the wild tribes of the interior has not made the progress which might have been fairly looked for; but the military and naval forces at the disposal of the captain-general have always been small when the extent of his authority is considered. In fact, many conquests have had to be abandoned from inadequacy of strength to maintain them. The ecclesiastical influences, which have been established among the idolatrous tribes, are weak when they come in contact with any of the forms of Mahomedanism, as in the island of Mindanao, where the fanaticism of Mussulman faith is quite as strong as that among the Catholics themselves. Misunderstandings between the Church and State could hardly be avoided where each has asserted a predominant power, and such misunderstandings have often led to the effusion of blood and the dislocation of government. Mutual jealousies exist to the present hour, and as the friars, in what they deem the interests of the people, are sometimes hostile to the views of the civil authority, that authority has frequently a right to complain of being thwarted, or feebly aided, by the local clergy.

While shortly recording the names of the captains-general to whom the government of the Philippines has been confided, I will select a few episodes from the history of the islands, which will show the character of the administration, and assist the better understanding of the position of the people.

Miguel Lope de Legaspi, a Biscayan, upon whom the title of Conqueror of the Philippines has been conferred, was the first governor, and was nominated in 1565. He took possession of Manila in 1571, and died, it is said, of disgust and disappointment the following year. The city was invaded by Chinese pirates during the government of his successor Guido de Lavezares, who repulsed them, and received high honours from his sovereign, Philip II. Francisco de Saude founded in Camarines the city of Nueva Caceres, to which he gave the name of the place of his birth. He was a man of great ambition, who deposed one and enthroned another sultan of Borneo, and

31

modestly asked from the king of Spain authority to conquer China, but was recommended to be less ambitious, and to keep peace with surrounding nations. Rinquillo de Peñarosa rescued Cagayan from a Japanese pirate, and founded New Segovia and Arévalo in Panay; his nephew succeeded him, and in doing honour to his memory set the Church of St. Augustin on fire; it spread to the city, of which a large part was destroyed. In 1589, during the rule of Santiago de Vera, the only two ships which carried on the trade with New Spain were destroyed by a hurricane in the port of Cavite. The next governor, Gomez Perez Dasmariñas, sent to Japan the missionaries who were afterwards put to death; he headed an expedition to Moluco, but on leaving the port of Mariveles his galley was separated from the rest of the fleet; the Chinese crew rose, murdered him, and fled in his vessel to Cochin China. His son Luis followed him as governor. A Franciscan friar, who had accompanied the unfortunate expedition of his father, informed him that he would find, as he did, his patent of appointment in a box which the Chinese had landed in the province of Ilocos, and his title was in consequence recognised. Francisco Tello de Guzman, who entered upon the government in 1596, was unfortunate in his attempts to subdue the natives of Mindanao, as was one of his captains, who had been sent to drive away the Dutch from Mariveles.

In the year 1603 three mandarins arrived in Manila from China. They said that a Chinaman, whom they brought as a prisoner, had assured the Emperor that the island of Cavite was of gold, that the Chinaman had staked his life upon his veracity, and that they had come to learn the truth of his story. They soon after left, having been conducted by the governor to examine Cavite for themselves. A report speedily spread that an invasion of the Philippines by a Chinese army of 100,000 was in contemplation, and a Chinese called Eng Kang, who was supposed to be a great friend of the Europeans, was charged with a portion of the defences. A number of Japanese, the avowed enemies of the Chinese, were admitted to the confidence of the governor, and communicated to the Chinese the information that the government suspected a plot. A plot there was, and it was said the Chinese determined on a rising, and a general massacre of the Spaniards on the vespers of St. Francis' day. A Philippine woman, who was living with a Chinaman, denounced the project to the curate of Quiapo, who advised the governor. A number of the conspirators were assembled at a half-league's distance from Manila, and Eng Kang was sent with some Spaniards to put down the movement. The attempt failed, and Eng Kang was afterwards discovered to have been one of the principal promoters of the insurrection. In the evening the Chinese attacked Quiapo and Tondo, murdering many of the natives. They were met by a body of 130 Spaniards, nearly all of whom perished, and their heads were sent to Parian, which the insurgents captured, and besieged the city of Manila from Dilao.

The danger led to great exertions on the part of the Spaniards, the ecclesiastics taking a very active part. The Chinese endeavoured to scale the walls, but were repulsed. The monks declared that St. Francis had appeared in person to encourage them. The Chinese withdrew to their positions, but the Spaniards sallied out from the citadel, burnt and destroyed Parian, and pursued the flying Chinese to Cabuyao. New reinforcements arrived, and the flight of the Chinese continued as far as the province of Batangas, where they were again attacked and dispersed. It is said that of 24,000 revolted Chinese only one hundred escaped, who were reserved for the galleys. About 2,000 Chinese were left, who had not involved themselves in the movement. Eng Kang was decapitated, and his head exposed in an iron cage. It was three years after this insurrection that the Court of Madrid had the first knowledge of its existence.

Pedro de Acuña, after the suppression of this revolt, conquered Ternate, and carried away the king, but died suddenly, in 1606, after governing four years. Cristobal Tellez, during his short rule, destroyed a settlement of the Japanese in Dilao. Juan de Silva brought with him, in 1609, reinforcements of European troops, and in the seventh year of his government, made great preparations for attacking the Dutch, but died after a short illness. In 1618, Alonzo Fajardo came to the Philippines, with conciliatory orders as regarded the natives, and was popular among them. He punished a revolt in Buhol, sent an unsuccessful mission to Japan, and in a fit of jealousy killed his wife. Suspecting her infidelity, he surprised her at night in a house, where she had been accustomed to give rendezvous to her paramour, and found her in a dress which left no doubt of her crime. The governor called in a priest, commanded him to administer the sacrament, and, spite of the prayers of the ecclesiastic, he put her to death by a stab from his own dagger. This was in 1622. Melancholy took possession of him, and he died in 1624. Two interim governors followed. Juan Niño de Tabera arrived in 1626. He brought with him 600 troops, drove the Dutch from their holds, and sent Olaso, a soldier, celebrated for his deeds in Flanders, against the Jolo Indians; but Olaso failed utterly, and returned to Manila upon his discomfiture.

A strange event took place in 1630. The holy sacrament had been stolen in a glass vase, from the cathedral. A general supplication (*rogativa*) was ordered; the archbishop issued from his palace barefooted, his head covered with ashes, and a rope round his neck, wandering about to discover where the vase was concealed. All attempts having failed, so heavy were the penitences, and so intolerable the grief of the holy man, that he sank under the calamity, and a fierce contest between the ecclesiastical and civil functionaries was the consequence of his death.

In 1635 there was a large arrival of rich converted Japanese, who fled from the fierce persecutions to which the Christians had been subjected in Japan; but a great many Catholic missionaries hastened to that country, in order to be honoured with the crown of martyrdom. Another remarkable ecclesiastical quarrel took place at this time. A commissary, lately arrived from Europe, ordered that all the friars with beards should be charged with the missions to China and Japan; and all the shorn friars should remain in the Philippines. The archbishop opposed this, as the Pope's bulls had no regulations about beards. Fierce debates were also excited by the exercise of the right of asylum to criminals, having committed offences, either against the military or the civil authority. The archbishop excommunicated—the commandant of artillery rebelled. The archbishop fined him—the vicar apostolic confirmed the sentence. The Audiencia annulled the proceedings—the Bishop of Camarines was called on as the arbiter, and absolved the commandant. Appeals followed, and one of the parties was accused of slandering the Most Holy Father. The Jesuits took part against the archbishop, who called all the monks together, and they fined the Jesuits 4,000 dollars. The governor defended the Jesuits, and required the revocation of the sentence in six hours. The quarrel did not end here: but there was a final compromise, each party making some concessions to the other.

The disasters which followed the insurrection of Eng Kang did not prevent the influx of Chinese into the islands, and especially into the province of Laguna, where another outbreak, in which it is said 30,000 Chinese took part, occurred in 1639. They divided themselves into guerrillas, who devastated the country; but were subdued in the following year, seven thousand having surrendered at discretion. Spanish historians say that the hatred of the Indians to the Chinese awaked them from their habitual apathy, and that in the destruction of the intruders they exhibited infinite zeal and activity.

In the struggles between the natives and the Spaniards, even the missionaries were not always safe, and the Spaniards were often betrayed by those in whom they placed the greatest confidence. The heavy exactions and gabelles inflicted on the Indians under Fajardo led to a rising in Palopag, when the Jesuit curate was killed and the convent and church sacked. The movement spread through several of the islands, and many of the prisoners were delivered in Caraga to the keeping of an Indian, called Dabao, who so well fulfilled his mission, that when the governor came to the fortress, to claim the captives, Dabao seized and beheaded his Excellency, and, with the aid of the prisoners, destroyed most of the Spaniards in the neighbourhood, including the priests; so that only six, among whom was an Augustine barefooted friar, escaped, and fled to the capital. Reinforcements having arrived from Manila, the Indians surrendered, being promised a general pardon. "The promise," says the Spanish historian, "was not kept; but the leaders of the insurrection were hanged, and multitudes of the Indians sent to prison." The governor-general "did not approve of this violation of a promise made in the king's name," but ordered the punishment of the Spanish chiefs, and the release of such natives as remained in prison.

In 1645, for two months there was a succession of fearful earthquakes. In Cagayan a mountain was overturned, and a whole town engulfed at its foot. Torrents of water and mud burst forth in many places. All the public buildings in the capital were destroyed, except the convent and the church of the Augustines, and that of the Jesuits. Six hundred persons were buried in Manila under the ruins of their houses, and 3,000 altogether are said to have lost their lives.

De Lara was distinguished for his religious sentiments. On his arrival in 1653 he refused to land till the archbishop had preceded him and consecrated the ground on which he was to tread. He celebrated a jubilee under the authority of the Pope, by which the country was to be purified from "the crimes, censures, and excommunications" with which, for so many years, it had been afflicted. The archbishop, from an elevated platform in Manila, blessed the islands and their inhabitants in the presence of an immense concourse of people. Reconciliations, confessions, restitutions followed these "days of sanctity;" but the benedictions seem to have produced little benefit, as they were followed by earthquakes, tempests, insurrections, unpunished piracies, and, in the words of a Spanish writer, "a web of anxieties and calamities." Missionaries were sent to convert the Mahomedans, but they were put to death, and many professed converts turned traitors. Kung Sing, the piratical chief, who had conquered Formosa, and who had 1,000 junks and 100,000 men under his orders, had sent an envoy to Manila demanding the subjection of the islands to his authority or threatening immediate invasion. The threat created a general alarm: the Chinese were all ordered to quit the country; they revolted, and almost all were murdered. "It is wonderful," says De Mas, "that any Chinaman should have come to the Philippines after the repeated slaughters" of their countrymen at different periods, though it is certain they have often brought down the thunderbolt on their own heads. De Lara, having been accused of corruption, was fined 60,000 dollars, pardoned, and returned to Spain, where he became an ecclesiastic, and died in Malaga, his native city.

The "religiosity," to use a Spanish word, of De Lara was followed by a very different temper in his successor, Salcedo, a Belgian by birth, nominated in 1663. He quarrelled with the priests, fined and condemned to banishment the archbishop, kept him standing while waiting for an audience, insulted him when he had obtained it; and on the death of the archbishop a few months afterwards, there were royal *fiestas*, while the services *De Profundis*, in honour of the dead, were prohibited as incompatible with the civil festivities. The Inquisition interfered in the progress of time, and its agents, assisted by an old woman servant, who held the keys, entered the palace, found the Governor asleep, put irons upon him, and carried him a prisoner to the Augustine convent. They next shipped him off to be tried by the Holy Office in Mexico, but he died on his way thither. The King of Spain cancelled and condemned the proceedings, confiscated the property of those who had been concerned in them, and directed all that had been seized belonging to Salcedo to be restored to his heirs.

Manuel de Leon, in 1669, obtained great reputation among the ecclesiastics. He governed for eight years and left all his property to *obras pias*. His predecessor, Manuel de la Peña Bonifaz (nominated provisionally), had refused to surrender his authority. He was declared an intruder, his goods were confiscated, and his arrest was ordered, but he sought refuge in the convent of the Recoletos, where he died. A quarrel took place between the competitors for the provisional government—the one appointed enjoyed his authority only for six months. He was, on his death, succeeded by his competitor, who was displaced by Juan de Vargas Hurtado in 1678. Great misunderstandings between the clergy and the civilians took place about this time. The governor was excommunicated, having been ordered on every holiday to appear in the cathedral and in the churches of Parcan and Binondo, barefooted and with a rope round his neck. Refusing to submit to such a degradation, he lived a solitary life, excluded from all intercourse, on the banks of the river, until he obtained permission to embark for New Spain; he died broken-hearted on the voyage.

It must be remembered, in looking over the ancient records of the Philippines, that the sole historians are the monks, and that their applause or condemnation can hardly be deemed a disinterested or equitable judgment. Hurtado is accused by them of many acts of despotism: they say that, in order to accomplish his objects, he menaced the friars with starvation, and by guards, prevented food reaching the convents; that he interfered with the election of ecclesiastics, persecuted and ordered the imprisonment of Bonifaz, his immediate predecessor (provisionally appointed), who fled to a convent of Recoletos (barefooted Augustines), and was protected by them. The Jesuits denied his claim to protection, but during the controversy Bonifaz died, and the records remain to exhibit another specimen of the bitterness of the *odium theologicum* and of the unity and harmony of which the Church of Rome sometimes boasts as the results of her infallibility. The archbishop was at this time quarrelling with the civil tribunals, to which he addressed his *mandamus*, and answered their recalcitrancy by reminding them that *all* secular authority was subordinate to ecclesiastical. The archbishop was placed under arrest and ordered to be banished by the Audiencia. He was conveyed by force in his pontifical robes to the vessel which transported him to Pangasinan. The Dominicans, to whose order the archbishop belonged, launched their excommunications and censures, and troops were sent to the convent to prevent the ringing of bells and the alarm and gathering of the people. The provincial, who had taken the active part in resistance, was, with other friars, ordered to be banished to Spain. When about to be removed, the dean commanded the soldiers present to kiss the provincial's feet and do him all honour while he poured out his benedictions on the recalcitrant friars. In the midst of all this confusion a new governor (Curuzcalegui) arrived, in 1684, who took part with the clergy, and declared himself in favour of the banished archbishop, and condemned his judges to banishment. One of them fled to the Jesuit's College, a sanctuary, but was seized by the troops. This by no means settled the quarrel, the following out of which is too complicated and too uninteresting to invite further scrutiny here.

In 1687 the King of Spain sent out a commissioner to inquire into the troubles that reigned in the Philippines. The Pope had taken up the cause of the more violent of the clergy, and Pardo (the archbishop), thus encouraged in his intemperance, declared the churches of the Jesuits desecrated in which the bodies of the civilians had been buried, who had adjudicated against the monks. Their remains were disinterred, but most of the judges who had defended the rights of the State against the ecclesiastical invasions were dead before the commissioner arrived; and, happily for the public peace, the turbulent prelate himself died in 1689. Curuzcalegui also died in 1689. After a short provisional interregnum (during which Valenzuela, the Spanish minister, who had been banished to the Philippines by Charles II., on his return homeward, was killed by the kick of a horse in Mexico), Fausto Cruzat y Gongora, was in 1690 invested with the government. His rule is most remarkable for its financial prosperity. It lasted for eleven years, for his successor, Domingo de Zubalburo, though nominated in 1694, did not arrive till 1701. He improved the harbour, but was dismissed by the King of Spain in consequence of his having admitted a Papal Legate *à latere* without requiring the presentation of his credentials. The Audiencia demanded them, and the

Legate replied he was surprised at their venturing to question his powers. He frightened the people by this assumption, and proceeded to found a college in the name of St. Clement. The king was so exasperated that he ordered the college to be demolished, fined the *Oidores* (judges) a thousand dollars, and removed the dean from his office. Martin de Ursua y Arrimendi arrived in 1709, and died much regretted in 1715; he checked the influx of the Chinese, and thus conciliated popular prejudices. The interim governor, Jose Torralba, was accused of peculation to the amount of 700,000 dollars. He was called on by royal order to reimburse and find security for 40,000 dollars; but failing was sent to prison in fetters. He was ordered afterwards to be sent to Spain, but agreed to pay 120,000 dollars. He had not the money, and died a beggar. Fernando Bustillo (Bustamente) landed in 1717. He spent large sums in useless embassies, and lived ostentatiously and expensively. He set about financial reforms, and imprisoned many persons indebted to the State. He seized some of the principal inhabitants of the capital, menaced the judges, who fled to the convents for protection. The governor took Torralba into favour, releasing him from prison, and using him to undermine the authority of the Audiencia, by investing him with its powers. He ordered that on the discharge of a piece of artillery, all the Spaniards should repair to the palace: he arrested the archbishop, the chapter of the cathedral, several prelates and ecclesiastics, when a tumult followed; crowds rushed to the palace; they killed the governor and his son, who had hurried thither to defend his father. Francisco de la Cuesta was called upon to take charge of the government. The remaining children of Bustillo were sent to Mexico, and the Audiencia made a report of what had taken place to the king, who appointed Toribio José Cosio y Campo, and directed the punishment of those who had caused the former governor's death; but under the influence of a Franciscan monk, Cosio was induced to consent to various delays, so that nothing was done in the matter, and the government in 1729 was transferred to Fernando Valdes y Tamon, who reformed the military exercises, sent an expedition to conquer the island of Palaos, failed in the attempt, and was succeeded by a Fleming, Gaspar de la Torre, in 1739. He dealt so severely with the fiscal Arroyo as to cause his death. He was disliked, became morose and solitary, and died in 1745. The bishop elect of Ilocos, father John Arrechedera, was the next governor, and the Sultan of Jolo, who desired to be baptized, visited him in Manila. The archbishop, to whom the matter was referred, declared that the Sultan had been received into the bosom of the Church by the Dominican friars of Panogui. The Marquis of Obando took possession of the government in 1750. The archbishop, whom he displaced, had received orders from the Spanish Cabinet to expel the Chinese from the islands; but whether from the honest conviction that the execution of the order would be pernicious to the permanent interests of the Philippines—in which judgment he was perfectly right—or (as the natives avow) from an unwarrantable affection for the Chinese, he, on various pretexts, delayed the publication of the royal mandate. Obando involved himself in quarrels with the Mussulman inhabitants of Mindanao, for which he had made no adequate preparation. He determined to restore the Sultan of Jolo, but on reaching Zamboanga he proceeded against the Sultan for unfaithfulness (*infidencia*), sent him to Manila, and caused him to be put into prison. The Mahomedans revolted. Obando desired to take the command against them. The Audiencia objected to the exposure of the person of the governor. The expedition failed, and disorders increased. He left the government in a most unsatisfactory state, and died on his way homewards. Pedro Manuel de Arandia assumed the government in 1754. He had some successes against the Mahomedans (or Moors, as they are generally called by Spanish writers). He intended to restore the Sultan of Jolo, but he involved himself in quarrels with the clergy, and his proceedings were disapproved by the Spanish Court. His unpopularity led to a fixed melancholy, under whose influences he died in 1759. Though he left his property for charitable purposes, the fact of its amounting to 250,000 dollars is urged as evidence of the corrupt character of his administration. The Bishop of Zebu, followed by the Archbishop of Manila, Manuel Royo, held the government provisionally on the death of Arandia. It was Royo who surrendered Manila, and transferred the island to the British in 1762.[1] He was made a prisoner, and died in prison in 1764, of grief and shame it was said. Simon de Anda y Salazar, one of the judges of the Royal Audiencia, was charged with the government during the possession of the capital by the English, and established his authority in Pampanga, where he maintained himself till the arrival of Francisco de la Torre, who was provisionally appointed by the Crown, and who, through Anda, received back Manila from the British. José Raon took possession of the government in 1766.

The Sultan of Jolo, replaced on his throne by the English, caused great molestations to the island of Mindanao, against Raon, who was unable to protect his countrymen. The expulsion of the Jesuits having been determined on, the secret purpose was communicated to the Governor. He was accused of having divulged, and of concealing a writing-desk supposed to contain important documents. He was ordered to be imprisoned in his own house, where he died.

One of the monkish historians gives the following account of the manner in which the rebellious Indians were disposed of:—"Arza, with the efficacious aid of the Augustin fathers, and of the faithful (who were many), went to Vigan, and repeated what he had done in Cagallan; for he hanged more than a hundred, and among them Doña Gabriela, the wife of Silang, a mestiza of *malas mañas* (bad tricks), not less valiant than her husband, the notary, and a great many *cabecillas* (heads of groups of families), who fled to the mountains of Alva; as to the rest of the rabble of this revolted crew, he was satisfied with giving them each two hundred lashes, while exposed on the pillory. He sent 3,000 Ilocos triumphant and rich with booty to Pangasinan. This was in 1763."[2]

After the capture of Manila by the British, they were naturally suspected and accused of fomenting and encouraging the many insurrections which followed that event. The impetuous and despotic character of Anda, who assumed the governorship of the islands, had made him many enemies, and he seems to have considered all opposition to his arbitrary measures as evidence of treacherous confederation with the English. No doubt their presence was welcomed, especially by the Mussulman population of the southern islands, as affording them some hopes of relief from Spanish oppression; but even the Philippine historians do justice to the British authorities, and state that they punished the piratical acts of their allies, without distinction of persons. The Spaniards, however, encouraged Tenteng, a Mahomedan *dato* (chieftain), to attack the British, whose garrison, in Balambangan, was reduced by sickness from 400 men to seventy-five infantry and twenty-eight artillery. But it was, says De Mas, "solely in expectation of booty." From the woods in the night they stole down on the English while they were asleep, set fire to the houses, and murdered all but six of the garrison, who escaped in a boat with the English commandant; they then hoisted the white flag, and did not spare the life of a single Englishman left on shore. The Mahomedans seized much spoil in arms and money. The Sultan of Jolo and the datos, fearing the vengeance of the English, disclaimed all participation in the affair; but on Tenteng's reaching Jolo, and delivering up his plunder to the authorities, they, "thinking there were now arms and money enough to resist both Spaniards and English," declared Tenteng to be a hero, and well deserving of his country. A few months afterwards, a British ship of war appeared, and obtained such reparation as the case allowed.

Anda had won so much credit for resisting the English, that he was rewarded by his sovereign with many honours, made Councillor of Castile, and returned as governor to Manila, in 1770. He imprisoned his predecessor, many of the judges, the government secretary, a colonel, and other persons. He sent some to Spain, and banished others from the capital. He involved himself in ecclesiastical quarrels, met with many vexations, and retired to the estate of the Recoleto friars, where he died in 1766. De Mas says, in reference to this period:—"For more than two centuries, the Philippines had been for the crown of Spain a hotbed of so many disputes, anxieties, and expenses, that the abandonment of the colony was again and again proposed by the ministers; but the Catholic monarchs could never consent to the perdition of all the souls that had been conquered, and which it was still hoped to conquer, in these regions." After a short interregnum temporarily filled by Pedro Sarrio, José Basco arrived in 1778. He established the tobacco monopoly, sent off to Europe three judges, and compelled other functionaries to quit the capital, but, after two years' occupation of the gubernatorial seat, he returned to Spain, and obtained other employment from the crown. Pedro Sarrio was again invested with the temporary authority. Felix Berenguer de Marquina arrived in 1788, and ruled six years. He was accused of corruption, but absolved by the king. Rafael Maria de Aguilar was nominated in 1793.

In 1800 the governor-general having consulted the assessor on the conduct to be observed towards the Mussulman pirates who had entered the port of Manila, received a reply which is somewhat grandiloquent:—"It is time all the royal wishes should be fulfilled, and that these islands cease to be tributaries to a vile and despicable Mahomedan. Let him feel the direful visitations of a nation, whose reputation has been so often offended and outraged, but which has tolerated and concealed its wrongs the better to inflict its vengeance; let the crown be cleansed from the tarnish, which in this port, and in the sight of so many European nations, it has received from the low rabble (*canalla*). The repeated disasters of the Indians appear to have rendered Spaniards insensible; yet is there a man who, having witnessed the desolation, murders, ruin of families, has not his soul moved with a desire of revenge against the desolator and destroyer? Were they our wives, sons, fathers, brothers, with what clamour should we call on the authorities to punish the criminal, and to restore our freedom.... Justice, pity, the obligation of *your* consciences, upon which the royal conscience reposes, all plead together.... Eternal memory for him who shall release us from the yoke which has oppressed us for ages!"

A treaty was concluded between the government of Manila and the Sultan of Mindanao in 1805. The Sultan's minister of state was a Mexican deserter; the ambassador of the Spaniards a Mexican convict. He was, in truth, hardly dealt with, for, after making the treaty, he was ordered to fulfil the term of his transportation.

In 1811, a conspiracy broke out in Ilocos, where a new god was proclaimed by the Indians, under the name of Lungao. There was a hierarchy of priests appointed in his honour. They made their first attempts to convert the idolaters in Cagayan, and to engage them to take part against the Spaniards. The Catholic missionaries were the special object of their dislike, but the information which these ecclesiastics gave to the authorities enabled them to suppress the rebellion and to punish the leaders.

The cholera invaded Manila in 1819. A massacre of foreigners and Chinese was the consequence, who were accused (especially the English) of poisoning the wells. Robberies and other excesses followed the murders. The Host was paraded in vain through the streets. The carnage ceased when no more victims were to be found, but Spanish persons and property were respected.

Under the government of Martinez, in 1823, a rising took, place, headed by Novales, a Manilaman in the Spanish service. As many as 800 of the troops joined the movement. They took possession of the palace, murdered the king's lieutenant, and, according to all appearances, would have overthrown the government, had there been any organization or unity of purpose. But a few courageous men gathered around them numbers faithful to the king and the royalist party. Soldiers arrived; the insurgents faltered; the inconstant people began to distrust the revolutionary leaders, and Novales was left with one piece of artillery, and about 300 to 400 followers. Overpowered, he fled, but was compelled to surrender. He was brought to a drumhead court-martial, declared he had no accomplices, but was the sole seducer of the troops, and was shot with one of his sergeants the same day. Amnesty was proclaimed, after twenty non-commissioned officers had been executed.

A serious insurrection broke out in Tayabas during the short rule of Oraa (1841–43). The Spaniards say it was the work of a Tagál called Apolinano, lay-brother of the convent of Lucban, not twenty years old, who established a brotherhood (*Cofradia*) exclusively confined to the native Indians. The object does not seem to have been known, but the meetings of the Cofrades excited alarms and suspicions. The archbishop called on the captain-general to put down the assemblies, which in some places had sought legalization from the authorities. The arrest of Apolinano was ordered, upon which he fled to the mountains, where he was joined by 3,000 Indians, and it was reported in Manila that he had raised the cry of rebellion in Igsavan. On this the Alcalde mayor, accompanied by two Franciscan friars, a few troops, and two small pieces of artillery, marched upon the denounced rebels. They fired upon the Spaniards and killed the Alcalde. On the news reaching the capital, a force of about 800 men was collected. It is said the positions held by Apolinano were impregnable, but he had not kept the promises he had made to the Indians, that sundry miracles were to be wrought in their favour. Only a few advanced to meet the Spaniards, and many of these were killed and the rest took to flight. Almost without loss on their own side, the Spaniards left above 240 Indians dead on the field, and shot 200 whom they made prisoners. Apolinano, in endeavouring to cross a river, was seized by two of his own people, bound, and delivered over to the authorities. He was accused of aspiring to be King of the Tagálos. He averred that the objects of his Cofradia were purely and simply religious. He was shot on the 4th of November, 1841. De Mas says he knew him, and that he was a quiet, sober, unobtrusive young man, exhibiting nothing of the hero or the adventurer. He performed menial services at the convent of Lucban; and as far as I can discover, the main ground of suspicion was, that he admitted no Spaniards or Mestizos into his religious fraternity; but that so many lives should have been sacrificed to a mere suspicion is a sad story.'

Between 1806 and 1844 no less than fourteen governors followed one another. Among them Narciso Claveria (1844–49) is entitled to notice. He added the island of Balanguingui to the Spanish possessions. One of his declarations obtained for him great applause—that "he had left Spain torn by civil dissensions, but that he should make no distinctions between his countrymen on the ground of political differences, but forget all title except that of *Español y Caballero* (Spaniard and gentleman)." Since that time Ramon Montero has been their Governor *ad interim*, viz., in 1853, 1854, and 1856. The Marquis of Novaliches took possession of the government in 1854, but held it only for about eight months. Don Manuel Crespo arrived in November, 1854, and the present Governor-General, Don Fernando de Norzagaray, on the 9th of March, 1857.

It is worthy of note that during the period in which there have been seventy-eight governors, there have been only twenty-two archbishops; the average period of the civil holding being four years—that of the ecclesiastical, eleven and a-half years.

1

The account given by Spanish writers of the taking of Manila by the British forces, and here translated from Buzeta's narrative, seems given with as much fairness as could be expected.

"In 1762, the city of Manila had reached to wonderful prosperity. Its commercial relations extended to the Moluccas, Borneo, many parts of India, Malacca, Siam, Cochin China, China, Japan—in a word, to all places between the Isthmus of Suez and Behring's Straits. But at the end of this year a disaster visited the city which prostrated it for many years after. The English, then at war with Spain, presented themselves with considerable forces. The most illustrious Archbishop Don Manuel Royo, then temporarily in charge of the government, had received no notice of any declaration of war, and had made no preparations for defence. The enemy's fleet was the bearer of the news. The garrison was composed of the regiment *del rey*, which ought to have numbered 2,000 men, but was reduced to 500, by detachments, desertion and disease. There were only 80 artillerymen, all Indians, who knew little about the management of guns. In this state of matters, the English fleet suddenly appeared on the 22nd September, 1762. It consisted of thirteen ships, with 6,830 excellent troops. In total ignorance of public affairs, the fleet was supposed to be one of Chinese *sampans*. Some defensive measures were adopted, and an officer was sent to inquire of the commander of the fleet what was his nation, and what the object of his unannounced visit. The messenger returned the following day, accompanied by two English officers, who stated that the conquest of the islands was the purpose of the expedition. They were answered that the islands would defend themselves. On the night of the 23rd/24th, the enemy effected their disembarkation at the redoubt of St. Anthony Abbot. An attempt was made to dislodge them; it failed. They were fired upon in the morning of the 24th, but with little effect, so well were they entrenched and protected by various buildings. In order to arrest their proceedings, it was determined to make a vigorous sally, whose arrangement was left to M. Fallu, a French officer in the service of Spain; but this valiant soldier soon found that the foreign troops were too numerous to be dealt with by his forces. He fought during the night, and did not return to the citadel till 9 A.M. of the following day. There was a suspension of hostilities, and the invaders sent a flag of truce to the city. The bombardment continued on the 25th, and our grape-shot did much damage to the enemy. On the 28th, in the morning, the English general asked for the head of an officer who, having been the bearer of a flag of truce two days before, had been decapitated by the Indians. He demanded also the delivery of the persons who had committed the crime, and, if refused, threatened horrible reprisals. The requirement was complied with; and the Archbishop, who was exercising the functions of government, and directing the defence of the city, showed himself on horseback to the camp of the enemy, but without result. On the 29th, the English squadron received a reinforcement of three ships, which bore 350 Frenchmen from Pondicherry, who sought an opportunity to turn upon the English, and nominated two of their confidants to arrange their desertion and the accomplishment of their purpose; but the two confederates were supposed by the Indians to be Englishmen, and, instead of being welcomed, were slain. The English, being informed of what had taken place, secured themselves against further treachery on the part of the French. On the 3rd of October, a large force of Pampangan Indians having arrived, a sally was resolved upon: it was very bloody, but of no benefit for the defence. The following day the besiegers made a breach in the Fundicion bulwarks. A council of war was held, and the military decided that a capitulation was imperative: the citizens were for continuing the defence. Unfortunately the Archbishop was carried away from this opinion, which led to so many disasters for Manila. On the 4th, there was a general conviction that this city would soon be compelled to surrender; and the title of the Lieutenant to the Government having been conferred on the judge (*oidor*) Simon de Anda y Salazar, in order that he might transfer the seat of Spanish authority to some other part of the island, and provide for its defence, he left the same evening at 10 P.M., in a launch with a few rowers, a Tagál servant, 500 dollars in silver, and forty sheets of official stamped paper. These were his resources against an enemy having sixteen vessels in the bay, and who were on the point of entering the city. Thus without an army or a fleet, a man of more than threescore years reached Bulacan, determined on pertinacious opposition to those conquerors who were about to enter the capital. They did enter on the following day, leaving their entrenchments and advancing in three columns to the breach, which was scarcely practicable. Forty Frenchmen of Pondicherry led and found no resistance. The fortress was compelled to surrender. The city was sacked for forty hours, neither the churches nor the palace of the Archbishop or Governor finding any mercy. The loss of the Spaniards during the siege was three officers, two sergeants, fifty troops of the line, and thirty civilians of the militia, without reckoning the wounded; the Indians had 300 killed and 400 wounded. The besiegers lost about 1,000 men, of whom 16 were officers. The fleet fired upon the city more than 5,000 bombs, and more than 20,000 balls. It might have been hoped that a sack of forty hours and the capitulation of the garrison would have satisfied the enemy; it was not so, for during the sackage the English commander informed the Archbishop that all the inhabitants would be massacred if two millions of dollars were not immediately paid in coin, and two millions more in drafts on the Spanish treasury. To this it was necessary to accede, and the charitable funds and the silver ornaments of the churches were devoted to the payment.

While the events of Manila had this tragic termination, Anda collected in Bulacan the Alcalde, the ecclesiastics, and other Spaniards, showed them his authority, which was recognised with enthusiasm. On the evening of the same day news of the fall of Manila was received, and Anda published a proclamation declaring himself Governor and Captain-General of the Philippine Islands, and chose for the seat of his government Bacalor in Pampanga. He thus for fifteen months carried on the war, notwithstanding the insurrections fomented by the English, especially among the Chinese, and notwithstanding the general disorganization of the provinces. In fact, he almost kept the English blockaded in Manila, from whose walls they scarcely dared to venture. In Malenta, a property of the Augustin friars, a French sergeant, named Bretagne, who deserted from the English, and induced some thirty of his countrymen to follow his example, was made captain, and directed operations against the invaders, to whom he appears to have given much trouble by intercepting provisions, and attacking stragglers from the city. The English offered 5,000 dollars for the delivery of Anda alive into their hands. But on the 3rd July, 1763, a British frigate arrived announcing an armistice between the belligerent powers, and directing the cessation of hostilities. In March, 1764, news arrived of the treaty of peace; the English evacuated Manila, and Spanish authority was re-established. The mischief done by the English was repaired by Governor Basco." †

2

MS. of the Siege of Manila, by Fr. Juan de Santa Maria. †

CHAPTER IV.

GEOGRAPHY—CLIMATE, ETC.

INTERIOR OF THE CRATER OF THE VOLCANO AT TAAL.

The generally accepted theory as to the formation of the Philippines is, that they all formed part of a vast primitive continent, which was broken up by some great convulsion of nature, and that these islands are the scattered fragments of that continent. Buzeta supposes that from Luzon the other islands were detached.[1]

The Indians have a tradition that the earth was borne on the shoulders of a giant, who, getting tired of his heavy burden, tumbled it into the ocean, leaving nothing above the waters but the mountains, which became islands for the salvation of the human race.

I do not propose to give a detailed geographical description of the Philippine Islands. Buzeta's two octavo volumes will furnish the most accurate particulars with which I am acquainted as to the various localities. The facts which I collected in the course of my personal observation refer specially to the islands of Luzon, Panay, and Mindanao. The more general information has been derived from Spanish authorities on the spot, or has been found in Spanish books which I have consulted. I cannot presume to consider the present volume as complete or exhaustive, but it will contribute something to augment that knowledge which is already possessed.

The extent of the Philippine Archipelago is about 300 leagues from north to south, and 180 leagues from east to west. The islands of which it is composed are innumerable, most of the larger ones having some Spanish or mestizo population. A range of irregular mountains runs through the centre of the whole. Those known by the name of the Caraballos, in Luzon, are occupied by unsubdued races of idolatrous Indians, and extend for nearly sixty leagues. Several large rivers have their sources in the Caraballos. At the top of Mount Cabunian, whose ascent is very difficult, there is a tomb worshipped by the pagan Igorrotes. There are large lakes in several of the islands, and during the rainy season some of them become enormously extended. These inundations are naturally favourable to the vegetable productions by fertilizing vast tracts of land. *Mindanao*, which means "Men of the lake," has its Indian name from the abundance of its inward waters, in the same way that *La Laguna* has been adopted by the Spaniards as the designation of the province bordering on the Lake of Bay. In this latter district are many mineral and thermal springs, which have given to one of its pueblos the name of Los Baños (the baths). One of them issues from the source at a temperature of 67° of Reaumur. They are much visited by the inhabitants of Manila. There are boiling springs in the pueblo of Mainit.

The climate of the Philippines is little distinguished from that which characterizes many other tropical regions of the East. It is described in a Spanish proverb as—

> Seis meses de polvo,
>
> Seis meses de lodo,
>
> Seis meses de todo.

"Six months of dust, six months of mud, six months of everything;"—though it may generally be stated that the rainy season lasts one half, and the dry season the other half of the year. There are, however, as the distich says, many months of uncertainty, in which humidity invades the ordinary time of drought, and drought that of humidity. But from June to November the country is inundated, the roads are for the most part impassable, and travelling in the interior is difficult and disagreeable. Even in the month of December, in several districts of Luzon, we found, as before mentioned, places in which carriages are necessarily abandoned, the palanquin bearers being up to their thighs in mud; and other places in which we were compelled to open a new way through the woods. The heat is too oppressive to allow much active exertion in the middle of the day, and the *siesta* is generally resorted to from 1 to 3 o'clock P.M., before and after which time visits are paid and business transacted. The pleasant evening time is, however, that of social enjoyment, and the principal people have their *tertulias*, to which guests are welcomed from half-past 8 o'clock to about 11 o'clock P.M.

The variations of the thermometer rarely exceed 10° of Reaumur, the maximum heat being from 28° to 29°, the minimum 18° to 19°. Winter garments are scarcely ever required.

The difference between the longest and shortest day is 1h. 47m. 12s. On the 20th June, in Manila, the sun rises at 5h. 33m. 12s., and sets at 6h. 26m. 48s.; on the 20th December, it rises at 6h. 26m. 48s., and sets at 5h. 33m. 12s.

The minimum fall of rain in Manila is 84 inches, the maximum 114. Hailstorms are rare. There is no mountain sufficiently high to be "snow-capped;" the highest, Banaho, is between 6,000 and 7,000 feet above the level of the sea.

Like other tropical climates, the Philippines are visited by the usual calamities gathered by the wild elements round that line which is deemed the girdle of the world. Violent hurricanes produce fearful devastations; typhoons cover the coasts with wrecks; inundations of rivers and excessive rains destroy the earth's produce, while long-continued droughts are equally fatal to the labours and the hopes of husbandry. Earthquakes shake the land, overturn the strongest edifices and sport destructively with the power of man; volcanic mountains inundate the earth with their torrents of burning lava. Clouds of locusts sometimes devour all that is green upon the surface of the ground; and epidemic diseases carry away multitudes of the human race. The ravages caused by accidental fires are often most calamitous, as the greater part of the houses are constructed of inflammable materials. When such a disaster occurs, it spreads with wonderful rapidity, and, there being no adequate means of extinction, a whole population is often rendered houseless.

During the change of the monsoons especially, the storms are often terrific, accompanied by very violent rains, fierce lightning and loud thunder. If in the night, the darkness thickens. Many lose their lives by lightning strokes, and houses are frequently carried away by the vehemence of the torrents.

Bagyo is the Indian name for hurricane. These violent outbreaks are generally announced in the morning by a light smoky mist which appears on the mountains; it gathers, and darkens, and thickens into heavy clouds, and before day closes breaks out with its fearful and destroying violence, raging from an hour and a half to two hours. M. de Gentil says that in the torrid zone the clouds which bring the most destructive tornadoes are at an elevation not exceeding 400 toises of perpendicular height.

The largest of the volcanoes is that of Mayon in Luzon. It is in the shape of a sugar-loaf, perfectly conical. Its base covers several leagues in the provinces of Albay and Camarines, and it is one of the most prominent objects and landmarks visible from the sea; there is a constant smoke, sometimes accompanied by flames; its subterranean sounds are often heard at a distance of many leagues. The country in the neighbourhood is covered with sand and stone, which on different occasions have been vomited forth from the crater. There is a description by the Alcalde of an eruption in 1767, which lasted ten days, during which a cone of flame, whose base was about forty feet in diameter, ascended, and a river of lava was poured out for two months, 120 feet in breadth. Great ruin was caused to the adjacent villages. The lava torrent was followed about a month afterwards by enormous outpourings of water, which either greatly widened the beds of the existing rivers, or formed new channels in their rush towards the sea. The town of Malinao was wholly destroyed, and a third part of that of Casana. Many other villages suffered; forests were buried in sand; which also overwhelmed houses and human beings. The ravages extended over a space of six leagues.

From an eruption at Buhayan, sixty leagues from Zamboanga, in the island of Mindanao, in 1640, large masses of stone were flung to a distance of two leagues. The ashes fell in the Moluccas and in Borneo. Dense darkness covered Zamboanga. Ships at sea lighted their lamps at 8 A.M., but the light could not be seen through the clouds of sand. The mountain whence the explosion originated disappeared, and a lake was formed and still remains in the locality as a record of the agitation. The waters of the lake were long white with ashes. The noise of the eruption was heard in Manila.

About twenty leagues from Manila is the province of Batanga. In one of the bays is an island called by the natives *Binintiang Malagui*, remarkable for its beauty, for the variety of its vegetation, and the number of animals which inhabit it. The eastern part of the island is a mountain, whose extinct volcano is seen in the form of a truncated cone of enormous extent, surrounded by desolation. The flanks of the mountain have been torn by vast channels, down which the lava-streams must have flowed. The sides are covered with ferruginous and sulphurous pyrites and scoriæ, which make the ascent difficult. It is most accessible on the southern side, by which we reach the mouth of the crater, whose circumference exceeds three miles, and whose deep and wild recesses exhibit astounding evidences of the throes and agitations which in former times must have shaken and convulsed this portion of the earth. A Spanish writer says it looked "like an execrable blasphemy launched by Satan against God." There are still some signs of its past history in the smoke which rises from the abyss; but what characterizes the spot is the contrast between the gigantic wrecks and ruins of nature on one side, and the extreme loveliness and rich variety of other parts of the landscape. Descending into the crater by the help of cords round the body, a grand platform is reached at the depth of about 600 feet, in which are four smaller craters, one constantly and the others occasionally emitting a white smoke, but they cannot be approached on account of the softness and heat of the soil. To the east is a lake from which a stream runs round the craters over beds of sulphur, which assume the colour of emeralds. Formerly this lake was in a state of boiling ebullition, but is now scarcely above the natural temperature; it blackens silver immediately. Frequent earthquakes change the character of the crater and its neighbourhood, and every new detailed description differs from that which preceded it. The Indians have magnificent notions of the mineral riches buried in the bosom of the mountain, the sulphur mines of which were advantageously worked a few years ago, when a well-known naturalist (Lopez, now dead) offered to the Spanish government large sums for the monopoly of the right of mining the district of Taal.

On the 21st of September, 1716, sounds like those of heavy artillery proceeded from the Taal volcano, and the mountain seemed to be in a state of ignition over a space of three leagues towards Macolot. Gigantic towers of boiling water and ashes were thrown up, the earth shook on all sides, the waters of the lake were agitated and overran its banks: this lasted for three days. The water was blackened, and its sulphurous smell infested the whole district. In 1754 a yet more violent eruption, lasting eight days, took place, with terrible explosions, heavings of the earth, darkness, and such clouds of dust and ashes that all the roofs of the houses at Manila, at a distance of twenty leagues, were covered. Great masses of stones, fire and smoke were thrown from the mountain. The lake boiled in bubbles. Streams of bitumen and sulphur ran over the district of Bong-bong. The alligators, sharks, tunnies, and all the large fish, were destroyed in the river and flung upon the banks, impregnating the air with stench. It is said that subterranean and atmospheric thunders were heard at a distance of 300 leagues from the volcano, and that the winds carried the ashes to incredible distances. In Panay there was midday darkness. Many pueblos were wholly destroyed; among them Sala, Janavan, Lipa, and Taal: others bearing the same names have been since founded at a greater distance from the mountain.

Lopez gives a description of his descent into the crater. He employed 100 men for eight days to make a slope for his going down. He says the crater is oval, two miles in diameter; that the lake within the crater is surrounded by level and solid ground; that there was a deep chasm which had been recently ignited: there was sulphur enough to load many ships. He saw a cube of porphyry 20 to 25 feet square. The crater wall is perpendicular on all sides; that on the north 1,200 feet high, the lowest exceeding 900 feet. He says he believes the south sides to be of porphyry. At night, midway of the descent, he saw "thousands of millions" of jets, whose gas immediately inflamed on coming in contact with the atmosphere, and he heard many small detonations. The waters of the lake were impregnated with sulphuric acid, and 12 lbs. of the water, when distilled, left a mineral residuum weighing 2½ lbs.

There are many remarkable caves in the Philippines. I translate a description of one in the province of Tondo. Two stony mountains unite, and on their skirt is the road towards a branch of the main river. On the left is a cave whose entrance fronts the south. The mouth is almost covered with tangling vegetation, but it is arched, and, being all of marble, is, particularly in the sunshine, strikingly beautiful. You enter by a high, smooth, natural wall like the façade of a church, over which is a cavity roofed as a chapel. The interior pathway is flat, about four yards in breadth and six in height, though in some places it is much loftier. The roof presents a multitude of graceful figures, resembling pendent pineapples, which are formed by the constant filtration and petrifaction of the water. Some are nearly two yards in length, and seem sculptured into regular grooves; others are in the shape of pyramids whose bases are against the roof. Arches, which may be passed both from above and below, are among these wonderful works. Not far from the door is a natural staircase, mounting which you enter a large chamber, on whose right hand is another road, which, being followed, conducts to a second staircase, which opens on the principal communication. Suspended on one wing are immense numbers of bats, who occupy the recesses of the ceiling. Though there is mud in some of the paths, the ground is generally of stone, which, on being struck, gives a hollow sound as if there were passages below. Penetrating the cave for above 200 yards, a loud noise is perceived coming from a clear bright river, by the side of which the cave is continued under a semicircular roof. The great cave has many smaller vaults and projections of a grotesque and Gothic character. The course of the stream is from the north-west to the south-east.

The destructive ravages and changes produced by earthquakes are nowhere more remarkable than in the Philippines. They have overturned mountains, they have filled up valleys, they have desolated extensive plains; they have opened passages for the sea into the interior, and from the lakes into the sea There are many traditional stories of these territorial revolutions, but of late disasters the records are trustworthy. That of 1796 was sadly calamitous. In 1824 many churches in Manila were destroyed, together with the principal bridge, the barracks, great numbers of private houses; and a chasm opened of nearly four miles in length. The inhabitants all fled into the fields, and the six vessels in the port were wrecked. The number of victims was never ascertained. In 1828, during another earthquake, the vibration of the lamps was found to describe an arch of four and a half feet; the huge corner-stones of the principal gate of the city were displaced; the great bells were set ringing. It lasted between two and three minutes, rent the walls of several churches and other buildings, but was not accompanied by subterranean noises, as is usually the case.

There are too few occasions on which scientific observations have been made on the subject of earthquakes, which take men by surprise and ordinarily create so much alarm as to prevent accurate and authentic details. A gentleman who had established various pendulums in Manila for the purpose of measuring the inclination of the angles and the course of the agitation, states that, in the slight earthquakes of 20th and 23rd June, 1857, the thermometer being at 88°, the direction of the first shock was from N.N.E. to S.S.E., the duration 14 seconds, and the oscillation of the pendulum 1½ degrees; time, 2h. 0m. 40s. P.M.: 20th June. Second shock from N.E. to S.W.; duration, 26 seconds; oscillation of pendulum, 2 degrees; time, 2h. 47m. P.M.: 20th June. Third shock S.W. to N.; duration of the shock, 15 seconds; greatest oscillation, 6 degrees, but slight movements continued for a minute, and the oscillations were observed from 2 degrees to three-quarters of a degree; time, 5 P.M.: 23rd June.

Earthquakes have produced great changes in the geography of the Philippines. In that of 1627, one of the most elevated of the mountains of Cagayan disappeared. In 1675, in the island of Mindanao, a passage was opened to the sea, and a vast plain was emerged. Successive earthquakes have brought upon Luzon a series of calamities.

Endemic diseases are rare in the Philippines. Intermittent fevers and chronic dysentery are among the most dangerous disorders. There have been two invasions of cholera, in 1820 and 1842. Elephantiasis, leprosy, and St. Anthony's fire are the scourges of the Indians; and the wilder races of the interior suffer from a variety of cutaneous complaints. The biri biri is common and fatal. Venereal diseases are widely spread, but easily cured. Among the Indians, vegetables alone are used as medicaments. Chinese quack-doctors have much influence. In the removal of some of the tropical pests, no European can compete with the natives. They cure the itch with great dexterity, and are said to have remedies for pulmonary phthisis. Their plasters are very efficacious in external applications. They never employ the lancet or the leech. Surgical science is, of course, unknown.

There have been generally in the Philippines a few successful medical practitioners from Europe. Foreigners are allowed to exercise their profession, having previously obtained the authority of the Spanish Government; but the natives seldom look beyond their own simple mode of dealing with the common diseases of the islands; and in those parts where there is little or no Spanish population, no one is to be found to whom a surgical operation could safely be intrusted. The vegetable world furnishes a great variety of medicinal herbs, which the instinct or the experience of the Indian has turned to account, and which are, probably, on the whole, as efficacious as the more potent mineral remedies employed by European science. Quinine, opium, mercury, and arsenic, are the wonder-workers in the field of Oriental disease, and their early and proper application generally arrests the progress of malady.

I found practising in the island of Panay Dr. Lefevre, whom I had known in Egypt more than twenty years before, and who was one of the courageous men who boldly grappled with the current superstitions respecting the contagious character of the Oriental plague, and the delusions as to the efficacy of quarantine regulations, so really useless, costly, and vexatious. He placed in my hand some observations which he had published at Bombay in 1840, where vessels from the Red Sea were subjected to sanatory visitations. He asserts that plague is only generated at particular seasons, in certain definable conditions of the atmosphere, and when miasma is created by the decomposition of decaying matter; that endemic plague is unknown in countries where proper attention is paid to hygienic precautions; that severe cold or intense heat equally arrests the progress of the plague; that the epoch of its ravages is always one when damp and exposed animal and vegetable substances emit the greatest amount of noxious gases; and that plague has never been known to originate or to spread where the air is in a state of purity. I was glad to rediscuss the matter with him after so long an added experience, and to find he had been more and more confirmed in his former conclusions by prolonged residence in the tropics, where endemic and epidemic diseases partake of the pestilential character, though they do not assume the forms, of the Levant plague. Dr. Lefevre affirms that quarantines have done nothing whatever to lessen the dangers or check the ravages of the plague, but much to encourage its propagation. He complains of the deafness and incredulity of those whom the examination of a "thousand indisputable facts" will not convince, and he thus concludes:—"If I had not with peculiar attention studied the plague in the midst of an epidemic, and without any more precautions than if the danger was nothing—if, subsequent to the terrible visitation of 1835 in Egypt, I had not been frequently a witness to the scourge —if, finally, since that epoch I had not given myself up, with all the warmth of passion, to the constant study of this malady, to the perusal of histories of the plagues which have ravaged the world, and to the examination of all sorts of objections—I should not have dared to emit such a decided opinion—an opinion respecting the soundness of which I do not entertain the slightest doubt."

One cannot but be struck, in reference to the geographical character of these islands, with the awful serenity and magnificent beauty of their primeval forests, so seldom penetrated, and in their recesses hitherto inaccessible to the foot of man. There is nothing to disturb their silence but the hum of insects, the song of birds, the noises of wild animals, the rustling of the leaves, or the fall of decayed branches. It seems as if vegetation revelled in undisturbed and uncontrolled luxuriance. Creeping plants wander from tree to tree; lovely orchids hang themselves from trunks and boughs. One asks, why is so much sweetness, so much glory, wasted? But is it wasted? To the Creator the contemplation of his works, even where unmarked by human eye, must be complacent; and these half-concealed, half-developed treasures, are but reserved storehouses for man to explore; they will furnish supplies to awaken the curiosity and gratify the inquiry of successive ages. Rove where he may— explore as he will—tax his intellect with research, his imagination with inventions—there is, there will be, an infinite field around and above him, inexhaustible through countless generations.

1

Diccionario geográfico, estadístico, histórico de las Islas Filipinas. 2 vols. Madrid, 1850.

CHAPTER V.

GOVERNMENT—ADMINISTRATION, ETC.

The Administration of the Philippine Archipelago has for its head and chief a captain and governor-general, who resides in Manila, the capital of the islands, and who is not permitted to quit them without the authority of the sovereign of Spain. Next to the government of Cuba, it is the most important and the most lucrative post at the disposal of the Cabinet of Madrid, and has unfortunately been generally one of the prizes wrested from the unsuccessful, and seized by the predominant, political party. It was rather a melancholy employment for me to look over the collection of portraits of captains-general, and many vacant frames waiting for future occupants, which ornament the walls of the handsome apartments in which I dwelt at the palace. Since 1835 there have been five provisional and eleven formal appointments to the governor-generalship. Some of these only held their authority for a few months, being superseded by ministerial changes at Madrid. Of other high functionaries, I observe that there have been only two archbishops since 1830, while it is understood that the service of heads of departments is assured for ten years. To the public interests the mischiefs which are the results of so uncertain a hold of the supreme authority are incalculable. The frequent and sudden removals and nominations are, indeed, little consistent with the principles of monarchical and hereditary government, however accordant with the republican institutions of the Western world; and among the causes of the slow development of the immense resources of these beautiful islands, the fluctuation of the superintending rule is assuredly one of the most prominent.

The titles of the captain-general occupy a page, and embrace the usual attributes of government, with the exception of authority over the fleet, which is subject to the Ministry of Marine in Spain, and a somewhat limited jurisdiction in ecclesiastical matters, which is a consequence of the exclusive establishment of the Roman Catholic faith.

The lieutenant-governor, who takes the place of the captain-general in case of his death, is called the *Segundo Cabo*, or second head.

The Philippine Islands are divided into provinces, subject either to politico-military governors or alcaldes mayores, who are generally civilians.

When the government is military, an assistant lieutenant-governor, who must have graduated as a lawyer, exercises the preliminary jurisdiction (*de primera instancia*), but the alcaldes hold that jurisdiction in their own persons. Both dispose in their provinces of the military authority, and have the controlling direction of the collection of the revenues, under responsibility to the General Administrator of Tributes.

The provinces are divided into *pueblos* (towns or villages), over each of which a native Indian or mestizo, called a *gobernadorcillo* (diminutive of governor) is placed. He is assisted in the discharge of his functions by native lieutenants and alguacils, whose number depends upon the extent of the population. This body, which, when gathered together, is called the *principalia* of the pueblo, settles all minor matters of police and civil questions between the natives as to rights of persons and property. In districts where the Chinese or their descendants are sufficiently numerous (they are known by the name of *Sangleyes*), they are allowed, under special authority of the government, to select principalia from their own body, independently of Indian jurisdiction. These principalia are really popularly chosen municipalities, and they are specially charged to assist the clergy in all matters connected with public worship and ecclesiastical authority. They determine questions up to the amount of two taels of gold, or forty-four silver dollars. They collect evidence in criminal cases, which is submitted to the provincial chief; they assist in the collection of the royal revenues, circulate the ordinances of the government among the people, and are authorized to levy a small but defined contribution in support of their dignity.

Besides these, there are in every pueblo certain functionaries who are called *Cabezas* (heads) *de Barangay*. A barangay is a collection of the chiefs of families, or persons paying tribute, generally amounting to forty or fifty. They are under the special charge of the cabeza, who must dwell among them, and, under bond, collect the tribute due to the State. He is required to settle misunderstandings and to maintain peace and order, to apportion the various charges among the members of the barangay, and to collect the taxes for payment to the gobernadorcillo, or to the functionary appointed for the purpose. The cabezas are also considered the *procuradores*, or law advisers, of these little communities.

In ancient times there is little doubt that the office was hereditary; and there are yet localities where the hereditary right is maintained; but it is generally elective: and when a vacancy occurs, the gobernadorcillo in council, with the other cabezas, presents a name for the approval of the superior authority, and the same steps are taken when the increase of population requires a new cabeza to be nominated. The cabezas, their wives and first-born, who are required to assist in the collection of the tribute, are exempted from its payment.

In some provinces the cabezas are only chosen for three years; after which they form part of the principalia, and take the title of Don. I remember, in one locality, that the principalia who came to pay their respects consisted of more than seventy persons. The government complains of the number who, under this state of things, are exempted from taxation, and I understand some measures are in contemplation for limiting the extent of the privileges.

The elections of the gobernadorcillo are annual, and take place on the 1st of April. An extraordinary excitement generally prevails, the post (a really important, popular, and influential one) being an object of much ambition. Three names are selected, one of whom must have already served as gobernadorcillo, for submission to the superior authority, on or before the 15th of May, and the chosen gobernadorcillo enters on his functions on the 1st of June. There is, however, some alteration of dates, where, as in the tobacco districts, the period of election interferes with harvest time.

The head of the province ordinarily presides over the elections, to which the principal ecclesiastic is also invited. In case of their absence, any native-born Spaniard may be nominated by the principal authority to preside.

There are thirteen electors for each pueblo—the gobernadorcillo and twelve inhabitants—half of whom must have been gobernadorcillos or cabezas, and the other half be in the actual exercise of those functions; they must also have some well-recognized means of existence: domestic servants to the authorities are excluded; as also those who have been punished as criminals.

It is further required that the gobernadorcillo be a native Indian or mestizo, an inhabitant of the locality where he serves, and above twenty-five years old; having passed the subordinate offices of lieutenant or cabeza, having his accounts in order, holding no land from the community, and no monopoly (*estanco*) from the government. Similar recommendations are insisted on for the first lieutenant and the principal (native) magistrates appointed for the settlement of questions regarding seed-sowing, police, and cattle. These magistrates must have enjoyed the rank of gobernadorcillo. As regards the minor officers of justice and their attendants, a list is to be made out by the gobernadorcillo before quitting office, which is to be presented to the authority presiding over the elections, and having heard the clergyman (*cura*) and the committee of election, the president approves the list for transmission to the supreme authority; but if he finds discordance and irreconcilable opinions between the parties before him, he is authorized himself to recommend the officers for nomination.

All the proceedings are the subjects of record, and to be signed by the president, the curate (if present), the electors, and the public notary, and to be remitted to the supreme authority, except in the provinces adjacent to the capital. The president may attach to the record any observations of his own connected with the returns. A decree of 1850 required the general adoption of the system which has been described, and which appears to me well worthy of note, showing how many valuable elements of good government are to be found in the popular institutions of the Philippine Indians.

The Chinese of the capital may elect Christian converts of their own body, under the presidency of the alcalde mayor of Manila, to the offices of gobernadorcillo, first lieutenant, and principal *alguacil* (bailiff). The dependent subordinate officers of justice are called *bilangos*, and are appointed by the gobernadorcillo on his election. The recovery of the tribute or taxes from the Chinese is not left to their principalia, but is effected by the alcalde mayor or superior chief. An officer is appointed to classify the Chinese, and apportion the quota of their contributions according to the wealth of the payer, who is charged for what is called a *patente industrial*.

The gobernadorcillos and officers of justice are entitled to sit in the presence of the provincial chiefs, who are to require the parochial clergy to treat them with due honour and regard.

M. Mallat, whose Geographical History of the Philippines was published in 1846, remarks that, of all colonies founded by Europeans, these regions are perhaps the least known, and the most worthy of being known. The number of islands which compose the archipelago,—their vast extent and boundless variety,—the teeming population of many of them,—the character of the climate,—the wonderful fertility of the soil,—the inexhaustible riches of hill, valley, and plain,—all offer to cultivation and its civilizing influences abundant rewards. But as regards the "industrious habits" of the natives, I cannot place that consideration, as M. Mallat does, among the elements of hope. It is the want of these "industrious habits," among four or five millions of inhabitants, which has left the Philippines in a position so little advanced.

Java under the government of the Dutch, and Cuba subjected to the Spanish rule, present, no doubt, far more favourable pictures than do the Philippines; but many of the difficulties which surround the captain-general of Manila,— difficulties both religious and social,—do not embarrass the governor of Batavia; the island of Java, the most productive of Netherlands India, being peculiarly free from these difficulties; and it cannot be said that Sumatra and Borneo are even on a level with the more advanced of the Philippine Islands.

To the character of the original conquest and of the earlier government of the Philippines may be traced many of the impediments which now stand in the way of improvement. In America and the West Indies all the brutality of military conquerors was exhibited, and the possession and plunder of new territories were encouraged by the Spanish court, and were the main object of the Spanish invader. But far different was the policy adopted in the Philippines, where only a small body of soldiers was accompanied by zealous missionaries, whose purpose was rather to convert and christianize the Indians than to pillage and destroy them. These friars gradually obtained a paramount influence over the Indians. The interests of trade have ever been the predominant consideration among Dutch colonizers, and among British adventurers the commercial element has always been intimately associated with the desire for territorial occupation. To the Spaniards it must be conceded that the religious purpose—be its value what it may—has never been abandoned or forgotten. Ecclesiastical jurisdiction and authority are interwoven in the Philippines with the machinery of government and the daily concerns of life.

And such ecclesiastical action has been comparatively little interfered with in the Philippines. The development which mental emancipation has given to many Protestant countries and their dependencies has reached few Catholic colonies; nor is that emancipation, indeed, consistent with the more rigid discipline and doctrines of Rome. But in the case of the most prosperous instances of colonization by the British, the native races have either wholly disappeared or are in progress of extinction, while the infusion of Spanish and foreign blood into the colonies of Spain has not only allowed the increase of the indigenous population, but has been insufficient to change or do more than slightly modify their national characters. It has undoubtedly been the boast of the Catholics that Francis de Xavier and his followers won more for the Roman Church in the East than Luther or Calvin ever tore away from it in the West; but the value of the conquests, contrasted with that of the losses and sacrifices, if fairly estimated, would hardly be deemed unsatisfactory to the Protestant cause.

No doubt the great remoteness of the Philippines from Europe, the difficulties and infrequency of communication, gave to the local authorities more of independent action than would otherwise have been allowed to them; and in case of the death of the governor, the archbishop was generally the functionary who filled his place; his adjacency to the government, and frequent direction of it, naturally led to the strengthening of his own authority and that of all ecclesiastics dependent upon him.

In the earlier periods of Eastern colonization, too, the Portuguese, jealous of all European intercourse but their own with nations east of the Cape, did all in their power to prevent any other than the Lusitanian flag from being seen in Oriental waters. But as regards missionary objects their views were to some extent concurrent with those of the Spanish priests, and their proceedings were in harmony with those of the Spaniards, especially in so far as both received their direction from the Pontiff at Rome. It ought not, however, to be forgotten that whatever may have been the progress of Christianity in the Philippines, the persecutions, disasters, discomfiture, and death of so many professing Christians in Japan, are probably attributable to the ill-guided zeal of the Portuguese preachers of the Gospel in these still remoter regions. It is well for the interests of truth, as most assuredly it is for the interests of commerce and civilization, that a more temperate and tolerant spirit has for the last century been associated with the progress of European influence in the East.

The comparatively small number of Spanish settlers in the Philippines would not allow them, even if such had been their purpose, which it does not appear to have been, unnecessarily to interfere with the usages of the Indians, or their forms of administration and government, except in so far as their conversion to Christianity compelled the observance of the Christian rites; and the friars willingly accommodated their action to the social habits of the people, respecting, as to this hour are respected, most of the patriarchal forms of administration and government which had existed among them from immemorial time.

There have been speculations—and M. Mallat is among the sanguine anticipators of such an advent—that in process of time the Philippines may become the dominant political power of the Eastern world, subjecting to its paramount influence the Netherlands Archipelago, the Pacific, Australia, and even China and Japan, and that Manila is destined to be the great emporium for the eastern and south-eastern world. M. Mallat even goes further, and says: "Manila might easily become the centre of the exports and imports of the entire globe." It must be contented with a less brilliant futurity. Certainly its commercial relations might be greatly extended, and the Spanish archipelago be much elevated in value and in influence; but in the vast development of commercial relations in the Oriental world, the Philippines must be contented with a moderate though a considerable share of benefit, even under the best administration and the adoption of the wisest policy.

Tropical regions fail to attract permanent settlers from the West. The foreign merchant comes to realize what he deems an adequate fortune, and to withdraw; the superior public functionary is among, or above, but never of, the people. What must be looked to is the popular element. Of what are the millions composed, and how can the millions be turned to account? There is no reason to apprehend that these millions will aspire to political power or sovereignty. Their pristine habits would permit of no general organization. The various races and clans would never unite in a national object, or recognize one native chief. All that is found of order and government among them is local; except through and for their masters, the different islands have little or no intercourse with one another. The Tagál and the Bisayan have no common sympathies. Dissatisfaction might produce disorder, which, if not controlled, would lead to anarchy, but not to good government.

The Philippines are free from the curse of slavery. Time will settle the controversy as to whether the labour of the freeman can, in the long run, be brought into competition with that of the slave, especially in the tropics; but that the great tide of tendency flows towards the abolition of slavery, that civilizing opinion and enlightened Christian legislation must sweep the ignominy away, is a conviction which possesses the minds of all who see "progress" in the world.

As it is, the Philippines have made, and continue to make, large contributions to the mother country, generally in excess of the stipulated amount which is called the *situado*. Spain, in her extreme embarrassment, has frequently called on the Philippines to come to her aid, and it is to the credit of the successive governors-general that, whatever may have been the financial disorders at home, the dependants upon the Manila treasury have had little motive for complaint, and while the Peninsula was engaged in perilous struggles for her independence, and even her existence as a nation, the public tranquillity of her island colonies was, on the whole, satisfactorily maintained, and interruptions to the ordinary march of affairs of short endurance.

There would seem to be no legislation defining the powers of the viceroy, or captain-general; but whenever any important matter is under discussion, it is found that reference must be made to Madrid, and that the supreme rule of this vast archipelago is in the leading strings of the Spanish Cabinet, impotent to correct any great abuses, or to introduce any important reforms. The captain-general should be invested with a large amount of power, subject, of course, to a personal responsibility as to its becoming exercise. As he must, if properly selected, know more, being present, than strangers who are absent, his government should be trusted on account of that superior knowledge. Well does the Castilian proverb say, "Mas sabe el loco en su casa que el cuerdo en la agena"—"The fool knows more about his own house than the sage about the house of another." He should be liberally paid, that the motives for corruption be diminished. He should be surrounded by a council composed of the best qualified advisers. Many objects would necessarily occupy the attention of such a body, and it would naturally have to create becoming local machinery and to furnish the materials for improved administration, such as surveys and statistics of the land and population, which would lead to a more satisfactory distribution of provinces, districts and pueblos. A simple code of civil and criminal law would be a great blessing, and should be grounded, in so far as the real interests of justice will allow, upon the customs and habits of the people, while employing, when compatible with those interests, the administrative local machinery in use among the natives.

Nothing would be more beneficial to the interests of Manila than the establishment of an efficient board of works, with provincial ramifications, to whose attention the facilitating communications should be specially recommended. The cost and difficulty of transport are among the principal impediments to the development of the resources of the islands, and the tardy progress of the few works which are undertaken is discouraging to those who suggest, and disappointing to those who expect to benefit by them. In many of the provinces the bridges are in miserable condition, and the roads frequently impassable. Even in the populous island of Panay delays the most costly and annoying interfere with the transport of produce to the capital and naturally impede the development of commerce. There is, no doubt, a great want of directing talent and of that special knowledge which modern science is able to furnish. The construction of bridges being generally left to the rude artists who are employed by the Spanish functionaries, or to the direction of the friars, with whom the *stare super antiquas vias* is the generally received maxim, it is not wonderful that there should be so many examples of rude, unsafe and unsightly constructions. Moreover, estimates have to be sent to the capital of all the proposed outlay, and it is hardly to be expected but that sad evidence should be found—as elsewhere—of short-sighted and very costly economy. The expense, too, almost invariably exceeds the estimates—a pretty general scandal; then the work is arrested, and sometimes wholly abandoned. Funds there are none, and neither policy nor patriotism will provide them. Even when strongly impelled, the Indian moves slowly; self-action for the promotion of the public good he has none. There is no pressure from without to force improvements upon the authorities, and hence little is to be hoped for as to improvement except from direct administrative action.

I can hardly pass over unnoticed M. de la Gironière's romantic book,[1] as it was the subject of frequent conversations in the Philippines. No doubt he has dwelt there twenty years; but in the experience of those who have lived there more than twice twenty I found little confirmation of the strange stories which are crowded into his strange volume. He was a resident of the Philippines at the time of my visit, and I believe still lives on the property of which he was formerly—but I was told is no longer—the possessor.[2] I did not visit his "Paradise," but had some agreeable intercourse with a French gentleman who is now in charge. I did not find any of that extraordinary savagery with which M. de la Gironière represents himself to be surrounded; and the answer to the inquiries I made of the neighbouring authorities as to the correctness of his pictures of Indian character was generally a shrug and a smile and a reference to my own experience. But M. de la Gironière may have aspired to the honour of a Bernardin de St. Pierre or a Defoe, and have thought a few fanciful and tragic decorations would add to the interest of his personal drama. "All the world's a stage," and as a player thereon M. de la Gironière perhaps felt himself authorized in the indulgence of some latitude of description, especially when his chosen "stage" was one meant to exhibit the wonders of travel.

As to M. de la Gironière's marvellous encounters and miraculous escapes from man and beast; his presence at feasts where among the delicacies were human brains, steeped by young girls in the juice of sugar-cane, of which he did not drink, but his servant did; his discoveries of native hands in "savory" pots prepared for food; his narratives where the rude Indians tell elaborate tales in the lackadaisy style of a fantastic novel; his vast possessions; his incredible influence over ferocious bandits and cruel savages;—all this must be taken at its value. I confess I have seen with some surprise, in M. de la Gironière's book, two "testimonies" from M. Dumont d'Urville and Admiral La Place, in which, among other matters, they give an account of the hatching of eggs by men specially engaged for this purpose.[3] They saw, as any one may, in the villages on the Pasig River, prodigious quantities of ducks and ducklings, and were "puzzled" to find how such multitudes could be produced; but they learnt the wonderful feat was accomplished by "lazy Tagál Indians," who lay themselves down upon the eggs, which are placed in ashes. The patient incubators eat, drink, smoke, and chew their betel, and while they take care not to injure the fragile shells, they carefully remove the ducklings as they are brought into being (pp. 358 and 362). Now it may well be asked who takes care when the lazy Tagáls are asleep; and, if our worthy witnesses had reflected for a moment, they would have known that, if *all* the inhabitants were employed in no other office than that of egg-hatching, they would be hardly sufficient to incubate the "prodigious" numbers of ducklings which disport on the banks of the Pasig. The incubation is really produced by placing warm paddy husks under and over the eggs; they are deposited in frames; a canvas covering is spread over the husks; the art is to keep up the needful temperature; and one man is sufficient to the care of a large number of frames, from which he releases the ducklings as they are hatched, and conveys them in little flocks to the water-side. The communities are separated from one another by bamboo fences, but there is scarcely a cottage with a river frontage which has not its *patero* (or duckery).

1

There is an English translation—"Twenty Years in the Philippines." Vizetelly. 1853.

2

I learn from the Captain-General that Messrs. de la Gironière and Montblanc are now charged with "a scientific mission to the Philippines," under the auspices of the French government.

3

I find in Mr. Dixon's book on Domestic Poultry the merits of this discovery in the science of incubation attributed to an ancient couple, whose goose having been killed while "sitting," the old man transferred the "cooling" eggs to their common bed, and he and the old lady taking their turns, safely brought the goslings into being. I ought to mention that confirmatory proofs of M. de la Gironière's narrative are added from Mr. H. Lindsay; but Mr. Lindsay guards himself against endorsing the "strange stories" with which M. de la Gironière's book abounds.

CHAPTER VI.

POPULATION.

In the last generation a wonderful sensation was produced by the propagation of the great Malthusian discovery—the irresistible, indisputable, inexorable truth—that the productive powers of the soil were less and less able to compete with the consuming demands of the human race; that while population was increasing with the rapidity of a swift geometrical progression, the means of providing food lagged with the feebleness of a slow arithmetical advance more and more behind; that the seats at nature's table—rich and abundant though it was—were being abundantly filled, and that there was no room for superfluous and uninvited guests; in a word, to use the adopted formula, that population was pressing more and more upon subsistence, and that the results must be increasing want, augmenting misery, and a train of calamities boundless as the catalogue of the infinite forms of mortal wretchedness.

How often, when threading through the thousand islands of the Philippine Archipelago, did the shadow of Malthus and the visions of his philosophy present themselves to my thoughts. Of those unnumbered, sea-surrounded regions, how many there are that have never been trodden by European foot, how few that have been thoroughly explored, and fewer still that are now inhabited by any civilized or foreign race! And yet they are covered with beautiful and spontaneous vegetable riches above, and bear countless treasures of mineral wealth below; their powers of production are boundless; they have the varieties of climate which mountains, valleys and plains afford —rains to water—suns to ripen—rivers to conduct—harbours for shipment— every recommendation to attract adventure and to reward industry; a population of only five or six millions, when ten times that number might be supplied to satiety, and enabled to provide for millions upon millions more out of the superfluities of their means.

To what a narrow field of observation must the mind have been confined that felt alarm at a discovery, in itself of so little importance, when brought into the vast sphere of the world's geography! Though the human race has been increasing at a rapid and almost immeasurable rate, it will be probably found that famines, and plagues, and wars, and those calamitous visitations which were deemed the redressers of the balance—the restorers of the due proportions between man's wants and man's supplies—were far more disastrous in ancient than in modern times, if the smaller number of then existing human beings be taken into consideration.

The nobler and higher axiom is that "progress" is the law of Providence, which never fails, while the race of man proceeds in ever-augmenting numbers, to provide ample means for their maintenance and happiness. Neither land nor sea is exhausted nor in process of exhaustion. What myriads of acres, whether in cold, temperate, or tropical climes, remain to be appropriated! what still greater amount to be improved by cultivation! And while in the more densely peopled parts of the world outlets may be required for those who are ill at ease and born to no inheritance but labour, how wonderfully are locomotive facilities increased, so that the embarrassment to ambulatory man is less to discover a fit place for his domicile, than to select one amid the many which offer themselves to his choice! If the poverty-struck Irish could emigrate in such multitudes to American or Australian regions, far greater are the facilities possessed by those better conditioned labouring masses of Europe who are still heavily pressed by the competition of neighbours more fortunate than themselves.

It is a matter of surprise that the Spanish colonies should not have attracted a greater number of Spaniards to settle in them; but the national spirit of the Iberian peninsula has ceased to be ambulatory or adventurous. Spain itself is thinly peopled, and offers great resources to its satisfied peasantry. "God," they say, "has given everything to Spain which He had to give. Our land is an Eden—why should we desert it?" Yet Spain, backward, inert and unenergetic, as she has proved herself to be in the rivalry of active nations, has taken her part in the proud history of human advancement. The more enterprising invaders of Gothic or Anglo-Saxon blood have frequently extirpated the indigenous races of the remote countries in which they have settled. One wave of emigration has followed another; commerce and cultivation have created a demand for, and provided a supply of, the intrusive visitors. But Spain has never furnished such numbers as to dislodge the aboriginal tribes. Her colonists have been always accompanied by large bodies of ecclesiastics, bent upon bringing "the heathen" into the Christian fold. These missionaries have no doubt often stood between the cupidity of the conqueror and the weakness of the conquered. They have preserved, by protecting the Indian clans, and it may be doubted whether ultimately the permanent interests of man will not have been served by influences, whose beneficial consequences may remain when the most prominent evils connected with those influences may be greatly modified or wholly pass away.

My observations and my reflections, then, lead to this conclusion—that, whatever exceptional cases there may be, the great tide of advancement rolls forward in ever-growing strength;—that the course of the Divine government is

> From seeming evil still educing *good*,
> And BETTER thence again, and BETTER still,
> In infinite progression;—

that the human family, taken as a whole, is constantly improving;—that every generation is wiser and better than that which preceded it;—that the savage and least improvable races will continue to be supplanted or absorbed by those of a higher intelligence;—that the semi-civilized will only be perpetuated by contact with a greater civilization, which will raise them in the scale of humanity. A middle race, such as China contributes in the shape of emigrating millions, is wonderfully advancing the work of civilization. The process is everywhere visible in the remoter Eastern world. The mestizo descendants of Chinese fathers and Indian mothers form incomparably the most promising portion of the Philippine population. In Siam, Burmah, Cochin China, profitable employments are mainly absorbed by Chinese settlers. In Netherlands India they are almost invariably prosperous. To them Sumatra, Borneo, and the other islands, must look, and not to the indigenous peoples, for any considerable development of their resources. In our Straits Archipelago they have superseded the *Klings* in all the most beneficial fields of labour, as the Klings had previously superseded the less industrious *Malays*. The progress of the higher capabilities, and the depression of the lower, may be traced in the extinction of so many rude languages and the spread of those which represent civilization in its most advanced stages. It may be foretold, I think, without presumption, that in some future time the number of tongues spoken on the face of the globe will be reduced to a very small amount. In the course of a century many a local idiom utterly perishes, and is invariably replaced by one of more extensive range and greater utility. When it is remembered that the *written* language of China is understood by one-third of the human race; that probably more than one-tenth of mankind have an acquaintance with *spoken* English—the language which has far more widely planted roots, and more extensive ramifications, than any other; when the daily decay of the provincial dialects of France, Germany, Spain, and Italy is watched, good ground will be discovered for the anticipation that many of the existing instruments for oral communication will be extinguished, the number of dead languages will be much augmented, and of living proportionally decreased.

I know not on what authority M. Mallat estimated, in 1846, the population of the Philippines at 7,000,000,—an augmentation, he says, of more than 50 per cent from 1816, when he states the population to have been 4,600,000. He says that it quadrupled itself from 1774 to 1816. He attributes the enormous increase from the later period to the introduction of vaccination and the general tranquillity of the country; but the correctness of the data may well be doubted.

The Christian population of the Philippines is stated by Father Juan Fernandez to be—

——	Pueblos.	Souls.
Under the Archbishopric of Manila	185	135,000
Bishopric of New Segovia	132	745,000
" " Bishopric of New Caceres	104	480,000
" " Bishopric of Zebu	306	1,200,000
" " In all	727	3,560,000

The population of the Philippines is generally supposed to be about four millions; but, as the Indians who dwell in the interior of several of the islands —those especially who occupy the unexplored forest and mountainous districts—cannot be included in any official census, any calculations can only be deemed approximative. The returns furnished by the government to the *Guia de Foresteros* for the year 1858 give the following results:—

Provinces.	Natives paying tribute.	Mestizos and Chinese Tributaries.	Total Population.	Births.	Deaths.	Marriages.
Manila	86,250	25,418	276,059	11,346	9,251	1,956
Bulacan	91,551	12,119	214,261	8,789	5,172	1,542
Pampanga	79,912	9,631	170,849	9,101	4,407	2,237
Nueva Ecija	40,949	...	74,698	5,963	2,547	1,176
Bataan	17,473	3,176	42,332	1,941	1,171	347
Cavite	41,471	6,943	56,832	8,867	2,619	868
Batangas	115,359	3,063	247,676	11,133	6,270	1,956
Moron	20,288	1,964	43,010	1,900	1,508	553
La Laguna	65,177	1,866	132,264	5,935	4,295	1,553
Zambales	28,023	149	31,116	2,320	1,191	635
Mindoro	7,335	...	15,135	734	645	191

Pangasinan	97,786	1,551	272,427	9,172	6,368	2,756
La Union	39,044	117	45,657	3,894	1,526	1,165
Ilocos Sur	77,974	2,293	179,407	7,305	3,647	1,801
Ilocos Norte	70,305	16	140,226	6,189	3,695	1,536
Cagayan	27,784	71	54,457	2,443	1,489	638
Abra	8,009	200	36,737	782	354	407
Nueva Biscaya	6,116	...	19,754	452	387	131
La Isabela	14,112	...	26,372	1,040	757	265
Camarines	78,012	125	209,696	6,273	3,456	1,770
Albay	103,928	990	204,840	7,458	6,722	1,099
Tayabas	44,940	154	102,210	3,049	2,124	949
Burias	470	...	525	17	12	1
Masbate of Ticao	5,421	27	10,992	249	103	55
Zebu	81,457	4,267	267,540	12,653	3,740	2,374
Negros	24,522	394	113,379	4,499	2,688	804
Calamianes	4,003	...	17,964	730	279	172
Bohol	64,760	692	175,686	5,924	2,476	1,452
Samar	61,586	437	117,866	6,161	3,437	1,863
Leite	66,371	790	134,493	5,582	2,168	1,387
Antique	25,567	42	77,639	4,810	1,708	664
Iloilo	174,884	1,442	527,970	17,675	9,231	3,697
Capiz	66,614	8	143,713	9,810	4,199	1,187
Surigao	13,801	148	18,848	944	525	181
Misamis	23,729	266	46,517	2,155	845	396
Zamboanga	3,871	16	10,191	429	956	55
Basilan	167	4	447	43	71	
Bislig	4,686	21	12,718	394	143	112
Davao	304	...	800	21	9	18
Romblon	3,517	...	17,068	892	375	149
Totals	1,787,528	78,400	4,290,371	184,074	102,466	40,093

Proportion of natives to mixed races	96.00 per cent.
" natives (paying tribute) to	29.00
" " " population	" "

69

		mixed races to population	1.75
„	„ „	births to population	„ „ 4.00
„	„ „	deaths to population	„ „ 2.33
„	„ „	marriages to population	„ „ .90
„	„ „	births to deaths	„ „ 64.00 to 36.00
„	„ „		„
		births to marriages	„ 2.70
„	„ „		„ „

Imperfect returns are given from Corregidor and Pulo Caballo, 370 inhabitants in all: From Benguet, 6,803, of whom 4,639 are pagans, and 15 Christian tributaries: From Cayan, 17,035, the whole population, of which 10,861 tributaries.

The number of European Spaniards settled in the Philippines bears a very small proportion to that of the mixed races. There are 670 males and 119 females in the capital (Manila and Binondo). Of these there are 114 friars, all living in Manila, eight ecclesiastics, forty-six merchants, fourteen medical practitioners, and the majority of the others military and civil functionaries. But in none of the islands does the proportion of Spaniards approach that which is found in the capital. Probably the whole number of European Spaniards in the islands does not amount to two thousand.

There are ninety-six foreigners established in Binondo—eighty-five males and eleven females (none in Manila proper). Of these fifty are merchants or merchants' assistants. There are twenty-two British subjects, fifteen French, fifteen South Americans, eleven citizens of the United States, nine Germans, and nine Swiss.

Independently of European Spaniards, there are many families which call themselves *hijos del pays* (children of the country), descendants of Spanish settlers, who avoid mingling with native Indian blood. They have the reputation of being more susceptible than are even the old Castilians in matters of etiquette, and among them are many who have received a European education. They are generally candidates for public employment, but are said to be less steady, and more addicted to play and to pleasure, than their progenitors; but they are eminently hospitable. They dress in European style when they appear in public, but at home both men and women use the loose and more convenient Indian costume. They complain, on their part, that barriers are raised between them and their countrymen from the Peninsula; in a word, that the spirit of caste exercises its separating and alienating influences in the Philippines, as elsewhere.

The mestizos, or mixed races, form a numerous and influential portion of the Filipinos; the number settled in the islands of women of European birth is small, and generally speaking they are the wives of the higher Spanish functionaries and of superior officers in the army and navy, whose term of service is generally limited. Though the daughters of families of pure Spanish blood generally marry in the colony and keep up a good deal of exclusiveness and caste, it is seldom that the highest society is without a large proportion of mestiza ladies, children of Spanish fathers and native mothers. The great majority of the merchants and landed proprietors belong to this class, and most of the subordinate offices of government are filled by them. There are very many descendants of Chinese by native women; but the paternal type seems so to absorb the maternal, that the children for whole generations bear the strongly marked character which distinguishes the genuine native of the flowery land, even through a succession of Indian mothers. I shall have occasion to speak of a visit I made to a district (Molo, near Iloilo), which in former times had been the seat of a large Chinese colony, where the Chinese race had disappeared centuries ago, but the Chinese physiognomy, and the Chinese character, had left their unmistakable traces in the whole population. I found nowhere among the natives a people so industrious, so persevering, so economical, and, generally, so prosperous. Almost every house had a loom, and it is the place where the best of the piña fabrics are woven. We were invited to a ball at which the principal native ladies were present, and I had to answer a *discurso* delivered in excellent Castilian by the leading personage. I was informed that the young women were remarkable for their chastity, and that an erring sister obtained no forgiveness among them. Their parents object to their learning Spanish lest it should be an instrument of seduction. Of the mestizos of Chinese or Mongolian descent, De Mas says:—"They are called *Sangley*, which means Chinese merchant or traveller. They inherit the industrious and speculative spirit of their forefathers. Most of them have acquired riches and lands, and the largest part of the retail trade is in their hands. They form the middle class of the Filipinos. Their prosperity and better education produce the natural results, and their moral and intellectual character is far superior to that of the Indians. They are luxuriously dressed, are more elegant and handsome than the Indians; some of their women are decidedly beautiful. But they preserve most of the habits of the Indians, whom they exceed in attention to religious duties because they are superior in intelligence. This race is likely to increase in numbers and in influence, and, in consequence of the large importation of Chinamen, to augment in the localities of their settlements at a greater rate than the Indian population."[1]

There can be no doubt that the predominance of the characteristics of the father over those of the mother has improved, through successive generations, the general character of the race of mestizo Chinese. They are more active and enterprising, more prudent and persevering, more devoted to trade and commerce, than the Indios. They all preserve the black hair, which is characteristic of China, "the black-haired" being one of the national names by which the people of the "middle kingdom" are fond of designating themselves. The slanting position of the eyes, forming an angle over the nose, the beardless chin, the long and delicate fingers (in conformity with Chinese usage they frequently allow the middle nail of the left hand to grow to a great length), their fondness for dress and ornament, distinguish them. They exercise great influence over the Indians, who believe them to be masters of the art of money-getting. The children of a Spanish mestizo by a Chinese mestiza, are called *Torna atras*, "going back;" those of a Chinese mestizo by an Indian woman are considered as Chinese and not Indian half-castes. The mingling of Chinese blood is observable in all the town populations. The number of mestizos of European descent is trifling compared with those of Chinese origin. Their houses are invariably better furnished than those of the natives. Many of them adopt the European costume, but where they retain the native dress it is finer in quality, gayer in colours, and richer in ornament. Like the natives, they wear their shirts over the trousers, but the shirt is of piña or *sinamay* fastened with buttons of valuable stones; and a gold chain is seldom wanting, suspended round the neck. The men commonly wear European hats, shoes and stockings, and the sexes exhibit no small amount of dandyism and coquetry.

The great mass of the indigenous population of the Philippine Islands may be divided into two principal races—the *Tagálos* occupying the north, and the *Bisáyos* the south. Of these, all who inhabit the towns and villages profess Christianity, and are much under the influence of the regular clergy, who administer the religious ordinances in the various provinces, which are, for the most part, submitted to the ecclesiastical jurisdiction of different orders of brotherhood. There are a few instances of the Indians being invested with the full rights of priesthood, though they generally reach no higher post than that of assistants to the friars. At the great ceremony which I attended of the *Purisima Conception* at Manila, an Indian was chosen to deliver the sermon of the day; it was, as usual, redolent with laudations of the Virgin, and about equal to the average style of flowery Spanish preaching. But as we recede from the towns, religious ordinances are neglected, and in the centre and mountainous parts of the islands Christianity ceases to be the profession of the inhabitants; the friars deplore their ignorant and abandoned state, and occupy themselves in the endeavour to bring them into their fold, and to enforce the payment of that *tributo* from which they, as well as the government, derive their revenues. If this be paid, if the services of the Church be duly performed, confession made, fit co-operation given to the religious processions and festivals (which are the native holidays), matters go on well between the clergy and the people. I found many of the friars objects of affection and reverence, and deservedly so, as guardians and restorers of the family peace, encouragers of the children in their studies, and otherwise associating their efforts with the well-being of the community; but removed, as the ecclesiastics frequently are, from the control of public opinion, there is often scandal, and good ground for it.

Father Zuñiga opines that the Philippines were originally colonized by the inhabitants of America; but he fails altogether in the proofs he seeks in the analogy of languages. The number of Malayan words in Tagal and Bisayan is greater than any to be traced to American dialects; and here I may remark, by the way, that there is no topic on which so much absurdity has been committed to the press as on the derivation and affinity of languages—a subject in which Spanish authority is seldom of much value. El Señor Erro, for example, in his book on the antiquity of the Bascuence, gives a description and picture of a jar found in a well in Guipuscoa, which had on it the words "Gott erbarme dein armes Würmchen!" This he reports to be a Biscayan inscription in honour of the priestesses of the sun anterior to the introduction of Christianity, and he doubts not that the vase (a piece of coarse modern German pottery) was used in the sacred services of the temple!

De Mas supposes that the Indians employed alphabetical writing anterior to the arrival of the Spanish, and gives five alphabets as used in different provinces, but having some resemblance to one another. I doubt alike the antiquity and authenticity of the records; but give a specimen which he says is a contract upon Chinese paper for a sale of land in Bulacan, dated 1652.

My own inquiries led to no discoveries of old records, or written traditions, or inscriptions of remote times, associated with Indian history. There is sufficient evidence that some rude authority existed—that there were masters and slaves —that the land was partially cultivated and the sea explored by labourers and fishermen, leading necessarily to a recognition of some rights of property— that there were wars between hostile tribes, which had their leaders and their laws. The early records of the missionaries give the names of some of the chiefs, and detail the character of the authority exercised by the ruling few over the subject many. They say that gold would procure the emancipation of a slave and his reception among the *Mahaldicas*, or privileged class. Prisoners of war, debtors, and criminals, were held in bonds. The daughter of a Mahaldica could be obtained in marriage, where the lover was unable to pay her money value, by vassalage to her father for a certain number of years. If a man of one tribe married the woman of another, the children were equally, or as nearly as possible, divided among the two tribes to which the parents belonged. Property was partitioned among the sons at the father's death, the elder enjoying no rights over the younger.

Local superstitions prevailed as to rocks, trees, and rivers. They worshipped the sun and moon; a blue bird called *tigmamanoquin*; a stag named *meylupa*, "lord of the soil;" and the crocodile, to which they gave the title of *nono*, or "grandfather." A demon named Osuang was supposed to torment children, to cause pains in childbirth, to live on human flesh, and to have his presence announced by the *tictic*, a bird of evil augury. Naked men brandished swords from the roof and other parts of the *choza* to frighten the fiend away, or the pregnant woman was removed from the neighbourhood of the tictic. The *Manacolam* was a monster enveloped in flames, which could only be extinguished by the ordure of a human being, whose death would immediately follow. The *Silagan* seized and tore out the liver of persons clad in white. The *Magtatangal* deposited his head and entrails in the evening in some secret place, wandered about doing mischief in the night, and resumed his "deposit" at break of day. So strange and wild are the fancies of credulity! Sacrifices were offered in deprecation of menaced evils, or in compliment to visitors, by female priestesses called *Catalona*, who distributed pieces of the sacrificed animal. There were many witches and sorcerers, exercising various functions, one of whom, the *Manyisalat*, was the love inspirer and the confidant of youths and maidens.

On entering a forest the Indian supplicated the demons not to molest him. The crackling of wood, the sight of a snake in a cottage newly built, were deemed presages of evil. In the house of a fisherman it was deemed improper to speak of a forest, in that of a huntsman of the sea. A pregnant woman was not allowed to cut her hair, lest her child should he horn hairless.

The price paid for a woman given in marriage was regulated by the position of the parties. The mother had a claim, as well as the nurse who had had charge of the childhood of the bride. Whatever expense the daughter had caused to the father he was entitled to recover from the bridegroom. Among opulent families there was a traditional price, such as the father or grandfather had paid for their wives. If the bride had no living parents, her price was paid to herself. Three days before the marriage the roof of the parental dwelling was extended, and an apartment, called a *palapala*, added for the wedding festival; the guests brought their presents to the bride, and, whatever the value, it was expected that when, on future occasions, the relations of hosts and guests were changed, an offering of not less value should be given. Among the ceremonies it was required that the lovers should eat from the same plate and drink from the same cup. Mutual pledges and promises of affection were given, and the catalona pronounced a benediction. Sad scenes of drunkenness and scandal are said to have followed the ceremony in the after festivities, which lasted three days. In the northern islands only one wife was allowed, but any number of handmaids and slaves; in the south, where, no doubt, Islamism was not without its influence, any number of legitimate wives was permitted: circumcision was also practised.

Hired mourners, as well as the members of the family, were gathered round the corpse, and sang hymns proclaiming the virtues of the dead. The body was washed, perfumed, dressed and sometimes embalmed. The poor were speedily buried in the *silong* over which their huts were constructed. The rich were kept for several days, laid out in a coffin made of a solid trunk, the mouth covered with gold-leaf, and the place of sepulture any favourite spot which the deceased might have selected; if on the bank of a river, the passage of boats was interdicted for some time, lest the dead should interfere with the concerns of the living, and a guard had charge of the tomb, near which the garments, usual food and arms of the departed were placed in a separate box —in the case of a woman, her loom and instruments of labour. Where a chief of distinction was interred, a building was erected, in which two goats, two deer, and two pigs were imprisoned and a fettered slave belonging to the deceased, who was ordered to accompany his master to the other world, and died a miserable death of starvation. It was supposed on the third day after the interment that the dead man visited his family: a vase of water was placed at the door, that he might wash and free himself from the dirt of the grave; a wax light was left burning through the day; mats were spread and covered with ashes, that the footmarks of the dead might be traced; and the door was opened at the accustomed time of meals, and a splendid repast laid out for the expected visitor. No doubt it was disposed of by the attendants in the same way as other costly sacrifices. The Indians of the north put on black, those of the south white, mourning robes.

INDIAN FUNERAL.

In the administration of justice the elders were consulted, but there was no code of laws, and the missionaries affirm that the arbitrators of quarrels were generally but too well paid for their awards. Murder committed by a slave was punished with death—committed by a person of rank, was indemnified by payments to the injured family. When a robbery took place, all the suspected persons were ordered to bring a load of grass; these loads were mixed in a heap, and if the stolen article was found it was restored to the owner, and no inquiry made as to the bringer of the bundle in which it was concealed. If this method failed, they flung all the suspected into a river, and held him to be guilty who came first to the surface, on the theory that remorse would not allow him to keep his breath. Many are said to have been drowned in order to escape the ignominy of rising out of the water. They sometimes placed candles of equal length in the hands of all the accused, and he was held to be guilty whose candle first went out. Another mode was to gather the accused round a light, and he towards whom the flames turned was condemned as the criminal. Adultery was condoned for by fine to the wronged persons.

Gold was used by weight as the medium of exchange, but there was no coined or stamped currency. The largest weight was called a *gael*, but it represented a dollar and a quarter in silver, nearly corresponding to the Chinese ounce or tael; a *gael* consisted of two *tinga*, a *tinga* of two *sapaha*;[2] a *sapaha* was divided into *sangraga*, a very small bean, which was the minimum weight. Accounts were kept by heaps of stones of different sizes. Their measures were the *dipa* (brace = 6 feet), the *dancal* (palm), *tumuro* (span), *sangdamac* (breadth of the hand), *sangdati* (breadth of the finger). Thus, as among many rude nations (the vestiges are still to be traced in the phraseology of civilization) every man carried with him his standard of mensuration.

Time was reckoned by suns and moons, in the Philippines as in China. In Chinese the same words designate day and sun, moon and month, harvest and year. The morning was called "cock-crowing," the evening "sun-leaving."

No Indian passed another without a salutation and a bending of the left knee. An inferior entering the house of a superior crouched down until ordered to rise. Earrings were worn by women and sometimes by men; the chiefs had coloured turbans, scarlet if they had killed an enemy, striped if they had killed seven or more. Peace was made by the mingling blood with wine, and each drank of the blood of the other. This was the most solemn of their oaths.

Chastity seems to have been unknown, though a price was always exacted for a woman's favours.

Many Mahomedan superstitions and usages had found their way to the interior, and among them the rite of circumcision.

All the Indians are born with a circular dark spot on the buttock, of the size of a shilling; as their skins darken the mark extends, becomes lighter in colour, and in age is scarcely distinguishable.

There is a tradition that the Indians were formerly in the habit of punishing an unpopular person by a penalty which they called *Cobacolo*, and which was inflicted on any who had misled them by false counsels. The whole population assembled, went to the house of the offender, every one bearing a cudgel; some surrounded the house to prevent escape, and others entered and, by blows, drove the victim to the balcony, from whence he was compelled to leap, and he was then chased out of the neighbourhood, after which the house was razed to the ground, and all that it contained destroyed. The tradition is preserved in many popular proverbs and phrases, in which the *Cobacolo* is used as a menace to evil-doers.

Among the most celebrated books on the Philippines are the "Cronicas Franciscanas," by Fr. Gaspar de S. Agustin, an Augustine monk of Madrid, who lived forty years among the Indians, and from whose descriptions I have made a few selections; but there are remarkable contrarieties of opinion among different writers. Their fields of observation are different, and natural temperament has much to do with the judgment formed. Our friar does not give the natives a favourable character. According to him they are generally "inconstant, distrustful, malicious, sleepy, idle, timid, and fond of travelling by rivers, lakes, and seas."

"They are great consumers of fish, which are found in immense abundance. After rains the fields and marshes and ponds are filled with them. Fish two palms long are often pulled up from among the paddy. As the waters dry up, the fish retreat to any muddy recess, and the Indians catch them with their hands, or kill them with sticks." I have seen many Indians fishing in the paddy grounds, and what becomes of the fish in the times of drought, when no "muddy recesses" are to be found, it is hard to say, but where there is water fish may invariably be sought for with success.

"They eat three meals a day, consisting principally of rice, the sweet potato, and a small quantity of fish or meat; the daily cost of the whole being half a rial" (= 3*d.* sterling). "As labourers they get half a rial in addition to their food. They willingly borrow money, which they do not repay, and he who will not encourage ingratitude must show them no favour; to exact a promise is to ensure a falsehood. They are the ingrates described in the 36th Psalm. They never shut the door they have opened; they return nothing to its place; they never do the work they have been paid for beforehand, yet they do not fail to ask for an advance: the carpenter must have money to buy wood; the washerman to get soap; and they even practise their devices upon the parish priest! They have the art of blundering about everything; they fold all garments the wrong way; turn a shirt inside out, always present the back where the front should be." The father is somewhat severe, and of my own experience I can say there was at least about as much chance in such matters of the Indians doing right as wrong. Alava said of the Indians that their brains were in their hands.

The padre continues:—"They are envious, ill-bred, and impertinent. They will even ask a padre, 'Whence do you come? where are you going?' If you are reading a letter, they will look over your shoulders, though not able to read themselves; and if two people are talking in secret, the Indians will come near, though not understanding a word." Grave charges these. "They enter houses, and even convents, without leave, and seem to make themselves at home in a manner to excite wonderment and anger; even when the padre is asleep, they make a great noise in trampling the floor, though in their own houses they walk with as much care as if treading among eggs. They use no chairs at home, but absolutely wear out those of the convents by sitting and lounging on them, particularly in the balconies, where they can get a look at the women."

These extracts are as characteristic of the monk as of the Indian. "They care nothing for dog, cat, horse nor cow; the game-cock is their great concern; him they visit at dawn; him they caress through the day; they will contemplate him with eyes fixed for half an hour at a time: the passion never decays; many of them think of nothing else. The government patronizes cock-fights. Last year they produced 40,000 dollars" (in 1859, 86,000 dollars); "sad resource this for so many tears, crimes, and punishments! What quarrels, what lawsuits, what appeals! And in their gambling they pass the night till sunrise. The chief of the Barangay (clan) loses the tribute-money he has collected; his doom is the prison, or a flight to the mountains. They hate to live in houses or convents where they would be placed beyond even the odour of women. They take care of their own plates, and exhibit in their dwellings some possessed before the arrival of the Spaniards, but in convents and houses they break plates enough to ruin their masters. This is because of their stupidity, or that they are thinking of their beloved, or of anything but what ought to occupy their thoughts; and if they let fall a dish, it is passed over by the Spaniards, or they are only called 'brute! animal! savage!' In their own house, however, the breaking a piece of earthenware would be followed with a good number of cane blows, and this is of more efficacy than all Cicero's Philippics (*sic* in orig.) They cannot be trusted with a sword, mirror, glass, gun, watch, nor any delicate thing; they are sure to spoil it. You may confide to them a bamboo, a stick, a piece of timber, a palm-branch, and to a few of them a ploughshare.

"They are bold and insolent in making unreasonable requests, careless of the when or the how. They remind me in their petitions of what happened to Sancho Panza in the island of Barataria, when troubled with that impertinent and intrusive rustic Michael Turra. For their four eggs they want a hundred dollars. I never see an Indian coming towards me with a gift—something worthless, of course, and of no use to himself—flowers or fruits, but I exclaim, in the words of Laocoon to the Trojans" (grandiloquent friar!) "'Timeo Danaos dona ferentes.' The Bishop of Troya, Don Francisco Gines Barrientes, a most circumspect prelate, told me that an Indian brought him a handkerchief of Guava fruit and asked him for the loan of fifty dollars. And when the Lord Marquis de Villasierra, Don Fernando de Valenzuela, was in the castle of Cavite, an Indian gave him a cock, for which the Marquis ordered him to be paid six times its value, and the Indian said he expected eighty cavans of rice, and this, too, was in the time of scarcity, when every cavan was worth two dollars. It matters little, however, for they are just as well pleased when they fail as when they succeed, for they do not value anything given them by a Spaniard, not even by a priest! In selling they will ask thirty and accept six; they take the chance of cheating, and, knowing the great goodness (*la suma bondad*) of the Spanish character, they do not apprehend any expression of anger in consequence of an absurd pretension."

The friar thus describes a negotiation between an Indian peasant and a merchant:—"The peasant has two or three hundredweight of indigo for sale; he does not come alone, but with his relations, friends, and sometimes the women, for the indigo belongs to several who form the suite of the seller. Every offer has to be communicated to the party, who are crouched in a circle round the negotiator; the offer being discussed, they agree to the reduction of a dollar in the price—the buyer requires three; this matter being settled, another discussion begins; some of the indigo is damp and dirty, and an allowance must be made, and thus the negotiation goes on harassing and never-ending, so that very few Spaniards will tolerate such impertinence and importunity, and the conference ends by a dry inquiry, 'Will you? yes! or no!' If no, the Indians are angrily ordered into the street, but the more patient mestizos and Chinese make the Indians their guests, feed them and lodge them, and get these commodities on their own terms, in Chinese style, for the Indian is very stupid in trading matters." And then the father gives abundant evidence of their simplicity. "In fine, the Indian prefers the rial of a Chinese to the dollar of a Spaniard." Who can wonder, then, at the prosperous condition of the Chinese in the Philippines? "The Indians show great indifference to danger: they will not move out of the way of a restive horse, nor, if in a small boat, give place to a large one. In the river, if they see crocodiles approaching, they take no notice and adopt no precautions. The Koran says that every one has his fate written in the marks on his forehead; so think the Indians, not that they have read the Koran, but because of their own folly, which exposes them to daily misfortunes." "They are very credulous among themselves, yet believe nothing but what is unfavourable about the Spaniards. It is evident that the act of faith is supernatural when they acknowledge the divine mysteries taught by the Spaniards. In other matters they believe in nothing which is adverse to their interests. They do not object to rob Spaniards, not even the ministers of religion. Of this we have irresistible evidence, so that there can be no doubt, and we can only regret that no remedy can be found."

The Augustine provincial friar of Ilocos, reporting on the insurrection of 1807 in that province, says:—"Here, as elsewhere, there are abundance of robbers and pilferers; it is of no use to bring them to Manila, they should be punished in the locality; but they can be no more extirpated than can the rats and mice. Indeed there is an Indian proverb which says:—'Robbers and rats will disappear together.'" I cannot endorse the friar's indiscriminating censures, for I have heard extraordinary evidences of extraordinary integrity. The Alcalde of Cagayan told me that, though he had frequently left uncounted dollars in the care of the Indians, he had never discovered a single fraud.

One would suppose that the rich and potent friars were tolerably well protected against the Indians, yet one of them writes:—"The Indians do not now employ lances and arrows against our ministry, but papers, pens, tales, jokes and calumnies. So much have they been taught politics in Manila that now in all the pueblos are obscure scribblers, pettifoggers, pretenders, who are clever enough in writing memorials on stamped paper, to be presented to the Royal Audiencia. So if the parish priest reprove or punish them for their evil and scandalous lives, they meet together, drink wine, and fill a folio paper with their crosses, and march off to Manila, to the tribunal which they deem the most impressionable, from whence great vexations are caused to the poor parish priest. And much courage is required to bear this species of martyrdom, which is sufficiently common in the Indies."—(Abbé Amodea.)

I do not know how lately there have been perquisitions against witches, but in the middle of the last century I find the record of a most diligent pursuit and rigorous punishment against the witches of Pampanga. The proceedings were superintended by a friar named Theodore of the Mother of God, who made a special report to the Mexican Inquisition. He says:—"There are witches in every pueblo, and in some they form a third part of the population. These slaves of the devil are divided into sundry classes: *lamias*, who suck the blood of infants; *striges*, who are wanderers on the face of the earth; *sagas*, who dwell in houses, and convey to the devil all the information he requires; *larvas*, who devote themselves to carnal delights; *temures*, who prepare love filtres; but all unite to do mischief to the human race."

Of the credulity of the Indians there is no end of examples. In 1832, when the *Santa Ana* arrived with 250 soldiers, a report spread like wild-fire that the King of Spain had ordered all the children of the Indians to be collected, that their blood might be spilt upon the Spanish mines to make them more productive. The women fled to their homes, seized their children, and sought an asylum in the houses of the Spanish ladies in Manila. The men armed themselves with spears, and rushed tumultuously through the streets. The agitation was appeased with some difficulty. What any man reputed as a sage among the Indians avers, acquires immediate authority, and is not to be controlled by the influence of the priests; the words "Vica ng maruning," meaning "The wise say so," is the ready answer to all impugners. "God preserve us," says the friar, "from Indian sages! for the Indians are proud, and will not obey the priest, nor the friar, nor the chaplain, unless obliged by fear, and they are not always afraid, though they feel thoroughly convinced of the superiority of the Spaniard, and are governed in spite of themselves. They imitate the Spaniard in all that is evil—his love of dress, his swearing habits, addiction to gaming, and all the vicious practices of the *zaramullos* (fops or busy-bodies); but Spanish courtesy and urbanity and good education they neither study nor copy; but revels and drunken bouts, and riotous weddings and burial excesses and tyrannical acts of all sorts they have inherited from their ancestors, and still preserve, so that they have Spanish vices added to their own."

They show much deference to everything that is aristocratic among themselves. The jacket-wearing principalia are treated with great deference, and their rank religiously respected. First, the gobernadorcillo; then the ex-gobernadorcillos, who are called passed captains, in order of seniority; then the acting lieutenant, who must be the head of a barangay; then the heads of barangays according to age; then passed lieutenants, and so on; and their rank is recognized by the adjacent communities.

GIRLS BATHING.

Bathing is universal, men and women in the same place. The men wear pantaloons, the women cover themselves with a garment which they throw off when they enter the water. No scandal is caused by the habit, and several attempts of the Spanish authorities to interfere with the ancient usage have failed.

The Indians embrace by touching noses; but lip-kissing often accompanies the act. When the nostril is contracted (as in the act of smelling), and the Indian looks towards a person at a distance, it is deemed an invitation to a closer embrace. Strange stories are told of the exquisite sense of smell possessed by the Indians; that by it they can distinguish the dresses of their masters and mistresses, and lovers ascertain the state of each other's affections. Inner garments are interchanged which are supposed to be impregnated with the passions of the owners. In disregard of the monks, the Indians secretly circumcise their children. The banian-tree (*Balete, Ficus Indica*) is held sacred. They burn incense under it, which they obtain from the friars under various pretences. How strangely are the rites of idolatry mingled with Christian observances! This is not the case alone in the Philippines. One of Dr. Gutzlaff's renowned converts in Hong Kong used to say that to please the missionary he had added another god—the Christian's God—to those he worshipped before; and I have known of secret visits to heathen temples on the part of Chinese professing Christians, when they were about to enter upon any important undertaking. "There is no driving out of them," says the padre, "the cursed belief that the spirits of their ancestors are in the woods and among the roots of bamboos, and that they can bring good or evil upon them. They will offer sacrifices to them; and all our books and all our preachings have failed to remove the impressions left by any old man whom they choose to call 'a sage.'" "The curates," says De Mas, "profess to believe that these superstitions are passing away; no doubt the Indian conceals them as much as he can from his father confessor, but I have on many occasions convinced myself of their existence and influence." Who, indeed, knowing anything of the credulity of the less instructed classes, and not these alone, among ourselves, can wonder at the state of "the religious mind" of the Philippine Indian? And so little are the priests themselves wholly free from infirmity, that a Philippine curate, Mallares, committed and caused to be committed no less than fifty-seven assassinations in the town of Magalan, believing that he should thus save his mother from being bewitched. Mallares was executed in 1840; and in his report the fiscal expresses his horror of "the incredible and barbarous prodigality of bloodshed by this monster."

"The Indian knows no medium," again to quote from the father. "Ask for tepid water, he will bring it boiling; say it is too hot, and you will get it quite cold. He lives in a circle of extremes. He rejoices if you lose patience and give him a beating, for he goes and boasts of having put his master into a passion. To irritate the Indian, you must take no notice of his short-comings. The sagacious men among them say that the Indian and the cane (for his correction) always grow together. They have another proverb: 'The Spaniard is fire, and the Indian snow, and the snow puts out the fire.'" One of the padres reports that his servant-boy said to him: "You are a new comer, and are too indulgent: if I do amiss you ought to chastise me. Don't you know the proverb, 'The Indian and the cane grow together?'" "They blaspheme and abuse God when their prayers are not granted, and use language which would indeed be horrible were it not known how thoughtless they are, and how impossible it is for them to conform themselves to the Divine will."

They are fond of religious dramas, especially of one in Tagál representing the passion and death of Christ; but these religious representations and gatherings give rise to scandal and abuse, and the birth of many illegitimate children. The priests have generally prohibited these exhibitions at night, and sometimes disperse them, whip in hand; at other times the singers are denounced, and get flogged for their pains—or pleasures.

It is amusing to read the contradictory opinions of the friars respecting their flocks. One says:—"Their confessions are false; they never own to any but three sins: first, that they have neglected church-going; second, that they eat meat during Lent; and third, that they have sworn profanely." Another reports

—"No Spaniard can be more devout and fervid than the Indians of Manila in their confessions. They obey the instructions they receive, and I have the same good account from many padres of many Indians in the provinces." No doubt the ecclesiastical statistics would be curious, if obtainable. In Lilio, the curate reports that of 1,300 persons paying tribute in 1840, 600 never confessed, and "this pueblo is not of the most remiss." In Vigan, of 30,000 inhabitants, the attendance at church did not exceed from 500 to 800 (De Mas), except on the yearly festival of the Virgin, patroness of the pueblo. Father Agustin's indignation is vehemently expressed as regards confession: —"The infernal Macchiavel Satan has taught them a policy as good for their bodies as bad for their souls, which is that they own their errors and crimes to one another, and conceal them, however excessive, from the spiritual father, from the Spanish alcalde, notwithstanding their personal quarrels, and, as they call them, murder-enmities; so that there is among them no greater offence than to tell the padre or the alcalde what has happened in the pueblo, which they say is *mabibig*, the most abominable of sins; indeed, the only offence which they hold to be sin."

The friars speak in general more favourably of the women than of the men. They are more devout, more submissive, more willing to listen to their ghostly fathers, one of whom says:—"Did all mankind hang upon a single peg, and that peg were wanted by an Indian for his hat, he would sacrifice all mankind. They have no fear of death, but this is an infinite mercy of the Divine Being, who knows how fragile they are; they talk about death, even in the presence of the dying, without any concern. If condemned to the scaffold, they exhibit equal indifference, and smoke their cigar with wonted tranquillity. Their answer to the attendant priest is invariably, 'I know I am going to die. I cannot help it. I have been wicked—it was the will of God,—it was my fate,' But the approach of death neither interferes with their sleep nor their meals." "The tree must bear its fruit," he continues. "God in his wisdom has made many races of men, as He has made many varieties of flowers, and at last I reconciled myself to seeing the Indians do everything differently from what we should do, and keeping this in view, I could mould them like wax to my purpose."

As a general result I have not found among these Indian races any one distinguished for intellectual superiority. A few were not backward in their knowledge of the mechanical arts; one or two examples there were of genius as sculptors; a universal love and devotion to the musical art, and some appreciation even of the merits of European composers; but, it must be added, little or nothing is done to develop such capacities as the Indians possess; the field of public instruction is narrowed alike by religious and official influences, and the social tone of the opulent classes, to which alone the Indian can look up, is greatly below that of the Spanish peninsula. Literature is little cultivated: the public newspapers are more occupied with the lives of saints, and preparation for, or accounts of, religious *fiestas*, than with the most stirring events of the political world. The Spaniards have never been celebrated for very busy inquiries, or very active virtues; but it is to be hoped that the *mañana*, to which everything is referred, will at last become an *hoy dia*.

It has been said of the Indian that he is more of a quadruped than a biped. His hands are large, and the toes of his feet pliant, being exercised in climbing trees, and divers other active functions. He is almost amphibious, passing much of his time in the water. He is insensible alike to the burning sun and the drenching rain. The impressions made upon him are transitory, and he retains a feeble memory of passing or past events. Ask him his age, he will not be able to answer: who were his ancestors? he neither knows nor cares. He receives no favours and cannot, therefore, be ungrateful; has little ambition, and therefore little disquiet; few wants, and hence is neither jealous nor envious; does not concern himself with the affairs of his neighbour, nor indeed does he pay much regard to his own. His master vice is idleness, which is his felicity. The labour that necessity demands he gives grudgingly. His health is generally good, and when deranged he satisfies himself with the use of herbs, of whose astringent or laxative powers he has had experience. He uses no soap to wash, no razor to shave; the river is his bathing-place, and he pulls out the hairs in his face with the assistance of a sharp shell; he wants no clock to tell him of the flight of time—no table, nor chairs, nor plates, nor cutlery, to assist him at his meals; a *hacha*, or large knife, and bag are generally hung at his waist; he thinks no music equal to the crowing of his cock, and holds a shoe to be as superfluous as a glove or a neck-collar.

I certainly have not discovered among the Indians that enduring "à tout jamais" horror of foreigners upon which M. Mallat dwells, and which he represents as specially and properly directed against Englishmen. On the contrary, I found many Englishmen settled in the Philippines objects of great confidence and affection; and I have heard mestizos and Indians say that they put greater trust in English commercial probity than in that of any other nation. I have witnessed the cordiality with which the old Spanish proverb, "Paz con Ynglaterra y con todo el mundo guerra," has been quoted in large assemblies of the Filipinos. And assuredly there is no nation which has contributed more than England to the prosperity of the Spanish archipelago.

Evidence enough will be found in the course of this narrative of the kindness shown to Englishmen.

It has been said that the Spaniards have very discreetly and successfully used the "divide et impera" among the Indian races as a means of preserving their own authority. There is little sympathy, it is true, between the remoter races; but that their separation and aberration form a part of the Spanish policy may be disproved by the fact that in Binondo nearly one-third of the resident inhabitants are Indians from distant provinces.

The numerical power of the Spaniards is small, that of the armed natives great, were there among them a disposition to rebel against their rulers: I believe there is little of such disposition. Lately the Tagál soldiers have been called into active service in a foreign country (Cochin China), and involved in a quarrel where the Spanish interest is not very discernible. No complaints have been made of their conduct, though they have been exposed to much privation.

There is a pretty custom among the peasantry of the interior. Little bamboo frames are seen either supported by a post, or projecting from a window of the choza, on which is to be found, covered with plantain leaves, a supply of food, or fruits, provided from the Indian's garden, which invariably surrounds his dwelling. Any passing traveller supplies himself, paying nothing if he be poor, but otherwise leaving such compensation as he may deem proper. No sort of reproach attaches to the person who, without the means of payment, partakes of the proffered bounty. These hospitable receptacles are most common in the least peopled localities, and reminded me of the water and the lamp which I have found in the tombs of sainted Mussulmans, who had themselves discharged, or required their followers thus to discharge, the claims of humanity, and in the arid desert provided these grateful, silent, and touching welcomes to the thirsty and weary traveller.

The tact or talent of imitation is strong among the Indians, and facilitated the efforts of the friars, but very various and contradictory reports are found of their aptitudes. Those of Pampanga, Cagayan, Pangasinan, Ilocos, and Zebu are reported to be valiant, generous, laborious, and frequently exhibiting artistical taste. I found the love and the practice of music universal, and saw some remarkable specimens of sculptural ability, but of painting nothing Indian was ever presented to my attention, and the examples of persevering dedication to any sort of labour were few indeed. As servants, the Tagáls are in all respects inferior to the Chinese; as soldiers, the officers generally reported of them favourably. The Indians settled in Manila are said to be the worst of their races: no doubt great cities are the recipients of the dregs of a people, but they attract at the same time the highest order of merit. The courtesies which we received as their guests seemed boundless; no effort too great to do us honour: something, indeed much, could not but be attributed to the guidance of the priests and the presence of the authorities, but there were a thousand marks of spontaneous kindness, such as no external influence could have commanded.

1

The Chinese seem everywhere to preserve the same characteristics. The British Consul-General of Borneo writes to me:—"Chinese settlers cannot flourish under Malay rule. We have a few hundreds, but the country would absorb hundreds of thousands. In the interior I found among the aborigines a lively remembrance of the former Chinese pepper-growers; they have been all destroyed or driven away by civil dissensions. There remain a few of their descendants, who speak the language of their fathers, but they are not distinguishable from the natives. A Chinese merchant was speaking disparagingly of one of the chiefs, who turned round, and, much to the astonishment of the Chinaman, accosted him in very tolerable Fokien. The little pepper-growing that remains is partly conducted by the mixed races. The produce is slightly increasing, and a few Chinese with native wives are beginning to try it again." |

2

Both *gael* and *sapaha* are terms probably introduced by traders with China. *Tael* and *sapeque* are the names given by Europeans to the *liang* and *tsien* of the Chinese, the silver ounce and its thousandth part. |

CHAPTER VII.

MANNERS AND SUPERSTITIONS OF THE PEOPLE.

Far more than the fair portion of domestic and social cares falls upon the Indian female, and she has far less than her becoming share of enjoyments. Barbarous practices are frequently associated with parturition. The *Mabuting hilot*, the good midwife, is called in. If the birth be delayed, witches are supposed to be the cause, and their dispersion is effected by the explosion of gunpowder from a bamboo cane close to the head of the sufferer. The new-born infant is laid on a mat or pillow and exposed to the air, to facilitate the escape of evil influences from the body, which is brought about by burning three wax tapers placed on the two cheeks and chin of the babe, often to its great peril. These practices are to some extent checked and controlled by the priests, who provide where they can for the baptism and registration of the infant.

The patriarchal custom of serving in the house of the father in order to obtain the hand and heart of the daughter, is by no means abolished in the Philippines; nor is the yet more intimate intercourse of plighted lovers, which is reported to be still in usage in the ruder parts of Wales, and with the same perilous consequences to the feebler sex. The domestication of the lover in the house of his intended father-in-law leads to the birth of great numbers of illegitimate children, to frequent violations of vows and promises, to domestic quarrels and much misery. The influence of the friars is generally employed for the protection of the frail one. They are opposed both by duty and interest to these irregularities, matrimonial fees being among the most productive contributions to their revenues.

I find one of the priests giving the following instructions to the Indians as to marriage:—"It is not right," he says, "to marry heedlessly, nor to hurry the sacred ceremony as if it were to be got rid of as soon as possible. Let the parties consult the padre, who will learn if they are really disposed to marry. You Indians say the male naturally runs after the female and obtains her consent (an Indian proverb); but this is not decorous; the proper mode of courting is for the priest to say, 'Will you be the spouse of ——, according to the arrangements of our holy mother Church?' This is first to be asked of the woman, and then an inquiry is to be made of the man whether he will have the woman, and the ancient and immodest usages of past times must then be abandoned." In the same spirit is the common saying of the Indians, "Savangmatovir ang ihinahatol nang mañga padre" (The counsels of the padre are always right). And again—"There is no Christian road but through the Roman Catholic Church."

F. de los Santos says there is no instance of a Tagála woman making advances in the way of marriage, nor of a father or mother looking out a bridegroom for their daughter; that it would be a great affront were any girl to seek the favour of the person whom she wished to be her mother-in-law in order to win the son. No woman was ever heard to say, "Manciganguin mo aco" (Make me thy daughter-in-law).

The same friar asserts that the Indians have learnt the meaning which the Europeans attach to "horns," and that the corresponding Tagál word *sungayan* (horned animal) cannot be used indiscreetly without giving great offence. He is very angry with the nonsense (*boberias* and *disparates*) which he says the natives address to their children. A mother will call her babe father, and mother, and aunt, and even king and queen, sir and madam, with other extravagant and unbecoming outbreaks of affection, which he reproves as altogether blameworthy and intolerable.

Though there is some variety in the houses of the Indians, according to their opulence, they preserve a common character, having bamboo floors, nipa roofs, and wooden pillars to support them. A speculation was entered into near Manila to provide more comfortable domestic accommodation for the natives by introducing imported improvements; but the houses were unoccupied, and the adventure proved a losing one. I have seen handsome lamps suspended from the roofs, and pictures hung upon the walls, of some of the Indian dwellings; while among the mestizos many aspire to all the decorations of Spanish luxury, competing with the richest among the European settlers. But religious ornaments are never forgotten, such as images and pictures of the Virgin and her child, vessels for holy water and crucifixes.

The beds of the Indians are merely mats on which the whole family repose indiscriminately. Here they smoke their cigars, chew their betel, and fall asleep. The domestic utensils are "a mortar for grinding rice, bamboos for all purposes, cup and spoons of the cocoa-nut shell, pots and kettles, a knife called a *goloc*, a bench against the wall, a stool which serves for a table, a Chinese basin for oil, a clay lamp, some cotton wicks, torches of the resin-cane, an image of the Virgin, a crucifix, mats, a jar of betel leaves, some areca nuts and lime ready for use, and sometimes a flute or guitar."—(Buzeta.)

The Indians have a very vague idea of distance. *Tahanan* and *Bitañgan* are the names given to places of rest between different localities. Instead of the Spanish word league, they say "taval," which is the distance an ordinary burthen can be carried without stoppage.

The forty days' labour which is exacted every year from the Indians is called *atag* or *bayani*. This is in addition to the *tributo* of a dollar and one-third; but exemption from the *atag* may be obtained by the payment of three dollars. The tribute is called *bovis* or *buvis*. "Buvis aco sa balañgay ni covan' (I am tributary to such and such a balangay).

A curious illustration of the passion for gaming, so general among the Filipinos, is given by the statistical commission, in the report on Binondo. Among the not prohibited games is that called by the natives *Panguingui*. It is played with six packs of cards, and five or six persons make a party. This game is most popular among all classes. The authorities prohibit its being played during the hours of labour, but it is permitted from twelve to two P.M., and from sunset to ten P.M., on ordinary days, and there is no restriction on festival days. The commission determined to visit without notice the different tables where the game was played; they found on an average 200 tables occupied, but there were 39 ready for play unoccupied.

Players	at the 200 tables, 867 men and 313 women.
Spectators	405	353
" " " "	" "	"

This did not include the tables in private houses, to which the commission had no access. It is to be presumed that these visits took place during the authorised hour of play, but this is not stated by the commission.

Though games of hazard are prohibited to the multitude, the great game of the lottery is monthly played for the profit of the government and the perdition of the people. Its existence and its temptations encourage that gambling passion which is one of the greatest plagues of the Filipinos. The newspapers are constantly occupied with long lists of persons condemned to heavy fines and imprisonments for indulging in what may be called the besetting sin of the Indians, from which, however, neither mestizos, Chinese nor Europeans are by any means free.

But the passion for play is most strikingly and universally exhibited in the cock-fights, so characteristic that I can scarcely avoid entering upon some details.

A writer on the Philippines, after showing the antiquity of cock-fighting, and tracing its history through most of the civilized nations of the world, thus concludes:—"In Spain there is a notable affection for cock-fights, and great is the care with which the birds are trained to the combat. In America this amusement is a dominant passion, and the Filipinos are not a whit behind the Americans. Nay, here the passion is a delirium, and no law can check the number or the duration of the fights, accompanied by slaughter of the combatants, which may be well called perfidious" (*i.e.* in violation of protecting regulations). "In other places they sharpen the spurs of the cocks. In the Philippines they are armed with razors, and chance more than skill decides the contest. Every day countless numbers perish, but the race is not diminished. There is hardly a locality which has not more cocks than human inhabitants. On the Puente Grande of Manila, at between four and five A.M., hundreds and hundreds of 'the shrill clarions' are heard on all sides, and from vast distances; it is a string of signals passed from mouth to mouth, from the port of Bangui, in North Ilocos, to Manog, the southernmost point of Albay. There are cocks in every house, at every corner, at the foot of every tree, along the quays and shores, on the prows of every coasting ship, and, as if the living were not enough, they are sculptured, they are painted and charcoaled (not artistically) on every wall for public admiration, and public admiration recognizes the portraiture, though the information is not placed there—as by the painter of old—to announce, 'This is a cock.'"

The following is a translation of an advertisement from a Manila newspaper: —"*Principal Cock-fight of Tondo.*—The subscriber informs the public that on all cock-fighting days a great crowd from all parts, nearly half of them Chinese, attend, so that on a single day there are from 90 to 100 combats, and this not only from the convenience of the place, which is made of tiles, but because the doubloons (*onzas*) which circulate there are honest doubloons (*son de recibo*).—Dalmacio Oligario."

It is considered a discourtesy to touch an Indian's game-cock, and permission is always asked to examine a favourite bird. He is the object of many a caress; he eats, crows, and sleeps in the arms of his master; and, whatever else may be forgotten, the cock is in continual remembrance. I have found him celebrated in verse in terms the most affectionate. A cock that has been frequently victorious is subjected to the most minute criticism, in order to discover by external marks what may serve to characterize his merits. The scales of his legs are counted, their form and distribution, the bent of the rings on the spurs, and whether the two spurs resemble each other; the shape of the toes and their nails, the number and colours of the wing-feathers (eleven being the favourite quantity); white eyes are preferred to chesnut; a short comb falling over the eye and beak is a recommendation. Cocks of different colours bear different names—white, *puti*; red, *pula*; white with black spots, *talisain*; red body and black tail and wings, *bulic* or *taguiguin*; black, *casilien*, or *maitin*; black and white, *binabay*; ash-colour, *abuen*; black and white, having black legs, *tagaguin*; and many others. The wild cock is called *labuyo*.

Of cock-fighting I translate Buzeta's description:—"The Indians have an inveterate passion for the sport, which occupies the first place in their amusements. The cock is the first object of their care, their general companion, which accompanies them even to the church-door, and is fastened to a bamboo plug outside, when they enter for the service of the mass. For no money will they dispose of a favourite bird. Some possess as many as half-a-dozen of these inappreciable treasures, for whose service they seem principally to live.

"Every pueblo has its *gallera*, or amphitheatre, for the cock-fights, from which the government draws a considerable revenue. The galleras are large buildings constructed of palm-trunks, bamboo, and nipa leaves, consisting of a hall, lighted from windows in the roof. In the centre is a stage, raised about five feet high, surrounded by bamboo galleries, which are reached by the spectators, who pay according to the adjacency and convenience of the seats. The gallera is generally crowded. The Indian enters with his cock under his arm; he caresses the favourite, places him on the ground, lifts him up again, smooths his feathers, talks to him, blows his cigar-smoke over him, and, pressing him to his breast, tells him to fight bravely. The cock generally crows aloud in defiance and in pride. His rival appears, a sharpened spur, or rather two-edged knife, or razor, is fastened to the natural spur of the bird, and after being for some time presented to each other the sign of combat is given, which is carried on with extraordinary excitement, until an alguacil announces that the betting is closed. The announcement is followed by universal silence. The owners of the cocks withdraw at another signal, and the combatants contemplate each other, their feathers agitated and erect; they bend their necks, shake their heads, and spring upon one another; the fight continues until one is mortally wounded and falls. The conqueror springs upon him, and crows in token of victory; but it is not unusual for the wounded cock to rise and turn upon his victor. If the victor should fly (as is sometimes the case), he is condemned to ignominious death; his feathers are plucked, and he is suspended almost naked on the outside of the gallera. The wounds of the living bird are staunched by an infusion of tobacco leaves in cocoa-nut wine. He becomes from that hour a favourite to be betted on, and if disabled for future frays, he is carefully provided for by his master. There are cock-doctors and receiving-houses devoted to the healing of their wounds.

GALLERA, OR COCK-PIT.

"In the neighbourhood of the gallera are stalls, where wines, sweetmeats, chocolate, and other refreshments, are sold, prepared by Indians and Chinese. A whole day is devoted to the combat, and even the charms of the *siesta* are forgotten, and the Indian often returns to his home after sunset a wretched and a ruined man."

The Indians were sometimes desirous that we should witness the exhibition, and brought their favourite cocks to be admired; but I had little curiosity to witness such a display, picturesque as it was no doubt—more picturesque than humane.

Don Ildefonso de Aragon passes this severe judgment upon the sport:
—"Perpetual idlers," the Indians, "they go from cockpit to cockpit, those
universities of every vice, which the owners think themselves privileged to
keep constantly open and accessible; hence they come forth consummate
masters of roguery, jugglery, frauds, ready for acts of violence in private and
in public, in town and in country."

Kite-flying (introduced by the Chinese, among whom it is an amusement both
for young and old, and who have made their kites musical by day and
illuminated by night) is popular in the Philippines, as are fire-balloons and
other pyrotechnic displays.

Except on suitable occasions, the Indian is sober and economical, but he
makes great efforts at display when desirous of honouring his guests. On two
or three occasions we sat down to meals, which a gastronomer would scarcely
have ventured to criticise; a variety of wines, health-drinking, and even
speech-making, music and firing of guns, accompanying the festivity.
Smoking never fails to form a part of the entertainment; pure cigars of various
sizes, and paper cigarritos, being always at hand. St. Andrew's day, kept in
celebration of the delivery of the Philippines from piratical Chinese, is one of
great rejoicing.

In religious ceremonies the Indian takes a busy part, and lends a very active
co-operation. When they take place after sunset, crowds attend with burning
tapers. Gun-firing, music and illuminations are the general accompaniments
of the great *fiestas*. I have more than once mentioned the universality of the
musical passion, which is easily trained to excellent performances. An Indian,
we heard, was not selected to the band unless he could play for eight hours
without cessation. The national music of Spain is generally studied, and, in
honour to us, in some places they learnt our "God save the Queen!" We were
not hypercritical upon the first attempts, but such tributes from a race, that
only sought to do our sovereign, our country, and ourselves all honour, could
not but greatly gratify us.

When at Guimbal (Iloilo), we were waited on at table wholly by Indian
female children, prettily dressed; whose bright eyes expressed extreme
curiosity, and whose anxiety to understand and to administer to every wish
was very charming. They were much pleased to exhibit the various garments
they wore of the piña cloth. I remarked one who went to the friar, and
whispered in his ear, "But where are the golden garments of the general?"
meaning me, and the padre had to explain to the children that "golden

garments" were only worn on State occasions, which did not seem satisfactory, as the occasion of our arrival in the pueblo was one of unprecedented excitement and display. They crowded round me, however, and looked into my face, and expressed admiration at my long soft hair. Their associating finery with rank reminded me of a visit once paid me by a young Abyssinian prince, who was taken up the narrow staircase by some mistake of the servants, and who (his interpreter told me) afterwards said to him, "You told me I was to see a great man—had ever a great man so small a staircase?" At his next visit, he was conducted through the principal portals up the wide marble steps of the house in which I lived, and he expressed extreme satisfaction, and said, "Ah! this is as it should be."

A few of the Indians reach the dignity of the priesthood, but they are generally *asistentes* to the friars. I have heard from the lips of Indian priests as pure Castilian as that spoken in Madrid.

"I have observed," says Father Diaz, "that the word of an Indian is more to be trusted when he uses one of the ancient forms of speech, such as '*totoo nang totoo*' (it is as true as truth, or, it is truly true), than when called on to take a solemn oath in the name of God or of the cross." A youth always seeks to get the promise of his sweetheart made according to the old Tagál usage, and it is held as the best security of veracity in all the relations of life.

Many of the padres complain that, notwithstanding all the religious instruction given, the taint of idolatry still exists among the converted Indians. There is a sort of worship of ancestors which is seen in many forms. They attach to the word *nono* (forefather) the same spiritual meaning which the Chinese give to *Kwei*. These nonos are often addressed in prayer, in order to bring down blessings or to avert calamities. If an Indian gather a flower or fruit, he silently asks leave of the nono. Certain spots, woods and rivers, he never passes without an invocation to these departed genii. Pardon is asked for short-comings or actions of doubtful character. There is a disease called *pamoao* which is attributed to the influence of the nonos, to whom petitions and sacrifices are offered to obtain relief. These idolatries, says one of the friars, are so deeply rooted and so widely spread as to demand the utmost vigilance for their extirpation.

So, again, they have their native devil, in the shape of a little black old man, a wild horse, or monster. As a protection against this fiend, however, they apply to their rosary, which certainly affords evidence that *he* is an orthodox demon of whom the padres cannot fairly complain.

Witches and witchery are called in to discover thieves and to unbewitch bewitched persons; but scapularies and saints, especially St. Anthony of Padua, are auxiliaries in undoing the mischiefs menaced or done. The cauldrons of the weird sisters in *Macbeth* would find counterparts among the people of the Philippine Islands, but there must be a mingling of Christian texts and Catholic superstitions to complete the identity. One author says these incantations are used for the attainment of riches, beautiful wives, success in battle, escape from justice, and other objects of desire. Father Ortiz will have it that the secrets of these supernatural influences are treasured up in various manuscript works "which ought to be burned." Their preservation and publication (if they exist) would be more serviceable, because more instructive, to mankind.

Indian women are seldom seen without some religious ornaments. They have rosaries of corals or pearl beads, medals of copper or gold, having figures of Our Lady of Mexico or Guadalupe. The scapulary is generally found hanging by the rosary. Many of the Indians are associated in the Cofradias, whose different emblems they preserve with great veneration; such as St. Augustine's string, St. Francis' cord, St. Thomas's belt; but they also hang upon their children's necks crocodiles' teeth as a preservative against disease.

The ancient Indian name for God was *Bathala*, to whom they attributed the creation of the world. Remnants of the old idolatry remain among the people, and the names of some of the idols are preserved. A few phrases are still retained, especially in the remoter parts, as, for example, "Magpabathala ca" (Let the will of Bathala be done), and the priests have been generally willing to recognize the name as not objectionable in substitution for *Dios*. The Tagál word adopted for idolatry is *Pagaanito*, but to the worship of images they give the term *Anito*. I find among the records reference to an idol called *Lacambui*, probably the god of eating, as the Spaniards call him *Abogado de la Garganta* (the throat-advocate). The idol *Lacanpate* was the god of the harvest, and was equally male and female; "an hermaphrodite devil," he is called by one of the friars. *Linga* was the god who cured diseases. *Lachan bacor* protected the growing crops. *Aman Sinaya* was the fisherman's god, and was appealed to when the nets were cast. *Ama ni Caable* was the protector of huntsmen. An ill-famed idol named *Tumano* was believed to wander about at night among human habitations; the Indians threw ashes upon him, and calling out, "Iri, iri," he fled, being "a cowardly devil." *Mancucutor* was the patron of a particular class of Indians, but the traditions are very obscure.

There is a bird called by the natives *Tigmamanoquin*, and if, when they are going to a festival, this bird flies from the right to the left, it is considered of auspicious augury, but disastrous if it fly from the left to the right. The bird (I know not its classical name) is never killed by the Indians, but if caught it is set free with the words, "Hayona tigmamanoquin, lunchan mo nang halinging" (Be gone, bird! and sing sweetly for me).

The Indians believe that a guardian angel is born at the birth of every Christian child, to whose special care through life the infant is confided. In some parts this angel is called *Catotobo*, in others *Tagatanor*. But the Tagáls habitually employ the Castilian words *angel* and *angeles* in the Catholic sense. I remember to have heard a clever Dutchman say that Java was well governed by knowing how to use properly two Arabic words—*Islam* (faith), which was never to be interfered with; and *Kismet* (fate), under whose influence Mussulmans cheerfully submit to their destiny. The *Santa Iglesia madre* is the charm by which the Philippines are ruled.

The Indian women are generally cleanly in their persons, using the bath very frequently, and constantly cleaning and brightening their black and abundant hair, which they are fond of perfuming and tying in a knot behind, called the *pusód*, which is kept together by a small comb and gilded needles, and is adorned with a fragrant flower. They are proud of their small foot, which the Chinese call golden lily, and which has a slipper, often embroidered with gold or silver, just supported by the toes. Their walk is graceful and somewhat coquettish; they smoke, eat betel, and are rather given to display a languid, liquid eye, for which they have an Indian expression, "Mapuñgay na mata."

The dress of the Filipinos is simple enough. It consists of a shirt worn outside a pair of pantaloons; but the shirt is sometimes of considerable value, woven of the piña, handsomely embroidered, and of various colours, bright red being predominant. I asked an opulent Indian to show me his wardrobe, and he brought out twenty-five shirts, exhibiting them with great pride; there were among them some which may have been worth a hundred dollars each. It is difficult to fix a limit to the money value of the more exquisite specimens of weaving and embroidery. A small pocket handkerchief sent to the Queen of Spain is said to have cost five hundred dollars. One or two doubloons (*onzas*) of gold are asked for the *pañuelos* (kerchiefs) usually sold in the shops of the capital. The finest qualities are woven in the neighbourhood of Iloilo. The loom is of the rudest and simplest construction; one woman throws the shuttle, another looks after the threads. The cloth is sent to Manila to be embroidered. The women wear gowns of the fabrics of the country, into which, of late, the silks of China and the coloured yarns of Lancashire have been introduced. The better-conditioned wear an embroidered shawl or kerchief of piña. This is the representative of female vanity or ambition.

When we passed through the towns and villages of the interior, a handsomely adorned piña handkerchief was the flag that often welcomed us from the windows of the native huts, and sometimes the children bore them about and waved them before us in the processions with which they were wont to show their pleasure at our presence.

The dress of the Indians is nearly the same throughout the islands; the pantaloons of cotton or silk, white or striped with various colours, girded round the waist with a kerchief, whose folds serve for pockets, and a shirt over the pantaloons of cotton. Sinamay (a native cloth), or piña for the more opulent, is universally employed. Straw hat or kerchief round the head; but the favourite covering is a huge circular cap like a large inverted punch-bowl, made generally of bamboo, but sometimes of tortoise-shell, and having a metal spike or other ornament at the top; it is fitted to the head by an internal frame, and fastened by a ribbon under the chin. This *salacot* is used by many as a protection against sun and rain; it appeared to me too heavy to be convenient.

Among the Indian women the opulent wear costly embroidered garments of piña, and many of them possess valuable jewels, and are decorated on occasions of festivity with earrings, necklaces and bracelets of pearls, diamonds and other precious stones. A few of them speak Spanish, and during our visits became the interpreters for the others, as the Indian women generally took a part in the graceful but simple ceremonials which marked our progress; sometimes forming a line through the towns and villages, and waving many-coloured flags over us as we passed, escorted by the native bands of music. In some families the garments which were worn a century ago are still preserved. Many of the petty authorities are the hereditary possessors of local rank, and on grand occasions make displays of the costumes of their forefathers. There is some variety in the mode of dressing the hair. The Tagálas clean it with lemon juice, and employ cocoa-nut oil made fragrant by infusions of odoriferous flowers. They clean their hands with pumice-stone. In many parts the thumbnail of the right hand is allowed by both sexes to grow to a great length, which assists playing on the guitar, and divers domestic operations. The under garments of the women are tightened at the waist, and their *camisas* have long and wide sleeves, which are turned back upon the arms, and embroidered in more or less costly taste. They all chew the areca, and, as age advances, they blacken their eyebrows and wear false hair like their patrician mistresses. They sometimes paint their nails with vermilion, and to be entitled a *Castila*, which means European, is recognized as a great compliment.

Rice is the ordinary food of the Indians. It is boiled for half an hour, and then called *canin*. The capsicum, or chile, is used for a condiment. They eat three meals a day, out of a large dish, helping themselves with their fingers, and sometimes using a plantain leaf for a plate. They also have sauces round the central dish, into which they dip the canin. They introduce the thumb first into the mouth, and very dexterously employ the fingers to push forward the food. The luxuries of the native are pretty nearly reduced to the cigar and the betel-nut. Indeed these can scarcely be called luxuries; they are more necessary to him than his simple food, which consists generally of boiled rice, sometimes flavoured with fish or vegetables, and his sweetmeat the sugar-cane. As he obtains his cigarritos at the estanco for less than two cuertos a dozen, and can make them, or buy them from a contrabandista, at not even half that price, and as the cost of the areca is extremely small, his wants and his enjoyments are easily and cheaply supplied. His garments are few and economical, and such as in most parts of the islands are supplied by the rude family loom; but the source of his ruin is in his *gallo* and his passion for play, to which nine-tenths of the miseries of the Indian are to be traced. Out of his embarrassments the Chinaman makes his profit, buying the labour of the indebted and extorting its maximum with coarse and often cruel tyranny. The Chinese have a proverb that the Indian must be led with rice in the left hand of his master and a bamboo in the right.

There is in some of the islands abundance of deer and wild boars; they are killed by arrows of two kinds—one barbed with a clove from the wild palm, shot direct; another with an iron head, shot upwards and falling down upon the animal. The Indians make a dry venison (called *tapa*) of the flesh and send it to the Manila market. Much wild fowl is found in the forest, especially of the gallinaceous species. The Bisayan caves are frequented by the swallows which produce the edible bird's-nests, and which are collected by the natives for exportation to China.

Multitudes of Indians get their living by the fisheries. The fish most esteemed is the *sabalo*, which is only found in the Taal Lake, whose water is fresh and flows into the sea. In the centre of the lake is an island, with its always burning volcano. At the season when the sabalo quit the lake for the sea, an estocade of bamboos is erected across the river, the top of which does not reach the surface of the water; three or four yards below, another estocade is placed, raised five or six feet above the surface, and the two estocades are united by a bamboo platform. The fish leap over the first barrier, and fall on the platform, where they are caught: some of them are as large as salmon. The *Bay* Lake is celebrated for the *curbina*, an excellent fish. By the banks of the river enormous nets are seen, which are sunk and raised by a machinery of bamboo, and the devices employed for the capture of fish are various and singular. In the Bisayans the Indians make faggots, which they kindle, and, walking on the banks with a spear in their right hand, the fish approach the light and are harpooned and flung upon the shore. I understand the sea-slug, which the Indians call *balate*, is thus captured. It is a well-known delicacy among the Chinese. Turtle are caught by watching their approach (the watcher being concealed) and simply turning them on their backs when they are at a certain distance from the water. Native divers bring up the mother-of-pearl oyster, but the pearl fishery is not of much importance. These divers also discover the enormous shell-fish which serve as receptacles for holy water in the churches.

LAKE OF TAAL, AND VOLCANO.

CHAPTER VIII.

POPULATION—RACES.

Though the far greater number of the *pagan Indians*, as they are called by the Spaniards, belong to the same races as those who inhabit the towns, there are many exceptional cases. Independent and separated from the pagans, there are numerous Mahomedans, especially in the island of Mindanao, of which only a small tract along the coast has been subjected by the Spaniards; these, whom the Spaniards designate as *Moros*, a name to which traditional and national associations attach great abhorrence, are probably of Malayan descent. There, as in every region where missionaries have sought to undermine or depreciate the authority of the Koran, the attempt has wholly failed. I saw some of these people at Zamboanga, and found them familiar with the Arabic formula of Islamism, and that many of their names, such as Abdallah, Fatima, and others, were such as are common to the Mussulmans. They are understood to be in amity with the Spaniards, who have treaties with the reigning Sultan; but I found no evidence of their recognition of Spanish authority.

The enmity between the Mahomedan races (*Moros*) and the Spaniards may be deemed hereditary. The answer given by the Rajah Soliman of Tondo to Legaspi, the first governor of the Philippines, who solicited his friendship, is characteristic:—"Not until the sun is cut in two, not until I seek the hatred instead of the love of woman, will I be the friend of a Castila" (Spaniard).

Living in the remotest mountainous regions of Mindanao, never, I believe, explored by European adventurers, there is a race in the very lowest stages of barbarism, I cannot say of civilization, for of that they present no trace. They are said to wear no garments, to build no houses, to dress no food. They wander in the forest, whose wild fruits they gather by day, and sleep among the branches of the trees by night. They have no form of government, no chief, no religious rites or usages. I saw one of the race who was brought for sale as any wild animal might have been to the governor of Zamboanga. He refused to purchase, but retained the lad, who was apparently of about eight or nine years of age. At Iloilo, he was waiting, with other native servants, at table, and he appeared to me the most sprightly and intelligent of the whole— bright-eyed, and watching eagerly every sign and mandate of his master. He was very dark-coloured, almost black; his hair disposed to be woolly; he had neither the high cheeks nor the thick lips of the African negro, but resembled many specimens I have seen of the Madagascar people. I was informed that the whole tribe—but the word is not appropriate, for they are not gregarious —are of very small stature; that they avoid all intercourse with other races, collect nothing, barter nothing, and, in fact, want nothing. I had once occasion to examine in the prison of Kandy (Ceylon) one of the real "wild men of the woods" of that island, who had been convicted for murder; the moral sense was so unawakened, that it was obvious no idea of wrong was associated with the act, and the judge most properly did not consider, him a responsible being on whom he could inflict the penalties of the law. There was little resemblance between the Filipino and the Cingalese in any external characteristic. Ethnological science would be greatly advanced if directed to the special study of the barbarous aboriginal races of whom specimens yet remain, but of which so many have wholly disappeared, who can have had no intercourse with each other. I believe there are more varieties of the human family than have hitherto been recognized by physiologists, amongst whom *no* affinity of language will be found. The theories current as to the derivation of the many varieties of the human race from a few primitive types will not bear examination. Civilization and education will modify the character of the skull, and the differences between the crania of the same people are so great as to defy any general law of classification. The farther back we are enabled to go, the greater will be the distinction of types and tongues; and it will be seen that the progress of time and commerce and knowledge and colonization, has annihilated many an independent idiom, as it has destroyed many an aboriginal race.

Against the wilder savages who inhabit the forests and mountains of the interior, expeditions are not unfrequently directed by the government, especially when there has been any molestation to the native Christian population. Their chiefs are subjected to various punishments, and possession is taken of their villages and strongholds; but these are not always permanently held, from the insufficiency of military force to retain them. But it is clear that these rude tribes must ultimately be extinguished by the extension of cultivation and the pressure of a higher civilization.

De Mas lays down as a principle that the *Igorrotes* of Luzon are heathens of the same race as the converted Indians, but in a savage state. The *Aetas*, or *Negritos*, are a separate race, not indigenous, but the descendants of invaders and conquerors. He had many opportunities of intercourse with them, and speaks favourably of his reception among them. The men had no other covering than a belt of bark fibres, the women a sort of petticoat of the same texture. Unmarried girls wore a species of collar made from the leaves of a mountain palm, whose ends met between their naked breasts. The females played on a rude guitar, the case being a piece of bamboo, with three strings from the roots of a tree, and which they tuned by tightening or loosening with their left hand. When it rained, they covered themselves with large palm-leaves, which they also used as shelter from the sun. He says they resisted all attempts upon their chastity. They brought wax, honey and deer, and sought for tobacco and rice in exchange. For money they cared not. The mode of showing respect is to offer water to the superior—no son can accept it from, but must hand it to, his father. They exhibit much fear of the evil spirits that are in the forests, but all information they gave was at secondhand. They had not seen the spirits, but others had, and there was no doubt about *that*. The friars report them to be short lived—their age seldom exceeding forty years. Father Mozo says: "They have their localities, in which they group themselves and which they unwillingly leave: fixed abodes they have none, but shift from place to place within a circumference of four to five leagues. They drive four rough sticks into the ground, surround them with the flexible branches of the *ylib*, fling down some palm-leaves, bring in a piece of wood for a pillow, and have their house and bed ready. The game killed by one belongs to all—the head and neck being thrown to the dogs. The community ordinarily consists of twenty to twenty-five persons, who select the most courageous of their number as chief. In the summer they locate themselves on the banks of rivers, but during the rainy and windy seasons they confine themselves to their rude huts. If a death take place, they bury the corpse, but flee from the locality, lest others be summoned away. When they seek wild honey in the woods, the finder of a swarm marks the tree where the bees are, and the property is deemed his own until he has time to return and remove the comb. A fire is lighted at the foot of the tree—the smoke drives away the bees —the Indian mounts, bearing a broad palm-leaf folded in the shape of a vase, into which he turns the honey-comb, ties it over, and descends. All his wants are supplied when, in addition to his matches for fire, his bow and arrows, and his rude cutlass, he has a small supply of tobacco for his luxury. If food be scarce, he drinks hot water and ties a cord tightly round his body; he eats also of a root called *sucbao*, but in the warm weather indigenous fruits are never wanting." After a string of quotations from the classics, illustrating the pains, penalties and passions of civilized existence, with the serenity, stupidity and satisfaction of these children of nature, the padre says: "Finally, in admiration of their manner of life, if they were but enlightened by our holy faith—if they only suffered what they suffer for the sake of God—I verily believe they would not be paralleled by the austerest monk of the Thebaïd. True it is they commit the sin of divorce—true it is that a slip before marriage is seldom heard of; but they are cruel, they are murderers!" Such is the consistency of ecclesiastical judgment.

There are many speculations as to the origin of the darker, or black races, who now occupy the northern and central mountainous and little visited regions, and from whom one of the islands, *Negros*, takes its name. They principally dwell in the wilder part of the provinces of Ilocos South, Pangasinan, Cagayan, and Nueva Ecija. They are of small stature, have somewhat flattened noses, curled hair, are agile, have no other dress than a covering of bark over their genitals, are dexterous hunters, have no fixed dwellings, but sleep wherever sunset finds them. Their whole property consists of their bow, a bamboo quiver and arrows, a strip of skin of the wild boar, and the girdle, which the Spaniards call the *tapa rabo* (tail cover). The *Negritos* are held to be the aboriginal inhabitants of the islands, which were invaded by those now called *Indios*, who much resemble, though they are a great improvement on, the Malayan race. The Negritos retired into the wilder districts as the Tagáls advanced, but between the two races there exists a great intensity of hatred. The Negritos are the savages of the Philippines, and are divided into many tribes, and it is said every grade between cannibalism and the civilization of the Indian is found among them. They generally live on the wild fruits and vegetables which grow spontaneously, though some cultivate rice, and attend to the irrigation of their fields. Some make iron weapons, and the *Itaneg*, according to the friars, only want conversion to be in all respects equal to the Indios. This race has a mixture of Chinese blood, the *Ifugaos* of that of the Japanese. The ruder savages ornament their cabins with the skulls of their enemies. The *Apayos* live in comfortable houses, and employ for floors polished planks instead of the interwoven bamboos of the Tagáls. They carry on a trade in wax, cocoa and tobacco, and deck their dwellings with China earthenware. The *Isinay* Negritos profess Christianity. In the island of Luzon there are estimated to be 200,000 heathens, in that of Mindanao 800,000 idolators and Mussulmans. But it is impossible to follow out the mixed races in all their ramifications and peculiarities. Among the characteristics of the wilder races is the separation of the toes, which enables them to pick up even minute objects, so if they let anything fall they use foot or hand with equal facility; they will descend head downwards the rigging of a ship, holding on with their feet; the great toe is much more separated from the others than in the white races. Their sense of smelling is exquisite, and they profess, without the aid of language, to discover the state of the affections from the breath.

Though they have a pantheon of gods and goddesses (for most of their divinities have wives), they have no temples, and no rites of public worship. They consult soothsayers (usually old women) in their diseases and difficulties; and there are sacrifices, outpouring and mingling of blood, libations of fermented liquors, violent gesticulations, and invocations to

Cambunian (God), the moon, and the stars, and the ceremonials end with eating and drinking to excess. They sacrifice a pig to pacify the Deity when it thunders, and adore the rainbow after the storm. Before a journey they kindle a fire, and if the smoke do not blow in the direction they intend to take they delay their project. The flight of birds is watched as an important augury, and the appearance of a snake as a warning against some approaching calamity.

The mountain tribes are subject to no common ruler, but have their separate chieftains, called *barnaas*, to whom a certain number of dependants is assigned. On the death of a barnaas, the intestines are extracted, examined and burnt, for the purpose of ascertaining by the arts of divination the future destiny of the tribe. The body is placed in a chair, relations and friends are invited, and a great festivity of eating and drinking provided from the flocks and rice-fields of the deceased, with shouts and songs celebrating the virtues of departed barnaas. The banquet closes with all species of excesses, and both sexes remain drunk, exhausted or asleep on the ground about the corpse. It is said that the flesh of the departed is distributed among the guests, and Buzeta avers that such a case lately occurred at Tagudin (Ilocos South); but as he attributes it to the poverty of the deceased who had not left behind wherewithal to provide for the festival, the carnal distribution could hardly have been deemed an honour. The stories of the cannibalism of the natives must be received with distrust, there being a great disposition to represent them as worse savages than they really are. The arms of a warrior are gathered together after his death, and his family will not part with them. A vessel into which wine has been poured is placed at the foot of the trophies, in order that it may imbibe the virtue and valour of the departed, and obtain his auspices.

In case of the murder of an individual, the whole of the tribe unite to revenge his death. Prisoners taken in war are made slaves, and sell for from ten to twenty-five dollars each. Old men are bought, upon whom to try the poisonous powers or sharpness of their weapons. Adultery and the third offence of robbery are punished with death. Polygamy is not allowed, but there is no difficulty about divorce.

A great variety of languages is to be found among the wild people of the interior; not only are dialects of the various tribes unintelligible to each other, but sometimes a language is confined to a single family group. Where there has been no intercourse there is no similitude. Words are necessary to man, and language is created by that necessity. Hence the farther the study of idioms is pursued back into antiquity, the greater will their number be found. Civilization has destroyed hundreds, perhaps thousands, of idioms, and is still carrying on the work by diminishing the number of languages in which man holds intercourse with man. It is no bold prophecy to aver that in the course of centuries the number of separate tongues will be reduced to a small amount. In France, the French; in Italy, the Tuscan; in Spain, the Castilian; in Germany, the Saxon; in Great Britain, the English;—are becoming the predominant languages of the people, and have been gradually superseding the multitude of idioms which were used only a few generations ago. Adelung recorded the names of nearly 4,000 spoken and existing languages, but a list of those which time has extinguished would be far more extensive.

That such large portions of the islands should be held by independent tribes, whether heathen or Mahomedan, is not to be wondered at when the geographical character of the country is considered. Many of their retreats are inaccessible to beasts of burden; the valleys are intolerably hot; the mountains unsheltered and cold. There is also much ignorance as to the localities, and the Spaniards are subject to be surprised from unknown ambushes in passes and ravines. The forests, through which the natives glide like rabbits, are often impenetrable to Europeans. No attempts have succeeded in enticing the "idolaters" down to the plains from these woods and mountains, to be tutored, taxed and tormented. Yet it is a subject of complaint that these barbarians interfere, as no doubt they do, with the royal monopoly of tobacco, which they manage to smuggle into the provinces. "Fiscal officers and troops," says De Mas, "are stationed to prevent these abuses, but these protectors practise so many extortions on the Indians, and cause so much of discontent, that commissions of inquiry become needful, and the difficulties remain unsolved." In some places the idolaters molest "the peaceful Christian population," and make the roads dangerous to travellers. De Mas has gathered information from various sources, and from him I shall select a few particulars; but it appears to me there is too much generalization as to the unsubjugated tribes, who are to be found in various stages of civilization and barbarism. The *Tinguianes* of Ilocos cultivate extensive rice-fields, have large herds of cattle and horses, and carry on a considerable trade with the adjacent Christian population. The Chinese type is said to be traceable in this race. The women wear a number of bracelets, covering the arm from the wrist to the elbow. The heaviest Tinguian curse is, "May you die while asleep," which is equivalent to saying, "May your death-bed be uncelebrated." It is a term of contempt for an Indian to say to another, "Malubha ang Caitiman mo"—Great is thy blackness (*negregura*, Sp.). The Indians call Africans *Pogot*.

There are many Albinos in the Philippines. They are called by the natives Sons of the Sun; some are white, some are spotted, and others have stripes on their skins. They are generally of small intellectual capacity.

Buzeta gives the following ethnological table, descriptive of the physical characteristics of the various races of the Philippines:—

	Pure Indians.	Mestizos.	Negritos.
Size	Handsome, middle, sometimes tall.	The same.	Handsome, small and thin.
Skin	Copper or quince colour, fine.	Lighter, somewhat yellow.	Dark copper.
Body	Slight, well-formed, strong.	Heavy.	Slight and agile.
Hair	Black, even, thick, harsh.	Less thick.	Black, curly, but less so than the Africans.
Head	Medium or small, round, and flat behind.	Generally large.	Small and rounder.
Forehead	Open, often narrow.	Open.	Narrow.
Eyes	Black, brilliant.	Less uniform.	Large, penetrating, brilliant.
Eyebrows	Thick and arched.	Less arched.	
Eyelids	Long.		Very long.
Nose	Medium, generally flat.	Thicker.	Medium, slightly flat.
Mouth	Large, medium sometimes.	Larger.	Medium.
Lips	Medium.	Thicker.	Medium, rounder.
Teeth	White, regular, strong.	Strong and large.	Long, very strong.
Upper Mandible	Ordinary size.	High, salient.	Ordinary.
Lower Mandible	Ordinary and strong.	Strong, open.	Well-formed.
Breast	Wide; woman's hard and firm.	Firm but narrow.	Firm but narrow.
Carriage	Graceful, elegant.	Graceful.	Easy and careless.
Buttocks	Broad and hard.	Broad, hard.	Broad, hard.
Muscles	Small.	Small.	Small.
Thighs	Small.	Small.	Small.
Feet	Small.	Small.	Small and well-formed.
Flesh	Hard.	Hard.	Hard.

Hair (body)	Lightly spread.	None.	Little.
Beard	None.	Little.	Little.
Genitals	Small.	Small.	Small.

The Altaban Indians have an idol whom they call *Cubiga*, whose wife is *Bujas*. The Gaddans give the name of *Amanolay*, meaning Creator of Man, to the object of their worship, and his goddess is *Dalingay*. There are no temples nor public rites, but appeals to the superior spirits in cases of urgency are generally directed by the female priest or sorceress, who sprinkles the idol with the blood of a buffalo, fowl or guinea-pig, offers libations, while the Indians lift up their hands exclaiming, "Siggam Cabunian! Siggam Bulamaiag! Siggam aggen!" (O thou God! O thou beautiful moon! O thou star!) A brush is then dipped in palm wine, which is sprinkled over the attendants. (This is surely an imitation of Catholic aspersions.) A general carousing follows.

The priests give many examples of what they call Indian ignorance and stupidity, but these examples generally amount only to a disclaimer of all knowledge respecting the mysteries of creation, the origin and future destiny of man, the nature of religious obligations, and the dogmas of the Catholic faith. It may be doubted whether the mere habitual repetition of certain formulas affords more satisfactory evidence of Christian advancement than the openly avowed ignorance of these heathen races.

If an Indian is murdered by one of a neighbouring tribe, and the offence not condoned by some arranged payment, it is deemed an obligation on the part of the injured to retaliate by killing one of the offending tribe.

The popular amusement is dancing; they form themselves into a circle, stretching out their hands, using their feet alternately, leaping on one and lifting the other behind; so they move round and round with loud cries to the sounds of cylindrical drums struck by both hands.

The skulls of animals are frequently used for the decoration of the houses of the Indians. Galvey says he counted in one dwelling, in Capangar, 405 heads of buffaloes and bullocks, and more than a thousand of pigs, causing an intolerable stench.

They use the bark of the Uplay in cases of intermittent fever, and have much knowledge of the curative qualities of certain herbs; they apply hot iron to counteract severe local pain, so that the flesh becomes cauterized; but they almost invariably have recourse to amulets or charms, and sacrifice fowls and animals, which are distributed among the attendants on the sick persons.

Padre Mozo says of the Italons (Luzon) that he has seen them, after murdering an enemy, drink his blood, cut up the lungs, the back of the head, the entrails, and other parts of the body, which they eat raw, avowing that it gave them courage and spirit in war. The skulls are kept in their houses to be exhibited on great occasions. This custom is probably of Bornean origin, for Father Quarteron, the vicar apostolic of that island, told me that he once fell in with a large number of savages who were carrying in procession the human skulls with which their houses were generally adorned, and which they called "giving an airing to their enemies." The teeth are inserted in the handles of their hangers. After enumerating many more of the barbarous customs of the islands, the good friar Mozo exclaims:—"Fancy our troubles and labours in rescuing such barbarians from the power of the devil!" They sacrifice as many victims as they find fingers opened after death. If the hand be closed, none. They suffer much from cutaneous diseases. The Busaos paint their arms with flowers, and to carry ornaments bore their ears, which are sometimes stretched down to their shoulders. The Ifugaos wear on a necklace pieces of cane denoting the number of enemies they have killed. Galvey says he counted twenty-three worn by one man who fell in an affray with Spanish troops. This tribe frequently attacks travellers in the mountains for the sake of their skulls. The missionaries represent them as the fiercest enemies of Christians. Some of the monks speak of horrible confessions made by Igorrote women after their conversion to Christianity, of their intercourse with monkeys in the woods, and the Padre Lorenzo indulges in long details on the subject, declaring, moreover, that a creature was once brought to him for baptism which "filled him with suspicion." De Mas reports that a child with long arms, covered with soft hair, and much resembling a monkey, was exhibited by his mother in Viyan, and taught to ask for alms.

De Mas recommends that the Spanish Government should buy the saleable portion of the Mahomedan and pagan tribes, convert them, and employ them in the cultivation of land; and he gives statistics to show that there would be an accumulation of 120 per cent., while their removal would set the Indians together by the ears, who would destroy one another, and relieve the islands from the plague of their presence. This would seem a new chapter in the history of slave-trade experiments. He calculates that there are more than a million pagans and Mahomedans in the islands. Galvey's "Diary of an Expedition to Benguet in January, 1829," and another to Bacun in December, 1831, are histories of personal adventures, many of a perilous character, in which many lives were lost, and many habitations destroyed. They are interesting as exhibiting the difficulties of subjugating these mountain races. Galvey conducted several other expeditions, and died in 1839.

There are few facts of more interest, in connection with the changes that are going on in the Oriental world, than the outpouring of the surplus Chinese population into almost every region eastwards of Bengal; and in Calcutta itself there is now a considerable body of Chinese, mostly shoemakers, many of whom have acquired considerable wealth, and they are banded together in that strong gregarious bond of nationality which accompanies them wherever they go, and which is not broken, scarcely even influenced, by the circumstances that surround them. In the islands of the Philippines they have obtained almost a monopoly of the retail trade, and the indolent habits of the natives cannot at all compete with these industrious, frugal, and persevering intruders. Hence they are objects of great dislike to the natives; but, as their generally peaceful demeanour and obedience to the laws give no hold to their enemies, their numbers, their wealth, their importance increase from year to year. Yet they are but birds of passage, who return home to be succeeded by others of their race. They never bring their wives, but take to themselves wives or hand-maidens from the native tribes. Legitimate marriage, however, necessitates the profession of Christianity, and many of them care little for the public avowal of subjection to the Church of Rome. They are allowed no temple to celebrate Buddhist rites, but have cemeteries specially appropriated to them. They pay a fixed contribution, which is regulated by the rank they hold as merchants, traders, shopkeepers, artisans, servants, &c. Whole streets in Manila are occupied by them, and wherever we went we found them the most laborious, the most prosperous of the working classes. Thousands upon thousands of Chinamen arrive, and are scattered over the islands, but not a single Chinese woman accompanies them from their native country.

In the year 1857, 4,232 Chinamen landed in the port of Manila alone, and 2,592 left for China.

Of the extraordinary unwillingness of the women of China to emigrate, no more remarkable evidence can be found than in the statistics of the capital of the Philippines. In 1855, there were in the fortress of Manila 525 Chinamen, but of females only two women and five children. In Binondo, 5,055 Chinamen, but of females only eight, all of whom were children. Now, when it is remembered that the Philippines are, with a favourable monsoon, not more than three or four days' sail from China, that there are abundance of opulent Chinese settled in the island, that the desire of having children and perpetuating a race is universal among the Chinese people, it may be easily conceived that there must be an intensely popular feeling opposed to the emigration of women.

And such is undoubtedly the fact, and it is a fact which must prove a great barrier to successful coolie emigration. No women have been obtainable either for the British or Spanish colonies, though the exportation of coolies had exceeded 60,000, and except by kidnapping and direct purchase from the procuresses or the brothels, it is certain no woman can be induced to emigrate. This certainty ought to be seriously weighed by the advocates of the importation of Chinese labourers into the colonies of Great Britain. In process of time, Hong Kong will probably furnish some voluntary female emigrants, and the late legalization of emigration by the Canton authorities will accelerate the advent of a result so desirable.

During five years, ending in 1855, there were for grave crimes only fourteen committals of Chinamen in the whole of the provinces, being an average of less than three per annum; no case of murder, none of robbery with violence, none for rape. There were nine cases of larceny, two of cattle-stealing, one forgery, one coining, one incendiarism. These facts are greatly creditable to the morality of the Chinese settlers. Petty offences are punished, as in the case of the Indians, by their own local principalia.

A great majority of the shoemakers in the Philippines are Chinese. Of 784 in the capital, 633 are Chinamen, and 151 natives. Great numbers are carpenters, blacksmiths, water-carriers, cooks, and daily labourers, but a retail shopkeeping trade is the favourite pursuit. Of late, however, many are merging into the rank of wholesale dealers and merchants, exporting and importing large quantities of goods on their own account, and having their subordinate agents scattered over most of the islands. Where will not a Chinaman penetrate—what risks will he not run—to what suffering will he not submit—what enterprises will he not engage in—what perseverance will he not display—if money is to be made? And, in truth, this constitutes his value as a settler: he is economical, patient, persistent, cunning; submissive to the laws, respectful to authority, and seeking only freedom from molestation while he adds dollar to dollar, and when the pile is sufficient for his wants or his ambition, he returns home, to be succeeded by others, exhibiting the same qualities, and in their turn to be rewarded by the same success.

When encouragement was first given to the Chinese to settle in the Philippines, it was as agricultural labourers, and they were not allowed to exercise any other calling. The Japanese were also invited, of whom scarcely any are now to be found in the islands. The reputation of the Chinese as cultivators of the land no doubt directed the attention of the Manila authorities towards them; but no Chinaman continues in any career if he can discover another more profitable. Besides this, they were no favourites among the rural population, and in their gregarious nature were far more willing to band themselves together in groups and *hwey* (associations) than to disperse themselves among the pastoral and agricultural races, who were jealous of them as rivals and hated them as heathens. They have created for themselves a position in the towns, and are now too numerous and too wealthy to be disregarded or seriously oppressed. They are mostly from the province of Fokien, and Amoy is the principal port of their embarkation. I did not find among them a single individual who spoke the classical language of China, though a large proportion read the Chinese character.

When a Chinese is examined on oath, the formula of cutting off the head of a white cock is performed by the witness, who is told that, if he do not utter the truth, the blood of his family will, like that of the cock, be spilt and perdition overtake them. My long experience of the Chinese compels me to say that I believe no oath whatever—nothing but the apprehension of punishment— affords any, the least security against perjury. In our courts in China various forms have at different times been used—cock beheading; the breaking of a piece of pottery; the witness repeating imprecations on himself, and inviting the breaking up of all his felicities if he lied; the burning of a piece of paper inscribed with a form of oath, and an engagement to be consumed in hell, as that paper on earth, if he spoke not the truth;—these and other ceremonies have utterly failed in obtaining any security for veracity. While I was governor of Hong Kong an ordinance was passed abolishing the oath-taking, as regards the Chinese, and punishing them severely as perjurers when they gave false testimony. The experiment has succeeded in greatly fortifying and encouraging the utterance of truth and in checking obscurity and mendacity. I inquired once of an influential person in Canton what were the ceremonies employed among themselves where they sought security for truthful evidence. He said there was one temple in which a promise made would be held more binding than if made in any other locality; but he acknowledged their tribunals had no real security for veracity. There is a Chinese proverb which says, "Puh tah, puh chaou," meaning "Without blows, no truth;" and the torture is constantly applied to witnesses in judicial cases. The Chinese religiously respect their written, and generally their ceremonial, engagements —they "lose face" if these are dishonoured. But little disgrace attends lying, especially when undetected and unpunished, and the art of lying is one of the best understood arts of government. Lies to deceive barbarians are even recommended and encouraged in some of their classical books.

CHAPTER IX.

ADMINISTRATION OF JUSTICE.

The supreme court of justice in the Philippines is the *Audiencia* established in Manila, which is the tribunal of appeal from the subordinate jurisdiction, and the consultative council of the Governor-General in cases of gravity.

The court is composed of seven *oidores*, or judges. The president takes the title of Regent. There are two government advocates, one for criminal, the other for civil causes, and a variety of subordinate officers. There are no less than eighty barristers, matriculated to practise in the Audiencia.

A *Tribunal de Comercio*, presided over by a judge nominated by the authorities, and assisted, under the title of *Consules*, by gentlemen selected from the principal mercantile establishments of the capital, is charged with the settlement of commercial disputes. There is a right of appeal to the Audiencia, but scarcely any instance of its being exercised.

There is a censorship called the *Comercia permanente de censura*. It consists of four ecclesiastics and four civilians, presided over by the civil fiscal, and its authority extends to all books imported into or printed in the islands.

There are fourscore lawyers (*abogados*) in Manila. As far as my experience goes, lawyers are the curse of colonies. I remember one of the most intelligent of the Chinese merchants who had settled at Singapore, after having been long established at Hong Kong, telling me that all the disadvantages of Singapore were more than compensated by the absence of "the profession," and all the recommendations of Hong Kong more than counterbalanced by the presence of gentlemen occupied in fomenting, and recompensed for fomenting, litigations and quarrels. Many of them make large fortunes, not unfrequently at the expense of substantial justice. A sound observer says, that in the Philippines truth is swamped by the superfluity of law documents. The doors opened for the protection of innocence are made entrances for chicanery, and discussions are carried on without any regard to the decorum which prevails in European courts. Violent invectives, recriminations, personalities, and calumnies, are ventured upon under the protection of professional privilege. When I compare the equitable, prompt, sensible and inexpensive judgments of the consular courts in China with the results of the costly, tardy, unsatisfactory technicalities of judicial proceedings in many colonies, I would desire a general proviso that no tribunal should be accessible in civil cases until after an examination by a court of conciliation.

The extortions to which the Chinese are subjected, in Hong Kong, for example—and I speak from personal knowledge—make one blush for "the squeezing" to which, indeed, the corruption of their own mandarins have but too much accustomed them. In the Philippines there is a great mass of unwritten, or at least unprinted, law, emanating from different and independent sources, often contradictory, introduced traditionally, quoted erroneously; a farrago, in which the "Leyes de Indias," the "Siete partidas," the "Novisima recompilacion," the Roman code, the ancient and the royal fueros—to say nothing of proclamations, decrees, notifications, orders, bandos—produce all the "toil and trouble" of the witches' cauldron, stirred by the evil genii of discord and disputation.

Games of chance (*juegos de azar*) are strictly prohibited in the Philippines, but the prohibition is utterly inefficient; and, as I have mentioned before, the Manila papers are crowded with lists of persons fined or imprisoned for violation of the law; sometimes forty or fifty are cited in a single newspaper. More than one captain-general has informed me that the severity of the penalty has not checked the universality of the offence, connived at and participated in by both ecclesiastics and civilians.

The fines are fifty dollars for the first, and one hundred dollars for the second, offence, and for the third, the punishment which attaches to vagabondage— imprisonment and the chain-gang.

Billiard-tables pay a tax of six dollars per month. There is an inferior wooden table which pays half that sum.

The criminal statistics of five years, from 1851 to 1855 present the following total number of convictions for the graver offences. They comprise the returns from all the provinces. Of the whole number of criminals, more than one-half are from 20 to 29 years old; one-third from 30 to 39; one-ninth from 40 to 49; one-twentieth from 15 to 19; and one-forty-fifth above 50.

They consist of 467 married, 81 widowers, and 690 unmarried men.

During the said period 236 had completed the terms of their sentences, 217 had died, and 785 remained at the date of the returns.

Adultery	1	Brought forward	259
Adultery, with homicide	1	Murder, with wounding and	
Prohibited arms	7	robbery	314
Abandonment of post	6	Robberies	390
Bigamy	1	Robberies, with violence	120

Drunkenness	2	Robberies of Tobacco	6
Horse and cattle stealing	21	Robberies on bodies (Dacoits)	36
Conspiracy	17	Wounding in quarrels	44
Smuggling	1	Wounding (causing death)	7
Deserters	126	Incendiarism	4
Rape	14	Incendiarism, with robbery	16
Rape and incest	4	Incest	6
Rape and robbery	6	Mutiny	7
Poisoning	2	Nonpayment of fines	3
Forging passports	13	False name	1
Fraudulent distilling	1	Parricide	2
Vagabonds	35	Resistance to military	18
Coining	1	Escape from prison	5
Carried forward	259	Total	1,238

In the city of Manila there was only one conviction for murder in five years. The proportion of the graver offences in the different provinces is nearly the same, except in the island of Negros, where of forty-four criminals, twenty-eight were convicted of murder.

CHAPTER X.

ARMY AND NAVY.

The army of the Philippines, with the exception of two brigades of artillery and a corps of engineers which are furnished by Spain, is recruited from the Indians, and presents an appearance generally satisfactory. They are wholly officered by Europeans.

There are nine regiments of native infantry, one of cavalry, called the Luzon Lancers, and there is a reserve corps of officers called *Cuadro de Remplazos*, from whom individuals are selected to fill up vacancies.

There is a small body of *Alabarderos de servicio* at the palace in the special service of the captain-general. Their origin dates from A.D. 1590, and their halberds and costume add to the picturesque character of the palace and the receptions there.

There are also four companies called the Urban Militia of Manila, composed of Spaniards, who may be called upon by the governor for special services or in cases of emergency.

A medical board exercises a general inspection over the troops. Its superior functionaries are European Spaniards. Hospitals in which the military invalids are received are subject to the authority of the medical board as far as the treatment of such invalids is concerned. The medical board nominates an officer to each of the regiments, who is called an *Ayudante*.

Of late a considerable body of native troops has been sent from Manila to Cochin China, in order to co-operate with the French military and marine forces in that country. They are reported to have behaved well in a service which can have had few attractions, and in which they have been exposed to many sufferings, in consequence of the climate and the hostile attitude of the native inhabitants. What object the Spaniards had in taking so important a part in this expedition to Touron remains hitherto unexplained. Territory and harbours in Oriental regions, rich and abundant, they hold in superfluity; and assuredly Cochin China affords nothing very inviting to well-informed ambition; nor are the Philippines in a condition to sacrifice their population to distant, uncertain, perilous, and costly adventures. There is no national pride to be flattered by Annamite conquests, and the murder of a Spanish bishop may be considered as atoned for by the destruction of the forts and scattering of the people, at the price, however, of the lives of hundreds of Christians and of a heavy pecuniary outlay. France has its purposes—frankly enough disclosed—to obtain some port, some possession of her own, in or near the China seas. I do not think such a step warrants distrust or jealousy on our part. The question may be asked, whether the experiment is worth the cost? Probably not, for France has scarcely any commercial interest in China or the neighbouring countries; nor is her colonial system, fettered as it always has been by protections and prohibitions, likely to create such interest. In the remote East, France can carry on no successful rivalry with Great Britain, the United States, Holland, or Spain, each of which has points of geographical superiority and influence which to France are not accessible. One condition is a *sine quâ non* in these days of trading rivalry—lowness of price, associated with cheapness of transport. France offers neither to the foreign consumer in any of the great articles of supply: she *will* have high prices for *her* producers.

The maritime forces are under the orders of the commandant of the station. They consist of four steamers and one brig-of-war, six gunboats, and a considerable number of *faluas* (feluccas), which are employed in the coasting service and for the suppression of piracy.

CHAPTER XI.

PUBLIC INSTRUCTION.

Public instruction is in an unsatisfactory state in the Philippines—the provisions are little changed from those of the monkish ages.

In the University of St. Thomas there are about a thousand students. The professorships are of theology, the canon and civil law, metaphysics and grammar; but no attention is given to the natural sciences, to the modern languages, nor have any of the educational reforms which have penetrated most of the colleges of Europe and America found their way to the Philippines. In the *colegios* and schools what is called philosophy, rhetoric and Latin are the principal objects of attention. The most numerously attended of these establishments were founded two or three centuries ago, and pursue the same course of instruction which was adopted at their first establishment. There are several colleges and convents for women. That of Santa Potenciana was established under a royal decree, dated A.D. 1589, which requires that girls (*doncellas*) be received and taught to "live modestly" (*honestamente*), and, under sound doctrine, to "come out" for "marriage and propagation of the race" (*hagan propagacion*). There is a nautical school, of which I heard a favourable report, and an academy of painting, which has hitherto produced no Murillo or Velasquez. The best native works of art which I saw were two heads of the Virgin and St. Francisco, carved by an Indian in ivory, and which adorn the convent of Lucban, in the province of Tayabas. The good friars attributed to them almost miraculous virtues, and assured me that, though heavy rains preceded and followed the processions in which the images were introduced, a bright and beautiful sunshine accompanied them in their progress.

Among the novel objects that meet the eye in Manila, especially on the morning of religious *fiestas*, are groups of veiled women, wearing a dark mysterious costume, who visit the different churches. Their dress is a black woollen or silken petticoat, over which is a large shining mantilla, or veil, of a deep mulberry colour; others wear the ancient hooded Andalusian black cloak. There are the sisterhoods called the *Colegialas de los Beaterios*—religious establishments in which young women receive their education; some supported by "pious foundations," others by voluntary contributions. The rules of these convents vary, as some of the nuns never quit the buildings, others visit the churches under the guardianship of a "mother;" in some it is

119

permitted to the colegiala to join her family at certain seasons, and to participate in social enjoyments at home or abroad. These pay for their education sums varying from two to eight dollars a month, according to the regulations of the different beaterios, which have also their distinguishing costumes in some of the details, such as the colour of the lining of their dress. It is said there is scarcely a family of respectability in Manila that has not one daughter at least in a beaterio. In that of Santa Rosa the monthly pay is five dollars. Its inmates rise at five A.M., to chant the *trisagio* (holy, holy, holy), to hear mass and engage in devotion for the first part of the rosary till six; then to wash and dress; breakfast at half-past six; instruction from seven to ten; dinner at half-past eleven in the refectory; siesta and rest till half-past two P.M.; devotion in the chapel, going through the second part of the rosary; instruction from half-past three till half-past five; at the "oration," they return to the chapel, recite the third part of the rosary, and engage in reading or meditation for half an hour; sup at eight P.M.; enjoy themselves in the cloister or garden till nine; another prayer, and they retire to their cells. In the beaterio of St. Sebastian of Calumpang the inmates rise at four A.M.: the pay is five dollars; but the general arrangements are the same as those described. In the beaterio of Santa Catalina de Sena they are not allowed to leave the convent. The pay is eight dollars: it has the reputation of superior accommodation, and less economical food. The beaterio of the Jesuits has about 900 inmates; but this number is much exceeded in Lent, when great numbers enter to perform their spiritual exercises. The pay is only two dollars per month; but much sewing and washing is done within the convent for its support. When the Jesuits were expelled, the direction of this beaterio passed to the vicar-general of the archbishopric.

The beaterio of Pasig is solely devoted to the reception of Indian orphans, and its founder required that they should be taught "Christian doctrine, sewing, reading, writing, embroidery, and other instruction becoming the sex."

There are many charitable institutions in Manila. The Jesuits, afterwards expelled from the Philippines by Carlos II., founded several of the most important. The Hospital of San Juan de Dios has 112 beds; that of San José de Cavite 250, of which 104 are for soldiers, and the rest for paupers and criminals. There is an *Administracion de Obras Pias*, under the direction of the archbishop, the regent, and some of the superior civil authorities, which lends money to the Indians to the value of two-thirds of their landed property, one-half of their value on plate and jewellery, and insures vessels employed in the coasting trade. A *caja de comunidad* exacts half a rial (3¼d.) annually from the Chinese and Indians for the payment of "schoolmasters, vaccinators, defence of criminals, chanters, and sacristans of churches." The fund is administered by the directing board of finance.

The history of the Hospital of St. Lazarus, under charge of the Franciscan friars, is not without interest. It was constructed for the use of the natives in 1578, was enlarged, and twice consumed by fire. In the year 1632, it received 150 Christian lepers exiled from Japan, and thence took its present name. It was demolished by the captain-general in 1662, when the Chinese pirates menaced the capital, as it was deemed an impediment to the defence of the place. The inmates were removed; and another hospital was built, which was again destroyed in 1783, in consequence of its having been useful to the English in their invasion in 1762; but a few years afterwards the present edifice was built on lands which belonged to the Jesuits before the extinction of their society in the Philippines.

CHAPTER XII.

ECCLESIASTICAL AUTHORITY.

There are in the Philippines one archiepiscopal and three episcopal sees. The metropolitan archbishopric of Manila was founded by Clement VII. in 1595, and endowed by Philip II. with a revenue of 500,000 maravedis (= 200*l.* sterling). The bishopric of New Segovia was created at the same time with a similar endowment. The see is now (1859) vacant. The bishopric of Cebu was established in 1567, soon after the conquest of the island by the Spaniards. Nueva Caceres has also a bishop. The selection of candidates for these ecclesiastical honours has been generally left to the religious brotherhood who are most numerous in the district where there is a vacancy, and the candidate, being approved by the sovereign of Spain, is submitted to the Pope for confirmation. Some nominations have taken place where the bishop elect has not been willing to quit the mother-country for the colonies, which I was informed had caused the adoption of a resolution not to install a bishop until he has taken possession of his see. Most of the ecclesiastical authority is in the hands of the friars or regular clergy. There are proportionally few secular priests in the islands. The Dominicans and Augustine monks have large possessions, especially in the central and southern provinces; the Franciscans are most numerous in the northern. To the hospitality and kindness of the friars during the whole of my journey I bear a willing and grateful testimony. Everywhere the convents were opened to us with cordial welcome, and I attribute much of the display of attention on the part of the Indians to the reception we everywhere experienced from the Spanish padres. The Dominican monks have charge of the mission to Fokien, in China, and Tonquin.

The ecclesiastical records of the Philippines overflow with evidences of the bitter, and sometimes bloody, controversies of the Church with the civil authority, and with quarrels of the religious bodies among themselves. In the year 1710 the Dominicans declared themselves not subject to the jurisdiction of diocesan visits. One of their resolutions says:—"The provinces hold it for evident and certain that such visits would lead to the perdition of religious ministers, which is the opinion that has been for many years held by grave and zealous ecclesiastics and superior prelates who have dwelt in the province." In 1757 the Augustine friars (*calzados*) were menaced with the confiscation of their property if they denied the supreme authority and the admission of parochial curates regularly appointed; and they resolved that such submission "would be the ruin of their institution and to the notable detriment of souls." In 1767 Benedict XIV. published a bull insisting on the recognition of the metropolitan authority, which was still resisted by the Augustines. In 1775 a royal mandate was issued at Madrid insisting that all regular curates be submitted to their provincial in questions *de vitâ et moribus*, to the bishop, in all matters of spiritual administration, and to the captain-general as vice-regal patron. Whether the ecclesiastical police is better kept by the interference of the higher authorities, or by the independent action among themselves of the different religious orders, is a question much debated, but the substantive fact remains that the friar has an enormous and little-controlled influence in the locality of his *cure*, and that where abuses exist it is very difficult to collect evidence, and still more so to inflict punishment in case of his misdoings.

It cannot be denied that, in the language of Tomas de Comyn, "the missionaries were the real conquerors of the Philippines; their arms were not, indeed, those of the warrior, but they gave laws to millions, and, scattered though they were, they established by unity of purpose and of action a permanent empire over immense multitudes of men." Up to the present hour there are probably few parishes in which the gobernadorcillo, having received a mandate from the civil authority, fails to consult the friar, and the efficiency and activity of the Indian functionary in giving effect to the mandate will much depend on the views the padre may take of the orders issued.

Religious processions are the pride and the passion of the Filipinos, and on great festivals they bring together prodigious crowds both as actors and spectators. The most brilliant are those which take place after sunset, when some thousands of persons carry lighted wax candles, and the procession is sometimes a mile long, composed of all the military and civil authorities and of the ecclesiastical functionaries, vying with each other in the display of their zeal and devotion. On these occasions splendidly dressed images of the various objects of veneration form an important part of the ceremonial. I was assured that the jewels worn by the image of *Nuestra Señora de la Imaculada Concepcion* on the day of her festival exceeded 25,000 dollars in value. Numerous bands of music accompany the show. One of the most interesting parts of the exhibition is the number of little girls prettily and fancifully dressed in white, who follow some of the images of the saints or the *palio* of the archbishop. One of the processions witnessed was forty minutes in passing, and of immense length, the whole way being lined with bearers of wax lights on both sides. There seems a rivalry among the religious orders as to whose displays shall be the most effective and imposing. The images are of the size of life, and clad in gorgeous garments encumbered with ornaments.

They are borne on the shoulders of their votaries, occupying a platform, whence they are visible to the crowd.[1]

These religious ceremonials, so dear to, and so characteristic of, the Filipinos, are called *Pentacasi*. Everybody seems to take a part, whether within or without doors. All invite or are invited, and busy hands are engaged in making sweetmeats, preparing meats, or adorning apartments (with furniture borrowed from all sides, a favour to be reciprocated in turn), musicians are collected, strangers are sought for, and universal bustle pervades the locality.

"On the eve preceding the festival," says a native author, describing what takes place in the neighbourhood of Manila, "the pueblo exhibits all the activity of preparation. In the streets, handsome arches are constructed of bamboo, covered with painted linen, and representing various orders of architecture; graceful drapery is suspended over the arch, which has sundry openings or windows, in which variegated lanterns are placed (an art taught, no doubt, by the Chinese, who possess it in perfection). Within the lanterns ornamented figures are kept in perpetual movement by the heated atmosphere. Nosegays of artificial flowers, groups of fruits, and various devices decorate the houses, and the local musicians serenade the priests and the authorities; while the whole population crowd the church for the vesper service. The *dalagas* (girls) prepare their gayest attire to take part in the procession, in which queens and saints and various scriptural personages are represented by the Zagalas or females of the leading families, in garments of velvet and gold, with all the jewels that can be collected—not that always the costume testifies to much classical or historical knowledge; it is, however, very gay and gorgeous, satisfactory to the wearers, admired and applauded by the spectators. Popular songs are sung to the music of the guitar, and the gaieties are carried on to the midnight hour. At eight o'clock on the following morning mass is attended, a sermon preached, a procession follows, and all retire to their dwellings to escape the heat of the day; but in the principal houses repasts are ready for any guests who may call, and a considerable variety of Indian dishes are laid out upon the table. At four P.M., the military arrive with their music, and generally the village musicians and the church choir assemble near the church, and welcome the many visitors who come from the capital. So great is the crowd of carriages, that they are not allowed to pass through the streets, but their occupiers quit them at the entrance of the pueblo, and make their way to the hosts who have invited them. A great number of Spanish ladies from Manila are generally seated at the windows to witness the busy scene. Not only are the streets crowded by the gaily dressed inhabitants, but multitudes of Indians come from the interior to take part in the festivity. The native authorities, preceded by music, then visit the various houses to collect the Zagalas, who come forth in their regal robes and crowns, with a suite of attendants. There is a great display of fireworks, rockets, and balloons, and the procession proceeds to the church. It is a grand day for the gallera, or cockpit, which resembles the bull-fight arena in Spain: it is filled to suffocation with noisy and excited actors and spectators; immense bets are laid; booths surround the place, where food and drink are sold, and among the delicacies roasted sucking-pigs abound. The procession usually starts at six P.M. All those who take part bear a lighted wax-candle: first, the children of the pueblo; then the soldiers; then the image of the Virgin, with an escort of veiled women; then the image of the saint of the day or of the place, the car drawn by a number of dalagas in white garments, bearing garlands and crowns of flowers, followed by the authorities and by the priest in his golden cope; then a military band and cavalry soldiers; then the principal Zagala, whose queenly train is borne by eight or ten Indian girls, in white garments, adorned with flowers. Other Zagalas, personifying the Christian virtues, follow—Faith, Hope, Charity, with their characteristic attributes. Sometimes there are cars in which scenes of Scripture are exhibited by living actors; others displaying all the fancies of devotees. The procession parades the streets till the night is far advanced; the images are then restored to the church, and other amusements begin. The principal guests are invited to an open, but temporarily erected building, handsomely curtained, and brilliantly lighted, in the centre of which is a large table, covered with delicacies, and ornamented with groups and pyramids of flowers. The first attentions are shown to the ecclesiastics, and then to the other visitors, according to their rank and position. The streets and houses being illuminated as the night advances, the principal inhabitants gather their guests together, and at ten P.M. there are displays of fireworks and balloons, in which the rivalry of the pyrotechnic artists of the capital have a fine field for exercise. Most of the pueblos around Manila have their festival days, and in the competition for giving glory to their local saints and patrons, they seek to outdo the capital itself. Santa Cruz, which is an opulent and populous locality, rejoices in the protection of St. Stanislaus, and outbids most of the rest for ostentatious show, in which the inhabitants of Manila take an active part. The Chinese have their day in celebrating St. Nicholas in Guadalupe. Tondo has its distinguished festivals. Binondo is great and gorgeous on the day of "Our Lady of the Rosary of Saint Dominic." Sampaloc claims "Our Lady of Loreto." Santa Ana worships "Our Lady of the abandoned ones" (*de los desamparados*). Pandacan has its gatherings in honour of "The sweet name of Jesus," and its beautiful scenery adds to the attractions of the place. St. Sebastian processionizes its silver car, in which "Our Lady of Carmel" is conveyed in state. The suspensions caused by the rainy months, Lent, and a few other interruptions, are compensated by the extra ceremonials and festivities of the holy weeks, and other seasons of Catholic gratulation. The mere list of all these *fiestas* would occupy pages, and it was my good fortune to visit the islands at a time when I had an opportunity of witnessing many of these characteristic exhibitions.

The opulence of the individual monks, and of some of the monkish fraternities in the islands, has often and naturally been a subject of reproach. The revenues received by individuals are in many localities very large, amounting in remote districts to eight or nine thousand dollars a year, and much more, it is reported, in such populous pueblos as Binondo. Some of these communities also possess large tracts of land, whose management is superintended at periodical meetings held in the capital, when friars from the different provinces, and of the same brotherhood, are summoned to give an account of their stewardship, and to discuss the general interests of the fraternity. The accumulations of the friars pass to the convents at their death, but they have little difficulty in disposing of them while living.

It has been said that the policy of the friars in the Philippines is to conduct the Indian to heaven by a pathway of flowers. Little molestation will he experience from his ghostly father, if he be strict in his religious observances, pay his regular contributions to Church and State, and exhibit those outward marks of respect and reverence which the representatives of the Deity claim as their lawful heritage; but there are many thorns amidst the flowers, and drawbacks, on the heavenly road; and the time may come when higher and nobler aspirations than those which now satisfy the poor untutored, or little tutored, Indian, will be his rule of conduct.

The personal courtesies, the kind reception and multifarious attentions which I received from the friars in every part of the Philippines naturally dispose me to look upon them with a friendly eye. I found among them men worthy of being loved and honoured, some of considerable intellectual vigour; but literary cultivation and scientific acquirements are rare. Occupied with their own concerns, they are little acquainted with mundane affairs. Politics, geography, history, have no charms for those who, even had they the disposition for study, would, in their seclusion and remoteness, have access to few of its appliances. Their convents are almost palatial, with extensive courts, grounds and gardens; their revenues frequently enormous. Though their mode of life is generally unostentatious and simple, many of them keep handsome carriages and have the best horses in the locality; and they are surrounded generally by a prostrate and superstitious population, upon whose hopes and fears, thoughts and feelings, they exercise an influence which would seem magical were it not by their devotees deemed divine. This influence, no doubt, is greatly due to the heroism, labours, sufferings and sacrifices of the early missionaries, and to the admirably organized hierarchy of the Roman Church, whose ramifications reach to the extremest points in which any of the forms or semblances of Christianity are to be discovered. Volumes upon volumes—the folio records of the proceedings of the different religious orders, little known to Protestant readers—fill the library shelves of these Catholic establishments, which are the receptacles of their religious history.

The most extensively influential brotherhood in the Philippines is that of the Augustines (*Agostinos Calzados*), who administer to the cure of more than a million and a half of souls. The barefooted Augustines (*Agostinos Descalzos*, or *Recoletos*) claim authority over about one-third of this number. The Dominicans occupy the next rank, and their congregations are scarcely less numerous than those of the barefooted Augustines. Next come the Franciscans, who are supposed to rank with the Dominicans in the extent of their authority. Independently of the monastic orders and the superior ecclesiastic authorities, there are but a small number of parochial or secular clergy in the Philippines.

On occasions of installations under the "royal seal," the ceremonies take place in the church of the Augustines, the oldest in Manila, where also the regimental flags receive their benediction, and other public civil festivals are celebrated. A convent is attached to the church. Both the regular Augustines and the Recoletos receive pecuniary assistance from the State. The Franciscans rank next to the Augustines in the number of their clergy.

A source of influence possessed by the friars, and from which a great majority of civil functionaries are excluded, is the mastery of the native languages. All the introductory studies of ecclesiastical aspirants are dedicated to this object. No doubt they have great advantages from living habitually among the Indian people, with whom they keep up the most uninterrupted intercourse, and of whose concerns they have an intimate knowledge. One of the most obvious means of increasing the power of the civil departments would be in encouragement given to their functionaries for the acquirement of the native idioms. I believe Spanish is not employed in the pulpits anywhere beyond the capital. In many of the pueblos there is not a single individual Indian who understands Castilian, so that the priest is often the only link between the government and the community, and, as society is now organized, a necessary link. It must be recollected, too, that the different members of the religious brotherhoods are bound together by stronger bonds and a more potent and influential organization than any official hierarchy among civilians; and the government can expect no co-operation from the priesthood in any measures which tend to the diminution of ecclesiastical authority or jurisdiction, and yet the subjection of that authority to the State, and its limitation wherever it interferes with the public well-being, is the great necessity and the all-important problem to be solved in the Philippines. But here, too, the *Catholic* character of the government itself presents an enormous and almost invincible difficulty. Nothing is so dear to a Spaniard in general as his religion; his orthodoxy is his pride and glory, and upon this foundation the Romish Church naturally builds up a political power and is able to intertwine its pervading influence with all the machinery of the civil government. The Dutch have no such embarrassment in their archipelago.

The Captain-General has had the kindness to furnish me with the latest returns of the ecclesiastical corporations in the Philippines (dated 1859). They are these:—

	Tributaries.	Souls.	Baptisms.	Marriages.	Deaths.
RECOLETOS					
Archbishopric of Manila	29,899	122,842	5,335	1,166	3,334
Province of Zebu	90,701	454,279	18,559	4,166	6,500
Total	120,600	577,121	23,894	5,332	9,834
FRANCISCANS					
Archbishopric of Manila	60,936	227,866	7,988	1,923	7,896
Bishopric of New Caceres	72,477	289,012	9,957	2,505	7,020
Bishopric of Zebu	57,778	237,583	9,941	2,260	4,691
Total	191,191	754,461	27,886	6,688	19,607
AUGUSTINES					
Archbishopric of Manila	162,749	678,791	28,826	6,194	20,669
Bishopric of Ilocos	85,574	357,218	15,775	4,218	8,383
Bishopric of Zebu	136,642	607,821	27,049	4,049	16,361
Total	384,965	1,643,830	71,650	14,461	45,413

DOMINICANS					
Archbishopric of Manila	20,803	74,843	3,230	603	2,806
New Segovia	77,314	352,750	1,374	3,909	9,216
Total	98,117	427,593	4,604	4,512	12,022

The Dominicans have charge of the missions to the province of Fokien in China and Tonquin. They report in 1857:—In Fokien: 11,034 confessions and 10,476 communions, 1,973 infant and 213 adult baptisms, 284 marriages and 288 confirmations. In Eastern Tonquin: 3,283 infant and 302 adult baptisms, 4,424 extreme unctions, 64,052 confessions, 60,167 communions and 658 marriages. In Central Tonquin: 5,776 infant and 400 adult baptisms, 32,229 extreme unctions, 141,961 confessions, 131,438 communions and 1,532 marriages.

There may be some interest in the following details, as a specimen; but it is by no means one of the most distinguished.

Programme of the Procession of the Holy Interment, proceeding from the Church of San Domingo, and returning thither through the principal streets of Manila:—

Civil guards on horseback.
Files of bearers of wax lights along the line of procession.
Military, under their several heads and colours.

Carabineers of the Hacienda, bearing lights, 8.
Company of Engineers,   ditto,   8.
Carabineers of Public Safety, ditto,   8.
Cavalry (Lancers),   ditto,   32.
Infantry (Borbon),   ditto,   32.
Ditto (Princesa),   ditto,   32.
Ditto (Infante),   ditto,   32.
Ditto (Fernando VII.),   ditto,   32.
Artillery Brigade, No. 1,   ditto,   32.
Ditto, No. 2,   ditto,   32.
Infantry (Rey),   ditto,   32.

Peasants bearing lights.
Officers of the army and marine and public functionaries.
Collegiates of St. John of Lateran.

Secular clergy.

Brotherhood of St. Domingo.

Two files of sisterhood (Beatas).

The centre of the procession to consist of

Band of music of Infantry (Rey).

Standard.

Ten representations of the Passion, carried by the clergy at appropriate distances.

Six collegiates of St. John of Lateran with cirios (large wax lights).

Image of St. John the Evangelist.

Eleven representations of the Passion, carried by the clergy.

Six collegiates of St. John with cirios.

Image of St. Mary of Magdalene.

Band of music of Infantry (Ferdinand VII.).

Ten representations of the Passion, as before.

Musical choir chanting the *Miserere*.

Eight collegiates of St. Thomas with cirios.

Car conveying *The Lord*.

By the side of the car, eight Halberdiers, with funeral halberds.

Music of Infantry (No. 7).

Pall (palio) carried by collegiates of St. John of Lateran.

Brotherhood of the interment, in semicircle.

Six collegiates of St. John of Lateran with cirios.

Image of Santa Maria Salomé.

Six collegiates of St. Thomas with cirios.

Image of Santa Maria Jacoba.

Choir of music, singing *Stabat Mater*.

Six collegiates of St. Thomas in file with cirios.

Image of our Lady de los Dolores.

Pall carried by six collegiates of St. Thomas.

Preste (celebrator of high mass) in his black cope, with two sacristans at the right and the left.

H. E. the Governor-General, at his left the Lieutenant-Governor, at his right the Prior of St. Domingo, President of the Brotherhood of the Holy Interment.

Preceding these are all the supreme authorities of the islands in full dress, followed by the military and naval officers of high rank.

Brigade of European Artillery, with officers.

Drums (muffled) playing funeral march.

Bands of music (as at funerals).

European brigade, with muskets reversed.

Escort of Captain-General on horseback.

Note—That in this religious procession perfect equality is to be preserved.

CHAPTER XIII.

LANGUAGES.

The Tagál and Bisayan are the most widely spread of the languages of the Philippines, but each has such a variety of idioms that the inhabitants of different islands and districts frequently are not intelligible to one another, still less the indigenous races who occupy the mountainous districts. The more remarkable divisions are the dialects of Pampangas, Zambal, Pangasinan, Ilocos, Cagayan, Camarines, Batanes, and Chamorro, each derived from one of the two principal branches. But the languages of the unconverted Indians are very various, and have little affinity. Of these I understand above thirty distinct vocabularies exist. The connection between and the construction of the Tagál and Bisayan will be best seen by a comparison of the Lord's Prayer in each, with a verbal rendering of the words:—

Tagál.

Ama nanim[1]   sungma[2]   sa langit ca[3],   sambahin[4]   ang ngalan   mo;   mupa sa anim ang
Father our (to us)   art   in heaven thou, worshipped (be)   the   name thine; come to   us   the
caharian   mo;   sundin   angloob   mo dito sa lupa para na sa langit; bigianmo camin
kingdom thine;   done (be) the will thine here in earth   so as in heaven; given (be)   us
ngai-on nang anim canin sa arao-arao[5] at patauarvin-mo camis nang animg manga-otang,
   now   the   our rice of day day,   and forgiven (be)   us   the   our   faults,
para nang pagpasawat nanim sa   nangagcacaoton   sa   anim; at huvag-mo
   as   if   pardoned (are)   our   those who have committed faults against   us; and   let not
caming ipahuintulot[6] sa   tocso;   at yadia-mo camis sa dilan masama.
   us   fall   in temptation; and   deliver   us   in all   ill.

Bisayan.

Amahan namu nga itotat   ca sa langit, ipapagdayat[7] an imong ngalun; moanhi[8] canamun
Father   our   who   art   thou in heaven, praised be   the   thy   name;   come   to us
an imong pagcahadi[9]; tumancun an imong buot dinhi si yuta maingun sa langit; ihatag mo
the   thy   kingdom;   done (be) the thy   will here in earth   as   in heaven; given (be)
damsin an canun namun sa matagarvlao, ug pauadin-mo[10] canir san mga-sala namu,
   us   the rice   our   on every day,   and pardoned (be)   us   the   sins   our,
maingun ginuara[10] namun san mganacasala danum; ngan diri imo   tugotan   cami
   as   pardoned   our   those   sin   against us; not by thee permitted (be) us
maholog sa manga-panulai sa amun manga caauai[11]; apan   baricun-mo cami sa
   fall   in   temptations of our   enemies;   also   delivered (be)   us of
manga-maraut ngatanan.
     evil   all.

The following table of numerals (extracted from De Mas) will show the affinities between several of the idioms of the Philippines with one another, and with the Malay language:—

—	Ilocos.	Tagál.	Bisayan.	Cagayan.	Malay.
1	Meysa.	isá; sang; ca.	usá.	tadd ay.	salu; sa.
2	Dua.	dalauá.	duhá.	dua.	dua.
3	Tal.	tat-ló.	toló.	tálu.	tigga talu.
4	Eppa.	ápat.	upát.	áppa.	ámpat.
5	Lima.	lima.	lima.	lima.	lima.
6	Niném.	ánim.	unúm.	ánnam.	anam.
7	Pitó.	pitó; pipito.	pitó	pitar.	túgàu.
8	Oaló.	ualo.	ualó.	ualu.	diapan; dalapan.
9	Siam.	siam.	siam.	siam.	sambilan.
10	Sangapulo.	sampu; povo; sang povo.	napulo.	mafulu.	pulo; napulo.
11	Sangapulo qet maysa.	labin isa.	napulo ugusa.	caraladay.	sa blas.
12	Sangapulo qet dua.	labin dalava.	napulo ugdua.	caradua.	dua blas.
20	Duàpulo.	daluanpú; dulavangpovo.	caloháan.	dua fulù.	dua pulo.
30	Talcopulo.	tat lonpu.	catloan.	talu fulù.	tiga pulo.
50	Limapulo.	limanpu.	caliman.	lima fulu.	lima pulo.
100	Sangagasùt.	isam daán; dansandang.	usa cagatós.	magattu.	ratus; sarátus.
200	Dua nga gasùt.	dalauan daán.	dua cagatós.	duagattu.	dua ratus.
1,000	Sang aribo.	libo; isan libo.	usa ca libó.	marifu.	ribu; saribu.
10,000	Dua nga ribo.	sampon libo.	napálo calibo.	mafulu rifu.	lagsa.
100,000	Sang agasùt aribo.	isandaán libo; sang yolo.	usa cagatós calibo.	magatu farifu.	kati; sakiti.
1,000,000	....	sangañgaonúgao.	....	....	....

A vocabulary of the Tagal was printed in 1613 by Padre San Buenaventura; and a folio *Vocabulario* by Fr. Domingo de los Santos, in Sampaloc (Manila), 1794. This vocabulary consists of nearly 11,000 terms, the same word conveying so many meanings that the actual number of Tagal words can scarcely exceed 3,500. The examples of distinct interpretations of each are innumerable.

Another *Vocabulario de la Lengua Tagala*, by "various grave and learned persons," corrected and arranged by the Jesuit Fathers Juan de Noceda and Pedro de San Lucar, was published in Valladolid in 1832. The editor says he would fain have got rid of the task, but the "blind obedience" he owed to his superior compelled him to persevere. Rules for the accurate grammatical construction of the language cannot, he says, be given, on account of the exceptions and counter-exceptions. The confusion between active and passive participles is a labyrinth he cannot explore. There are more books on the language (*artes*), he avers, than on any dead or living language! He has consulted no less than thirty-seven, among which the first place is due to the Tagál Demosthenes (Father Francis de San José), to whose researches none have the knowledge of adding anything valuable. He professes to have given all the roots, but not their ramifications, which it is impossible to follow. But the *Vocabulario* is greatly lauded by the "Visitador," as "an eagle in its flight," and "a sun in its brilliancy." It is reported to have added three thousand new words to the vocabulary. The editor himself is modest enough, and declares he has brought only one drop to a whole ocean. The work, which had been in many hands, occupied Father Noceda thirty years, and he allowed no word to pass until "twelve Indians" agreed that he had found its true meaning. He would not take less, for had he broken his rule and diminished the numbers, who knows, he asks, with what a small amount of authority he might have satisfied himself? There can be no doubt that to find absolute synonymes between languages so unlike as the Castilian and the Tagáloc was an utterly impossible task, and that the root of a word of which the editor is in search is often lost in the inflections, combinations and additions, which surround and involve it, without reference to any general principle. And after all comes the question, What is the Tagáloc language? That of the mountains differs much from that of the valleys; the idiom of the Comingtang from those of the Tingues.

The word Tagála, sometimes written Tagál, Tagálo, or Tagáloc, I imagine, is derived from *Taga*, a native. Taga Majayjay is a native of Majayjay. A good Christian is called *Ang manga taga langit*, a native of heaven; and it is a common vituperation to say to a man, "Taga infierno," signifying, "You must be a native of hell."

The Tagál language is not easily acquired. A Spanish proverb says there must be *un año de arte y dos di bahaque*—one year of grammar and two of *bahaque*. The *bahaque* is the native dress. The friars informed me that it required several years of residence to enable them to preach in Tagál; and in many of the convents intercourse is almost confined to the native idioms, as there are few opportunities of speaking Spanish.

The blending of nouns and verbs into a single word, and the difficulty of tracing the roots of either, is one cause of perplexity, the paucity of words requiring many meanings for the same sound. Thus *ayao* means, enough, passage of merchandise, dearness, and is a note of admiration; *baba* signifies brace, beard, lungs, perchance, abscess; *bobo*, a net, to melt, to frighten, to spill; *alangalang*, courtesy, elevation, dignity. Hence, too, the frequent repetitions of the same word. *Aboabo*, mist; *alaala*, to remember; *ñgalañgala*, palate; *galagala*, bitumen; *dilidili*, doubt; *hasahasa*, a fish.

So a prodigious number of Tagál words are given to represent a verb in its various applications, in which it is difficult to trace any common root or shadow of resemblance. Noceda, for the verb *give* (*dar*, Spanish) has 140 Tagál words; for (*meter*) *put*, there are forty-one forms; for (*hacer*) *do*, one hundred and twenty-six. The age of the moon is represented by twelve forms, in only two of which does the Tagál word for moon occur.

It is scarcely necessary to say that a language so rude as the Tagál could never become the channel for communicating scientific or philosophical knowledge. Yet M. Mallat contends that it is rich, sonorous, expressive, and, if encouraged, would soon possess a literature worthy of a place among that of European nations!

A folio dictionary of the Bisayan and Spanish language, as spoken in the island of Panay, was published in 1841 (Manila), having been written by Father Alonzo de Mentrida. The Spanish and Bisayan, by Father Julian Martin, was published in the following year.

The letters *e, f, r*, and *z* are wanting, and the only sound not represented by our alphabet is the *ñg*. The Tagála Indians employ the letter *p* instead of the *f*, which they cannot pronounce. *Parancisco* for *Francisco*, *palso* for *falso*, *pino* for *fino*, &c. The *r* is totally unutterable by the Tagálos. They convert the letter into *d*, and subject themselves to much ridicule from the mistakes consequent upon this infirmity. The *z* is supplanted by *s*, which does not convey the Castilian sound as represented by our soft *th*.

In many provinces, however, of Spain, the Castilian pronunciation of *z* is not adopted. There is in the Tagál no vowel sound between *a* and *i*, such as is represented in Spanish by the letter *e*.

In teaching the Tagal alphabet, the word *yaou*, being the demonstrative pronoun, is inserted after the letter which is followed by the vowel *a*, and the letter repeated, thus:—*Aa yaou* (*a*), *baba yaou* (*b*), *caca yaou* (*c*), *dada yaou* (*d*), *gaga yaou* (*g*), *haha yaou* (*h*), *lala yaou* (*l*), *mama yaou* (m), *nana yaou* (*n*), *ñgañga yaou* (*ñg*), *papa yaou* (*p*), *sasa yaou* (*s*), *tata yaou* (*t*), *vava yaou* (*v*). The *ñg* is a combination of the Spanish *ñ* with *g*.

Nouns in Tagal have neither cases, numbers, nor genders. Verbs have infinitive, present, preterite, past, future, and imperative tenses, but they are not changed by the personal pronouns. Among other singularities, it is noted that no active verb can begin with the letter *b*. Some of the interjections, and they are very numerous in the Tagaloc, are of different genders. How sad! addressed to a man, is *paetog!* to a woman, *paetag!*

The Tagáls employ the second person singular *icao*, or *co*, in addressing one another, but add the word *po*, which is a form of respect. In addressing a woman the word *po* is omitted, but is expected to be used by a female in addressing a man. The personal pronouns follow instead of preceding both verbs and nouns, as *napa aco*, I say; *napa suja*, it is good.

One characteristic of the language is that the passive is generally employed instead of the active verb. A Tagal will not say "Juan loves Maria," but "Maria is loved by Juan." Fr. de los Santos says it is more elegant to employ the active than the passive verb, but I observe in the religious books circulated by the friars the general phraseology is, "It is said by God;" "it is taught by Christ," &c.

Though the Tagál is not rich in words, the same expression having often a great variety of meanings, there is much perplexity in the construction. The padre Verduga, however, gives a list of several species of verbs, with modifications of nouns subjected to the rules of European grammar.

In adopting Spanish words the Tagals frequently simplify and curtail them; for example, for *zapato* (shoe) they use only *pato*; *Lingo* for Domingo; *bavay*, *caballo* (horse). The diminutive of Maria is *Mariangui*; whence *Angui*, the ordinary name for Mary.

In looking through the dictionary, I find in the language only thirty-five monosyllables, viz., *a*, *ab*, *an*, *ang*, *at*, *ay*, *ca* [with thirteen different meanings —a numeral (1), a personal pronoun (they), four substantives (thing, companion, fright, abstract), one verb (to go), and the rest sundry adjectival, adverbial, and other terms], *cay*, *co*, *con*, *cun*, *di*, *din*, *ga*, *ha*, *i*, *in*, *is*, *ma* (with eighteen meanings, among which are four nouns substantive, eight verbs, and four adjectives), *man*, *mi*, *mo*, *na*, *ñga*, *o*, *oy*, *pa* (seven meanings), *po*, *sa*, *sang*, *si*, *sing*, *ta*, *ya*, and *yi*.

Watches are rare among the Indians, and time is not denoted by the hours of the clock, but by the ordinary events of the day. De Mas gives no less than twenty-three different forms of language for denoting various divisions, some longer, some shorter, of the twenty-four hours; such as—darkness departs; dawn breaks; light advances (*magumagana*); the sun about to rise (*sisilang na ang arao*); full day (*arao na*); sun risen; hen laying; (sun) height of axe; height of spear (from the horizon); midday; sun sinking; sun set (*lungmonorna*); Ave Maria time; darkness; blackness; children's bed-time; *animas* ringing; midnight near; midnight; midnight past (*mababao sa hating gaby*). And the phraseology varies in different localities. As bell-ringing and clock-striking were introduced by the Spaniards, most of the terms now in use must have been employed before their arrival.

Repetitions of the same syllable are common both in the Tagál and Bisayan languages. They are not necessarily indicative of a plural form, but frequently denote sequence or continuation, as—*lavay lavay*, slavery (continued work); *iñgiliñgil*, the growl of a dog; *ñgiñgiyao ñgiñgiyao*, the purring of a cat; *cococococan*, a hen calling her chickens; *pocto pocto*, uneven, irregular (there is a Devonshire word, *scory*, having exactly the same meaning); *timbon timbon*, piling up; *punit punit*, rags; *añgao añgao*, an infinite number; *aling aling*, changeable; *caval caval*, uncertain. Some Spanish words are doubled to avoid being confounded with native sounds; as *dondon* for *don*. These repetitions are a necessary consequence of the small number of primitive words.

Though the poverty of the language is remarkable, yet a great variety of designations is found for certain objects. Rice, for example, in the husk is *palay* (Malay, *padi*); before transplanting, *botobor*; when beginning to sprout, *buticas*; when the ear appears, *basag*; in a more advanced stage, *maymota*; when fully ripe in ear, *boñgana*; when borne down by the wind or the weight of the ear, *dayapa*; early rice, *cavato*; sticky rice, *lagquitan*; ill-formed in the grain, *popong*; rice cleaned but not separated from the husks, *loba*; clean rice, *bigas*; waste rice, *binlor*; ground rice, *digas*; roasted rice, *binusa*; roasted to appear like flowers, *binuladac*; rice paste, *pilipig*; fricasseed rice, *sinaing*; another sort of prepared rice, *soman*. There are no less than nineteen words for varieties of the same object. And so with verbs:—To tie, *tali*; to tie round, *lingquis*; to tie a belt, *babat*; to tie the hands, *gapus*; to tie a person by the neck, *tobong*; to tie with a noose, *hasohaso*; to tie round a jar, *baat*; to tie up a corpse, *balacas*; to tie the mouth of a purse, *pogong*; to tie up a basket, *bilit*; to tie two sticks together, *pangcol*; to tie up a door, *gacot*; to tie up a bundle (as of sticks), *bigquis*; to tie up sheaves of grain, *tangcas*; to tie up a living creature, *niquit*; to tie the planks of a floor together, *gilaguir*; a temporary tie, *balaguir*; to tie many times round with a knot, *balaguil*; tight tie, *yaguis*; to tie bamboos, *dalin*; to tie up an article lent, *pañgayla*. Of these twenty-one verbs the root of scarcely any is traceable to any noun substantive. For rice there are no less than sixty-five words in Bisayan; for bamboo, twenty.

There are numerous names for the crocodile. *Buaya* conveys the idea of its size from the egg to the full-grown animal, when he is called *buayang totoo*, a true crocodile. For gold there are no less than fifteen native designations, which denote its various qualities.

Juan de Noceda gives twenty-nine words as translations of *mirar* (to look); forty-two for *meter* (to put); seventy-five for *menear* (to move); but synonymes are with difficulty found in languages having no affinity, especially when any abstract idea is to be conveyed.

In family relations the generic word for brother is *colovong*; elder brother, *cacang*: if there be only three, the second is called *colovong*; the third, *bongso*: but if there be more than three, the second is named *sumonor*; the third, *colovong*. Twin brothers are *cambal*. *Anac* is the generic name for son; an only son, *bogtong*; the first-born, *pañganay*; the youngest, *bongso*; an adopted son, *ynaanac*. *Magama* means father and son united; *magcunaama*, father and adopted son; *nagpapaama*, he who falsely calls another his father; *pinanamahan*, a falsely called father; *maanac*, father or mother of many children; *maganac*, father, mother and family of children (of many); *caanactilic*, the sons of two widowers; *magca*, brothers by adoption.

A common ironical expression is, *Catalastasan mo aya a!* (How very clever!)

The Indian name for the head of a *barrio*, or barangay, is *dato*, but the word more commonly used at present is the Castilian *cabeza*; so that now the Indian generally denominates this native authority *cabeza sa balañgay*. The Tagal word for the principal locality of a district is *doyo*, in Castilian, *cabazera*.

The word *cantar* has been introduced for the music of the Church, but many of the ancient Indian words have been retained, such as *Pinanan umbitanan ang patay.*—They sing the death-song; *dayao*, the song of victory; *hune*, the song of birds. The noise of the ghiko lizard is called *halotictic*.

The following may serve as specimens of Tagál polysyllabic words:—

Anagnalaláqui	son.
Ananababai	daughter.

Cababulaánang	lie.
Malanuingiolog	thunder.
Pagsisisi	} suffering.
Paghahanducan	
Pagsisingsiñgan	finger.
Pagpapahopa	peace.
Palayanglayañgan	swallow.
Pañgañganyaya	damage.
Sangtinacpan	the world.
Solonmañgayao	comet; exhalation.
Magbabaca	} warrior, from *baca* to light.
Tagupagbaca	
Tangcastancasan	faggot.
Masaquit angmangapilipis anco	my head aches.
Hahampasinguita	I will flog thee (thou shalt be flogged by me).
Guiguisiñgincata	I will wake thee (thou shalt be waked by me).
Magpasavalabanhangan	everlasting.
Pananangpahataya	faith.
Mapagpaunbabao	deceitful.
Mapagpalamara	ungrateful.

Odd numbers in Tagál are called *gangsal*, even numbers *tocol*.

> Affirmative, Yes! Oo; tango.
> Negative, No!   Di; dili; houag; dakan.

Many Malayan words are to be traced, some in their pure, others in a corrupted form, not only in the Tagal and Bisayan, but in other idioms of the Philippines.[12] Such are *Langit*, heaven; *puti*, white; *mata*, eye; *vato*, stones; *mura*, cheap; and some others. Slightly modified are *dita* for *lina*, language; *babi*, for *babuy*, pig; *hagin* (Tag.) and *hangin* (Bis.) for *angin*, wind; *masaguit* for *sakit*, sick; *patay* for *mati* (Mal.), *mat* (Pers.), dead; *nagcasama* for *samasama*, in company; *matacut* for *takot*, fear; *ulan* for *udian*, rain; and a few others. The Malay word *tuan*, meaning honourable, and generally employed to signify the obedience and deference of the speaker to the person addressed, is mostly used by the Tagals in an ironical sense. *Ay touan co!* Honourable man indeed! "Do not *tuan* me," is equivalent to, "None of your nonsense."

The monks have introduced most of the Castilian words of Greek and Latin origin necessary for the profession of the Catholic faith, or the celebration of its religious rites, for few of which could any representatives be found in the aboriginal tongues.

Considering the long possession of many portions of the Philippines by tribes professing Mahomedanism, the number of current Arabic words is small: I heard *salam*, salute; *malim*, master; *arrac*, wine or spirits; *arraes* for *reis*, captain. And among the Mussulmans of Mindanao, *Islam*, *koran*, *rassoul* (prophet), *bismillah*, *kitab*, and other words immediately connected with the profession of Islamism, were quite familiar.

The only Chinese word that I found generally in use was *sampan*, a small boat, meaning literally three planks.

Many of the sounds in the Tagal are so thoroughly English that they fell strangely on my ear. *Toobig* is water; and *asin*, salt, when shouted out to the Indian servants at table, somewhat startled me, and I could not immediately find out what was the excess denounced, or the peccadillo committed. Most of the friars speak the native idioms with fluency, never preach in any other, and living, as most of them do, wholly surrounded by the Indian population, and rarely using their native Spanish tongue, it is not to be wondered at that they acquire great facility in the employment of the Indian idioms. Most of the existing grammars and dictionaries were written by ecclesiastics to aid in the propagation of the Christian doctrine, and small books are printed (all on religious subjects) for the instruction of the people. I could not discover that they have any historical records or traditions brought down from a remote antiquity.

The more my attention has been directed to the study of the idioms of distant countries, the more I am struck by the absurd fancies and theories which have obtained so much currency with regard to the derivation and affinities of languages. The Biscayans firmly hold their Euscaran idiom to have been the tongue of Adam and Eve in Paradise, and consequently the universal language of primitive man and the fountain-head of all others. More than one Cambrian patriot has claimed the same honour for the Welsh, insisting that all the dialects of the world have been derived from the Cymri. But it would be hard to prove that a single word has descended to the present times from the antediluvian world. Intercourse and commerce seem the only channels through which any portion of the language of any one nation or tribe has passed into the vocabulary of any other. The word *sack* is said to be that of the most general diffusion. A French writer contends it was the only word preserved at the time of the Babel confusion of languages, and it was so preserved in order that the rights of property might be respected in the general anarchy. In the lower numerals of remote dialects there are many seemingly strange affinities, which may be attributed to their frequent use in trading transactions. Savages, having no such designations of their own, have frequently adopted the higher decimal numbers employed by civilized nations, of which the extended use of the word *lac* for 10,000 is an example. *Muster*, among trading nations, is, with slight variations, the almost universally received word for pattern; so the words *account*, *date*, and many similar. How many maritime terms are derived from the Dutch, how many military from the French, how many *locomotive* from the English! The Justinian code has impregnated all the languages of Europe with phrases taken from the Roman law. To the Catholic missal may be traced in the idioms of converted nations almost all their religious phraseology. In the facilities of combination which the Greek in so high a degree possesses science has found invaluable auxiliaries. Our colonies are constantly adding to our stores, and happily there is not (as in France) any repugnance to the introduction of useful, still less of necessary words. Bentham used to say that *purity* of language and *poverty* of language were nearly synonymous. It is well for the interests of knowledge that the English tongue receives without difficulty new and needful contributions to the ancient stock. The well of pure English undefiled is not corrupted, but invigorated, by the streams which have been poured into it from springs both adjacent and remote. Language must progress with and accommodate itself to the progress of knowledge, and it is well that a language clear, defined and emphatic as our own—derived from many sources, whence its plasticity and variety—having much monosyllabic force and polysyllabic cadence—condensed and yet harmonious—should be the language having now the strongest holds and the widest extension.

Among the evidences of progress which the world exhibits, not only is the gradual extinction of the inferior by the advance of the superior races of man a remarkable fact, but equally striking is the disappearance of the rude and imperfect idioms, and their supplantation by the more efficient instruments of advancement and civilization found in the languages of the cultivated nations. The attempts which have been made to introduce the phraseology of advanced arts and sciences into tongues which only represent a low stage of cultivation, have been lamentably unsuccessful. No appropriate niches can be found in barbarian temples for the beautiful productions of the refined genius of sculpture. The coarse garments of the savage cannot be fitly repaired with the choice workmanship of the gifted artisan. And few benefits can be conceived of more importance to the well-being of the human family than that the means of oral intercourse should be extended, and that a few widely spread languages (if not a universal one, whose introduction may be deemed an utterly hopeless dream) will in process of time become the efficient instrument of communication for the whole world.

The poetry of the Tagals is in quantity of twelve syllables. They have the Spanish asonante, but words are considered to rhyme if they have the same vowel or the same consonant at a terminal, as thus:—

> In beautiful starlight
>
> Heaven's concave is drest,
>
> And the clouds as they part
>
> Make the brightness more bright.

So *stick* would rhyme with *thing*, *knot* with *rob*; and the Indian always chant their verses when they recite them, which, indeed, is a generally received Asiatic custom. The San tze King, or three-syllable classic, which is the universally employed elementary book in the schools of China, is always sung, and the verse and music naturally aid the memory. The music of the song sung by the Tagálas to tranquillize children, called the *helehele*, De Mas says, resembles that of the Arab.

I have found a few proverbs in verse, of which these are examples:—

> Isda acong yaga saprap
> Galataliptip calapad
> Caya naquiqui pagpusag
> Ang cala goyo y apahap.

> Weak men, by the helping aid
> Of the mighty, strong are made.

> Aba ayá casampaga
> Nang ponay na olila
> Un umumbo y pagscap na
> Valan magsopcop na ma.

> It is a very careless hen,
> Who will not stretch her pinions when
> The young brood for protection fly
> From storms and rains and threatening sky.

Ycao ang caou co	In going and coming on life's long stage,
Pacacaou so tomanda y	
Maguinguin bata pa	You may say as a certain truth,
Ang catacayac	That men may travel from youth to age,
Sucat macapagcati nang dagat.	But never from age to youth.

Coya ipinacataastaas.	Many few make a many.
Nang domagongdong ang cagpac.	The higher the flight the greater the fall. Tolluntur in altum ut lapsu graviore ruant.—*Claud.*

NOTE.—The chapter I had written on the language of the Philippines was, with many others of my MSS., submerged in the Red Sea by the *Alma* wreck, and much of their contents is utterly illegible; nor have I been able, from any materials accessible to me in this country, to present anything like a satisfactory sketch. Under the circumstances, my short-comings will, I doubt not, be forgiven.

1

Personal pronouns are *aco*, I; *anim*, we. The Tagál has no possessive pronouns; but employs instead the genitive of the personal.

2

Um, to be; *ungma*, thou art.

3

Ca, or *ycao*, personal pronoun, thou, always follows the verb; *mo* is the genitive.

4

Samba, adore; *sambahin*, the future tense.

5

Arao, sun, or day.

6

Tolot, to allow to escape.

7

Dayat, praise; the future passive is conveyed by *ipapag*.

8

From *anchi*, adverb, here.

9

From *hadi*, king. ↑

10

From *uara*, forgiveness. ↑

11

From *auai*, to quarrel. ↑

12

Mr. John Crawfurds's Dissertation in his Malayan Grammar. ↑

CHAPTER XIV.

NATIVE PRODUCE.

The *Leyes de Indias* emphatically recognize the wrongs and injuries of which the Indians are constantly the victims, and seek to furnish remedies against them: they annul dishonest contracts—they order the authorities rigorously to punish acts of oppression—they declare that the transactions of the Spanish settlers have frequently been "the ruin of the Indians"—they point out the mischiefs produced by the avarice in some cases, and inaction in others, of the mestizos, who are commonly the go-betweens in bargains of colonists with natives. The local *ordenanzas*, which are numerous and elaborate, have for their object to assure to the Indian the fruits of his labours—to protect him against his own imprudence and the usurious exactions of those to whom he applies in his difficulties; they provide against the usurpation of his lands, declare the sovereign the rightful owner of property which there are no heirs to claim, and insist that everywhere the Indian shall draw from the soil he cultivates the means of comfortable subsistence: the accumulation of properties acquired from the Indians by ecclesiastical bodies is prohibited, notwithstanding which prohibition enormous estates are held by the monkish fraternities. There are also arrangements for setting apart "common lands" for general use, independently of private estates. Many of the provisions are of so vague a character as to insure their non-observance, and others so particular and special in their requirements as to make their enforcement impossible. The 71st article, for example, compels the Indians "to plant useful trees, suited to the soil"—to sow wheat, rice, maize, vegetables, cotton, pepper, &c., in proper localities—to maintain "every species of appropriate cattle"—to have "fruits growing in their gardens and orchards round their houses"—to keep "at least twelve hens and one cock" (a very superfluous piece of legislation), and one "female sucking pig;" they must be encouraged to manufacture cloths and cordage; and failing in these duties for the space of two years, they are to lose their lands, which, by public proclamation, shall be appropriated to others. There is, in fact, no absolute territorial right of property among the Indians. It can always be seized and reappropriated by the Spanish authorities. Lands are held on condition that they are cultivated. There are lands possessed by Spaniards and by corporations of the clergy principally, which pay a nominal rental to the crown, but the rental is so small as to be of no account. There is no difficulty in obtaining gratuitous concessions of territorial surface on the sole obligation of bringing it into cultivation. Long usage and long possession have no doubt created supposed rights, which are able to maintain themselves even against competing private claims or the obvious requirements of public utility. Questions arise as to what is meant by "cultivation," and the country is full of controversies and lawsuits, of which land is generally the subject-matter. The larger proprietors constantly speak of the difficulty of obtaining continuous labour—of the necessity of perpetual advances to the peasant—of the robbery of the ripe harvests when raised. Hence they are accustomed to underlet their lands to petty cultivators, who bring small and unsatisfactory returns to the owners and to the market. They complain of the jealousy and ill-will of the Indians, their intrigues and open resistance to foreign settlers, and of the too indulgent character of the "Law of the Indies." It appears to me that there is abundant field for advantageous agricultural experiments, not perhaps so much in the immediate vicinity of large and populous places, as on the vast tracts of uncared-for territory, which demand nothing but attention and capital, perseverance and knowledge, to render a prodigal return. No doubt the agriculturist should have possession absolutely and irrevocably secured to him. Once installed by the government he must be protected against all molestation of his title. I do not believe in the invincible inertness of the Indians when they are properly encouraged. I heard of a native in one of the most distant villages I visited in Pinay, who had been recommended by a friar to take to sugar-growing. He did so, and obtained five hundred dollars for the produce which he, for the first time, took down to Iloilo. He will get a thousand the second year; and others were following his example. A little additional labour produces so much that the smallest impulse gives great results, especially where employed over a vast extent. But Indian indolence is not only prejudicial from the little assistance it offers to agricultural activity in preparing, sowing, watching and gathering the harvest; it is unable to furnish any of those greater appliances which must be considered rather of public than of private concern. Hence the absence of facilities for irrigation, the imperfect state of the river navigation, the rarity of canals, the badness of the roads in so many localities. The seasons bring their floods, and the mountain torrents create their gullies; but the water escapes into the sea, and the labourer brings his produce, as best he may, amidst the rocks and sand and mud which the cataracts have left behind them. I have seen beasts of burden struggling in vain to extricate themselves, with their loads, from the gulf into which they had fallen, and in which they were finally abandoned by their conductors. I have been carried to populous places in palanquins, whose bearers, sometimes sixteen in number, were up to their thighs amidst mire, slough, tangled roots, loose stones and fixed boulders. De Mas says that the labourer absorbs three-fifths of the gross produce, leaving two-fifths to the proprietor and capitalist; but the conditions of labour are so very various that it is difficult to reach any general conclusion, beyond the undoubted fact that neither capitalist nor labourer receives anything like the amount of profit which, under a better system, would be enjoyed by both; that the cost is far greater, and the returns far smaller, than they should be; and that the common prosperity suffers from the position of each. Whatever may be said of the enervating effects of climate and the want of motive to give activity to industry, it is probable that all nations, even the most industrious and the most opulent, have passed through their stages of indolence and inactivity. China affords an example that climate alone is no insuperable barrier to energetic exertions in all departments of the field of production, and that the possession of much is no necessary check upon the desire of obtaining and enjoying more. The value of lands is very various. De Mas says that the *quiñon* (of 1,000 square fathoms), in Pangasinan, sells for from 220 to 250 dollars; in the Laguna, 250 to 300; in Ilocos Sur, 300; in the neighbourhood of Manila, 1,000. He seems to consider sugar as, on the whole, the most profitable investment. He gives several tables of the cost and charges of sundry tropical productions, but the many elements of uncertainty, the cost of raising, the vicissitudes of climate, the attacks of insects, the fluctuations in the amount and value of accessible labour, and all the ebbs and flows of supply and demand, make all calculations only approximative. His *apuntes*, however, are well worth consulting by those interested in detailed inquiry. He gives as a result of rice cultivation a minimum profit of 24 per cent., a maximum profit of 76 per cent. per annum. This would seem sufficiently inviting, especially as the Spaniards are reported to be fonder of agriculture than of any other pursuit, and fonder of being owners of lands than of any other property, according to their old refrain:—

> "No vessel on the sea,
>
> But the house that's mine for me,
>
> And all the lands around which I've been used to see."[1]

Indigo will render, according to De Mas, 100 per cent. Coffee, on the same authority, will double its capital in four years. Cocoa returns 90 per cent. Attempts to introduce mulberry cultivation for silk have had little success, though the specimens sent to Europe have obtained prizes for their excellent quality. The worms require a more continuous attention than the Indians are willing to give, and the same may be said of those spices, nutmegs, cinnamon, and any produce which demands unremitting care. The spontaneous productions of the Philippines do not easily obtain the benefit of a more enlightened mode of culture.

The rights of property require thorough investigation and recognition in a country which has not been surveyed or cadastred; where the foreign population is migratory and uncertain; where documentary titles are, for the most part, wanting, and appropriation of the soil has been little controlled by the supreme authorities; where there is no land-tax, and the religious bodies hold immense territories generally underlet to the natives. The smallness of estates necessarily adds to the cost of production, and it would not be easy to induce wealthy capitalists to settle unless facilities were given for the acquisition and cultivation of extensive properties. Such capitalists would introduce the improvements in agricultural science which are now wholly wanting; they would bring with them able heads and hands to conduct, and better instruments to give practical effect to superior knowledge. A desire is frequently expressed for the formation of agricultural societies, but these are rather the children than the parents of progress, and the numerous and respectable body which already exists in Manila, the "Sociedad Economica," has not been instrumental in introducing any very important changes. There is in the Spanish mind too great a disposition to look to "authority" as the source and support of all reforms; but the best service of authority in almost all cases of productive industry is non-interference and inaction; it is not the meddling with, but the leaving matters alone, that is wanted; it is the removal of restrictions, the supersession of laws which profess to patronize and protect, but whose patronage and protection mean the sacrifice of the many to the few. Government, no doubt, can greatly assist the public weal by the knowledge it can collect and distribute. Nothing is more desirable than that the rich territorial capabilities of the Philippines should be thoroughly explored by efficient scientific inquiry. Geologists, chemists, mechanicians, botanists, would teach us much respecting the raw materials of these multitudinous islands, so inviting to the explorer, and so little explored. Mountains, forests, plains, lakes, rivers, solicit the investigation, which they could not fail to reward.

Of the indigenous productions found by the Spaniards the dry mountain rice seems to have been the principal article cultivated by the Indians for food, the arts of irrigation being little known, and the mode of culture of the simplest character. The missionaries taught the Indians to divide their lands, to improve their agriculture, to store their harvests, and generally to meliorate their condition by more knowledge and foresight. Maize and wheat were introduced from America, though for a long time the use of wheaten bread was confined to the service of the mass. There is now an adequate supply for the wants of the consumer. Melons, water-melons and various fruits, peas, pumpkins, onions, cucumbers, garlic and other vegetables, soon found their way from Mexico to the church gardens, and thence to more extensive cultivation. Coffee sprang up wild in the island of Luzon, ungathered by the natives. Tobacco was introduced under the patronage of the government, and is become the most important source of revenue. Pepper and cassia grew unnoticed, but the cocoa-nut tree and the plantain were among the most precious of the Indian's possessions, and the areca was not less valued. Indigo was indigenous, and the wild cotton-tree was uncared for; nor can it be other than a subject of regret that to the present hour so inadequate an attention has been paid to the natural production of the islands, and means so little efficient taken for improving their quality or extending their cultivation. At the present time there are few large estates having the benefit of well-directed labour and sufficient capital. Of those possessed by the religious communities little can be expected in the way of agricultural improvement, but the cultivated lands are generally in the hands of small native proprietors. Where the labourer is hired, his daily pay is from a half rial to a rial and a half (3½d. to 10d.), varying in the different provinces.

The *quiñon* is the ordinary measure of land; it is divided into 10 *baletas*, these into 100 *loanes*, which represent 31,250 Castilian varas. Three labourers are supposed sufficient for the cultivation of a quiñon. In 1841 the Captain-General Urbiztondo published a decree encouraging the importation of Chinese agricultural labourers by landed proprietors, and with a special view to the cultivation of sugar, indigo and hemp. The decree was expected to produce a beneficial revolution—it has been a dead letter. Imported labour, subject to all sorts of restrictions, cannot in the long run compete with free indigenous labour. The question is a very grave one in its ramifications and influence on colonial interests, when they come into the field against the free trade and the free labour of the competing world. I doubt altogether the powers of the West Indies—dependent upon imported and costly immigrants —to rival the rich fields of the East, when capital and activity shall turn to account their feracious soil, more genial climate, and more economical means of production. Progress there is but the natural development of the elements which Providence has allotted to them, whereas in the West India colonies everything is forced and unnatural, purchased at an immense cost and maintained by constant sacrifices.

1

Barco ninguno, casa la que vivas, tierras las que veas. †

CHAPTER XV.

VEGETABLES.

The money value of the tobacco grown in the Philippines is estimated at from 4,000,000 to 5,000,000 of dollars, say 1,000,000*l*. sterling. Of this nearly one half is consumed in the islands, one-quarter is exported in the form of cheroots (which is the Oriental word for cigars), and the remainder sent to Spain in leaves and cigars, being estimated as an annual average contribution exceeding 800,000 dollars. The sale of tobacco is a strict government monopoly, but the impossibility of keeping up any efficient machinery for the protection of that monopoly is obvious even to the least observant. The cultivator, who is bound to deliver all his produce to the government, first takes care of himself and his neighbours, and secures the best of his growth for his own benefit. Out of the capital of Manila scarcely anything is smoked but the *cigarro ilegitimo*; and in the capital you frequently get a hint that "the weed" is not from the *estanco real*. From functionaries able to obtain the *best* which the government brings to market, a present is often volunteered, which shows that they avail themselves of something *better* than that best. And in discussing the matter with the most intelligent of the *empleados*, they agreed that the emancipation of the producer, the manufacturer and the seller, and the establishment of a simple duty, would be more productive to the revenue than the present vexatious and inefficient system of privilege.

There has been an enormous increase in the revenues from tobacco. They gave nett—

		Annual Average.
From 1782 to 1785	260,597 dolls.	86,865 dolls.
1786 to 1800 (15 years)	4,950,101	330,006
,,	,,	,,
1801 to 1815 (15 years)	7,228,071	481,871
,,	,,	,,
1816 to 1830 (15 years)	8,403,368	560,225
,,	,,	,,
1831 to 1835 (5 years)	3,707,164	741,433
,,	,,	,,
1836 to 1839 (4 years)	4,990,011	1,247,503
,,	,,	,,

Since when the produce has more than quadrupled in value.

In 1810 the deliveries were 50,000 bales (of two arrobas), of which Gapan furnished 47,000, and Cagayan 2,000. In 1841 Cagayan furnished 170,000 bales; Gapan, 84,000; and New Biscay, 34,000. But the produce is enormously increased; and so large is the native consumption, of which a large proportion pays no duty, that it would not be easy to make even an approximative estimate of the extent and value of the whole tobacco harvest. Where the fiscal authorities are so scattered and so corrupt;—where communications are so imperfect and sometimes wholly interrupted;—where large tracts of territory are in the possession of tribes unsubdued or in a state of imperfect subjection;—where even among the more civilized Indians the rights of property are rudely defined, and civil authority imperfectly maintained;—where smuggling, though it may be attended with some risk, is scarcely deemed by anybody an offence, and the very highest functionaries themselves smoke and offer to their guests contraband cigars, on account of their superior quality,—it may well be supposed that lax laws, lax morals and lax practices, harmonize with each other, and that such a state of things as exists in the Philippines must be the necessary, the inevitable result. It is sufficient to look at the cost of the raw material and the value of the manufactured article to perceive what an enormous margin of profit there exists. A quintal of tobacco will produce—

		Dollars.
14 cases, each containing 1,000 cigars, whose value is, at 6½ dolls. per case		87·50
The quintal of tobacco costs	5·00 dolls.	
Manufacture	5·25	
	"	
14 cases at 2 rials	3·50	
	"	
		13·75
	Profit	73·75

Cheroots (cigars) are manufactured in two forms,—that of the Havana, the smaller end being twisted to a point,—or cut at both ends, the usual Manila form. They are of sundry qualities, as follows:—Largest size, 125 to a box— 1st Regalias, 1st Caballeros and Londres; second size, 250 to a box—2nd Regalias and 1st Cortados, 2nd Caballeros, 1st Havanas (ordinary size, and

such as are more commonly used, Nos. 2 and 3 being those in most demand);
500 to a box—Nos. 2, 3, 4, and 5 Havanas, 2 and 3 Cortados. Besides these,
enormous quantities of paper cigars (*cigarillos*) are consumed by the natives.
They are sold in packets of twenty-five, at 5 cuartes; thirty, at $5\frac{1}{3}$ cuartes;
thirty-six, at 5 5/7 cuartes.

The estanco prices for these cigars are, per box—

					Dollars.
Imperiales		box contains 125 cigars			3·750
Regalias and Caballeros			125		3·125
		,,	,,	,,	
1 Havanas, 1 Cortados			250		3·500
		,,	,,	,,	
2	2		500		4·000
,,	,,	,,	,,	,,	
3	3		500		3·500
,,	,,	,,	,,	,,	
4			500		3·000
,,		,,	,,	,,	
5			500		2·500
,,		,,	,,	,,	
Londres			125		1·875
		,,	,,	,,	

Upon these minimum prices biddings take place at the monthly public
auctions. So large is the demand that it is difficult to obtain any but fresh
cigars, which require to be kept for two or three years to ripen.

The collection of tobacco and the manufacture of cigars are under the charge
of an administration whose head-quarters are in Manila. The warehouses are
of immense extent, and 20,000 persons probably find occupation in the
preparation of this article of luxury, to say nothing of those employed in its
production. The provinces in which there are establishments for the collection
are Cagayan, La Isabela, New Ecija, La Union, Abra and Cayan. The largest
of the manufactures of cigars are in Binondo (Manila) and Cavite, in the
province of the same name.

Fr. Blanco thus describes the *Nicotiana tabacum* of the Philippines: "It is an
annual, growing to the height of a fathom, and furnishes the tobacco for the
estancos (licensed shops). Here, as everywhere else, its quality and taste vary.

General opinion prefers the tobacco of Gapan, but that of the Pasy districts, Laglag and Lambunao, in Iloilo, of Maasin or Leyte, is appreciated for its fine aroma; also that of Cagayan, after being kept for some years,—for otherwise, like the tobacco of the island of Negros, it burns the mouth. It is a narcotic, and will subdue recent tumours. It is salutary when smoked, and even a necessity in these regions; it disperses phlegm, protects from the bad consequences of humidity and the morning dews, and is only injurious to health when used in excess. Snuff relieves from headaches and disperses gloomy humours. A small piece of smoked tobacco at the end of a stick applied to the nose of the lizard, which is here called the *chacon* (probably the ghiko), causes its instant death. A cruel practice," (adds the father), "for the reptile is most useful, destroying cockroaches, centipedes, mice and other vermin; besides which its song may cheer the timid, who believe that while that song lasts there will be no earthquakes nor any excess of rain."—(Pp. 74–75.)

I am informed by the alcalde mayor of Cagayan that he sent last year (1858) to Manila from that province tobacco for no less a value than 2,000,000 dollars. The quality is the best of the Philippines; it is all forwarded in leaf to the capital. He speaks of the character of the Indians with great admiration, and says acts of dishonesty are very rare among them, and that property is conveyed in perfect safety through the province. The quantity of leaf transmitted was 300,000 bales, divided into seven qualities, of which the prices paid were from two to seven rials per quintal, leaving a large margin of profit. The tobacco used by the natives is not subject to the estanco, and on my inquiring as to the cost of a cigar in Cagayan, the answer was, "Casi nada" (Almost nothing). They are not so well rolled as those of the government, but undoubtedly the raw material is of the very best.

The demand for the important article of coffee in Australia and California will probably hereafter be largely supplied from the Spanish archipelago. Of the mode of cultivation, there is nothing particularly characteristic of the Philippines. The ground having been cleared (where on a large extent, by fire), it is fenced in, the soil prepared, and after having been steeped in water for two or three days, the sprouts are stuck into the holes which had been made for their reception, and in the following year are ready for cutting. The use of the plough largely increases the produce. The cultivation of sugar is rapidly extending. The harvest takes place generally from March to May. Four groups of labourers are employed: the cutters and the carters in the field, the grinders and the boilers in the manufactory. Improvements are gradually being introduced, as larger capitalists and more intelligent cultivators come forward; and the establishment of refineries now in progress will induce many beneficial changes. Much of the clayed sugar which I saw delivered at Manila for refining into loaves had rather the appearance of dirty mud than of a valuable commodity. Though slowly, the work of improvement goes on, and there could be no greater evidence of it than the presence of a number of Chinese employed in the various stages of the fabric. Nor do these Chinese labourers fail to bring with them much practical knowledge. They are mostly from Fokien, a province in which the production of sugar is great, and in which there are large sugar refineries, mostly, however, for the manufacture of sugar-candy, which is the form in which the Chinese usually purchase the sugar for consumption, pounding it into powder. I visited several extensive establishments at Chang-chow-foo, about thirty miles from Amoy, a port whence the exportation is large.

There are several varieties of the sugar-cane. The *zambales* is used principally as food; the *encarnado* (red), *morada* (purple), *blanca* (white), and *listada* (striped), give the syrup for manufacture. The planting of the sprouts takes place between February and May. Weeds are removed by ploughing, and the plants ripen in ten or twelve months. In some provinces crops are cultivated for three successive years; in others, the soil is allowed to rest an intermediate year, and maize or other produce grown. When cut, the canes are carried to mills called by the natives *cabayavan*, to be crushed. The mills consist of two cylindrical stones with teeth of the *molave* wood; a buffalo turns the wheel and the juice is conveyed to the boilers. The improvements of the West are being slowly introduced, and sundry economical processes have been adopted. Increasing demand, extended cultivation and, above all, the application of larger capitals and greater activity, will, undoubtedly, make the Philippines one of the great producing countries. A variety of tables have been printed, showing that the average annual profits on coffee cultivation are from 20 to 30 per cent.; in some provinces considerably more.

Rice being of far more general production, is estimated to give an average yearly profit of from 12 to 20 per cent.; sesame returns an average of about 20 per cent.; cocoa-nuts may be considered at about equal to rice in the yearly benefits they leave, but the conditions are so various that it may be difficult to generalize. It may, however, be asserted with tolerable certainty, that money employed with ordinary prudence in agricultural investments will give an interest of from 20 to 30 per cent.

The consumption of rice is universal, and the superfluity of the harvests is taken to the Chinese markets. The varieties of rice have been elsewhere spoken of, but they may be classed under the two general heads of water and mountain rice. The aquatic rice is cultivated as in Europe and America; the sowing of the dry rice usually precedes that of the water rice, and takes place at the end of May. It is usually broadcast on the hills, requires to be hoed and weeded, and is ripened in from three to four months and a half. It is harvested ear by ear.

Fr. Blanco describes four species of water-cultivated (*de agua*), and five of mountain-produced (*secano*) rice. Of the first class, the *lamuyo* (*Oryza sativa lamuyo*) is principally cultivated, especially in Batangas. The barbed rice (*Oryza aristata*) grows in Ilocos. Of the mountain rice, that called *quinanda* (*Oryza sativa quinanda*) is the most esteemed. The cultivation of the water rice begins by the preparation of the seed deposits (*semillero*), into which, at the beginning of the rainy season, the seed is thrown, after a thorough impregnation of the ground with water, of which several inches remain on the surface. Ploughing and harrowing produce a mass of humid mud. During the growth of the seed, irrigation is continued, and after six weeks the crops are ready for transplanting to the rice-fields. Men generally pull up the plants, and convey them to the fields, where women up to their knees in mire separate the plants, and place them in holes at a regular distance of about five inches from one another. They are left for some days to take root, when the grounds are again irrigated. The rice grows to the height of somewhat more than a yard, and after four months is ready for harvest. It is a common usage to cut every ear separately with an instrument whose Indian name is *yatap*. In some parts a sickle called a *lilit* is used. The lilit has a crook by which a number of ears are collected, and being grasped with the left hand, are cut by the serrated blade of the sickle held in the right hand. The crops of aquatic rice vary from thirty to eightyfold.

The mountain rice is sown broadcast after ploughing and harrowing, and buffaloes are employed to trample the seed into the ground. More care is sometimes taken, and holes made at regular distances, into which three or four grains of rice are dropped. Careful cultivation and great attention to the removal of weeds are said to produce hundred-fold crops.

It is stated by Father Blanco that a third of the rice harvest has been known to perish in consequence of the dilatory and lazy way in which the reaping is conducted.

There is no doubt that the Philippines offer great facilities for the cultivation of indigo, but it has been neglected and inadequate attention paid to the manufacture. The growers state that there is in Europe a prejudice against Manila indigo; but such prejudice can only be the result of experience, and would be removed by greater care on the part of the growers, manufacturers and exporters. The crops, however, are uncertain, and often seriously damaged or destroyed by tempestuous weather, and by invasions of caterpillars. The seed is broadcast, sown immediately after the temperate season. It grows rapidly, but requires to have the weeds which spring up with it cleared away. It is ready for harvesting in the rainy months, generally in June. The fermentation, straining, beating, cleaning, pressing, and final preparation are carried on, not according to the improved processes of British India, but as they were introduced by the Spaniards. The Indians, like the Chinese, employ the dye in its liquid state.

The consumption of the betel root is incredibly great. There are in the city of Manila, in the courts and ground floors of the houses, altogether 898 warehouses and shops, of which 429 (or nearly half the whole) are devoted to the sale of the prepared betel, or to the materials of which it is composed. There are two warehouses where the leaf in which the areca nut is wrapped is sold wholesale; there are 105 retail shops for the same article, and there are 308 shops in which is sold for immediate use the nut mixed with shell-lime, and served with the *buyo* (leaf of the piper betel), ready for conveyance to the mouth of the consumer, to whom it is from usage become an article of necessity even more urgent than the rice he eats or the water he drinks.

Of the areca, Fr. Blanco, in his *Flora de Filipinas*, gives the following account:—"This species of palm, with which everybody is acquainted, and which like its fruit is called *bonga* by the Indians, grows to about the average height of the cocoa-nut tree. Its trunk is smaller at the base than the top, very straight, with many circular rings formed by the junction of the leaves before they fall, which they do on growing to a certain size. The use of the nut, which is somewhat smaller than a hen's egg, is well known. When the bonga is wanting, the Indians employ the bark of the guava, or of the antipolo (*Artocarpus*). Mixed with lime and the pepper leaf, it makes the saliva red. The Indians apply this saliva to the navel of their children as a cure for the colic and a protection from the effects of cold air. When ripe, the fruit is red and, I believe, might be used as a red dye. With copperas it makes a black dye, but inferior to that of the aroma. The lower part of the leaves, called *talupac*, is very clean, broad, white and flexible, making excellent wrappers and serving many useful purposes. The sprouts are salted and eaten, and are agreeable to the taste, but when cut the tree perishes."—(P. 495.)

Father Blanco says of the piper betel (*Pimenta betel*), whose leaves are employed as envelopes to the areca nut and lime:—"This plant is universally known, in consequence of the immense consumption of the betel, or *buyo*, as the betel is called by the Spaniards. The betel of Pasay, near Manila, is much esteemed; that of Banang, in Batangas, is the best of that province, and probably superior to the betel of Pasay. The tree prefers a somewhat sandy soil, but if too sandy, as in Pasay, fish is used as a manure, or the rind of the *Ajonjoli* (sesame), or other oleaginous fruits. The tree must be frequently watered. The roots are renovated after a year, but if left to grow old they produce flowers like the litlit (*Piper obliquum*). The fruit is called by the natives *poro*. Of the *Piper parvifolium*, an inebriating liquor is made. The Indians use the leaves as a preservative against the cholera. All the species of *Piper* are useful against the poison of snakes. The wound is first scarified, and either the juice or bruised leaves of the plant applied and frequently changed. 'I was called,' says the author of the *Flora of the Antilles*, 'to a negro whose thigh had just been bitten by a snake. The poison had made frightful progress. All the remedies of art had been employed in vain. A negro appeared, and asked leave to apply the popular mode of cure. There was then no hope of the recovery of the patient—human life was at stake—I did not hesitate. In a few moments the progress of the poison was stopped by the simple application of the *Piper procumbens*. On the third application the cure was completed.'"—(Pp. 16, 17.)

Of the vegetation of the Philippines, the bamboo may be deemed the most extensive, the most useful, and the most beautiful. The graceful groups of *Cañas* (the Spanish name, the Tagál is *Bocaui*) are among the most charming decorations of the island scenery, and are scattered with great profusion and variety on the sides of the streams and rivers, on hills and plains, and always to be found adjacent to the residence of the native. Waving their light branches at the smallest breeze, they give perpetual life to the landscape, while they are of daily service to the people. The *Bambus arundo* grows to a great height, and its cane is sometimes more than eight inches in diameter. In it is sometimes found a small stone, called *Tabaxir*, to which the Indians attribute miraculous healing virtues. The *Bambus lumampao* and the *lima* are so hard that the wood is used for polishing brass. The bamboo serves for an infinity of uses; from the food that nourishes man or beast, to the weapons that destroy his life: for the comforts of home; for the conveniences of travel; for the construction of bridges, several hundred feet in length, over which heavy artillery can safely pass; for shipping and cordage; for shelter, and for dwellings and domestic utensils of all sorts; for vessels of every size to retain, and tubes to convey, water and other fluids; for mats, palings, and scaffoldings; for musical instruments, even organs for churches; for a hundred objects of amusement; and, indeed, for all the purposes of life the bamboo is distinguished. It is the raw material on which the rude artist makes his experiments—roots, trunks, branches, leaves, all are called into the field of utility. There is much of spontaneous production, but it may be multiplied by layers and cuttings. Some of the bamboos grow to an enormous size. That called by the natives *cauayang totoo*, and by the Spaniards *caña espino*, reaches the height of from forty to fifty feet, the diameter of the stalk or trunk exceeding eight inches. One of its divisions will sometimes hold two pecks of wheat. An infusion of this bamboo is poisonous to deer; but its leaves are eaten by horses and cattle and its young shoots as salad by man. The *cauayang quiling* (*caña macho* of the Spaniards) grows to about forty feet in height, its stem being of the size of a man's arm. From the thickness of the rind and the smallness of the hollow, it is the strongest of the bamboos, and is used for carrying burdens on the shoulders; a fourth part of the whole cane, of the length of two yards, when split, will support any weight that a man can carry. The cane has an elasticity which lightens the burden to the bearer. The varieties of the bamboo are scarcely to be counted. The interior of the *osin* gives a white substance, which is used as a cure for urinal and eye diseases.

I once heard a remark that the Crystal Palace itself could have been filled with specimens of various applications of the bamboo. Minus the glass, the palace itself might have been constructed of this material alone, and the protecting police furnished from it with garments, hats and instruments of punishment. The living trees would fill a conservatory with forms and colours of wondrous variety and beauty; and if paintings and poetry, in which the bamboo takes a prominent place, were allowed, not the walls of the Louvre could be sufficient for the pictures and the scrolls.

The various classes of canes, rattans and others of the *Calamus* family, have a great importance and value. The *palasan* is frequently three hundred feet long, and in Mindanao it is said they have been found of more than treble that length. They are used for cords and cables; but as the fibres are susceptible of divisions, down to a very fine thread, they are woven into delicate textures, some of which, as in the case of hats and cigar-cases, are sold at enormous prices. If not exposed to damp, the fibres are very enduring, and are safe from the attacks of the weevil.

The native name for hemp is *anabo*, the Spanish, *cañamo*; but the raw material known in commerce as Manila hemp, is called in the Philippines by its Indian name, *abacá*. It is become a very important article of export, and in the year 1858 no less than 25,000 tons were shipped for foreign countries from Manila alone. Of this quantity Great Britain received about one-fourth, and the greater portion of the remainder went to the United States. Next to sugar and tobacco, it ranks highest in the list of exported produce. It is employed not only for cordage, but for textile fabrics. It is the fibre of one of the plantain family—the *Musa trogloditarum textoria*. Dampier says that its growth is confined to the island of Mindanao; but the quantity there grown is, at the present time, trifling compared to the production of Luzon, Panay, and other islands of the archipelago. The finer qualities are in considerable demand for weaving, and these are, of course, subjected to a more elaborate manipulation. It readily receives red and blue dyes; the *morinda* and *marsdenia*, native plants, being employed for the purpose. The fruit is said to be edible, but I am not aware of ever having seen it introduced, nor would it be likely to compete with the best of the delicious plantains which the Philippines produce. Father Blanco says that of these there are no less than fifty-seven varieties. The native name is *saguing*. Curious traditions are connected with this fruit. The Arabs say it was introduced into the world by Allah, when the Prophet lost his teeth, and could no longer enjoy the date. It is sometimes called Adam's apron, on the supposition that it was the plant whose leaves he and Eve employed to cover their nakedness. Its use is universal, both in its natural state and cooked in various forms.

The cultivation of Coffee might be largely extended. For that, and indeed for every tropical produce, there is scarcely a limit to the unappropriated lands well suited to their production. Some of the coffee is of excellent quality, scarcely distinguishable from that of Arabia, but the general character is less favourable.

Indeed there is an obvious contrast between the great improvements which have taken place in the Dutch archipelago, the British colonies, Ceylon for example, and the stagnation created by the too stationary habits of the Indian producer. He is little attentive to the proper selection of soil, the temperature or elevation of the ground, the choice of the seed, the pruning of the tree, the care of the berry, the separation of the outer coatings, and other details, which may help to account for the comparatively small extension of coffee production, especially considering the enormously increased demand for the article, and the prodigious development of its cultivation in Netherlands India, Ceylon and elsewhere.

The quality of the Cocoa is excellent, and I have nowhere tasted better chocolate than in the Philippines, but the tree is principally planted for the private use of its possessors. In the convents particularly, the friars are proud of their chocolate, which is generally made under their own superintendence, and from fruit raised in their own grounds and gardens. A little attention is required in the selection of soil and locality; the fruit is gathered as it ripens, and after the removal of the cuticle simply requires to be sun-dried.

It is sown in the month of November, and the shade of the banana is sought for its protection. The cocoa of Zebu is reported to be equal in excellence to that of the Caracas. In the island of Negros there is a large spontaneous production. The Indian soaks the cocoa in sugar juice, and in many parts the beverage is taken twice a day.

The supply of Cotton is one of the most interesting of questions as regards our manufacturing population, and I have felt surprised at the small sagacity, the *parva sapientia*, which has been exhibited by many who have devoted their attention to the matter. The expectation that *Negroland* Africa will be able to fill up the anticipated *vacuum* of supply is a vain hope originating in ignorance of the character and habits of the native races, and it will end in disappointment and vexation. The capabilities of British India are great, and the elements of success are there; but the capabilities of China are vastly greater, and I believe that as in two or three years China was able to send raw silk to the value of ten millions sterling into the market, and immediately to make up for the absence of the European supply, so to China we may hereafter look for a boundless supply of raw cotton; she now clothes more than three hundred and fifty millions of her people from her own cotton-fields. The prices in China are so nearly on a level with those of India that though they allow an importation to the yearly value of two or three millions sterling in the southern provinces of China, importations into the northern are scarcely known. The quality, the modes of cultivation, of cleaning, of packing, are all susceptible of great improvements; their interests will make the Chinese teachable, and the Yang-tse-Kiang may be the channel for the solution of the cotton difficulty.

There seems no sufficient reason why cotton wool should not have been more largely exported from the Philippines. It is cheaply produced and might follow the crops of mountain rice. There is a domestic demand, and that seems to satisfy the grower, for cotton has almost ceased to be an article of foreign trade. The staple is said to be short. The plant is an annual and produces its crop in two or three months after it is sown. It is gathered in the midday sun before the advent of the rainy season, which destroys both shrub and seedpod.

Cocoa-nut trees (*Cocos nucifera*), called *Nioc* by the Tagals, eminently contribute to the ornament, comfort, and prosperity of the natives. Trunks, branches, leaves, fruit, all are turned to account. Oil, wine and spirits are made from its juices. The bark is employed for caulking and cables; the shell of the cocoa is wrought and carved in many ways for spoons, cups and domestic utensils; the burnt shell is employed for dyeing black. The trunk often forms the frame, the leaves the cover, of the Indian houses. The fibres of the leaves are manufactured into cloths for garments; the fibres of the fruit into brushes. The pulp is eaten or made into sweetmeats and the milk is esteemed for its medicinal virtues. The root, when roasted, is used as a decoction for the cure of dysentery.

A Spanish writer says that an Indian wants nothing but his *Cocal* (cocoa-nut palm garden) for his comfortable support. The tree will give him water, wine, oil, vinegar, food, cords, cups, brushes, building materials, black paint, soap, roofing for his house, strings for his rosaries, tow, red dye, medicine, plaister for wounds, light, fire, and many other necessaries. It produces fruit after seven years' growth. The *nipa* palm is almost, though not quite as useful. These spontaneous bounties of nature may not be the allies or promoters of civilization, but they are the compensations which make savage life tolerable and, if not of high enjoyment, not far from happy.

A very small quantity of Pepper is now grown, though it was formerly one of the most prized productions of the islands. It is said that the Indians destroyed all their pepper plantations in consequence of frauds practised on them by the Manila merchants.

Attempts to introduce some of the more costly spices, such as the Cinnamon and Nutmeg, have not been attended with success.

Fruits are abundant. There are no less than fifty-seven varieties of the banana. The fame of the Manila mango is universal in the East. There are many sorts of oranges, pines (*ananas*) in great quantities, guavas, rose-apples, and the mangosteen is found in Mindanao. The chico is a favourite fruit in winter, somewhat resembling the medlar, hut I must refer those who desire more extended information to Father Blanco's *Flora*, imperfect though it be.

Among the riches of the Philippine Islands, the forest trees occupy an important place. A collection of 350 specimens was sent to the Royal Exhibition in London in the form of square-based prisms. In the year 1858 Colonel Valdes published a report on the character and resistance of Philippine woods for buildings (*maderas de construction*). The specimens on which the experiments were made were cubes of one centimetre and prisms of one centimetre square by one metre of breadth. The woods were allowed one year's drying. Five experiments were made on each, and the average results adopted.

The abbreviations employed in the following tables, which give a synopsis of the results, are:—

E Elasticity.

F Strength of cohesion.

f Arc of flexion produced by a constant weight of 1 kilogram hung from the centre.

n Arc at which fracture took place.

P Weight applied at the centre of the arc.

c Distance between the supporters of the wood: in some 68 centimetres, in others 60.
Section of prisms, 1 square centimetre.
Length of the same, 1 metre.

R Weight producing fracture at the bend.

T Coefficient of fracture by bending, or of maximum bend.
Resistance is estimated in the direction of the fibres (diagonally) and perpendicularly upon them.

SCALE of RESISTANCE and SPECIAL QUALITIES of WOODS, extracted from the Table, pp. 266–71.

Those with an asterisk are little used for building, either on account of their cost, scarcity, or unsuitableness for the purpose.

1. RESISTANCE.				2. Elastici
Pressure.		**Tension or**	**Tortion.**	
Horizontal	**Perpendicular**	**Cohesion.**		
with the fibre.	**upon the fibre.**			
*Ebano.	*Ebano.	Pototan.	Molave.	Malatalisa
Alupag.	Palma-brava	Malabugat.	Bitoc.	*Malatapa
*Balibago.	*Camagon.	Baliti.	Malarujat.	Molave.
*Santol.	Camayuan.	Molave.	Yacal.	Laneti.
Molave.	Acre.	Alupag.	Guijo.	Bitoc.
*Alintatao.	*Alintatao.	*Balibago.	Alupag.	Malavidon
*Camagon.	Ypil.	Yacal.	*Camagon.	Ypil.
Palma-brava.	Molave.	*Ebano.	Camayuan.	Tangan.
Calamansanay.	*Santol.	Malavidondao.	Banabà.	Malabugat
*Narra.	*Malatapay.	Bitoc.	*Balibago.	Malacintu
*Malatapay.	Alupag.	Malacintud.	Amoguis.	Guijo.
Baliti.	Dongon.	*Pincapincahan.	Calamansanay.	*Narra.
Acre.	*Balibago.	Palo-Maria.	Laneti.	Yacal.
Calantas.	*Narra.	*Manga.	Malavidondao.	*Ebano.
Yacal.	Yacal.	Banabà.	Mangachapuy.	Calumpit.

*Tindalo.	Baliti.	Calumpit.	*Tindalo.	Palma-bra
Palusapis.	Palo-Maria.	Calamansanay.	*Manga.	Calamansa
Mangachapuy.	*Manga.	Palma-brava.	*Alintatao.	Bolongita.
Dongon.	Palusapis.	Palusapis.	Ypil.	*Balibago.
Camayuan.	Pototan.	Malarujat.	*Santol.	Palo-Maria
Ypil.	Panao.	Bolongita.	Palma-brava.	Sampaloc.
Pototan.	Aninabla.	Tugan.	Bolongita.	*Camagon
Palo-Maria.	Guijo.	Sampaloc.	Pototan.	Dongon.
Malacintud.	Mangachapuy.	*Santol.	Aninabla.	*Manga.
Panao.	Calamansanay.	Panao.	*Malatapay.	Acre.
*Manga.	Amoguis.	*Camagon.	Antipolo.	Amoguis.
*Pincapincahan.	Banabà.	Anonang.	Dongon.	Lauan.
Guijo.	Anonang.	*Malatapay.	Acre.	*Alintatao
Bolongita.	Bolongita.	*Alintatao.	Malacintud.	Tanguili.
Malavidondao.	Laneti.	Guijo.	Palo-Maria.	*Tindalo.
Banabà.	Malabugat.	Lauan.	*Pincapincahan.	*Pincapinc
Calumpit.	Malvidondao.	Tanguili.	*Narra.	Panao.
Anonang.	*Tindalo.	*Narra.	Calumpit.	Banabà.
Malarujat.	*Pincapincahan.	Dongon.	Sampaloc.	Palusapis.
Aninabla.	Malacintud.	Amoguis.	*Ebano.	Malarujat.
Bitoc.	Bitoc.	Antipolo.	Tagan.	*Santol.
Amoguis.	Tangulin.	Ypil.	Tanguili.	Camayuan
Laneti.	*Baticulin.	Calumpit.	*Baticulin.	Aninabla.
Tangan.	Sampaloc.	Malatalisay.	Calantás.	Antipolo.
Sampaloc.	Lauan.	Camayuan.	Panao.	Baneal.
Malabugat.	Calumpit.	Aninabia.	Malatalisay.	Alupag.
Tanguili.	Malarujat.	Acre.	Baliti.	Calantás.
Malatalisay.	Antipolo.	*Tindalo.	Lauan.	Pototan.
Antipolo.	Bancal.	Bancal.	Bancal.	Mangacha
Lauan.	Calantas.	Laneti.	Palusapis.	*Malacatb
Bancal.	Tangan.	Mangachapuy.	Malabugat.	*Baticulin.
*Baticulin.	Malatalisay.	*Malacatbun.	Anonang.	Anonang.
*Malacatbun.	*Malacatbun.	*Baticulin.	*Malacatbun.	Baliti.

— Name,	f.	n.	P.	c.	R.	Weight of	Resistance.
Description and Application.						the cubic decimetre.	To pressure by centimetres.
							With On the gr

		Cent.	Cent.	Kilo.	Cent.	Kilo.	Kilo.	the grain of the fibre. Kilo.	perpendic Kilo.
1	ACRE—Mimosa acre (Monodelphia dodecandria). *Abounds in the islands. Employed for buildings and shipping.*	1·6	13·0	4·78	68·0	1·10	1·12	498	340
2	ALINTATAO— Diospyros piloshantera (?) (Octandria monoginia). *Several varieties. Used for household furniture. Luzon and Visayas.*	1·3	6·3	6·21	68·0	1·25	0·91	598	300
3	ALUPAG ALOPAI— Euphoria litchi (Octandria monoginia). *Used for posts. Abounds.*	0·3	5·0	13·80	60·0	1·40	0·92	666	220
4	AMBOGUES or AMOGUIS— Cyrtocarpa quinquistila (Decandria pentaginia). *Suffers much from termites. Used for planks.*	1·4	9·0	5·06	68·0	1·40	0·98	338	130
5	ANINABLA or	1·2	7·0	4·83	68·0	1·15	0·59	340	146

	ANINAPLA—Mimosa conaria(?) (Monœcia dodecandria). *Used for house and boat building. Valued for light weight and long duration.*								
6	ANONANG—Cordia sebesteria (Pentandria monoginia). *Leaves, while growing, covered with worms. Wood used for drums and musical instruments.*	0.4	4.0	8·28	60·0	0·5	0·46	340	120
7	ANTIPOLO—Artocarpus incisa (Monœcia diandria). *For canoes, floors and machines. Garters are made from a gum that exudes.*	0·1	10·0	5·52	68·0	0·9	0·41	286	70
8	BALIBAGO—Hibiscus tellacius (Monodelphia poliandria). *Cords and paper made of the bark; gunpowder of the charcoal.*	1·0	10·0	5·52	68·0	0·9	0·46	616	200
9	BALITI—Ficus	0·2	0·6	14·95	60·0	0·7	0·40	498	176

	Indica (Monœcia triandria). *Banian tree. Chopped roots used for curing wounds.*							
10	BATICULIN— Millingtonia quadripinnata (Didinamia angiospermia). *White woods for moulds and sculpture. Lasts long without decay. Abounds.*	0·2	0·1	2·10	68·0	0·9	0·42	186	100
11	BANABA— Munchaustia speciosa (Poliadelphia poliandria). *Great tenacity; resists action of climate and water.*	0·7	0·7	5·06	68·0	1·3	0·65	348	126
12	BANEAL— Nauclea glaberrima (Pentandria monoginia). *Tenacious and enduring. Used for furniture and floors, ships, casks and quays.*	1·2	10·5	4·60	68·0	0·6	0·58	220	66
13	BITOC—Mirtica (?) *A strong wood to resist pressure.*	1·15	13·0	9·90	68·0	1·7	0·71	338	100
14	BOLONGUITA— Diospyros	0·9	10·8	8·40	68·0	1·2	0·90	360	120

(Octandria monoginia). *Solid texture for building. Abounds.*								
15 CALAMANSANAY— Gimbernatia calamansanay (Decandria monoginia). *Planks for flooring and building.*	1·0	10·0	8·74	68·0	1·3	0·86	533	130
16 CALANTAS (Native Cedar)—Cedrela odorata (Pentandria monoginia). *Found throughout the Philippines. Used for canoes.* Taratara, *a variety.*	1·0	7·0	5·06	68·0	0·85	0·40	470	60
17 CALUMPIT— Terminalia edulis (Decandria monoginia). *Abounds in Angol. Building. Great strength on the line of the fibres.*	1·0	11·2	8·68	68·0	1·0	0·60 to 0·80	348	90
18 CAMAGON— Variety of the Diospyros piloshantera (Alintatao). *Beautifully veined and spotted. Easily polished. Fine furniture.*	1·1	9·3	7·36	68·0	1·35	0·92	558	340

19	CAMAYUAN— Diospyros(?) *Used for building.*	1·2	14·8	8·74	68·0	1·3	0·94	434	340
20	DONGON—Variety of Herculia ambiformis (Monœcia adelphia). *Good building wood. Largely produced.*	1·3	7·57	6·44	68·0	1·1	1·02	435	200
21	EBANO—Variety of the Sapote negro Diospyros nigra; variety of Camagon and Alintatao. *Bears a very fine polish.*	0·35	7·5	1·45	51·6	1·1	1·91	688	470
22	GUIJO— Dipterocarpus guijo (Poliandria monoginia). *Shipbuilding, keels, carriage-wheels. Much esteemed and abundant.*	1·3	10·5	7·70	68·0	1·5	0·76	370	140
23	LANETI—Anaser laneti (Pentandria monoginia). *Elastic and suited for furniture.*	2·5	14·8	4·50	68·0	1·3	0·55	336	120
24	LAUAN or LANDANG— Dipterocarpus thurifera (Poliandria monoginia).	1·1	8·0	6·80	68·0	0·6	0·43	226	90

Gives resin for incense. Much used formerly for shipping. Not splintered by balls. Abounds. 25 MALACATBUN— Tetracera sarmentosa (?) (Poliandria tetraginia). *Of little use.*	1·5	6·0	3·00	68·0	...	0·63	146	60
26 MALACINTUD *Strong wood, fit for building.*	1·0	8·5	6·80	68·0	1·1	0·645	400	160
27 MALAVIDONDAO— Mavindalo (?) (Niota.) *Ship futtocks. Strong wood.*	1·0	9·0	0·81	68·0	1·3	0·78	350	116
28 MALATALISAY— Terminalia mauritania (Decandria monoginia). *Elastic and flexible. Shipbuilding.*	0·15	15·0	2·82	42·3	0·8	0·50	300	60
29 MALARUHAT or MALADUJAT— Mirtaceas (?) *Solid texture. Uses not mentioned.*	0·7	7·8	8·51	68·0	1·5	0·79	340	76
30 MALATAPAY or MABALO; also TALANG— Diospyros embriopteris (Poliandria monoginia).	2·0	12·3	7·25	68·0	1·15	0·78	500	290

	For furniture and building. Resembles ebony.							
31	MALABAGAT	0·7	8·5	4·00	68·0	0·5	0·89	330	120
	Building, especially for supporting longitudinal pressure.							
32	MANGA— Mangifera Indica (Pentandria monoginia) *Variety of Cuba mango. From value of fruit, wood little used.*	0·6	13·0	0·12	60·0	1·3	0·58	380	166
33	MANGACHAPUY or GUISON DILAO— Dipterocarpus magachapuy (Poliandria monoginia). *For ships and houses. Fine planks for floors.*	1·25	5·8	3·64	68·0	1·3	0·88	438	136
34	MOLAVE—Vilex geniculata altissima (Didinamia angiospermia). *Called by the natives Queen of Woods. Used for all purposes. Resists action of water and of lime; also attacks of insects.*	1·0	11·0	12·31	68·0	2·00	0·95 to	600	290
35	NARRA, or NAGA, or ASANG—	1·73	7·3	6·20	68·0	1·00	0.66	500	200

	Pterocarpus palidus santalinus (Diadelphia dodecandria). *Buildings, furniture, doors and windows.*								
36	PALO-MARIA, or BITANHOL— Calophilum mophilum (Poliadelphia poliandria). *Planks and shipping purposes.*	0·9	7·3	9·20	68·0	1·05	0.68	400	126
37	PALMA-BRAVA, or ANAJAO—Coripha minor (Hexandria monoginia). *Hard and enduring, especially under water. Used for piles.*	1·0	6·5	8·74	68·0	1·20	1.085	530	400
38	PALUSAPIS— Dipterocarpus palusapis (Poliandria monoginia). *Strong wood. Used for canoes.*	0·5	8·5	9·66	60·0	0·70	0.50	440	146
39	PANAO, or BALAO, or MALAPAJO— Dipterocarpus vernicephurus (Poliandria monoginia). *Buildings and ships. Incision in the trunk gives a*	...	...	...	60·0	0·80	0.69	393	146

fragrant resin, which, put in a hollow bamboo, is used for light by the Indians. Gives the talay oil, which destroys insects in wood. Used also for varnish.

40	PENCAPENCAHAN— Bignonia quadripinnata (Didinamia angiospermia). *Used principally for clogs and buoys.*	0·5	6·0	10·80	60·0	1·05	0.46	378	106
41	POTOTAN or BACAO— Rizophora gimaoriza (Dodecandria monoginia). *For piles, as resisting the action of water.*	0·2	7·0	19·78	60·0	1·20	0.69	420	146
42	SAMPALOC or TAMARIND— Tamarindus Indica (Triandria monoginia). *For tools and some building purposes.*	1·0	12·0	8·28	68·0	0·95	0.62	320	90
43	SANTOL— Sandoricum Indicum (Decandria monoginia). *For posts and*	0·5	7·0	9·00	60·0	1·20	0.46	630	...

pillars; not common.								
44 Tanguili— Dipterocarpus polispermum (Poliandria monoginia). *Building purposes.*	1·1	10·0	6·80	68·0	0·90	0.57	300	100
45 Tangan— Rizophora longissima (?) (Dodecandria monoginia). *Window frames, joints, &c.*	1·2	12·8	8·40	68·0	0·90	0.65	330	60
46 Tindalo—Eperna rhomboidea (Decandria monoginia). *For furniture; has a pleasant fragrance.*	1·6	5·5	4·60	68·0	1·30	0.89	450	106
47 Yacal— Dipterocarpus plagatus (Poliandria monoginia). *Used for ship and house building.*	0·8	10·8	11·50	68·0	1·30	1.105	450	200
48 Ypil—Eperna decandria (Decandria monoginia). *Generally for building. Abounds in Luzon.*	2·0	13·5	5·50	68·0	1·20	1.035	434	300

CHAPTER XVI.

ANIMALS.

The buffalo is, perhaps, the most useful of Philippine quadrupeds. Immense herds of wild buffaloes are found in the interior, but the tamed animal is employed in the labours of the fields and the transport of commodities, whether on its back or in waggons. His enjoyment is to be merged in water or mud. Such is the attachment of the mother to her young that she has been known to spring into the river and furiously to pursue the crocodile that had robbed her of her calf. Wild boars and deer abound.

A good deal of attention has been paid to improvement of the race of native ponies, and their value has much increased with the increasing demand. Till of late years the price was from forty to fifty dollars, but the Captain-General told me that the four ponies which he was accustomed to use in his carriage cost 500 dollars.

Though the accounts of the silent, concealed and rapid ravages of the white ants would sometimes appear incredible, credulity respecting them will outstrip all bounds. We had a female servant at Hong Kong who told us she had lent her savings in hard dollars to one of her relations, and, on claiming repayment, was informed that the white ants had eaten the dollars, nor did the woman's simplicity doubt the story. In the Philippines at sunset during the rains their presence becomes intolerable. One well-authenticated fact may serve as an illustration of the destructive powers of these insects, to whom beautiful gauze wings have been given, as to butterflies in the later stage of their existence, which wings drop off as they find a resting-place. In the town of Obando, province of Bulacan, on the 18th of March, 1838, the various objects destined for the services of the mass, such as robes, albs, amices, the garments of the priests, &c, were examined and placed in a trunk made of the wood called *narra* (*Pterocarpus palidus*). On the 19th they were used in the divine services, and in the evening were restored to the box. On the 20th some dirt was observed near it, and on opening, every fragment of the vestments and ornaments of every sort were found to have been reduced to dust, except the gold and silver lace, which were tarnished with a filthy deposit. On a thorough examination, not an ant was found in any other part of the church, nor any vestige of the presence of these voracious destroyers; but five days afterwards they were discovered to have penetrated through a beam six inches thick.

Few of the larger wild animals are found in the Philippines. The elephant must have been known in former times, as the names *gadya* (elephant) and *nangagadya* (elephant-hunting) are preserved in the Tagal language. Oxen, swine, buffaloes, deer, goats, sheep, a great variety of apes and monkeys, cats, flying squirrels, dogs, rats, mungoes and other quadrupeds, are found in various stages of domesticity and wildness.

The great insect pests of the Philippines are the white ants (*termes*) and the mosquitos. Fleas, bugs and flies are less numerous and tormenting than in many temperate regions.

Some of the bats measure from five to six feet from the tips of their wings.

There are incredible stories about a small black bird of the swallow race, which is said to make its nest in the tail of wild horses. De Mas quotes what he calls undoubtedly trustworthy authorities[1] for his arguments. There is an immense variety of gallinaceous fowls, pigeons and birds, whose Indian names would to European ornithologists bring little information; among which the *balicyao* is celebrated for its song; the *mananayom* (solitary), which always dies when captured; the *coling*, easily taught to talk; numerous parrots; the *calao*, which has a large transparent bill and crows like a cock; the *bocuit*, or bird of seven colours, which has a singularly sweet note; the *valoor*, a pigeon whose plumage is varied like that of the partridge; another called the *dundunay*, which is reported to be one of the most beautiful of birds.

Snakes, lizards and other reptiles abound; spiders of enormous size, tarantulas, &c. The *guiko* is very disturbing, from its noise. I was struck with the tenacity with which this creature held, even in the agonies of death, to a piece of timber on which it was placed; the soles of its feet seemed to have all the power of the sucker with which boys amuse themselves, and the animal was detached with great difficulty.

The fire-flies illuminate the forests at night. There are some trees to which they attach themselves in preference to others. Few objects are more beautiful than a bush or tree lighted by these bright and glancing stars. The brilliant creatures seem to have a wonderful sympathy with one another, sometimes by the production of a sudden blaze of beautiful fire, of a light and delicate green, and sometimes by its as sudden extinction.

Of aquatic creatures the tortoise is of considerable commercial importance. The natives, who watch the time of their coming on shore, conceal themselves, and, when a certain number are marching inland, run between the tortoises and the waves, turn them one after another on their backs, and return at their leisure to remove them. The large bivalve called by the natives *taclovo*, and which is used much in the churches as the receptacle for holy water, and is seen frequently at the entrance of houses, is captured by dropping a cord upon the body of the animal when the shell is opened, the animal immediately closes upon the cord, and is dragged to the surface with the greatest ease. I am not aware of the existence of any conchological work on the Philippines, though there is a great variety of land and water shells.

---

[1]

I am, however, informed by a friend of one of the gentlemen referred to by De Mas, that he disclaims having authorized the statement given under his name.

CHAPTER XVII.

MINERALS.

The Mining Laws, *Reglamento de Minas*, are of a liberal character and allow concessions to be made to any person, Spaniard, Indian, mestizo, naturalized or established foreigner, who shall discover and report the discovery of a mine, and undertake to work it. Sundry officials and all ecclesiastics are excluded from the privilege. The work must be entered upon in ninety days, under certain conditions; four months of continued suspension, or eight months of interrupted labour, within the year bring the loss of the conceded privilege. There must not be less than eight labourers employed. The mines are subjected to the inspection of the mining department The mining regulations were published by the Captain-General Claveria in January, 1846.

The gold of the Philippines is produced by washing and digging. In several of the provinces it is found in the rivers, and natives are engaged in washing their deposits. The most remarkable and profitable of the gold mines worked by the Indians are those of Tulbin and Suyuc. They break the rock with hammers, and crush it between two small millstones, dissolving the fragments in water, by which the gold is separated. They melt it in small shells, and it produces generally from eight to ten dollars an ounce, but its fineness seldom exceeds sixteen carats. It is found in quartz, but the nuggets are seldom of any considerable size. The inhabitants of Caraga cut in the top of a mountain a basin of considerable size, and conduct water to it through canals made of the wild palm; they dig up the soil while the basin is filling, which is opened suddenly, and exhibits for working any existing stratification of gold; these operations are continued till the pits get filled with inroads of earth, when they are abandoned; generally, when a depth has been reached which produces the most advantageous returns, the rush of waters conveys away much of the metal which would otherwise be deposited and collected. Gold is also found in the alluvial deposits which are ground between stones, thrown into water, and the metal sinks to the bottom. The rivers of Caraballo, Camarines, and Misamis, and the mountains of Caraga and Zebu, are the most productive. Many Indian families support themselves by washing the river sands, and in the times of heavy rains gold is found in the streets of some of the pueblos when the floods have passed. There can be no doubt of the existence of much gold in the islands, but principally in the parts inhabited by the independent tribes.

The Sociedad Exploradora is engaged in working gold-mines and washing auriferous sands in the province of New Ecija.

Gold dust is the instrument of exchange in the interior of Mindanao, and is carried about in bags for the ordinary purposes of life. The possession of California by the Spaniards for so many generations without the development of its riches may explain their inertness and indifference in the Philippines, notwithstanding the repeated averments of Spanish writers that the archipelago abounds in gold.

Iron also abounds, especially in the province of Bulacan; but it may be doubted whether it can be produced as cheaply as it may be imported, especially while roads are in so backward a state, and carriage charges so heavy. Many iron-works have been entered on and abandoned.

A coal-mine is being explored at Guila Guila, in the island of Zebu, on the river Mananga, at a distance of about six miles from the town of San Nicolas, which has nearly 20,000 inhabitants and is by far the largest town in the island. There are reported to be strata of coal from one to four feet in thickness. The proprietor informs me that he expects in the course of another year to be able to deliver coals on the coast at a moderate rate in Tangui, which is close to the town of Falisay.

Of the various objects of speculation, mining is probably the most attractive to the adventurer, from the high premiums which it sometimes brings to the successful. When the risk is divided among many shareholders, it partakes of the character of a lottery, in which the chances are proportioned to the stakes; but where, as in most of the mining speculations of the Philippines, the enterprises are conducted by individuals, without adequate means to overcome the preliminary difficulties and to support the needful outlay, disappointment, loss, ruin and the abandonment of probably valuable and promising undertakings are but of too frequent occurrence. I have before me some details of the attempts made to work the copper ores of Mancayan, in the district of Cagan (now called Lepanto), in South Ilocos (Luzon). They have been worked in the rudest way by the Igorrote Indians from time immemorial, and the favourable report of the richness of the ores which were sent to Europe led to renewed but inadequate attempts for their exploitation. A good deal of money has, I understand, been lost, without providing the necessary machinery for extracting the metal, or roads for its conveyance. A sample taken from a stratum ten feet in height and seven in breadth, on the side of a pit four yards deep, gave, as the results of an analysis, 44 per cent. of copper, 29 of sulphur, 18 of arsenic, and 9 of iron. The ruggedness of the rocks, the thickness of the forest jungle, the indolence of the natives, and, probably more than these, the absence of an intelligent direction and sufficient pecuniary resources, have produced much discouragement. Don Antonio Hernandez says there are 280 Indian (Igorrote) families occupied in Mancayan in copper digging and melting; that they only produce annually about 200 picos (of 137½ lbs. each), which they sell at from eight to nine dollars per pico on the spot; to the neighbouring Christian Indians at ten to twelve, who resell them on the coast at from thirteen to sixteen dollars.

The Indians in Ilocos and Pangasinan manufacture their own domestic utensils from the copper extracted by themselves.

Finely variegated marbles exist in the province of Bataan, and some have been used for ornamenting the churches; but their existence has excited little attention, and no sale was found for some large blocks quarried by a patriotic adventurer.

I have before mentioned that there are many mineral waters in the island—sulphurous and ferruginous—at Antipolo. In the Laguna there is a virgin patroness, whose festival lasts eighteen days, and immense crowds of all races come to drink the waters, and join the processions in her honour. The inhabitants of Manila attribute great virtues to the waters of Pagsanghan.

CHAPTER XVIII.

MANUFACTURES.

The art of weaving, or that of crossing threads so as to produce a wearable tissue, is one of the evidences of a transition from savage towards civilized life. In cold countries the painting the body, or covering it with furs and skins, or bark of trees, is the resource of a wild people; but the necessity for dress of any sort is so little felt in tropical regions that the missionaries claim the credit of introducing the loom, and of instructing the natives in all the matters most conducive to their comforts. For their houses they taught them to make lime and brick and tiles—staircases, windows and chimneys—and better to protect themselves against rain and storms; chairs, tables and domestic utensils followed; carriages for conveyance of commodities; but, above all, the friars boast of the application, and devotion, and success of the Indians in decorating the Christian churches, building and ornamenting altars, sculpturing virgins and saints, and generally contributing to the splendours of ecclesiastical ceremonials.

The science of ship-building made great advances. To the canoes (*barotos* is the Indian name) scooped out of a single trunk, and used only for river navigation, succeeded well-built vessels of several hundred tons, by which a commerce along the coast and among the islands was established. At first the planks were the whole length of the vessel, but European improvements have gradually been adopted, and the ships now built in the Philippines are not distinguishable from those of the mother country. We found many on the stocks on the banks of the river Agno, and the Indian constructors were desirous of looking into all the details of H. M.'s ship *Magicienne*, in which the captain and officers most courteously aided them, in order to avail themselves of any improvements which our vessel exhibited. The cost of construction was reported to be about 15*l*. sterling per ton. The *Bella Bascongada*, a vessel of 760 tons, built in Pangasinan, cost 54,000 dollars, or about 11,000*l*. sterling.

Little has been done for the introduction of improved machinery for the manufacture of tissues, which are made of silk, cotton, abacá, and, above all, the exquisitely fine fabrics produced from the fibre of the pine-apple leaf, called *piñas*. These are worked on the simplest looms, made of bamboos, and of a thread so fine that it is necessary to protect it, by the use of a fine gauze, from even the agitation of the wind. The Bisayan provinces, and especially the neighbourhood of Iloilo, are most distinguished for the manufacture of this beautiful tissue, which is sent to the capital for embroidery, and prices which seem fabulous are paid for the more elaborate specimens—one or two ounces of gold being frequently given for a small handkerchief. In Zebu handsome cotton rugs are made, and in Panay a variety of stuffs of sundry materials.

The Indians have the art of softening and manufacturing horn. In metals they make chains of silver and gold of great fineness, for which formerly there was a great demand in Mexico, but I believe European jewellery has supplanted the Indian craftsman.

Mats are a remarkable production of the islands. Many of them are very beautiful, of various colours, and are ornamented with gold and silver patterns. As mattresses are never used for beds, everybody sleeps on a mat, which in some cases, but not generally, is provided with a sheet and a long soft pillow, which is placed between the legs and deemed a needful appliance for comfortable repose.

Fibre-wrought hats and cigar-cases of various colours, the white, however, being the most costly and beautiful, compete with similar productions of the natives of Panama.

The tools and instruments employed by the Indians in manufacture are all of the simplest and rudest character.

The alcoholic beverage called *vino de nipa* is largely produced in the Philippines. It was made a monopoly as early as 1712 in the provinces near the capital, and then produced 10,000 dollars of annual revenue; the farm was abolished in 1780, and in 1814 the collection was transferred to the general administration. The juice is obtained by cutting a hole in a pulpy part of the palm, introducing a bamboo cane, and binding the tree over the receiving vessel. The sale of the nipa wine is a monopoly in the hands of the Government. The monopoly is much and reasonably complained of by the Indians. Excise duties leading to domiciliary visits, and interfering with the daily concerns of life, have been always and in all countries deemed one of the most vexatious and disagreeable forms of taxation. Man, whatever be his colour, is everywhere man, and everywhere exhibits, though in different forms, the same general dislikes and sympathies. The heavy hand of extortion and oppression does not crush the Filipinos, but a redistribution of the forms of taxation would be beneficial to the fiscal interest and satisfactory to the people.

CHAPTER XIX.

POPULAR PROVERBS.

The following collection of proverbs will be found curious and characteristic. They will serve to throw light upon the genius of the people, and are appropriate specimens of the Tagal idiom:—

Ang mañga casalanan ang nacasisira sa calolova.—Sins are the diseases of the soul.

Valan di dungmating na dalita t' saguit cay Job ay dili y saman nagogolorhianan ang coniyang loob.—Job had many troubles, but they did not affect the inner man.

Catotohin mo ang catatoro co.—Make thyself a friend of my friend.

Avatin mo angcoob mo sa quinauiuilihan niyang masama.—Separate thy will (purpose) from him whose love has a bad object.

Houag mong pitahin ang vala.—Desire not what *is* not (not attainable).

At cun ano caya ang pinagpipilitanan.—They dispute about what their dispute shall be (are determined to quarrel).

Masamang cahuy ang dinamomoñga.—Bad tree produces no fruit.

Maminsanminsan ay susulat ca at maminsanminsa y babata ca nang sulat.—Write now and then, read now and then.

Nang anoman at maca tomama sa olo ninyo.—Don't fling up a stone, it may fall on your own head.

Paombaychan ca at napapagal ca.—Sing a lullaby at your wedding.

Houag mo acong pangalatacan at dili aco hayop.—Don't drive me, for I am not a beast.

Ay at linologmocan mo iyang duma?—Why seat yourself in that dirty place?

Houag mo acong galavirin niyan osap na iyan.—Don't involve me in that quarrel.

Hindi matimoan, ang balat nang Buaya, nang anomang tilos.—A knife will not enter a crocodile's back.

Tiguis cang nag papacalouay.—What thou doest do quietly.

Tiñgalen mo ang balatic.—Lift up your eyes, and you will see the stars. (*Balatic*, the *Astilejos* of the Spaniards—Castor and Pollux.)

Magguimbal ca manguiguimbal.—The drummer should beat the drum.

Houag ninyong yñgayan ang natotolog.—Wake not what is sleeping.

Hindi nag aaya ang mañga ducha.—The poor have no nurse.

Mababao na loob.—He carries his heart in his hand.

Lumaclac ca un valan ynuman.—He would suck a horse-brush rather than not drink.

Nag babacobaco ca pala.—Listen! thou doest what thou knowest not.

Calouhalhatiang mañga gavang magagaling.—Good deeds are heavenly doings.

Nag cacaligalig tovina ang pañgiboghoin.—Disquiet is the constant companion of jealousy.

Papaslañgin mo iyang matologuin.—To make a sentinel of a sluggard (*dormilon*, Spanish).

Ang mahabang dila tapit gupitan.—A long tongue ought to be clipped.

Ang mañga cayamanan ay pain din nang demonio sa tavo.—Riches are the baits of the devil for man.

Ang mañga paguyac nang mañga ducha ay macadarating sa lañgit.—The cries of the wretched will reach Heaven.

Na aalinagnagan ang langsañgan nang ilao sa bahay.—A candle in a house will illumine a street.

Maguipag ani ca doon sa nag aani.—Reap thy rice with the reapers.

Si Adan ang nagtongtong mula sa atin.—There is no higher ancestry than Adam.

Caylan ca maoocan nang cahunghañgan mo?—When will you cast your fool's skin? (When will you be wise?)

Sucat parasuhan ang mañga magnanacao.—For thieves punishment and penitence.

Papagdalitin mo iyang marunung.—Let him make a song or sing one (to a pretender).

Caylan magcaca hapahap ang inyong ylog?—When will your river produce a conger eel? (to a boaster.)

Ang caiclian nang bait mo ay gaano!—How short must be the shortness of thy understanding.

Mabuti ang simbahan cung tabiñgan.—Beautiful is the church, but it must have its curtains (mysteries).

Nang magcatulay tulay na ang balita sa maraving tavo ay siyang ypinagcabalirbor.—Truth having passed through many (lips), becomes so entangled and altered, that it no longer resembles truth.

Maylomalong tamis sapolot at lacas sahalimao?—What is sweeter than honey, or stronger than a lion?

Ungmasoc lamang aco saujo.—Tell a lie to find a truth.

Houag mong ypanotnor sa maruming camay.—Trust not the disentanglement of the threads to a man with dirty hands.

Papasaylañginmo iyang nagbabanalbanalan.—If he be so virtuous, let him go to the wilderness (become a hermit).

Ayat sa lalandos cang naparito.—You come to the work and bring no tools.

Houag mong guisiñgin ang natotolog.—Wake not the sleeping.

Mapagsacasacang tavo sicuan.—Trust not the deceiver who says, "I'll do it by and by."

Houag mong ayoquin ang bavas nang catouirang justicia.—Bend not the straight rod of justice.

Ivinavasuas ang aguipo, nang dimipaling ang apuy.—He fans the ashes to keep up the fire.

Angpagal at ava nang Dios ang yquinayayaman co.—Labour and God's mercy bring riches.

Pinapananaligquita sa Dios ay nagbibiñgibiñgihanca.—I tell thee to trust in God, and thou makest thyself deaf.

Tionay mandin sa loob nang tavong mabait ang camuruhan.—An insult is a thorn that pierces the heart of an honourable man.

Sungmusubo ang polot.—Sweets have their froth (the saccharine matter of the sugar-cane).

Yaong nanacap pacsvarin mo sa palo.—For bravados, blows.

Ypinagbabalo balo mo saamin ang pagaayunar mo.—Thou wilt deceive by feigning fasting (religious hypocrisy).

Ang amo ay among dati paramtan man nang mabuti.—The monkey, however richly dressed, is but a monkey.

Aunque la mona se viste de seda, en mona se queda. (Spanish proverb.)—Though clad in silk, the monkey is a monkey still.

Houang cang mag hamalhamalan.—Do not seem to sniffle (through the nose) in the presence of a sniffler (*i.e.*, do not expose the defects of another).

Magyñgat cayo sapusang lambong.—Beware of a wild cat.

Ang magandanglalaqui huboma y mariguit—Even though naked, gentility will show itself.

Ang tapat na capitan may pinagcacapitanan.—Let governors govern.

Valangpalay ang amalong mo.—There is no rice in thy granary (to an empty-headed person).

Ymolos ang camay ay guinagat nang alopihan.—He struck a blow with his hand, and got bitten by a centipede.

Dino dolobasa ang dimaalan—Making ignorance your interpreter.

Nagcapalu na mandin ang canilan pagtatacapan.—Answer with nonsense the nonsense of others.

Anong ypinagpaparañgalanmo?—Why so jactant?—(a phrase to check boasting).

Maalam cang magsima sa taga?—Can he make the barb to the hook? (Is he clever?)

Mabuit ay nagpapatang patañgan finguin.—Being clever, he feigns stupidity.

Dibabao ang lañgit sa macasalanan.—Heaven is far off from sinners.

Gagadolong lisa iyan.—Serious as the bite of a louse's egg (nit).

Hindi macacagat ang valang ñgipin.—He who has no teeth cannot bite.

Malubha angpagpap aratimo samasaman gara.—Much obstinacy in an evil deed.

Iyang caratinanmo angy capapacasamamo.—Thy obstinacy will be thy perdition.

Pinag cayasalanan mo ang pañginoong Dios.—A sin against a neighbour is an offence against God.

Pinagbibiyayan an ninyo ang demonio.—To pay tribute to the devil.

Tingmitintinna ang darong magalao.—Turn lewdness to chastity.

Valan di dalita itong buhay natin.—Life is labour.

Mapaparari ang tova sa lañgit magparaling man san.—The joy of heaven will last and be perpetuated for ever and ever, and without end.

Cayañga t may tapal may sugat din.—Where the wound is, the plaister should be.

Houag cang omotang nang salapi.—Ask not for the money you lend.

Lubiranmo am navala ang pasilmo.—To play with the string when the top is lost. (A phrase used when a patron refuses a favour.)

Valan cabolohan ang logor dito sa lupa.—The pleasures of earth are not worth a hair.

Maytanim no sa mabato.—Sow not among stones.

Hungmo holangcapala aymarami panggava.—You are trifling while so much work is to be done.

Caya aco guinguinguiyacos dito.—I scratch myself because nobody will scratch me.

Napaguidaraan aco mya.—If I quarrel with myself, it shall be when I am alone.

Ano t guinagasaan mo aco?—If you scold me, why with so much noise?

Ang palagay na loob malivag magolorhanang.—Excesses are rare when the heart is at rest.

Caya co somosoyo siya y aco y tauong aba.—He must obey who is weak and poor.

Ang pagsisi anghuli ay valang guinapapacanan di baguin ang nañgag cacasaguit sa infierno. —Repentance is of little value when the penitent is in the hands of the devil (hell, or the executioner).[1]

Momoal moal mañgusap.—He who speaks with a full mouth will not be understood.

Hindi sosoco dito ang dimababa.—A short man will not knock his head against the roof.

Paspasin mo ang buñga at hunag mong pasapan ang cahuy.—In beating down the fruit, beat not down the tree.

Ang pagcatototo nang loob ang yguinagagaling nang lahat.—Unity of purpose brings certainty of success.

Nañgiñgisbigsiya nanggalit.—Petrified with rage (addressed to a person "borracho de colera," as the Spaniards say).

Aglahi si cabiri baquit mayag ang diti.—Saying No! with the lips, and Yes! with the heart.

Houag mong angcahan ang di mo masasacopan.—Do not adventure much until you are certain of the issue.

Some Spanish proverbs have made their way into Tagal.

Baquit siya y namong cahi ay siyang nabalantogui. Fué por lana y bolvió trasquilado.—He went for wool, and returned shorn.

I have selected most of these proverbs, aphorisms and moral and religious maxims from Fr. de los Santos' folio volume, and they would have some interest if they represented the thoughts and feelings of a civilized nation. That interest will hardly be less when the social code of semi-barbarians is studied in these short sentences. The influence and teachings of the priests will be found in many; others will be deemed characteristic of local usages, and some will find a recommendation in their grotesqueness and originality. I have thought these examples of the language might not be without their value to philologists.

---

[1]

There are many names for the public executioner, denoting the places in which he exercises his profession, and the instruments he employs for inflicting the punishment of death.

CHAPTER XX.

COMMERCE.

To foreign nations—to our own especially—the particular interest felt in the state of the Philippines is naturally more of a commercial than of a political character. They *must* grow in trading importance; already enough has been done to make a retrograde or even a stationary policy untenable. Every step taken towards emancipation from the ancient fetters which ignorance and monopoly laid upon their progress has been so successful and so productive as to promise and almost to ensure continuance in a course now proved to be alike beneficial to the public treasury and to the common weal. The statistics which I have been able to collect are often unsatisfactory and inaccurate, but, upon the whole, may be deemed approximative to the truth, and certainly not without value as means of comparison between the results of that narrow-minded exclusive system which so long directed the councils of Spain and the administration of *las Indias*, and the wiser and more liberal views which make their way through the dense darkness of the past.

The caprices and mischiefs of a privileged and protected trade and the curses which monopolies bring with them to the general interests, may, indeed, be well studied in the ancient legislation of Spain as regards her colonies. One vessel only was formerly allowed to proceed from the Philippines to Mexico; she was to be commanded by officers of the royal navy, equipped as a ship of war, and was subject to a variety of absurd restrictions and regulations: the adventurers were to pay 20,000 dollars for their privilege; and no one was allowed to adventure unless he were a *vocal de consulado*, which required a residence of several years in the islands, and the possession of property to the extent of 8,000 dollars. The privilege often passed clandestinely, by purchase, into the hands of friars, officials, women and other speculators—and it may well be supposed at what prices the goods had to be invoiced. Such being the licensed pillage in Asia, on arriving at Acapulco, in America, to which place the cargo was necessarily consigned, 33⅓ per cent. was imposed upon the valuation of the Manila invoices. And on the return of the ship similar or even more absurd conditions were exacted: she was only allowed to bring back double the value of the cargo she conveyed; but, as the profits were often enormous, every species of fraud was practised to give fictitious values to the articles imported—in fact, from the beginning to the end of the undertaking there seems to have been a rivalry in roguery among all parties concerned.

The establishment of the Company of the Philippines, in 1785, gave to monopoly another shape, but led to some development of colonial industry.

It is scarcely needful to follow the history of the commerce of the Philippines through the many changes which have produced its present comparative prosperity—a prosperity to be measured by the amount of emancipation which has been introduced. Had the Spanish authorities the courage to utter the magic words "Laissez faire, laissez passer!" what a cornucopia of blessings would be poured upon the archipelago!

But it could hardly be expected from a government constituted like the government of Spain, that, either of its own spontaneous movement, or by licence delegated to the Captain-General, so grand a work would be accomplished as the establishment of free production, free commerce, free settlement, and free education in the Philippines; and yet a step so bold and noble would, as I fully believe, in a few years be followed by progress and prosperity far beyond any calculations that have been ventured on. The little that has been hazarded for the liberty of trade, though hurriedly and imperfectly done, cannot but encourage future efforts; and in the meantime many beneficial reforms have been pressed upon the attention of the government with such conclusive statistics and irresistible logic, that, if it depended on these alone, the Philippines might hope to enter upon the early enjoyment of their heritage of future advancement. The reform of the tariffs— the removal of petty vexatious fiscal interferences—improvements in the navigation of the rivers—the cleansing the harbours—lighthouse, buoys and other appliances for the security of shipping—are among the more obvious and immediate claims of commerce. In Manila the absence of docks for repairing and harbouring vessels is much felt; the custom-house is on the wrong side of the river—though it were better it should exist on neither side; there are no means of regular postal communication with the islands from the Peninsula; tug-steamers, life-boats, quays and piers, seamen's houses, marine hospitals, are wanting, but their introduction has been so strongly advocated that its advent may be hoped for. In truth, it is pleasant to find in a country so remote and so long under the most discouraging and retarding influences, that inquiry, which is the pioneer and the handmaid of all improvement, is already busily at work and will not be at work in vain.

A communication was made to the Chamber of Commerce by the Governor-General in 1858, requesting that the merchants would point out to him the best possible means for developing the riches of the Philippine Islands by extending their foreign trade. The British merchants, after expressing a general wish that the islands should enjoy the benefits of that system of free trade and liberal commercial policy whose "great results" are manifest to all, point out the special grievances which demand immediate reform.

1. The present system of requiring *permits* for every cargo boat employed, leads to many needless charges, vexations and delays.

2. Reform of the tariffs which press very heavily on certain articles, for the protection of some small manufacturing interest in the island. This is specially the case with cotton goods intended for common use; those of the colours given by dyes produced in the island are selected for the heaviest impost, to give encouragement to native dyers. Many articles are estimated much beyond their real value, so that the percentage duty becomes excessive. Lawns, for instance, are tariffed at double their market price. Iron chains worth five dollars per cwt. are tariffed at twelve dollars. A small quantity of white, black, blue, purple and rose-coloured cotton twist being produced, there is a duty of from 40 to 50 per cent., while red, yellow, green, &c., which the natives cannot dye, are admitted duty free. These are striking exemplifications of the workings of a protective system.

Other blue goods are prohibited because the islands produce indigo; and for the protection of the native shoemakers (who, by the way, are almost invariably Chinese and mere birds of passage in the country), foreign boots and shoes pay from 40 to 50 per cent., to the great detriment of the public health, for the country-tanned leather will not keep out the rain and the mud, while the protective duty encourages the Chinese settler to become a manufacturer, who is less wanted than the agricultural labourer. In the same spirit the tailors are protected, *i.e.* allowed to overcharge the consumer to the extent of 40 to 50 per cent., the duty on imported clothes, which goes principally to the Chinese. Foreign fruits, preserves and liquors have to bear similar burdens, for cannot the Philippines give confectionary and sweets enough of their own? So runs the round of folly and miscalculation. One hundred dozen of Spanish beer entered the Philippines in 1857, and to protect and encourage so important an interest an excessive impost was levied on 350 pipes and nearly 100,000 bottles of beer *not* Spanish.

3. Then, again, the heavy differential duties in favour of Spanish ships are a well-grounded subject of discontent and highly prejudicial to the general interest. The levying tonnage duties upon ships entering and departing without cargoes is a grievance of which there are just complaints. The adjacency of so many free ports—Hong Kong, Macao and Singapore—and the more liberal system of the Australian and Polynesian regions, place the Philippine trade in a disadvantageous position. Among the documents which I collected is one from a native merchant, in which he says:—"The

demonstrations of political economists, and the practical results of free-trade legislation, establish the fact that public credit and public prosperity are alike benefited by the emancipation of commerce, and narrow is the view which, looking only to the temporary defalcation of revenue from the diminution of imports, forgets the enormous increase of all the sources of revenue from lowering prices and extending demand." In this way the great truths which have been silently and successfully revolutionizing our commercial legislation are spread on all the wings of all the winds, and will finally encircle the world in the great bonds of brotherhood, with peace and prosperity for attendants.

By a decree of the 18th June, 1857, the restrictions on the trade in rice and paddy were removed, and foreign grain was allowed to enter duty free, not, only into the ports opened to foreign trade, but into divers subordinate ports. Though the permission was then temporary, it has now become permanent, and I found that the emancipation of these important articles from all custom-house interference had been attended with the best results, by regulating and assimilating prices, without any detriment to native production. The more general the principles of free trade the more security will there be against dearth and famine on the one side, and superfluity and glut on the other.

Rice is sold by the cavan. Its price is ordinarily double that of paddy. The average fluctuations are from one to two dollars.

In 1810 the import trade of the Philippines amounted to only 5,329,000 dollars, of which more than half consisted of precious metals, sent from the Spanish colonies of America. From Europe and the United States the trade was only 175,000 dollars. The exports were 4,795,000 dollars, of which one-and-a-half million consisted of silver to China, and the whole amount of exports to Europe and the United States was 250,000 dollars. The great start took place in 1834, when the monopoly of the Philippine Company terminated, and commerce may be regarded as progressive from that time. Of the trade with the surrounding islands, that with Jolo, conducted principally by Chinese, is important. One of the leading articles of export is the edible bird's-nests, of whose collection a Spanish writer gives the following account: —"The nests are collected twice a year; those most valued from deep and humid caverns. Early training is needful to scale the localities where the nests are found, and the task is always dangerous. To reach the caves it is necessary to descend perpendicularly many hundred feet, supported by a rope made of bamboo or junk, suspended over the sea waves as they dash against the rocks." There is also from Jolo a considerable exportation of tortoise-shell. *Trepang* (sea-slug, *Holothuria*) and shark-fins are sent to the Chinese markets; also mother-of-pearl, wax and gold dust. The voyage from Manila to Jolo and return generally occupies seven to eight months. A trade in most respects resembling that of Jolo is carried on between Manila and the Moluccas. Spices are, however, added to the imports. There is a large trade between Singapore and Manila, and with Amoy, in China, the transactions are very important. Vessels are generally loading from and to that port. Rice, paddy, cocoa-nut oil, sugar, fine woods, table delicacies and a variety of minor articles, are exported; silks, nankins, tea, vermilion, umbrellas, earthenware and a thousand smaller matters, make up the returns.

Internal trade suffers much from the many impediments to communication and the various shiftings to which merchandise is exposed. It is said that in the transit from the north of Luzon to the capital there are as many as a hundred floating rafts upon which the goods must be carried across the different streams; at each considerable delay is experienced, as the raft (*balsa*) is seldom found when and where it is wanted. And during half the year inland conveyance is the only means of transport, as the monsoons make the sea voyage impossible for coasting vessels. Indeed, in the remoter islands months frequently pass without arrivals from the capital. Some of the fairs in the interior are largely attended by the Mahomedan and heathen natives, who will not visit the ports or larger towns. That of Yligan (Misamis, in Mindanao) is much visited by Moros, who bring thither for sale paddy, cocoa, coffee, gold dust, cotton fabrics, krises and weapons of war, with many other native articles, which they exchange mostly for European and Chinese wares. Panaguis, in Luzon, is another market much frequented by the Igorrote Indians. Many of the ancient river communications have been stopped by inundations, which have given a new direction to the stream, and by the invasion of snags, trees and rocks from the upper regions. There is a great deal of ambulatory petty trade in the interior; the Chinese especially are active pedlars and factors, and make their way to buy and to sell wherever there is a profit to be gained. They are to a great extent the pioneers of commerce, and in this way valuable auxiliaries and co-operators by opening new fields to be hereafter more extensively explored.

There are in Manila seven English, three American, two French, two Swiss and one German, commercial establishments. In the new ports there is no European house of business except at Iloilo, where there is an English firm, of which the British vice-consul is the directing partner.

Among the curiosities of commercial legislation is a decree of the governor of the Philippines, dated only a few years ago, by which it was ordered that no vessel should be allowed to introduce a cargo from China or the East Indies unless an engagement was entered into by the captain to bring to Manila *five hundred* living shrikes (*mimas?*), as the bird was reported to be most useful in destroying the insects which were at that time seriously damaging the harvests. I believe not a single bird was ever brought. It would have been about as easy and as reasonable to require them to import some slices of the moon, for the catching, and the caging, and the keeping, are scarcely within mortal capabilities, and 500 birds were the required *minimum* by every ship; nor was it the least remarkable part of the decree or requirement that they were all to be delivered gratis.

For the protection of the revenue there is an armed body called the *Carabineros de Real Hacienda*. It is composed of natives under European officers, and is charged with both land and sea service. They wear a military uniform and a broad hat resembling a large punch-bowl, which is, however, an admirable protection from the sun's rays.

Great Britain has a salaried consul and vice-consul in Manila and vice-consuls in Iloilo and Sual. France has also a salaried consul in the capital. The United States, Portugal, Belgium, Sweden and Chili, are represented by members of commercial establishments, who exercise consular authority in Manila. The American consul is Mr. Charles Griswold, and few are the visitors to these islands who have not enjoyed his hospitality and benefited by his experience.

The post-office establishments are imperfect and unsatisfactory and the charges for the conveyance of letters heavy. There is a weekly postal communication from the capital with the provinces in the island of Luzon, and southwards as far as Samar and Leyte, but all the other eastern and southern islands are left to the chances which the coasting trade offers and are frequently many months without receiving any news from the capital or the mother country. A regular service, providing for the wants of these important districts, Panay especially, with its population exceeding half a million, is greatly to be desired.

There is now a fortnightly service carried on by the steamers of the Peninsular and Oriental Company between Manila and Hong Kong, generally reaching forty-eight hours before the departure, and quitting forty-eight hours after the arrival, of the steamers from Europe. It is conducted with great regularity and the letters from Spain arrive in about fifty days; but many days would be saved were there a branch steamer from Malta to Alicant. For this service an annual sum (recoverable monthly) of 120,000 dollars is paid by the Manila government to the company. The steamers are freed from all port charges except pilotage.

The government has published proposals for the establishment of a steam-packet company for the service of the islands, offering 45,000 dollars annually as a State contribution, but I believe there is no immediate prospect of the adoption of the scheme.

The Banco Español de Isabel II. is a joint-stock company, whose capital is 400,000 dollars, in 1,000 shares of 400 dollars each. It was established in the year 1855, and has generally paid to the shareholders dividends at the rate of six to eight per cent. per annum. It issues promissory notes, discounts local bills of exchange and lends money on mortgage. The general rate of interest in the Philippines fluctuates from six to nine per cent. The yearly operations of the bank exceed 2,000,000 of dollars. The value of about half-a-million of bills of exchange is usually under discount. Its ordinary circulation does not exceed 200,000 dollars in promissory notes and it has deposits and balances to the value of about 1,750,000 dollars. The bank has afforded considerable facilities to commerce, and has answered one of its principal objects, that of bringing into circulation some of the hoarded money of the natives. Most of the foreign houses are shareholders.

The decimal system of accounts and currency was introduced into the Philippines by a royal decree, and an end put to all the complications of maravedis, quartos, and reales de ocho, by the simple adoption of the dollar, divided into one hundred cents. It would be, indeed, a wretched compliment to the population of England (let me say it in passing) if, as certain opponents of improvement have averred, they would never be brought to appreciate or comprehend a change to decimal denominations which the "untutored mind" of the "wild Indian" has already begun to adopt, using his digits as the instruments of the new philosophy, and aided now and then probably by the simple abacus of the Chinese shopkeeper, with whom he has much to do.

The weights and measures used in the Philippines are—

The Arroba	(25	lbs. Spanish)	=	25·36	English lbs.
The Quintal	(100	)	=	101·44	
		,,			,, ,,
The Catty			=	1·395	
					,, ,,
The Pecul of 137 catties (36 lbs. Spanish)			=	139·48	
					,, ,,
Cavan			=	25	gautas.
Gauta			=	8	chupas.

Pie		12	Spanish inches.

$$\text{Pie} = \begin{cases} 12 & \text{Spanish inches.} \\ \underline{11} & \text{English inches.} \end{cases}$$

$$\text{Vara} = \begin{cases} 3 & \text{pies.} \\ \underline{33} & \text{English inches.} \end{cases}$$

Cavan of rice (clean) weighs	132 lbs.	avoirdupois.
,, paddy ,, ,,	103½	,,
Jar of oil	96	,,

The following return gives the exports from Manila for the year 1858:—

EXPORTS FROM MANILA FOR 1858.

		United States, Atlantic.	California.	Continent of Europe.	Great Britain.
Hemp	Peculs.	289,953	10,140	6,650	105,633
Sugar		16,030	45,038	17,252	315,768
Sapan Wood	,,	10,594		2,491	21,295
Indigo	,, Qtls.	503		171	58
Leaf Tobacco				82,120	
Cigars	,, M.	4,613	3,416	209	8,244
Coffee	Peculs.	2,389	236	13,882	81
Cordage				2,751	
Hides	,,	999		113	3,619
Hide Cuttings	,,	2,929			62
Mother-of-Pearl Shell	,,			1,205	1,351

Tortoise-Shell	Catties.					260	1,931
Grass Cloth	Pieces.	57,224				547	
Gum Almasiga	Peculs.					2,113	3,571
Cowries	"						2,773
Rice	Cavans.						
Paddy	"						
Beche de Mer	Peculs.						
Liquid Indigo	Jars.						
Buffalo Horns	Peculs.					11	387
Birds' Nests	"						
Arrowroot	"			170		15	368
Gold Dust	Taels.						
Canes	M.					11	610
Cow Bones	Peculs.						
Hats	M.						408
Molave Logs	"					58	

EXPORTS FROM MANILA FOR 1858. (*Continued.*)

	Australia.	Batavia.	Singapore, and British Islands.	South America, Cape of Good Hope and Pacific Islands.	China.	Total.
Hemp		1,100		28	412,504	
Sugar	147,369		170	15,506	557,133	
Sapan Wood		1,200	4,607	27,031	67,218	
Indigo					732	
Leaf Tobacco					82,120	

Item						
Cigars	18,504	12,552	24,489	115	13,000	85,142
Coffee	6,764	55			1,556	24,963
Cordage	10,150	999	3,293		4,606	21,799
Hides					1,694	6,425
Hide Cuttings					884	3,875
Mother-of-Pearl Shell					36	2,592
Tortoise-Shell					314	2,505
Grass Cloth			350			58,121
Gum Almasiga	14		1,674			7,372
Cowries			165			2,938
Rice					21,361	21,361
Paddy					1,300	1,300
Beche de Mer					3,889	3,889
Liquid Indigo					4,805	4,805
Buffalo Horns						398
Birds' Nests					66	66
Arrowroot	263					816
Gold Dust					1,721	1,721
Canes						620
Cow Bones					906	906
Hats			120		1,372	1,900
Molave Logs					1,203	1,259

In the year 1855, Don Sinibaldo de Mas, having been charged with an official mission of inquiry into the state of these islands, published an article on the revenues of the Philippines, addressed to the finance minister of Spain.[1]

He begins his report by contrasting the population and commerce of Cuba with that of the Philippines; stating that Cuba, with less than a million of inhabitants, has a trade of 27,500,000 dollars, while the Philippines, which he says contained, in 1850, 4,000,000 of people in a state of subjection and 1,000,000 unsubdued, had a trade of less than 5,000,000 of dollars. He calculates the coloured population of Cuba at 500,000; the white population of the Philippines at from 7,000 to 8,000 persons. He deduces that, if the produce of the Philippines were proportioned to that of Cuba, it would be of the value of 250,000,000 dollars, and that the revenue should be 48,000,000 dollars, instead of about 9,500,000 dollars.

He avers that the soil is equal in its productive powers to any in the world; that the quality of the produce—sugar, coffee, tobacco, indigo, cocoa and cotton—is most excellent; that it possesses almost a monopoly of abacá (Manila hemp); and he goes on to consider the means of turning these natural advantages to the best account.

He altogether repudiates any extension of the existing system, or augmentation of taxation in its present forms; and states, what is most true, that to the development of agriculture, industry and commerce the Philippines must look for increased prosperity.

His three proposals are:—

1. Opening new ports to foreign trade.

2. Emancipating the production, manufacture and sale of tobacco.

3. Increasing the population of the islands.

By a royal decree, dated 31st March, 1855, three additional ports were opened to foreign trade—Zamboanga (Mindanao), Iloilo (Panay), and Sual (Luzon). The results have not responded to anticipations. One reason is obvious— custom-house officers, custom-house restrictions, custom-house vexations accompanied the seemingly liberal legislation. These are sufficient to check, if not to crush, the growth of intercourse. I doubt if in either of the new ports the custom-house receipts cover the costs of collection. The experiment should have been a free-trade experiment, but the jealousies and fears of the capital were probably influential. It ought not to have been forgotten that the new ports, charged with all the burdens which pressed upon Manila, offered none of its facilities, the creation of many generations—wharves and warehouses, accomplished merchants, capital, foreign settlers, assured consumption of imports and supply of exports; these counterbalanced the cost of conveyance of goods to or from the capital, while, on the other hand, the introduction of a custom-house has prejudiced the trade which previously existed—as, for example, the call of whalers at Zamboanga, unwilling to submit to the fiscal exactions now introduced. But if every port in the Philippines were made free from custom-houses a great impulse would be given to industry, commerce and shipping; the loss to the treasury would be inconsiderable, for the net proceeds of the customs duties is very insignificant, while other sources of revenue would be undoubtedly increased by the impulse given to the general prosperity. De Mas states that the extension of the trade of Cuba from the Havana to other ports led to an augmentation in its value from 2,000,000 to 30,000,000 dollars.

Two plans are suggested by Señor De Mas for the emancipation of the tobacco cultivation and manufacture from the existing State monopoly. One, the levying a heavy land tax on all lands devoted to the produce; the other, the imposition of a duty on exportation. He estimates that a *baleta* of land (1,000 brazas square) gives 1,500 plants, and 4 to 5 cwt. of tobacco, saleable at 4 to 5 dollars per quintal. The cost of manufacturing 14,000 cigars, which represent 1 cwt., 5¼ dollars, and boxes for packing, 3½ dollars. He says the value of the cigars is 6½ dollars per box (it is now considerably more), in which case the profit would be 77¼ dollars, and proposes a duty of 70 dollars per cwt., which is more than five times the cost of the article. He gives satisfactory reasons for the conclusion that cigars would be made much more economically by the peasantry than by the government, shows that the cost of the machinery of administration might be greatly diminished, asserts that the Indians employed at home would be satisfied with lower gains than the wages paid by the government, and supposes that the unoccupied houses of the natives would be dedicated to the making of cigars as a pleasant and profitable domestic employment. It may be doubted whether he estimates at its full value the resistance which the indolent habits of the Indian oppose to voluntary or spontaneous labour; but the conclusion I have reached by not exactly the same train of reasoning is the same as that arrived at by my friend whom I have been quoting, namely, that the government monopoly is less productive than free cultivation, manufacture and sale might become; that a reduction of prices would extend demand, leave larger benefits to the treasury and confer many advantages upon the people; and that the arguments (mostly of those interested in the monopoly) in favour of the existing system are not grounded on sound reasoning, nor supported by statistical facts.

The tobacco monopoly (*estanco*) was established in 1780 by Governor-General Basco; it was strongly opposed by the friars, and menaces of severe punishments were held over those who sought to escape the obligations imposed. But to the present hour there are said to be large plantations of tobacco which escape the vigilance of government, and cigars are purchaseable in many of the islands at one-fourth of the government price. The personal establishment for the protection of the tobacco monopoly consists of nearly a thousand officials and more than thirty revenue boats. It is, notwithstanding, cultivated largely in provinces where the cultivation is prohibited by law; and I find in a report from the Alcalde of Misamis (Mindanao) the following phrase: "The idea of interfering with the growth of tobacco for the benefit of the treasury must be abandoned, as the territory where it is produced is not subject to Spanish authority."

Attempts were made a few years ago to encourage the planting of tobacco in the province of Iloilo, by a company which made advances to the Indians; but the enterprise, discouraged by the government, failed, and I found, when I visited the locality, the warehouses abandoned and the company dissolved. There have been many expeditions for the destruction and confiscation of illicit tobacco; and on more than one occasion insurrections, tumults, serious loss of life and very doubtful results have followed these interferences. The statistical returns show that the consumption of the State tobacco varies considerably in the different provinces, being influenced by the greater or less difficulty of obtaining the contraband article.

There have been divers projects for augmenting the population of the Philippines—from China, from Switzerland, from Borneo and even from British India. The friars have never looked with complacency on any of these schemes. They all present elements which would not easily he subjected to ecclesiastical influence. The Chinese would not be willing cultivators of the soil if any other pursuit should promise greater profits, and it is quite certain that the indolent Indian will nowhere be able to compete with the industrious, persevering and economical Chinese. Many suggestions have been made for the introduction of Chinese women, with a view of attaching Chinese families to the soil; but hitherto nothing has sufficed to conquer the abhorrence with which a Chinese female contemplates the abandonment of her country, nor the general resistance to such abandonment on the part of the Chinese clans. Chinese female children have been frequently kidnapped for conveyance to the Philippines, and some horrible circumstances have come to the knowledge of British authorities in China, followed by the exposure and punishment of British subjects concerned in these cruel and barbarous deeds. An establishment of a sisterhood in China, called that of the *Sainte Enfance*, has been looked to as a means of christianizing female children, and conveying them to the Philippines; they have collected or purchased many orphans, but small success has attended these well-meant, but not well-directed labours. In 1855, it was stated in an official document (De Mas, p. 26) that in 1858, an annual entry of 2,500 children might be expected. The calculation has been a total mistake; the establishments in China are in a state of embarrassment and difficulty, and I am not aware that a single Chinese female has been supplied for the suggested purpose. Any number of orphans or abandoned children might be bought in the great cities of China, especially from the orphan asylums; but an increased demand would only encourage their abandonment by their mothers. These foundling hospitals are of very doubtful utility, and produce, probably, more misery than they cure.

The greatest impediment to the progress of the Philippines, and the development of their immense resources, is attributable to the miserable traditional policy of the mother country, whose jealousies tie the hands of the governors they appoint to rule; so that the knowledge and experience which are acquired in the locality are wholly subjected to the ignorance and shortsightedness of the distant, but supreme authority. Would the Spaniard but recognize the wisdom of one of their many instructive proverbs—*Mas sabe el loco en su casa que cuerdo en la agena* (the fool knows more about his own home than the wise man of the home of another)—more confidence might be reposed in those who are thoroughly cognizant of local circumstances and local wants. As it is, everything has to be referred to Madrid. A long delay is inevitable—an erroneous decision probable; circumstances are constantly changing, and what would have been judicious to-day may be wholly unadvisable to-morrow. Then there is the greatest unwillingness to surrender even the shadow of authority, or any of those sources of patronage which a government so enervate and corrupt as that of Spain clings to as its props and protection. Again, the uncertainty of tenure of office, which attaches to all the superior offices held under the Spanish Government, is alike calculated to demoralize and discourage. Before a governor has surveyed his territory and marked out to himself a course of action, he may be superseded under one of those multitudinous changes which grow out of the caprices of the court or the clamour of the people. It was a melancholy employment of mine to look round the collection of the various portraits of the captains-general which adorned my apartment, bearing the dates of their appointment and their supersession. Some of them only occupied their office for a few months, and were as carelessly and recklessly dismissed as a worthless weed is flung away. And there seemed no expectation of any change in this respect, for there were many blank frames made to receive the *vera effigies* of future excellencies. Our colonial system is wiser, as we appoint governors for six years, and, except under special circumstances, they are not dispossessed of their government. Whether there may be any moral deterioration connected with the possession of power, sufficient to counterbalance all the benefits which are furnished by long experience and local knowledge, may be a question for philosophy and statesmanship.

But other causes of backwardness are traceable to those very elements of wealth and prosperity, to which these islands must look for their future progress. A soil so feracious, a sun so bright, rains so bountiful, require so little co-operation from the aid of man that he becomes careless, indolent, unconcerned for the morrow. He has but to stretch out his hand, and food drops into it. The fibre of the aloe, which the female weaves with the simplest of looms, gives her garments; the uprights and the floors and the substantial parts of his dwelling are made of the bamboo, which he finds in superfluous abundance; while the nipa palm provides roofs and sides to his hut. Wants he has few and he cares little for luxuries. His enjoyments are in religious processions, in music and dancing, in his *gallo* above all. He may take possession without rent of any quantity of land which he is willing to cultivate. There is a tendency, no doubt, to improvement. Cultivation extends and good examples are not without effect.

In times of tranquillity Spain has nothing to fear for her Philippine colonies. So long as they are unmolested by foreign invaders and the government is carried on with mildness and prudence, there is little to be apprehended from any internal agitation; but I doubt the efficiency of any means of defence at the disposal of the authorities, should a day of trouble come. The Indian regular forces might for some time be depended on; but whether this could be anticipated of the *militia* or any of the urban auxiliaries is uncertain. The number of Spaniards is small—in most of the islands quite insignificant; indolence and indifference characterize the indigenous races; and if, on the one hand, they took no part in favour of intrusive strangers, on the other, they could not be looked to for any patriotic or energetic exertions on behalf of their Spanish rulers. They have, indeed, no traditions of former independence —no descendants of famous ancient chiefs or princes, to whom they look with affection, hope or reverence. There are no fragments left of hierarchies overthrown. No Montezumas, no Colocolos, are named in their songs, or perpetuated in their memories. There are no ruins of great cities or temples; in a word, no records of the remote past. There is a certain amount of dissatisfaction among the Indians, but it is more strongly felt against the native gobernadorcillos—the heads of barangay—the privileged members of the local principalia—when exercising their "petty tyrannies," than against the higher authorities, who are beyond the hearing of their complaints. "The governor-general is in Manila (far away); the king is in Spain (farther still); and God is in heaven (farthest of all)." It is a natural complaint that the tribute or capitation tax presses equally on all classes of Indians, rich or poor. The heads of barangay, who are charged with its collection, not unfrequently dissipate the money in gambling. One abuse has, however, been reformed—the tribute in many provinces was formerly collected in produce, and great were the consequent exactions practised upon the natives, from which the treasury obtained no profit, but the petty functionaries much. I believe the tax is now almost universally levied in money. All Spaniards, all foreigners (excepting Chinese), and their descendants are exempted from tribute. One of the most intelligent of the merchants of Manila (Don Juan Bautista Marcaida) has had the kindness to furnish me with sundry memoranda on the subject of the capabilities of the Philippine Islands, and the means of developing them. To his observations, the result of careful observation, much experience and extensive reading, I attach great value. They are imbued with some of the national prejudices of a Spanish Catholic, in whose mind the constitution of the Romish Church is associated with every form of authority, and who is unwilling to see in that very constitution, and its necessary agencies, invincible impediments to the fullest progress of intellect—to the widest extension of agricultural, manufacturing and commercial prosperity—in a word, to that great agitation of the popular mind, to which Protestant nations owe their religious reforms, and their undoubted superiority in the vast field of speculation and adventure.

He says:—"The social organization of the Philippines is the most paternal and civilizing of any known in the world; having for its basis the doctrines of the Gospel, and the kind and fatherly spirit of the Laws of the Indies." It may be admitted, in reference to the legislation of the colonies of many nations, that the Spanish code is comparatively humane and that the influence of the Romish clergy has been frequently and successfully excited for the protection and benefit of conquered natives, and of imported slaves; but M. Marcaida goes on to acknowledge and point out "the torpid and unimproving character of the existing system," and to demand important changes for the advancement of the public weal.

"The government moves slowly, from its complicated organization, and from the want of adequate powers to give effect to those reforms which are suggested by local knowledge, but which are overruled by the unteachable ignorance, or selfish interests, or political intrigues of the mother country."

As regards the clergy, he thinks the administration generally good, but that the progress of time and altered circumstances necessitate many important changes in the distribution of the ecclesiastical authority, a new arrangement of the pueblos, a better education of the church functionaries, a great augmentation of the number of parochial priests (many of whom have now cures varying from 3,000 to 60,000 souls). He would have the parish clergyman both the religious and secular instructor of his community, and for this purpose requires that he should be becomingly and highly educated—a consummation for which the government would have some difficulty in providing the machinery, and for which assuredly the Church would not lend its co-operation.

"For the administration of justice, the Philippines have one supreme and forty-two subordinate tribunals. The number is wholly insufficient for the necessities of 5,000,000 of inhabitants scattered over 1,200 islands, and occupying so vast a territorial space." There can be no doubt that justice is often inaccessible, that it is costly, that it is delayed, defeated, and associated with many vexations. Spain has never been celebrated for the integrity of its judges, or the purity of its courts. A *pleyto* in the Peninsula is held to be as great a curse as a suit in Chancery in England, with the added evil of want of confidence in the administrators of the law. Their character would hardly be improved at a distance of 10,000 miles from the Peninsula; and if Spain has some difficulty in supplying herself at home with incorruptible functionaries, that difficulty would be augmented in her remotest possessions. There seemed to me much admirable machinery in the traditional and still existing usages and institutions of the natives. Much might, no doubt, be done to lessen the dilatory, costly and troublesome character of lawsuits, by introducing more of natural and less of technical proceedings; by facilitating the production and examination of evidence; by the suppression of the masses of *papel sellado* (documents upon stamped paper); by diminishing the cost and simplifying the process of appeal; and, above all, by the introduction of a code applicable to the ordinary circumstances of social life.

He thinks the attempts to conglomerate the population in towns and cities injurious to the agricultural interests of the country; but assuredly this agglomeration is friendly to civilization, good government and the production of wealth, and more likely than the dispersion of the inhabitants to provide for the introduction of those larger farms to which the Philippines must look for any very considerable augmentation of the produce of the land.

"The natural riches of the country are incalculable. There are immense tracts of the most feracious soil; brooks, streams, rivers, lakes, on all sides; mountains of minerals, metals, marbles in vast variety; forests whose woods are adapted to all the ordinary purposes of life; gums, roots, medicinals, dyes, fruits in great variety. In many of the islands the cost of a sufficiency of food for a family of five is only a cuarto, a little more than a farthing, a day. Some

of the edible roots grow to an enormous size, weighing from 50 to 70 lbs.:—
gutta-percha, caoutchouc, gum-lac, gamboge, and many other gums abound.
Of fibres the number is boundless; in fact, the known and the unknown wealth
of the islands only requires fit aptitudes for its enormous development.

"With a few legislative reforms," he concludes, "with improved instruction of
the clergy, the islands would become a paradise of inexhaustible riches, and of
a well-being approachable in no other portion of the globe. The docility and
intelligence of the natives, their imitative virtues (wanting though they be in
forethought), make them incomparably superior to any Asiatic or African race
subjected to European authority. Where deep thought and calculation are
required, they will fail; but their natural dispositions and tendencies, and the
present state of civilization among them, give every hope and encouragement
for the future."[2]

---

[1]

Articulo sobre las Rentas de Filipinas y los medios de aumentarlas, por D. Sinibaldo de Mas
(afterwards Minister Plenipotentiary of Spain in China). Madrid, 1853.

[2]

M. Marcaida considers the best historical and descriptive authorities to be the Fathers Blanco, Santa
Maria, Zuñiga, Concepcion, and Buzeta. He speaks highly of Don Sinibaldo de Mas' *Apuntes*, of which
I have largely availed myself.

HAPTER XXI.

FINANCE, TAXATION, ETC.

The gross revenues of the Philippines are about 10,000,000 dollars. The budget for 1859 is as follows:—

RECEIPTS.	Dollars.	EXPENDITURE.	Dollars.
Contributions and taxes	1,928,607·92	Grace and Justice	679,519·11
Custom-houses	600,000·00	War	2,216,669·44
Monopolies	7,199,950·59	Finance (*Hacienda*)	5,367,829·83
Lotteries	253,500·00	Marine	904,331·27
State property	12,118·59	Government	272,528·62
Uncertain receipts	21,826·00	Remitted to and paid for Spain	1,011,850·00

Marine	1,338·00		
Total	10,017,341·10	Total	10,452,728·27

Thus about one-tenth of the gross revenue is received by the mother country in the following shapes:—Salaries of Spanish consuls in the East, 22,500 dollars; remittances to Spain and bills drawn by Spain, 680,600 dollars; tobacco and freights, 168,750 dollars; credits to French government for advances to the imperial navy, 140,000 dollars.

Of the direct taxes, 68,026·77 dollars are paid as tribute by the unconverted natives, 114,604·50 dollars by the mestizos (half-races), 136,208·78 dollars by the Chinese, and 1,609,757·87 dollars by the Indians (or tribes professing Christianity).

The produce of the customs is so small, and the expenses of collection so great—the cost of the coast and inland preventive service alone being 265,271·99 dollars; general and provincial administrations, between 70,000 and 80,000 dollars—that I am persuaded it would be a sound, wise and profitable policy to abandon this source of taxation altogether, and to declare all the ports of the Philippines *free*.

I have also come to the conclusion that the monopolies, which give a gross revenue to the treasury of more than 7,000,000 dollars, are, independently of their vicious and retardatory action upon the public weal, far less productive than taxation upon the same articles might be made by their emancipation from the bonds of monopoly. I leave here out of sight the enormous amount of fraud and crime, and the pernicious effects upon the public morals of a universal toleration of smuggling, as well as the consideration of all the vexations, delays, checks upon improvement, corruption of officials and the thousand inconveniences of fiscal interference at every stage and step; and only look at the acknowledged cost of the machinery—it amounts to about 5,000,000 dollars—so that the net produce to the State scarcely exceeds 2,000,000 dollars.

The whole receipt from the tobacco monopoly is 5,097,795 dollars. The expenses for which this department is debited are (independently of the proportion of the general charges of administration)—

	Dollars.	*Cents.*
PERSONAL—		
Collection of Tobaccos	24,604	0
Manufacture of Cigars	44,366	0
MATERIEL—		

Collection of Tobacco	66,741	75
Manufactures of Cigars	6,888	0
Purchase of Tobacco	1,412,503	30
Paper and other charges	62,865	3
Cost of sorting Tobacco	13,200	29
Cost of manufacturing	1,171,262	73
Charges for conveyance	259,321	76
Boxes, packing, warehousing, &c.	150,000	0
	3,211,752	86

So that the net rendering of this most valuable production is only 1,886,042·14 dollars, or 37 per cent. upon the gross amount, 63 per cent. being expended on the production of the tobacco and manufacture of the cigars. I am of opinion that from 4,000,000 to 5,000,000 dollars might be realized with immense benefit to the public by a tax upon cultivation, or the imposition of a simple export duty, or by a union of both. Production would thus be largely extended, prices moderated to the consumer and the net revenue probably more than doubled.

From the produce of the lottery, 253,500 dollars, there have to be deducted— expenses of administration, 4,472 dollars; prizes paid, 195,000 dollars; prizes not claimed, 1,000 dollars; commission on sales of tickets, 4,680 dollars;

making in all, 205,152 dollars; so that this fertile source of misery, disappointment, and frequently of crime, does not produce a net income of 50,000 dollars to the State. It may well be doubted if such a source of revenue should be maintained. The revenue derived from cock-fights, 86,326·25 dollars, is to some extent subject to the same condemnation, as gambling is the foundation of both, but in the case of the *galleras* the produce is paid without deduction into the treasury.

In the Bisayas palm wine has been lately made the object of a State monopoly which produces 324,362 dollars, but is very vexatious in its operation and much complained of by the Indians. The tax on spirituous liquors gives 1,465,638 dollars. The opium monopoly brings 44,333·34 dollars; that of gunpowder, 21,406 dollars. Of smaller sources of income the most remarkable are—Papal bulls, giving 58,000 dollars; stamps, 39,600 dollars; fines, 30,550 dollars; post-office stamps, 19,490 dollars; fishery in Manila harbour, 6,500 dollars.

It is remarkable that there are no receipts from the sale or rental of lands. Public works, roads and bridges are in charge of the locality, while of the whole gross revenue more than seven-tenths are the produce of monopolies.

Of the government expenditure, under the head of Grace and Justice, the clergy receive 488,329·28 dollars, and for pious works 39,801·83; Jesuit missions to Mindanao, 25,000. The cost of the Audiencia is 65,556; of the alcaldes and gobernadores, 53,332 dollars.

In the war department the cost of the staff is 154,148·80 dollars; of the infantry, 857,031·17 dollars; cavalry, 52,901·73 dollars; artillery, 192,408·71 dollars; engineers, 32,173 dollars; rations, 140,644·31 dollars; *matériel*, 149,727·10 dollars; transport, 112,000 dollars; special services, 216,673·89 dollars. In the finance expenses the sum of 310,615·75 dollars appears as pensions.

The *personnel* of the marine department is 235,671·82 dollars; cost of building, repairing, &c., 266,813·17 dollars; salaries, &c., are 155,294·98 dollars; rations, 190,740·84 dollars.

The governor-general receives, including the secretariat, 31,056 dollars; expenses, 2,500 dollars. The heaviest charge in the section of civil services is 120,000 dollars for the mail steamers between Hong Kong and Manila, and 35,000 dollars for the service between Spain and Hong Kong. There is an additional charge for the post-office of 6,852 dollars. The only receipt reported on this account is for post-office stamps, 19,490 dollars.

I have made no reference to the minor details of the incomings and outgoings of Philippine finance. The mother country has little cause to complain, receiving as she does a net revenue of about 5s. per head from the Indian population. In fact, about half of the whole amount of direct taxation goes to Spain, independently of what Spanish subjects receive who are employed in the public service. The Philippines happily have no debt, and, considering that the Indian pays nothing for his lands, it cannot be said that he is heavily taxed. But that the revenues are susceptible of immense development—that production, agricultural and manufactured, is in a backward and unsatisfactory state—that trade and shipping might be enormously increased —and that great changes might be most beneficially introduced into many branches of administration, must be obvious to the political economist and the shrewd observer. The best evidence I can give of a grateful remembrance of the kindnesses I received will be the frank expression of opinions friendly to the progress and prosperity of these fertile and improveable regions. Meliorations many and great have already made their way; it suffices to look back upon the state of the Philippines, "cramped, cabined and confined" as they were, and to compare them with their present half-emancipated condition. No doubt Spain has much to learn at home before she can be expected to communicate commercial and political wisdom to her dependencies abroad. But she may be animated by the experience she has had, and at last discover that intercourse with opulent nations tends not to impoverish, but to enrich those who encourage and extend that intercourse.

CHAPTER XXII.

TAXES.

Down to the year 1784 so unproductive were the Philippines to the Spanish revenues, that the treasury deficit was supplied by an annual grant of 250,000 dollars provided by the Mexican government. A capitation tax was irregularly collected from the natives; also a custom-house duty (*almojarifango*) on the small trade which existed, and an excise (*alcabala*) on interior sales. Even to the beginning of the present century the Spanish American colonies furnished the funds for the military expenses of Manila. In 1829 the treasury became an independent branch of administration. Increase of tribute-paying population, the tobacco and wine monopoly, permission given to foreigners to establish themselves as merchants in the capital, demand for native and consumption of foreign productions, and a general tendency *towards* a more liberal policy, brought about their usual beneficial results; and, though slowly moving, the Philippines have entered upon a career of prosperity susceptible of an enormous extension.

The capitation tax, or *tribute* paid by the natives, is the foundation of the financial system in the Philippines. It is the only direct tax (except for special cases), makes no distinction of persons and property, has the merit of antiquity, and is collected by a machinery provided by the Indians themselves. Originally it was levied in produce, but compounded for by the payment of a dollar (eight reales), raised afterwards to a dollar and a quarter, and finally the friars have managed to add to the amount an additional fifty per cent., of which four-fifths are for church, and one-fifth for commercial purposes.

The tribute is now due for every grown-up individual of a family, up to the age of sixty; the local authorities (*cabezas de barangay*), their wives and eldest or an adopted son, excepted. A cabeza is charged with the collection of the tribute of his cabaceria, consisting generally of about fifty persons. There are many other exceptions, such as discharged soldiers and persons claiming exemptions on particular grounds, to say nothing of the uncertain collections from Indians not congregated in towns or villages, and the certain non-collections from the wilder races. Buzeta estimates that only five per cent. of the whole population pay the tribute. Beyond the concentrated groups of natives there is little control; nor is the most extended of existing influences— the ecclesiastical—at all disposed to aid the revenue collector at the price of public discontent, especially if the claims of the convent are recognized and the wants of the church sufficiently provided for, which they seldom fail to be. The friar frequently stands between the fiscal authority and the Indian debtor, and, as his great object is to be popular with his flock, he, when his own expectations are satisfied, is naturally a feeble supporter of the tax collector. The friar has a large direct interest in the money tribute, both in the sanctorum and the tithe; but the Indian has many means of conciliating the padre and does not fail to employ them, and the padre's influence is not only predominant, but it is perpetually present, and in constant activity. There is a decree of 1835 allowing the Indians to pay tribute in kind, but at rates so miserably low that I believe there is now scarcely an instance of other than metallic payments. The present amount levied is understood to be—

For the Government	10 rials of plate.
For the tithe	1 „ „ „
Community Fund (*Caja de Comunidad*)	1 „ „ „
Sanctorum (Church)	3 „ „ „
	15 rials, or 1⅞ dollar.

Which at 4*s.* 6*d.* per dollar makes a capitation tax of about 8*s.* 6*d.* per head.

The *Sangleys* (mestizos of Chinese origin) pay 20 rials government tribute, or 25 rials in all, being about 14*s.* sterling.

There are some special levies for local objects, but they are not heavy in amount.

The Chinese have been particularly selected to be the victims of the tax-gatherer, and, considering the general lightness of taxation, and that the Chinese had been invited to the Philippines with every assurance of protection, and as a most important element for the development of the resources of the country, the decree of 1828 will appear tolerably exacting. It divides Chinese settlers into three classes:—

Merchants who are to pay a monthly tax of 10 dollars	£27 0 per annum.
Shopkeepers who are to pay a monthly tax of 4 dollars	10 16 „ „
All others who have to pay a monthly tax of 2 dollars	5 8 „ „

Not consenting to this, and if unmarried, they might quit the country in six months, or pay the value of their tribute in labour, and they were, after a delay of three months in the payment of the tax, to be fineable at 2 rials a day. At the time of issuing the decree there were 5,708 Chinese in the capital, of whom immediately 800 left for China, 1,083 fled to the mountains and were kindly received and protected by the natives, 453 were condemned to the public works, and the rest left in such a condition of discontent and misery that in 1831 the intendente made a strong representation to the government in their favour, and in 1834 authority was given to modify the whole fiscal legislation as regarded the Chinese.

The Chinese, on landing in Manila, whether as sailors or intending settlers, are compelled to inhabit a public establishment called the *Alcaiceria de San Fernando*, for which payment is exacted, and there is a revenue resulting to the State from the profits thereof.

CHAPTER XXIII.

OPENING THE NEW PORTS OF ILOILO, SUAL AND ZAMBOANGA.

The opening of the ports of Sual, Iloilo and Zamboanga to foreign trade, was of course intended to give development to the local interests of the northern, central and southern portions of the archipelago, the localities selected appearing to offer the greatest encouragements, and on the determination of the Spanish government being known, her Britannic Majesty's Consul at Manila recommended the appointment of British vice-consuls at Sual and Iloilo, and certainly no better selections could have been made than were made on the occasion, for the most competent gentleman in each of the ports was fixed upon.

Mr. Farren's report, which has been laid before Parliament, very fairly represents the claims of the new ports and their dependencies; each has its special recommendations. The population of the northern division, comprising Pangasinan, the two Ilocos (North and South), Abra and La Union, may be considered among the most industrious, opulent and intelligent of the Philippines. Cagayan produces the largest quantity of the finest quality of tobacco.

The central division, the most thickly peopled of the whole, has long furnished Manila with a large proportion of its exports, which, in progress of time, will, no doubt, be sent directly from the ports of production to those of consumption; while the southern, and the least promising at present, has every element which soil and climate can contribute to encourage the cultivation of vast tracts hitherto unreached by the civilizing powers of commerce and colonization.

The population in the northern division is large. In Ilocos, South and North, there are twelve towns with from 5,000 to 8,000 inhabitants; seven with 8,000 to 12,000; seven with from 12,000 to 20,000; and three with from 20,000 to 33,000. In Pangasinan, nine towns with from 5,000 to 12,000; seven with from 12,000 to 20,000; and three with from 20,000 to 26,000 inhabitants. The capital (Cabazera) of Cagayan has above 15,000 inhabitants. The middle zone presents a still greater number of populous places. Zebu has fourteen towns with 5,000 to 10,000 inhabitants, and nine towns of from 10,000 to 12,000; and in Iloilo there are seven towns with from 5,000 to 10,000 inhabitants;

fourteen towns with from 10,000 to 20,000; seven with from 20,000 to 30,000; two with from 30,000 to 40,000; and one (Haro) with 46,000 inhabitants.

These statistics for 1857 show a great increase of population since Mr. Farren's returns and prove that the removal of restrictions has acted most beneficially upon the common weal, imperfect as the emancipation has been. There cannot be a doubt that more expansive views would lead to the extension of a liberal policy, and that mines of unexplored and undeveloped treasure are to be found in the agricultural and commercial resources of these regions. The importance of direct intercourse with foreign countries is increased by the fact that, for many months of the year, the monsoons interrupt the communication of the remoter districts with the capital. The old spirit of monopoly not only denied to the producer the benefit of high prices, and to the consumer the advantage of low prices, but the trade itself necessarily fell into the hands of unenterprising and sluggish merchants, wholly wanting in that spirit of enterprise which is the *primum mobile* of commercial prosperity. For it is the condition, curse and condemnation of monopoly, that while it narrows the vision and cramps the intellect of the monopolist, it delivers the great interests of commerce to the guardianship of an inferior race of traders, excluding those higher qualities which are associated with commercial enterprise when launched upon the wide ocean of adventurous and persevering energy. How is the tree to reach its full growth and expansion whose branches are continually lopped off lest their shadows should extend, and their fruit fall for the benefit of others than its owner?

But in reference to the beneficial changes which have been introduced, their value has been greatly diminished by the imperfect character of the concessions. They should have been complete; they should, while opening the ports to foreign trade, have allowed that trade full scope and liberty. The discussions which have taken place have, however, been eminently useful, and the part taken in favour of commercial freedom by Mr. Bosch and Mr. Loney, both British vice-consuls, has been creditable to their zeal and ability. In the Philippines, the tendency of public opinion is decidedly in the right direction. The resistance which for so many years, or even centuries, opposed the admission of strangers to colonial ports, no doubt was grounded upon the theory that they would bring less of trade than they would carry away—that they would participate in the large profits of those who held the monopoly, but not confer upon them any corresponding or countervailing advantages.

Mr. Farren states that, in 1855, "the British trade with the Philippines exceeded in value that of Great Britain with several of the States of Europe, with that of any one State or port in Africa, was greater than the British trade with Mexico, Columbia, or Guatemala, and nearly ranked in the second-class division of the national trade with Asia, the total value of exports and imports approaching three millions sterling. The export of sugar to Great Britain and her colonies was, in 1854, 42,400 tons, that to Great Britain alone having gradually grown upon the exports of 1852, which was 5,061 tons, to 27,254 tons, which exceeds the exports to the whole world in 1852. The imports of British goods and manufactures, which was 427,020*l.* in value in 1845, exceeded 1,000,000*l.* sterling in 1853." It still progresses, and the removal of any one restriction, the encouragement of any one capability, will add to that progress, and infallibly augment the general prosperity.

The statistics of the island of Panay for 1857 give to the province of Iloilo 527,970; to that of Capiz, 143,713; and to that of Antique, 77,639; making in all 749,322, or nearly three-quarters of a million of inhabitants. The low lands of Capiz are subject to frequent inundations. It has a fine river, whose navigation is interfered with by a sandbank at its mouth. The province is productive, and gives two crops of rice in the year. The harbours of Batan and of Capiz (the cabacera) are safe for vessels of moderate size. The inhabitants of Antique, which occupies all the western coast of Panay, are the least industrious of the population of the island. The coast is dangerous. It has two pueblos, Bugason and Pandan, with more than 10,000 souls. The cabacera San José has less than half that number. The roads of the provinces are bad and communications with Iloilo difficult. The lands are naturally fertile, but have not been turned to much account by the Indians. There are only forty-two mestizos in the province. There is a small pearl and turtle fishery, and some seaslugs are caught for the Chinese market.

Iloilo has, no doubt, been fixed on as the seat of the government, from the facilities it offers to navigation; but it is much smaller, less opulent and even less active than many of the towns in its neighbourhood. The province of Iloilo is, on the whole, perhaps the most advanced of any in the Philippines, excepting the immediate neighbourhood of the capital. It has fine mountainous scenery, richly adorned with forest trees, while the plains are eminently fertile. All tropical produce appears to flourish. The manufacturing industry of the women is characteristic, and has been referred to in other places, especially with reference to the extreme beauty of the piña fabric. Of the mode of preparing the fabric Mallat gives this account:—

"It is from the leaves of the pine-apple—the plant which produces such excellent fruits—that the white and delicate threads are drawn which are the raw material of the *nipis* or piña stuffs. The sprouts of ananas are planted, which sometimes grow under the fruit to the number of a dozen; they are torn off, and are set in a light soil, sheltered, if possible, and they are watered as soon as planted. After four months the crown is removed, in order to prevent the fruiting, and that the leaves may grow broader and longer. At the age of eight months they are an ell in length, and six fingers in breadth, when they are torn away and stretched out on a plank, and, while held by his foot, the Indian with a piece of broken earthenware scrapes the pulp till the fibres appear. These are taken by the middle, and cautiously raised from one end to the other; they are washed twice or thrice in water, dried in the air and cleaned; they are afterwards assorted according to their lengths and qualities. Women tie the separate threads together in packets, and they are ready for the weaver's use. In the weaving it is desirable to avoid either too high or too low a temperature—too much drought, or too much humidity—and the most delicate tissues are woven under the protection of a mosquito net. Such is the patience of the weaver, that she sometimes produces not more than half an inch of cloth in a day. The finest are called *pinilian*, and are only made to order. Ananas are cultivated solely for the sake of the fibre, which is sold in the market. Most of the stuffs are very narrow; when figured with silk, they sell for about 10*s.* per yard. The plain, intended for embroidery, go to Manila, where the most extravagant prices are paid for the finished work."

Mr. Vice-Consul Bosch has written an interesting report on the capabilities of the province of Pangasinan, and of Sual, its principal port. The circumference of coast is from fifty to sixty miles on the south and east of the Gulf of Lingayen. The interior abounds with facilities for water communication, and the most important river, the Agno, enters the sea at St. Isidro, about one and a half mile from Sual. The Agno has about seventy to eighty miles of internal navigation, and brings produce from the adjacent provinces of La Union and Nueva Ecija, The exports to Manila are generally made from Sual, those for China from Dagupan. Dagupan is at the mouth of a large estuary, but a bar prevents the entry of any large vessel. The want of safe anchorage is the disadvantage of all the coast of the province, with the exception of the harbour of Sual. This harbour, though small, is safe: it is nearly circular. It would hold from twelve to fifteen large vessels and thirty to forty coasters, and is well protected on every side, but there is a somewhat dangerous bank within the port.

There are only about 400 houses in Sual: they are scattered on the plain in front of the harbour, and are of wood. There are, besides, 100 Indian huts (*chozas*) constructed of the nipa palm. The church is a poor, provisional edifice.

Sual is exhibiting some signs of improvement. The road to the neighbouring province of Zambales is in progress. The allied forces in Cochin China have been lately drawing provisions, especially cattle, from Sual. The value of the exports from Sual, for 1858, is 670,095 dollars; the imports of foreign goods and manufactures into the three ports of the province—Dagupan, Binmaley and Lingayen—amount to 464,116 dollars, all brought by coasting vessels, of which 75 belong to the province. The largest pueblo of the province is San Carlos, with 26,376 inhabitants; the second, Binmaley, with 24,911; the third, Lingayen, with 23,063; but the population of Sual is only 3,451. Rice and sugar are the leading articles of produce exported, but there is at Calasiao a considerable manufacture of hats, cigar-cases, mats and other fabrics of the various fibres of the country. There are no large estates, nor manufactures on an extensive scale. Everything is done by small proprietors and domestic industry. There are many places where markets (called *tiangues*) are periodically held, and articles of all sorts brought thither for sale. It is calculated that Pangasinan could give 20,000 tons of rice for exportation, after providing for local wants. The sugar, though it might be produced abundantly, is carelessly prepared. Much wood is cut for ship-building and other purposes. On the arrival of the N. E. monsoon commercial enterprise begins and many shipments take place; the roads are passable, the warehouses filled with goods: this lasts till the end of June or July. Then come on the heavy rains: the vessels for the coasting trade are laid up for the season; the rivers overflow; most of the temporary bridges are carried away by the floods; everybody is occupied by what the Spaniards call their "interior life;" they settle the accounts of the past year and prepare for that which is to come, and the little foreign trade of Sual is the only evidence of trading activity.

Labour is moderately remunerated. Taking fifty ship carpenters, employed in one yard, the least paid had 5 rials, the highest 10 rials per week (say 3*s.* to 6*s.*). They are also allowed two measures of rice and a little meat or fish. A field labourer (or *peon*) has a rial a day and his food. A cart with a buffalo and leader costs 1½ rial per day.

Almost all purchases are made by brokers (*personeros*), who, for a commission, generally of 5 per cent., and a guarantee of 2½ per cent., collect the products of the country from the cultivators, to whom they make advances —always in silver; and it sometimes passes through many hands before it reaches the labouring producer.

There are few native Spaniards in Pangasinan. A good many mestizos are devoted to commerce. In Lingayen, with 23,000 inhabitants, there are more than 1,000 mestizos; in Binmaley, with 24,000 inhabitants, only twenty-two mestizos: the first being a trading, the second an agricultural, pueblo. There are few Indians who have acquired opulence. The Chinese element has penetrated, and they obtain more and more influence as active men of business. No Oriental race can compete with them where patience, perseverance and economy can be brought into play. They are not liked; but they willingly suffer much annoyance and spread and strengthen themselves by unanimity of purpose. In Calasiao they are said in two years to have established nearly eighty shops, and were gradually insinuating themselves into all profitable occupations—attending the markets both as buyers and sellers, and establishing relations with the interior such as no native Indian would have ever contemplated. Nor in the ordinary transactions of life do they make the mistake of requiring extravagant profits. A Chinaman may, indeed, ask a high price or offer a low one in his different relations, but when he sees his way to a clear profit, he will not let the bargain escape him. There is an increasing demand for European merchandise, of which the Chinese are the principal importers; and they, above all other men, are likely to open new channels of trade. The current rate of interest is 10 per cent.; though the church funds are lent at 6 per cent. to those whom the clergy are disposed to favour, which indeed is the legal rate.

Mr. Bosch's return for the year 1858 shows that eight large vessels, with 7,185 tons, and 282 coasters, with 7,780 tons, entered the port of Sual. Only four of the former carried cargoes away, two having gone to repair damages, and two being Spanish government steamers for the remittal to Manila of money which amounted to 210,000 dollars.

CHAPTER XXIV.

ZAMBOANGA.

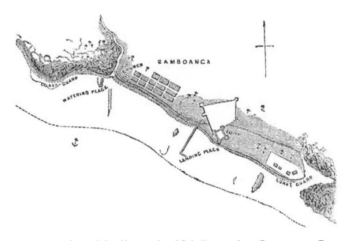

We steamed away from Manila on the 20th December. It was our first purpose to visit Labuan, which had become of some interest to me as Governor of Hong Kong, having been made of late the penal settlement for a certain number of Chinese convicts. Two groups of sixty each had been sent thither, and the Governor was desirous their number should be increased. I do not see how the settlement can be made a prosperous or productive one. The coals which it furnishes are not liked by our engineers, and seldom employed if English or Welsh coals can be obtained. A considerable quantity was reported to me as raised and lying on the shore without demand, but I found no willingness, either on the part of the naval authorities or of the merchants, to purchase it. I expect both China and Japan will be in a condition to provide this very important article on cheaper terms and of better quality than that of Labuan, or any part of Borneo. I should have been glad to have had an opportunity of forming an opinion, grounded on my own observations, as to the prospects of Sarawak. I am disposed to believe the Government has acted judiciously in refusing to buy the colony, and to encumber the treasury with the charges which its establishments would inevitably entail. The arguments which I have seen put forward in its favour by the advocates of the purchase, have certainly little weight. To represent the locality as of any importance as a place of call between Europe and China, is to display extraordinary geographical and commercial ignorance: it is hundreds of miles out of the regular course, and has in itself no attraction to induce any vessel to waste the time which must be expended in visiting it. It has a fertile soil, which may be said of the whole circumjacent region—of almost every island in the tropical archipelagos; but it must depend principally on imported labour, costly and capricious in its supply, and which must be directed by European machinery, still more costly and uncertain, for the climate is, and will long continue, unfriendly to the health of European settlers. The native population is too barbarous to labour; with few wants, they have few motives to exertion. I have had the advantage of much conversation with the Catholic Vicar Apostolic of Borneo, whose knowledge of the natives is probably greater than that of any other European, as he has lived so much among them in the discharge of the duties of his mission. He represents the different tribes as engaged in perpetual wars with one another, each taking any opportunity of pillaging or doing mischief to its neighbours; and our involving ourselves in the native quarrels, by ill-judged partisanship, must lead, he thinks, to much cruelty and injustice. He gave me many particulars of the savage practices of which he had been an eye-witness, particularly in the displays and processions of human heads as trophies of victory. Although I had not an opportunity of visiting Borneo and of witnessing there the progress that has been made under European influences, I have had so many means of studying the character of the native and unsubdued races in the territories of Spain and the Netherlands, that I feel quite justified in the conclusion, that little is to be expected from their co-operation, either as producers of tropical, or consumers of European, articles. The great element which is now revolutionizing these regions, is the introduction of Chinese labour, which has received a check not easily to be surmounted in the unfortunate outbreak at Sarawak, after the events in Canton; but the introduction of the Chinese must be spontaneous, and not forced. The Chinese field-labourer works unwillingly for a master who is to receive the profits of his labour; but far different are his feelings, his activity and perseverance, when the profits are all to be his own. Then, indeed, he becomes a valuable settler, from whom much is to be expected. Our new treaties—the presence of British shipping in so many ports of China—the supersession of the heavy junks by the square-rigged vessels of the West, which the habit of insuring that the Chinese are now adopting cannot fail to promote—will all assist in the transfer of the surplus population of China to regions where their industry will find a wider scope and a more profitable field. The adventurous spirit in China is becoming more and more active. The tens of thousands who have emigrated to California and Australia, and the thousands who have returned with savings which they have deemed a sufficiency, have given an impulse to the emigrating passion, which will act strongly and beneficially in all countries towards which it may be directed. In process of time, and with the co-operation of the mandarins, who are really interested in the removal of a wretched, sometimes starving and always discontented, social element, the difficulties attaching to the removal of females may in time be surmounted, and the Chinese may perpetuate, what they have never yet done, a Chinese community in the lands where they settle. No doubt the mestizo mixture of races—the descendants of Chinese fathers and Indian mothers—is now extensively spread, and is a great improvement upon the pure Malay or Indian breed. The type of the father is more strongly preserved than that of the mother; its greater vigour has given it predominance. The Chinese mestizo is physically a being superior to the Indian—handsomer in person, stronger in limb, more active in intellect, more persevering in labour, more economical in habits. The marvellous exodus of Chinese from their country is one of the most remarkable ethnological circumstances of modern history, and is producing and will produce extraordinary and lasting results. I do not believe any of the other Oriental races able to withstand the secret and widely spreading influences of Chinese competition and superiority. Dealt with justly and fairly, the Chinese are the most manageable of men, but they will be dangerous where despotism drives them to despair.

On the sixth day of our voyage we arrived at Zamboanga. Indian houses were visible through the plantain trees, and amidst the woodlands of the coast, and a large fortification, with the yellow and scarlet Spanish flag, advised us of our adjacency to the seat of government. We sent on shore, and found the guns and the garrison were not in a condition to return our salute, but we received an early and cordial communication from the governor, Colonel Navarro, inviting us to take up our abode at his residence, and we landed at a convenient wooden pier, which is carried out for some distance into the harbour. There was a small body of soldiers to meet us on landing. In walking about we found one street wholly occupied by Chinese shopkeepers, well supplied with European and Chinese wares; they generally appeared contented and prosperous, and will certainly find the means of supplying whatever the population may demand; they will leave nothing undone which is likely to extend their trade or augment their profits. There are about three hundred Chinese settled in Zamboanga, mostly men of Fokien. We walked to the fortification, and on our way met several of the Mahomedan women who had been captured in a late fray with natives; their breasts were uncovered, and they wore not the veils which almost invariably hide the faces of the daughters of Islam. We learnt that these females were of the labouring and inferior classes; but in the fortification we saw the wives and children of the chiefs, who had been captured, and they presented the most marvellous contrasts, between the extreme ugliness of the aged and the real beauty of some of the young. One mother especially, who had a child on her haunches, appeared to me singularly graceful and pleasing. Most of the captured chiefs had been sent to Manila; but in another part of the fortress there were some scores of prisoners, among whom, one seemed to exercise ascendency over the rest, and he repeated some of the formula of the Koran in Arabic words. The Spaniards represented them as a fierce, faithless and cruel race, but they have constantly opposed successful resistance to their invaders.

Next to Luzon, Mindanao is the largest of the Philippines. Though its surface is 3,200 square leagues in extent, the Spaniards do not occupy one-tenth of the whole. The number of Mahomedans (*Moros*) is great in the interior, and they are the subjects of an independent Sultan, whose capital is Selangan, and who keeps up amicable relations with the Spanish authorities. To judge by some of their native manufactures which I saw at Zamboanga, they are by no means to be considered as barbarians. The inland country is mountainous, but has some fine lakes and rivers little visited by strangers. There are many spacious bays. Storms and earthquakes are frequent visitants. The forests are said to be extensive, and filled with gigantic trees, but travellers report the jungle to be impenetrable. Mines of gold, quicksilver and sulphur are said to abound. Besides Zamboanga, the Spaniards have settlements in Misamis, Caraga and New Guipuzcoa, but they are reported to be unhealthy from the immense putrefaction of decaying vegetables produced by a most feracious soil, under the influence of a tropical sun. Beyond the Moros, and in the wildest parts of the mountains, are coloured races in a low state of savage existence. Mindanao was one of the earliest conquests of Magallanes (1521). The Augustine friars were the first missionaries, and they still retain almost a monopoly of religious instruction, but their success among the Mahomedans has been small. Many attempts have been made by the Spaniards to subdue the interior, but, however great their temporary success, they have never been able long to maintain themselves against the fanaticism of the Moros, the dangers and difficulties of the country and the climate, while supported only by inadequate military means. Misamis is used as a penal settlement. The Spaniards have not penetrated far into the interior of this part of the island, which is peopled by a race of Indians said not to be hostile, but, being frequently at war with the more formidable Mahomedans, they are considered by the Spaniards as affording them some protection, their locality dividing the European settlements from the territory of the Moors. But there is little development of agriculture or industry, and not one inhabitant in ten of the province pays tribute. The Jesuits had formerly much success in these regions; on their expulsion the Recolets (barefooted Augustines) occupied their places, but it would seem with less acceptance. The settlers and the Indians recognizing the Spanish authority have been so frequently molested by the Moors that their numbers are far less than they were formerly, and it is believed the revenues are quite inadequate to pay the expenses of the establishments; but it is said some progress is being made, and if all impediments to commercial intercourse were removed, a great amelioration in the condition and prospects of the natives would result. Caraga, from which New Guipuzcoa has been lately detached, has Surigao for its capital, and is on the north-east corner of the island. The dominions of the Sultan of Mindanao mark the limits of the province. A race of Indians remarkable for the whiteness of their skin, and supposed to be of Japanese descent, called Tago-balvoys, live on the borders of a creek in the neighbourhood of a town bearing the name of Bisig, a station of the Recolets. Some of this race pay tribute, and live in a state of constant hostility with the Moros. They are advanced in civilization beyond the neighbouring tribes. Butuan, in this province, was the last landing place of Magallanes; he planted a cross there, and the Indians took part in the ceremonials, and profess Christianity to the present hour. The Moros have destroyed some of the earlier establishments of the Spaniards. There are immense tracts of uncultivated and fertile lands. Teak is reported to abound in the forests, which are close to the habitations of the settlers. The orang-utan is common, and there are many varieties of apes and monkeys, wild beasts, particularly buffaloes and deer, and several undescribed species of quadrupeds. The Spaniards say that the province of Caraga is the richest of the Philippines; it is certainly one of the least explored. A Frenchman has been engaged in working the gold mines; I know not with what success. A favourite food of the natives is the wild honey, which is collected in considerable quantities, and eaten with fruits and roots. The Butuan River is navigable for boats. There are very many separate races of natives, among whom the Mandayos are said to be handsome, and to bear marks of European physiognomy. Some of the tribes are quite black, fierce and ungovernable. Cinnamon and pepper are believed to be indigenous. Wax, musk and tortoise-shell are procurable, but as the Spanish settlements are not much beyond the coast little is done for the encouragement of the productive powers of the interior. Gold, however, no doubt from the facility of its transport, is not an unimportant article of export, and the Spaniards complain that the natives attend to nothing else, so that there is often much suffering from dearth, and the insalubrity of the climate deters strangers from locating themselves. This is little to be wondered at, as the attacks of pirates are frequent and the powers of government weak. Along the coasts are towers provided with arms and ammunition for their defence; but the pirates frequently interrupt the communications by sea, on which the inhabitants almost wholly depend, there being no passable roads. On the approach of the piratical boats the natives generally abandon their own and flee to the mountains. There are many Mahomedan tribes who take no part in these outrages, such as the Bagobos, Cuamanes and others. Even the mails are interrupted by the pirates, and often delayed for days in localities where they seek shelter. All these drawbacks notwithstanding, the number of tributaries is said to have greatly increased, and the influence of the friars to have extended itself. I have compared various statistical returns, and find many contradictions and inconsistencies.[1] Some evidence that little progress has been made is seen in the fact that in the province of Surigao, where the census gives 18,848 Indians, there are only 148 mestizos; in that of Misamis, only 266 mestizos to 46,517 Indians; in Zamboanga, to 10,191 Indians, 16 mestizos; Basilan, 447 Indians and 4 mestizos; Bislig, 12,718 Indians and 21 mestizos; Davao, 800 Indians, no mestizo. This state of things assuredly proves that the island of Mindanao, whatever be its fertility, has few attractions for strangers, otherwise the proportion of the mixed races to the population would be very different from what it appears to be. Father Zuñiga, who, in 1799, published an account of the visit of General Alava, gives many particulars of the then state of the island, and suggests many plans for extending Spanish influence.

Zamboanga is not likely to become a port of much importance unless it is wholly emancipated from fiscal restrictions. The introduction of the custom-house has driven away the whalers that formerly visited the harbours; there is little capital, and the trading establishments are on a very small scale. The roads in the immediate neighbourhood are in very tolerable order; the villages have the general character of Indian pueblos; the country is rich in all the varieties of tropical vegetation; but the interior, even close to the cabaceras, is imperfectly known. Its produce is small in reference to the obvious fertility of the soil. Some companies of troops arrived during our stay at Zamboanga, and it is probable an effort is to be made to strengthen and widen the authority of the Spanish government.

Of the arms used by the Moros the governor had a large collection, consisting of long spears, swords of various forms, handsomely adorned kreeses, daggers and knives displaying no small amount of manufacturing art.

Confined as the Spaniards are to a narrow strip of land along the coast, it may be supposed there are few conveniences for locomotion, nevertheless a carriage was found, and a pair of horses, and harness such as it was, and an Indian driver, and thus we managed to obtain a very pleasant evening ride into the country, and had an opportunity of seeing its great fertility and its varied productions, leading to natural feelings of regret that so many of the boons of Providence should remain unenjoyed and unimproved, accompanied with the hope that better days may dawn. But the world is full of undeveloped treasures, and its "Yarrows unvisited" promise a bright futurity.

There would seem to have been some increase in the population of Zamboanga. In 1779 Zuñiga reports it to be 5,612 souls, "including Indians, Spaniards, soldiers and convicts;" in 1818 the number is stated to have been 8,640; in 1847, 7,190. The Guia of 1850 gives 8,618; that of 1858, 10,191, of whom 16 were mestizos, and tribute-payers 3,871; but I do not think much reliance can be placed on the statistical returns. The last states that the marriages were 55, the births 429, the deaths 956, which represents a fearful mortality. In the province of Misamis for the same period the proportion of births to deaths was 2,155 to 845.

A great value is attached to some of the canes which are found on the island of Palawan, or Paragua, especially where they are of variegated colours, or pure white, and without the interruption of a knot, so as to serve for walking-sticks. I was informed that two hundred dollars had been given for a fine specimen.

A gold-headed sticky with a silk cord and tassels, is the emblem of authority in the Philippines.

1

Buzeta may be consulted, especially under the head "Caraga," on which he has a long article.

CHAPTER XXV.

ILOILO AND PANAY.

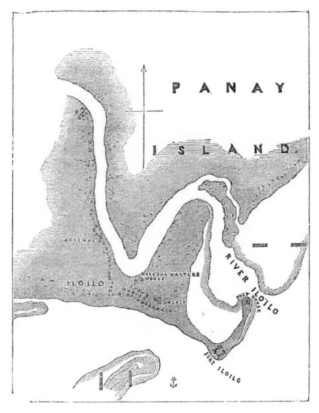

Of the three ports lately opened to foreign commerce, Iloilo is the most promising. The province of Iloilo is one of the most populous of the Philippines. It contains more than half a million of inhabitants, and though portions of the province are very thinly peopled, there is an average exceeding 2,000 inhabitants per square league. Independently of the pueblos which I visited, and of which some description will be given, Cabatuan has 23,000 inhabitants, Miagao 31,000, Dumangas 25,000, Janiuay 22,000, Pototan 34,600, and several others more than 10,000 souls. The province is not only one of the most numerously peopled, it is, perhaps, the most productive in agricultural, the most active in manufacturing, industry, and among the best instructed of the Philippines.[1] It has extensive and cultivated plains and forest-covered mountains; its roads are among the best I have seen in the archipelago. At the entrance of the channel are a number of islands called the Seven (mortal) Sins—*Los Siete Pecados*. The large island of Guimaras limits the channel on the south; it was visited by some of our party, who returned delighted with the extensive stalactite caverns which they explored, reaching them with some difficulty over the rocks, through the woods and across the streams which arrested their progress. The forests are full of game and the river Cabatuan abounds with crocodiles. There are many rivulets and rivers which greatly assist the cultivator, and we found a good supply of cattle. The ponies of Iloilo are among the best in the archipelago, and some attention is paid to the breeding of sheep. A good deal of salt is made, and there is a considerable fishery of *trepang* (sea-slug) and tortoises for the sake of the shells. But the island is most renowned for the piña fabrics called nipas and sinamays, some of which are of exquisite fineness and beauty; they are largely exported, and their perfection has given them a vast reputation even in Europe.

On the arrival of the Spaniards they found the district occupied by painted Indians, full of superstitions, which, notwithstanding the teachings of the Augustine friars, are still found to prevail, especially at the time of any public calamity. They are among the best formed of the Indians, speak a dialect of the Bisayan, which they called *Hiligueyna*, but in the remoter parts another idiom named the *Halayo* prevails. The Augustines boast of having converted fifty thousand families in 1566, but they were not able to induce them to cultivate their lands and to store their surplus produce, and the locusts having desolated the district, in the two following years more than half the population perished of hunger. But the missionaries made no progress among the *Negritos* who dwelt in the wilder parts of the mountainous regions, and who were joined by many desiring to escape from the authority of the invaders. These savages have not unfrequently attacked the villages of the converted Indians, but of late years have found it more prudent and profitable to bring down their wax and pitch, and exchange them for rice and garments. They have no general ruler, but each clan has its recognized head, and it is said that, when perplexed as to choice of a successor to a departed chief, they send deputations to the missionaries and ask their advice and assistance to regulate their choice. Formerly the district was frequently attacked by pirates, who committed great ravages and destroyed several towns. In 1716 the Dutch attacked the fortress of Iloilo, but were compelled to retire after a heavy loss both in killed and wounded. There has been a great increase in the population, which in 1736 numbered 67,708 souls; in 1799, 176,901; in 1845, 277,571; and by the last census, 527,970, of whom 174,874 pay tribute. There is a small number of Spaniards—of mestizos many, of whom the larger proportion are *sangleys*, the descendants of Chinese fathers and native mothers. The increase of the population must be great, the census in 1857 giving 17,675 births, and only 9,231 deaths.

The approach to Iloilo is by a channel between a sandbank (which has spread nearly a mile beyond the limits given in the charts) and the island of Guimaras. The town appears adjacent as it is approached, but the river by which vessels enter makes a considerable bend and passes round close to the town. We observed a large fortification, but it had not the means of saluting us, and we were therefore exonerated from the duty of exploding H. M.'s gunpowder; but if not in the shape of noisy salutations, the courtesies of the Spanish authorities were displayed in every possible way towards the officers and crew of our frigate, for whose service and entertainment everything was done. We were soon waited on by a gentleman from the British vice-consulate. The vice-consul returned to Iloilo the day after our arrival. It would indeed be well if all British functionaries possessed as much aptitude, knowledge and disposition to be useful as we found in Mr. Loney, to whom the commerce of the Philippines generally, and the port of Iloilo especially, is under great obligations. To him, more than to any other individual, the development of the trade of Panay will be due.

From the Governor of Iloilo, Colonel José Maria Carlès, especially I experienced great kindness. He was Buffering under a sore affliction—for affliction holds sway over every part of the world—the loss of an only and beloved son who had preceded him as governor of the province and was an object of so much affection that the people earnestly implored the Captain-General to allow the father to succeed him, which was granted. It was touching to hear the tales of the various displays of popular sympathy and sorrow which accompanied the death and the interment of Don Emilio Carlès, whom no less than fifty carriages followed to his grave in Arévalo. I passed the village more than once with the mourning father; at a time, too, when sorely suffering from sorrows of my own, I felt the consolation which is found in remembering and helping others to remember the virtues of the dead. These are their best monuments, though not written on tablets of stone.

The principalia of Molo came to invite us to a ball, and very prettily the ball was got up. It is a most industrious locality; in ancient times was a Chinese colony, and is now occupied by mestizos and their descendants, most of them having a mingling of Chinese blood. The pueblo has 16,428 inhabitants, of whom the mestizos are 1,106. It is one of the busiest towns in the island, and everything has a prosperous and active look. Some of the buildings have in the same apartment many looms occupied in making the piña stuffs. The place was gaily illuminated on occasion of the ball, and the gobernadorcillo made an oration in Spanish to the effect that the locality had been much honoured by our presence, and that the memory of the day would be long preserved. Many of the mestizos keep their carriages, which were placed at the disposal of our friends, and which fell into the procession when music and firing of guns and muskets accompanied us through the town. Molo is an island formed by two creeks, and entered by bridges on both sides. I believe it is one of the few localities served by a secular curate. It is about four miles from Iloilo, the road being good, and many Indian houses are seen on both sides of the way. Almost all these have their gardens growing plantains, cocoa-nuts, bread-fruits, cocoa, betel and other vegetable productions. Sugar planting appeared to be extending, and there are many paddy-fields and much cultivation of maize.

The Governor and British vice-consul accompanied us in our pleasant excursions to the interior, during which we visited some of the most populous pueblos of the provinces. We travelled in comfortable carriages, the friars or the gobernadorcillos providing us with relays of horses, and the convents were generally the places appointed for our reception, in which we invariably found most hospitable cheer. One day it was determined to visit Janiuay, and we first stopped at Jaro, a pueblo of more than 22,000 souls. The roads had their usual adornings: the Indian cottages exhibited their flags, the equestrian principalia came out to escort us, and the native bands of music went before us when we entered and when we quitted the populous part of the town. Jaro is deemed the most opulent place in the island of Panay. It was founded in 1584 or 1585. Cultivation extends to some distance around it. It boasts of its stone bridge, more than 700 feet in length and 36 feet in breadth, the erection of which, as well as the excellent roads by which the pueblo is approached, are due to the munificence of a curate knighted by his sovereign for his patriotic sacrifices. Though the country is level, the rich vegetation on the banks of the streams and by the borders of the highway make the scenery picturesque. The manufacture of fine stuffs and cotton, piña and silk, is very considerable. These fabrics are exposed for sale at a weekly market, held on Thursdays, which is crowded by people from every part of the province, being the largest of the Iloilo marts. From Jaro we proceeded to Santa Barbara, a pueblo of 23,000 souls. Here we were received at the convent of the Augustine friars, in whose hands are all the cures of Iloilo, to one of whom we had the pleasure of giving a passage to Manila, whither he was bound as the delegate to the annual assembly of the fraternity. Here, too, other Augustine friars visited us, all inviting us to partake of the hospitalities of their spacious convents. Santa Barbara is a modern town, built in 1759, and placed under the special protection of the saint whose name it bears. It has shared in the general prosperity of the province: in 1820 it had no manufactures; but it has now a weekly market for the sale of the produce of its looms, consisting principally of cottons, sail-canvas, quilts, coverlets, &c. The forests furnish fine timber for building and for cabinet work, and are crowded with wild bees, whose wax and honey form a considerable article of traffic. Excellent were the carriages and horses of the friars. Our next resting-place was Cabatuan, somewhat larger than Santa Barbara. Cabatuan was founded in 1732. It is on the banks of the river Tiguin; sometimes nearly dry, and at others deluging the country with its impetuous torrents. The numerous crocodiles make fishing unsafe; and the navigation even of small boats is often interrupted, either by the superfluity or insufficiency of its waters. There is a large production of rice and of cocoa-nut oil for lighting. From Cabatuan we went to Janiuay, which was the limit of the day's journey, and of our visit to the interior. It is called Matagul in the ancient maps of the province, and has about the same number of inhabitants as Santa Barbara. The convent and church are on a slightly elevated ground, and offer a pretty view of the pueblo and surrounding country. Many of the women are engaged in the labours of the loom, but agriculture is the principal industry of the neighbourhood. We had hoped to visit the Dingle mountain, one of whose caves or grottos is said to present the character of a temple of fantastic architecture, adorned with rock crystal and exhibiting masses of marble and alabaster which form its walls; another cave is formed of granite, which abounds in the locality: but we had to return to Iloilo to meet the principal people at a late dinner, succeeded as usual by a ball. The Governor's house being at some distance from the town, we were kindly accommodated at that of one of the native merchants, conveniently situated on the quay of the river. Several of the friars, who had been our hosts, were the guests of the merchants; and the kind hospitality we experienced did not justify the constant expression of courteous regrets for the inadequacy of the entertainment, the blunders of the native servants (sometimes amusing enough), and the contrasts between the accommodations of Europe and those which a remote Spanish settlement in the Philippines could afford; but there was so much of courtesy, good breeding and cordiality that it was impossible to feel otherwise than grateful and contented, and, after all, in this world to do all we can is to discharge every duty.

The next day we made our arrangements for visiting the different pueblos on the coast, and, starting in our carriages soon after daybreak, we passed through Molo and Arévalo to Oton. Arévalo has some celebrity in the annals of the Philippines, and had a special interest for the Governor, as here had been lately displayed the affection of the Indians for his son, whose funeral they had honoured with such special marks of sympathy and regret. Arévalo was formerly the residence of the governor—built by Ronquillo in 1581, who gave it the name of his birth-place. Molested by the Indians, attacked by pirates and the government quite disorganized, it was for a long time abandoned; and the seat of authority being removed to Iloilo, Arévalo presents few signs of activity: there are about 8,000 inhabitants in this district. At Oton we saw from the Augustine convent an interesting ceremony. It was on a Sunday; and on quitting the church the inhabitants were summoned by beat of drum to attend the reading of a proclamation of the government. They were all in their holiday garments, and men, women and children formed a circle round one of the native Indian authorities, who, in a loud voice, read in the Bisayan tongue the document which he had been ordered to communicate to the people. There was perfect silence during the reading, and a quiet dispersion of the crowd. Fortifications are erected along the coast, and a great variety of manufactures were brought to us for examination. A good deal of English cotton twist is sold, which forms the warp of most of the fabrics.[2] There were rugs of silk and cotton; varieties of coloured ginghams; tissues, in which the fibres of the abacá and the piña were mixed with our cotton thread, whose importation is, however, confined to the colours which the Indians are themselves not able to dye. Oton has nearly 23,000 inhabitants. I observe the proportion of births to deaths is as nearly four to one, and that while there are five births to one marriage, the deaths exceed the marriages by less than one-third, so that the increase of population must be very great. In 1818, it was less than 9,000. Tigbauan, with its 21,000 inhabitants, was our next halting place. Its general character resembles that of Oton. Rice is the principal agricultural production, but the women are mostly employed in weaving stuffs, which find markets in Albay and Camarines. We were accompanied from the Augustine convent by a friar of Guimbal, who obviously exercised much influence over his brethren and over the whole community. His conversation was both entertaining and instructive. He had a good stud of horses, a handsome carriage, and he certainly employs his large revenues with generous hospitality. Not to repeat what has been repeated so often, the Indians, on the whole line of our journey, made a holiday time for our reception, which partook everywhere of the character of a public festivity. After the principalia had accompanied us to the convents, and received their thanks from me, and their dismissal from the Governor and the friar, a number of little girls were introduced, to whom the service of the table and attendance on the guests were confided. There was a strange mixture of curiosity, fear and respect in their deportment; but they gathered round my arm-chair; their bright black eyes looked inquiringly into my face, and asked for orders; while one, who seemed rather a pet of the ghostly father, put her hand into the curls of my white hair, which she seemed to consider worthy of some admiration: but the friar told me they were discoursing among themselves whether it was possible I could be a general and a great man, who had no gold about my clothes; I was not dressed half as finely as the officers they had been accustomed to see. They were very proud of some of the piña garments they wore, and one after another came to display their finery. They took care to supply me with cigars, and that light should be ready whenever the cigar was extinguished, and when we sat down to our well-furnished repast, several of them were at hand to remove the plates, to provide others, and to see that we were well provided with the delicacies of the day. On our way back to Iloilo, we learnt that the principalia of Molo were to escort us in their carriages to our domicile; they were waiting for us in the main road, so that we made together quite a procession. They had before invited Captain Vansittart and the officers of the *Magicienne* to their ball, and many attended, keeping up the dance to an early morning hour.

We left Iloilo the following day. The Governor and several of the principal people, among whom was a large group of Augustine friars, accompanied us with music to the ship. Three loud shouts of grateful hurrah broke forth from our decks, cordially responded to by our hosts—and so farewell! and all happiness to Iloilo.

I have sent to Sir William Hooker, for the museum of the Royal Gardens at Kew, sixty specimens of woods grown in the northern and western districts of the island of Panay and the province of Antique, of which the most notable are—the *molave*, the most useful and compact of the Philippine woods, and applied to all purposes of building; *bancaluag*, for fine work; *duñgon*, for ship-building and edifices; *bago-arour*, building and cabinet-work; *lumati*, a species of teak; *guisoc*, a flexible wood for ships and houses; *ipil* has similar merits; *naga*, resembling mahogany, used for furniture; *cansalod*, planks for floors; *maguilomboy*, for the same purpose; *duca*, *baslayan*, *oyacya*, for ship-building; *tipolo*, for musical instruments; *lanipga*, a species of cedar used for carving and sculpture; *bayog*, spars for masts and yards; *bancal*, for internal roofs and carving; *malaguibuyo*, for flooring; *ogjayan*, flexible for joints, &c.; *lanitan*, guitars, violins, &c.; *janlaatan*, furniture; *lauaan*, spars for shipping; *basa*, in large blocks for building and shipping; *talagtag*, cabinet-work; *nino*, the bark used for dyeing both red and yellow; *bacan*, spars; *panao*, a medicinal wood used for sore eyes by the Indians; *banate*, a fine and solid box-wood, used for billiard-maces, has been exported to Europe; *bancolinao*, ebony; *casla* has a fruit resembling a French bean, whose oil is used by the natives for their lamps; *jaras*, for construction of houses. It will be observed that all these bear their Indian names, which are generally applied to them by the Spaniards.

As regards the commercial position and prospects of the whole of the central and southern islands of the Philippine Archipelago, the most satisfactory details which have reached me are those furnished in 1857 by the Vice-Consul of Iloilo, Mr. Loney, to the Consul of Manila, from which I extract the following information.

That portion of the Philippines called the Bisayas may be generally described as including the whole of the islands to the southward of Luzon, though, strictly speaking, it is understood to comprehend only those of Samar, Leyte, Panay, Negros, Cebu, Bohol (with their dependencies, Tablas, Romblon, Sibuyan, &c.), and four provinces—Misamis, Caraga, Zamboanga, and Nueva Guipuzcoa—of the important island of Mindanao, next to Luzon the finest and largest of the archipelago.

The administration of the revenue of the Bisayas was formerly in charge of a separate Government Intendency (*Gobierno Intendencia de Bisayas*) established in the city of Cebu; but this being abolished in 1849, all the provinces, as regards revenue, are now equally under control of the Superintendencia at Manila. While, however, the provinces and districts of Luzon (with the exception of Cavite, La Isabela, Nueva Viscaya, El Abra, San Mateo, and La Union) are presided over by civil functionaries (*alcaldes mayores*), those of the Bisayas are governed by military officers (*gobernadores militares y politicos*) of the rank of captain to that of colonel, assisted in most instances by a lieutenant-governor, a civilian, and usually a lawyer, who takes cognizance of all ordinary civil and criminal cases.

The Bisayan group is mostly inhabited by a race resembling, in all essential characteristics, the Tagálog, and other Malayan races of Luzon. Their language may be called a dialect of the Tagálog, though rather harsher in sound, and neither so copious, so refined, nor so subjected to grammatical rules, as this latter idiom. The Bisayan has more Malay words than have the dialects spoken in Luzon. The natives of these islands and those of Luzon imperfectly comprehend each other, though their languages are evidently derived from the same parent stock.

The Bisayas furnish a hardy, seafaring race; but, as a rule, the general tendency to indolence, attributed to the Philippine "Indian," applies, in a perhaps greater degree, to the inhabitants of the whole southern group, and constitutes at present, in the absence of any available means of coercion, one of the principal obstacles to a more rapid extension of agriculture by the introduction of European capital.

The christianized population of the Bisayas may be estimated as follows:—

Samar	118,000
Leyte	115,000
Romblon	16,600
Panay:—	
Capiz	135,000
Iloilo	450,000
Antique	80,000
Cebu and Bohol	385,200
Negros	108,000
Calamianes	18,000
Mindanao:—	
Misamis	44,500
Caraga (Surigao)	15,300
New Guipuzcoa (Bislig and Davao)	11,200
Zamboanga	12,000
Total	1,508,800

This estimate does not include the unsubdued tribes inhabiting the mountains in the interior, some idea of the number of which may be formed from a note of those ascertained to have existed in 1849, in the undernoted provinces:—

Misamis	66,000
Samar	25,964
Leyte (not ascertained).	
Negros	8,545
Panay	13,900
Cebu	4,903
Total	119,312

The largest number of unsubjected tribes (principally Mahomedan) inhabit Mindanao, the total population of which is generally asserted to amount to nearly one million souls.

The island of Panay, advantageously placed towards the centre of the Bisayas group, is distant at its nearest point—that of Potol, in lat. 11° 48′ N., long. 122° W. of Greenwich—180 miles in a right line from Manila. Its shape is nearly triangular, and it has a circumference of about 300 miles. It is the fifth in size of the Philippine Islands, coming in this respect after Luzon, which has a circumference of 1,059 miles; Mindanao, 900; Paragua, 420; and Samar, 390; but, though smaller than the islands just named, it is, next to Luzon, the most populous of the archipelago, if Mindanao, with the doubtful population of independent tribes above-mentioned, be left out of the question.

Panay is divided into the three provinces of Capiz, Antique, and Iloilo, which together contain a population of about 665,000.

Capiz occupies the whole of the northern portion of the coast of Panay, for a distance of seventy-seven miles.

Its limits towards the interior may be defined by a curved line, commencing from a little to the eastward of Point Bulacan, passing by the Pico de Arcangel, in the Siaurágan Mountains, and continued westward to Pandan, on the coast. Its chief town is Capiz, situated on the river of the same name. Though broken towards the southern and western portion by an irregular series of mountain chains, the greater part of the territory of Capiz consists of extensive low-lying plains, which produce rice in great abundance. It possesses a few good harbours, particularly that of Batan; and Capiz itself, situated at the confluence of the rivers Panay and Capiz, affords secure anchorage. Its tribute-paying population is officially reported to be 135,000 souls.

Antique takes up the western side of the island, to an extent of 84 miles—from Point Naso on the south to Pandan on the north—is of triangular shape, and limited on the north by the province of Capiz, on the south and east by that of Iloilo, and on the west by the sea. Antique is very mountainous, and, being comparatively thinly inhabited, does not at present produce much for export, especially as the greater development of its resources is retarded by the want of good harbours, of which it does not possess one along its whole line of coast. At its chief town and port, San José de Buenavista, a breakwater is in process of construction, which, if completed, will give a great impulse to the trade of the province, by enabling vessels to load there at all seasons of the year. At San José foreign whaling and other vessels not unfrequently call for water and fresh provisions. The number of its inhabitants, exclusive of the *remontados* and *monteses*, who occupy the mountainous districts, is computed to amount to 80,000 souls.

Iloilo extends over the south-eastern portion of the island, is also of triangular form, bounded on the north by Capiz, on the west by Antique, and on the south-east by the arm of the sea which separates it from the island of Negros.

This, the largest, richest and most peopled of the three provinces, deserves more particular notice.

Iloilo, its chief town, and the residence of its governor, distant 254 miles in a direct line from Manila, and placed by Spanish hydrographers in lat. 10° 48′ W. of the meridian of San Bernardino, is situated near the south-eastern extremity of the island, close to the sea, on the border of the narrow channel formed by the island of Guimarás, which lies opposite to it at a distance of two miles and a half from the Panay shore.

The town is built principally on low, marshy ground, subject to tidal influence, partly fronting the sea, and partly along the left bank of a creek, or inlet, which runs towards Jaro, and after describing a semicircle again meets the sea near Molo. Although the principal seaport and seat of the government of the province, its population is not so large as that of many of the towns in its vicinity. It does not at present exceed 7,500, while Jaro, Molo and Oton, towns in its immediate neighbourhood, possess 33,000, 15,000 and 20,000 respectively. This comparative scarcity of inhabitants is principally owing to the want of space for further extension on the narrow tongue of land on which the town is chiefly built. This obstacle to its further increase should in time cease to exist, as efficient measures are being taken to draw the population more inland; among others, the erection of a new government house and public offices at a more central point; the contemplated removal of the present church to a more advantageous and open site, beyond the tongue of land alluded to; and the convergence at this place of new and more direct roads (now in course of construction) leading to and from the adjacent populous towns.

Notwithstanding the drawback of limited space, the progress in size and importance of the town has of late years been very marked, while the European residents, who, in 1840, numbered only three, now, in 1857, amount to 31 in Iloilo, and 30 in the remaining towns of the province. A considerable portion of this number arrived during the past two years, and the effect of this increase of Europeans, though their number is so small, is already visible in the construction of new buildings, and projects for the erection of many others. The rise in house property may be illustrated by the fact that the house in which the vice-consulate is established—constructed of wood with a palm-thatched roof—is subject to a rental of 33 dollars per month, or about 80*l*. per annum. The value of land for building lots has also augmented in proportion.

The population of the province is given officially as 511,066; but there is reason to think it considerably exaggerated, and that 400,000, or at most

450,000, would be nearer the real amount.

The harbour of Iloilo, though well protected and naturally good, is not without inconveniences, capable, however, of being obviated with little trouble, and, provided with one of the excellent charts lately issued by the _Comisión Hidrográfica_ (and, if approaching from the north, with a pilot), large vessels may enter with safety.

The island of Guimarás, which is twenty-two miles long by three in breadth, forms in front of Iloilo a sheltered passage, running nearly north and south, of a width varying from two miles and a half to six miles, with deep water and good anchorage. The entrance to this passage from the south is a good deal narrowed by the Oton shoal (_Bajo de Oton_), which stretches for a considerable distance from the Panay shore, and contracts for about a mile in length the available channel at this part to the breadth of about two miles. This, however, will be no obstacle for large ships during the south-west monsoon (especially when the channel is properly buoyed off), the passage being perfectly clear as far as it extends; and with a contrary north-east monsoon they can work or drag through with the tide, keeping well over towards Guimaras, the coast of which is clear with deep water close in, anchoring, if necessary, on the edge of the shoal, which affords good holding-ground, and, being of soft sand, may be safely approached. The whole of this coast, protected as it is by Guimaras, the Panay shore, and, in a considerable degree, by the island of Negros, offers secure anchorage in the north-east monsoon; and situated on the south-west portion of Guimaras, the fine port of Buluanga, or Sta. Ana, of easy access and capable of admitting vessels of the largest tonnage, will afford shelter under almost any circumstances. The approach to the opposite or northern entrance is generally made by the coasting vessels through the chain of small islands (Gigantes, Pan de Azucar, Sicógon, Apiton, &c.), called collectively the _Silanga_, which lie off the north-east coast of Panay and afford an excellent refuge for a considerable distance to the vessels engaged in the trade with Manila and the southernmost Bisayas. But though there is good anchorage among these islands, particularly at Pan de Azucar and Tagú, it would be more prudent for vessels of large burden, in cases where there is no practical acquaintance with the set of the tides and currents, to take the outside channel between the Silanga and the island of Negros. After passing the Calabazas rocks and Pepitas shoal and making the castle or blockhouse of Banate (formerly erected, like many others along the Philippine coasts, for defence against the pirates of the Sooloo Sea), the route is due south until sighting a group of seven remarkable rocks, called the "Seven Sins," for which a direct course should then be made, the lead being kept going to avoid the Iguana Bank (which is well marked off on the charts referred to), and on getting south of the Iloilo Fort vessels of a certain tonnage may enter the creek, or, if too large, should bring up on the east side of the fort, where they are protected from the wind and the strength of the tides. The depth of water on the bar at the entrance to the creek is about five fathoms at low water; but at a short distance farther inside the water shoals to fifteen feet at low water, and then deepens again. The rise and fall being six feet, a vessel of 300 tons, drawing, when loaded, sixteen to eighteen feet, can easily obtain egress with a full cargo. A dredging machine employed to clear away the mud which has been allowed to accumulate at the shallower parts near the entrance, would enable ships of almost any burden to complete their cargoes inside. The *Santa Justa*, a Spanish ship of 700 tons, loaded, in 1851, part of a cargo of tobacco inside the creek, and finished her lading outside.

It should be mentioned that, the banks of the creek being of soft mud, there is little or no risk to be apprehended from grounding. Proceeding about a mile and a half up the creek (which varies in breadth from half a mile to three-quarters of a mile, and affords complete protection from wind and sea), the coasting crafts bring up at the jetties of their respective owners, and have the great advantage of discharging and loading at the stores without the necessity of employing boats.

Beyond this point, the creek stretches as far as Molo. Formerly the coasting vessels used, when necessary, to go on to Molo, but the drawbridge through which they had to pass having got out of repair, and the present bridge (now in very bad condition) affording no means of passage, they remain at Iloilo, to which place the Molo traders have had to transfer their warehouses.

The export trade of Iloilo, hitherto confined to the port of Manila and the adjacent islands, is at present chiefly carried on by four Spanish firms resident at Iloilo and owners of the better class of native craft sailing from this port; but to these are to be added a considerable number of mestizos, or half-castes, principally of Chinese descent, living at the neighbouring towns of Molo and Jaro, several of whom are also owners of vessels, and employ considerable sums in the trade.

The principal products exported are leaf tobacco, sugar, sapan-wood, rice in the husk (or paddy); hemp and hides, besides other articles in lesser quantity, including horns, beche-de-mer, mother-of-pearl shell, beeswax, canes, &c., and a considerable amount of native manufactured goods. Leaf, or unmanufactured tobacco, is at present the article of most importance, and the one which the Spanish traders have found most lucrative. It is purchased by them from the small native growers, and shipped to Manila for exclusive sale to the government, at prices fixed by the factory appraisers, according to the size and quality of the leaf. From Iloilo some 30,000 quintals were shipped last year for Manila, and from Capiz 20,000, giving about 50,000 as the exportable quantity of the leaf produced in Panay per annum.

The export of tobacco to Manila, until the year 1845, did not amount in this province to more than 10,000 quintals per annum; but in that year the agent of a Manila firm having raised the usual low prices given by the Iloilo traders from 10 rials to an average of 20 to 21 rials for the three first qualities, the export, in 1847, had rapidly reached 24,000 quintals.

The attention of the government being directed to its growing importance, it was resolved to institute a system of "Coleccion," through the governor and a staff of collectors, similar to those "Collecciones" that are established at Cagayan, La Union, and Nueva Ecija. By this system, the purchase for, and export to, Manila by private traders, though not positively interdicted (as is the case in the provinces just named), was so much prejudiced and interfered with by the unequal competition with the government (to which the private buyers had ultimately to sell what they shipped), that the total export from Iloilo fell during the six years from 1848 to 1853 from 25,000 to 18,900 quintals. In this latter year the coleccion was withdrawn. In 1853 a company formed at Madrid was allowed the exclusive privilege of the manufacture and export of cigars and leaf tobacco to foreign markets. A large and expensive stone-built factory was erected near Iloilo, the manufacture of cigars organized, and purchases of the leaf effected, and, latterly, the company's operations were extended to the cultivation of the plant in different parts of the province. A clause, however, in its charter rendered it incumbent on the company to furnish the factories at Manila, if required, with a considerable yearly amount both of leaf tobacco and cigars, equal, if necessary, to the amount annually derived in the province from other sources. As a consequence, the requirements made for the Manila factories (purposely augmented, it is said, by the hostility of the then Intendente de Hacienda to the company) were to such an extent as virtually to deprive it of all power to act on its own account; and, after an existence of nearly three years, its embarrassments were such as to compel its extinction, with the loss of a considerable portion of the capital originally sunk. Had the authorities at Manila favoured its development, the result, though necessarily cramped by the defective principle inherent in all monopolies, might have been favourable, as, with the liberty to manufacture for, and ship to, foreign markets, it could have afforded to give good prices, and might have extended the culture of the tobacco plant. It is a suggestive fact in connection with this subject that one of the Europeans formerly in the employ of the company has since had cigars manufactured for local consumption, which he has sold at 8 dollars per thousand, nearly, if not quite, equal in quality to the "Imperiales" occasionally manufactured at the factory at Manila at 25 dollars per thousand.

Since 1853, and coexistent with the company's operations, the purchase and shipment of tobacco by private individuals have been resumed on their original footing; and, while the amount so shipped has steadily, though very gradually, increased, prices have maintained a slight upward tendency. The maximum rates, however, which the local traders can afford to pay the native growers are not high enough to bring about a rapid extension of planting, or induce these latter to give time and labour enough to improve the quality of a plant, the proper culture of which requires special attention, and the application of more capital and intelligence than they have it in their power to bestow. The Iloilo shippers complain of the arbitrary manner in which the classification of qualities is made at Manila, and of the fact that, even after delivery of the tobacco at the government stores, it is held entirely at their risk until examined, repacked and ready for shipment to Spain. The qualities shipped at Iloilo are classed as 1st (of which a very small quantity is produced under the present system), 2nd, 3rd, 4th, and 5th; and any rejected by the examiners at Manila as under the 5th quality is retained and burnt, though no allowance on such portion is made to the vendor. The rates given by the factory for the above qualities are 7·75, 6·75, 5·25, 4, and 3 dollars per quintal respectively. The seedlings are planted out in January, and the greater part of the crop comes forward in May and June. The soil of the greater part of the Bisayas is favourable to the growth of tobacco. The island of Negros formerly produced about 8,000 quintals, of very good quality, which the Iloilo traders, through their agents, were in the habit of purchasing from the independent tribes inhabiting the interior; but the measures taken by the present governor to bring the latter into subjection having resulted last year in the slaughter of several hundreds and the dispersion of the rest, supplies from this source are at present stopped. Cebú produces about 15,000 quintals, of rather inferior quality. At Leyte, particularly in the district of Moasin, tobacco of very excellent quality and colour is grown, but it does not pay to produce in large quantity for export to Manila, and is consequently used almost exclusively in the Bisayas, where it is much appreciated. Samar also grows tobacco for local consumption. The manufacture of cigars is allowed throughout the Bisayas, but not for sale at Manila or elsewhere.

For the present the export of tobacco from Panay and the other islands possesses little direct interest for British or foreign merchants, the transactions with government, as at present conducted, not being of a satisfactory nature. It is, however, almost superfluous to say, that if the existing government monopoly of tobacco were abolished (substituted by a system of farming out lands, a direct territorial tax on the quantity under cultivation, or a duty on exports), and both the free manufacture for, and direct shipment to, a foreign market allowed, the export from Panay would immediately become of great importance to the foreign trade. The soil of a very great portion of the island being well adapted for the cultivation of the plant, the export, under the stimulus of much higher prices and the consequent employment of more and better-directed capital, would be capable of great expansion, particularly if, as would in all probability be the case, the culture were undertaken by Europeans, and the present system of small patches cultivated by natives gave place to estates on a large scale, as in Cuba. The benefits which would accrue to the native population by the opening up of larger sources of industry need not be pointed out.

The subject of the suppression of the existing monopoly is a most important one for the Philippines; and it is to be hoped that the government at Madrid, encouraged by the beneficial results of the abrogation, in 1819, of the monopoly in Cuba, will at no distant date resolve to overcome the difficulties which at present surround the question, particularly as its solution becomes yearly more urgent, and more called for on the part of both Europeans and natives.

Sugar, as an article of export, may be said to be as yet comparatively in the germ. By an abstract taken from notes of province cargoes given daily by the *Boletin Oficial* of Manila, it is seen that nearly 12,000 peculs went forward last year from this province to Manila, of which it may be estimated that about 3,000 were brought over from the Isla de Negros, and sent on to the capital as Iloilo sugar. So great has been the stimulus given by the high prices for this article which have lately ruled, that the quantity exported from Iloilo alone will not fall short of 20,000, or say, with contributions from Negros, about 25,000 peculs, or nearly 1,600 tons; and, were the present rapid extension of planting to continue in the same ratio for three years, the amount exportable would in that time, as there is no want of available land, reach about 80,000 peculs, or 5,000 tons, subject to further augmentation from other sources, should foreign vessels commence loading at this port.[3] At the island of Negros, from whence the voyage occupies from six to ten hours, the soil of which is eminently fertile, and which possesses immense tracts particularly adapted for the growth of sugar, a similar extension of culture is in progress, in spite of the great drawback of the comparative sparseness of its population, which alone prevents it from yielding sugar and hemp in larger proportion than any other province in the Philippines. At present Negros produces about 14,000 peculs, or nearly 900 tons, of sugar, of which more than two-thirds go to Manila direct, and the remainder by way of Iloilo. There is a further available source from whence sugar (in the event of foreign vessels loading at Iloilo) would be derivable at the contiguous island of Cebú, which produces upwards of 90,000 peculs, or 5,695 tons, for the Manila market, and is within easy distance of two to three days' sail from Iloilo.

The effective nature of the stimulus given by the present prices will be comprehended when it is considered that the value of Iloilo sugar, which in previous years up to 1855 had generally ranged from 2 to 2·10 dollars per pecul in the Manila market, is now 5·68¾ dollars per pecul at Manila, against 3·2 to 3·3 dollars, with 25 per cent. for prem. on silver, or equal to 4·06 dollars to 4·21½ dollars here, and as long as the rate obtainable at Manila does not recede below 3 dollars per pecul of 140 lbs., the extension of planting will be continued. Of late years, owing to the disproportionly low prices paid at Manila, sugar planting had in many districts been abandoned as unremunerative, but during the past and present year it has rapidly increased, particularly since the introduction of a more economical kind of furnace, in which the refuse cane is used to some extent in place of the large amount of wood formerly consumed.

The very defective nature of the process employed by the native and mestizo planters does not allow of the production in Iloilo of a superior class of sugar, and all that leaves for Manila may be described as "ordinary unclayed;" but the grain is usually very good, and on undergoing the ulterior processes in England and Australia, it yields a fine strong sugar, and has been much approved of for boiling purposes at the Glasgow refineries. Were a better system of crushing and boiling introduced here, sugar of an excellent quality would be produced, and it is greatly to be desired that a few Europeans with sufficient capital and experience would form estates in this neighbourhood. At present there is not a single iron-mill in the island. The unclayed sugars of the Philippines in ordinary times, even under the present defective and consequently expensive mode of production are held to be the cheapest in the world. The only Europeans now engaged in the cultivation of sugar in this quarter are a French planter, at Negros, who produces an excellent sugar (which always commands upwards of 1 dollar a pecul more than ordinary Iloilo), and a planter of the same nation, in this province, who has lately commenced on a limited scale.

Taking the prices quoted above as a basis (4·21½ dollars here against 5·68¾ dollars at Manila), the difference in favour of this, the place of production, is now 1·47¼ dollar per pecul; but supposing the additional 47¼ cents to be given here by the foreign exporter in order to secure such share of the crop as would be required to load a direct vessel, there would still remain an important saving of 1 dollar per pecul, or say 17½ per cent. less than the prime cost at Manila. The freight to Manila at present charged by the coasting vessels is 50 cents per pecul. The bulk of the sugar crop is delivered from February to March.

Sapan-wood is exported in considerable quantity from the province of Iloilo. It is chiefly produced in the vicinity of the southern coasting towns, Guimbal, Miagao, and San Joaquin (the farthest within twenty miles of Iloilo), from whence the greater part is brought round by sea to Iloilo for exportation to Manila, and the rest shipped direct from Guimbal. Last year, as reported in the imperfect notes of the *Boletin Oficial*, 32,723 peculs, or 2,045 tons, were shipped to Manila, and 789 peculs from Antique.

The high prices lately obtained at Manila have led to the formation of new plantations, which will still further increase the exportable amount. A large quantity is sent on yearly to Singapore and Amoy, and forms the bulk of the cargoes of such vessels as load at Manila for the former port.

The quality of the Iloilo sapan-wood would be much better were the natives to abstain from the practice of cutting down a large portion before the trees are sufficiently grown. When allowed to obtain its proper development, it is said to be quite equal or superior to that of Misamis or Bolinao, at present the best qualities brought to the Manila market. As both sellers and brokers endeavour to deliver the wood as soon as possible after it is cut, the loss in weight on the voyage to Manila is said to be sometimes as much as 12 to 14 per cent. The present price of sapan-wood delivered at Iloilo is, with the addition of 25 per cent. for cost of silver, 1·08 dollar per pecul against the Manila rate of 1·75 to 1·875 dollar, leaving a considerable margin in favour of vessels loading here for a foreign market. The freight to Manila is 31·25 cents per pecul.

Hemp (so called, though in reality the product of a variety of the plantain) produced in Iloilo is chiefly of a long, white fibre, equal to what is known in the London market as "Lupiz," used in the manufacture of the native fabrics, and at present little attention is paid to it as an article of export. But though Iloilo produces little or no surplus hemp, the small coasting craft annually bring here some 350 tons from the neighbouring islands and provinces of Leyte, Samar, Negros, Camarines, and Albay, received at those places in exchange for the paddy and native goods of this province.

Both Leyte and Samar now produce large quantities of excellent hemp for the Manila market, particularly the former island; and the voyage hither throughout the greater part of the year is so short (at present vessels take five to six days in going and two to return) that were the native traders to find a ready market at Iloilo, at prices relatively equivalent to those of Manila, it is more than probable that a considerable additional quantity would be directed to Iloilo instead of to the capital.

At the island of Negros the production is increasing very rapidly, a large quantity having been planted during the past year, several pueblos and districts possessing tracts of upwards of 100,000 and 200,000 plants, which will come into use during the next two years, and as the plant is remarkable for its great propagative power, the obtainable quantity should increase in duplicative ratio every year. The export of hemp from the Isla de Negros amounts at present to 13,000 to 14,000 peculs, or about 850 tons, per annum, chiefly from the port of Dumaguele, on the eastern side of the island.

When it is recollected that in 1831 the whole export of hemp from the Philippines did not amount to more than 346 tons, and that in 1837 it had already reached 3,585 tons, and that during 1856 no less than 22,000 tons left Manila for the United States and Europe, some idea may be formed of the future of this valuable article at the fertile island of Negros, even with the drawback already alluded to of a scanty population.

I am the more inclined to dwell on the facts regarding Negros, as from its close proximity it may almost be considered, in the event of direct exports from Iloilo, as an integral part of the island of Panay. The amount of hemp shipped from Capiz last year was 6,458 peculs, or 400 tons, chiefly, however, of an inferior description made from the fibres of the *pácul*, a wild variety of the plantain. As this inferior hemp, however, commands a remunerative price, I believe the plant producing the genuine article is now being more generally cultivated at Capiz. The rate for hemp here may be quoted at 5·375 dollars, or, with 25 per cent. for cost of silver, 6·715 dollars per pecul, against the Manila rate of 7·75 to 8 dollars. Freight to Manila, 50 cents per pecul.

Rice in the husk, or Paddy, is an important item in the agriculture of Panay, though at present of little actual interest in relation to the foreign trade. The yearly production of the province of Iloilo, though nothing definite is ascertained regarding it, may be supposed to be 850,000 cavans, of which probably 40,000 are exported to the neighbouring islands and Manila. Capiz may produce about 900,000 cavans, and export about 100,000 in the same way. Antique also contributes a considerable quantity for the consumption of the island, and exports upwards of 15,000 cavans. These amounts, however, must be looked upon as guesses at the actual quantities consumed and shipped.

The paddy exported is chiefly conveyed in small schooners (*pancos* and *barotos*) to the neighbouring islands of Leyte and Samar, and also to Camarines and Albay, in exchange for hemp and cocoa-nut oil (the latter obtained at Leyte), which are either brought to Iloilo for sale or taken on to Manila. When prices at Manila leave a sufficient margin (which they generally do throughout the year), some amount of paddy goes in that direction, forming a portion of the cargo of the vessels leaving for the capital.

The paddy shipped from Iloilo is chiefly drawn from the vast plains of Dumangas, Zarraga, Pototan, Santa Barbara and Barotac-viejo. Were a large portion of land brought under cultivation, the increased surplus of this grain would be available for an export to China, in which foreign vessels might be employed, as they frequently are at Sual, in Pangasinan; and it may not unreasonably be surmised that, in the course of time, ships frequenting the port of Iloilo, and proceeding to China, will naturally take part of their cargoes in rice, and thus give a further impetus to its cultivation. At present, owing to the late scarcity of rice in Camarines and Leyte, the price of paddy at Iloilo has risen to 10 rials per province cavan, which is equal to one and a half of the measure (*cavan del rey*) used at Manila. The other articles shipped from Panay likely to be of importance to the direct export trade are:—

Hides—Buffalo and cow, of which the last year's exports to Manila were 128 tons from Iloilo, 60 tons from Capiz, and 24 tons from Antique. Prices here (very high at present) may be quoted at 5 dollars to 8 dollars for buffalo, and 10 dollars to 14 dollars for cow hides, per pecul.

Horns—A limited quantity from the three provinces. Price, from 2 dollars to 3 dollars per pecul.

Cowries—430 cavans were shipped last year from Capiz, 42 from Antique, 33 from Iloilo. This article, formerly worth at Manila 2·50 dollars to 3 dollars per cavan, has lately risen to 15 dollars.

Gum Mastick—2,359 peculs, or 147 tons, were sent last year from Capiz to Manila, where its value is usually from 1·50 dollar to 3 dollars per pecul.

Mother-of-Pearl Shell—A small quantity is obtainable at this port, and at Capiz, chiefly brought from Sooloo, *viâ* Zamboanga, and from the adjacent islands of the Silanga. Quotation here usually about 18 dollars to 22 dollars per pecul.

Rattans or Canes—Used in packing produce at Manila; 401,000 went forward from Capiz in 1856, 104,000 from Iloilo, and 97,000 from Antique.

Mat Bags—Made from the leaf of the sago palm, used also for packing; 155,850 were shipped to Manila, from Capiz, in 1856.

Beeswax—A few peculs are annually shipped from the three provinces to Manila.

Gutta-Percha—Some quantity of this valuable substance has been sent from hence to Manila, but, either owing to adulteration, or ignorance of the proper mode of preparation, it has not obtained an encouraging price. The tree yielding it, called by the Bisayans *nato*, abounds in this province, and in Guimarás, and if it prove to be the real *Isonandra gutta* of the Straits and Borneo, should hereafter become of considerable importance. The monopoly of shipment from Manila, granted to Señor Elio, has an injurious effect on the production of this article.

Timber—for building, and woods, of various descriptions, for furniture, abound in Panay, and the islands of the Silanga and Guimarás are peculiarly rich in valuable trees. From thence are obtained the supplies for Iloilo and the neighbouring towns, and for the construction of vessels, occasionally built at Guimarás, where one of 350 tons is now (1857) on the stocks; but as yet little impression has been made on the immense quantity to be obtained.

Of other articles, which are either not adapted for European markets, or as yet produced in insignificant quantities, I will merely enumerate—cocoa, of excellent quality; arrowroot; vegetable pitch, of which a considerable quantity is sent to Manila; wheat, which grows freely in the elevated districts of the island, and of which 1,125 bags were sent from Iloilo and Antique in 1856; maize, beche-de-mer, dried vegetables (beans, &c., a large amount), sago, cotton, tortoise-shell, deer-skins, ginger and gold-dust.

Gums, dyes and drugs, of various descriptions, abound in Panay, and a scientific examination of the many products of this nature, of which little or no use is made, is a great desideratum. It should be borne in mind that most of the minor articles above-mentioned are also produced by the neighbouring islands, and may be therefore obtainable in increased quantities, should the anticipation of Iloilo becoming in a great measure the emporium of the trade of the Bisayas be realized in future.

Of the mineral wealth of the island little or nothing definite is known. Gold is found in the bed of a river near Abacá, in this province, and near Dumárao, in

Capiz. Iron and quicksilver are said to have been discovered, the former at various places in the island; and coal is reported to exist in Antique; but these are points which have hitherto received little attention. In a journey to the interior, made with the governor of Iloilo, through the Silanga, along the whole north-eastern portion of the province, and as for as the Capiz boundary, near Dumárao, Mr. Loney was shown several specimens of ore, apparently containing a large percentage of iron. With reference to this expedition, Mr. Loney adds from personal experience, his testimony in confirmation of the accounts of the fertility of the island, and the prosperous commercial future which seems to await it. The roads in general are tolerably good until the setting in of the heavy rains from August to October; but there is at present in many cases a want of efficient bridges, which impedes the free transit of produce towards the coast. The island does not afford a superficies large enough for the formation of any considerable streams, and the principal and only important river in this province, the Jalaur, which meets the sea near Dumángas, and by which a large quantity of paddy is conveyed to the coast, and forwarded to Iloilo, is only capable in the dry season of bearing craft of very small burden.

The system of purchases of produce at Iloilo is, as usual in nearly all the provinces, to employ brokers, or *personeros*, who buy the produce from the native and mestizo growers and dealers at the different pueblos in the interior and along the coast, and receive a commission of five per cent. on the amount delivered. It is generally necessary to make advances through these brokers against the incoming crop, in order to secure any quantity, and such payments in advance are always attended with a certain amount of risk. The price of the article to be received is commonly fixed at the time of paying over the advance, and for any overplus of produce received from the grower the current rate at the time of delivery is generally accepted. In the event of a permanent direct trade being established, it is likely that the practice will in time become more assimilated to that which obtains at Manila, *i. e.*, shippers may be able to purchase or contract on the spot from mestizo, Chinese or Spanish holders of produce, either directly or at the expense of a trifling brokerage.

Nearly all payments being made to the natives in silver—as they will seldom agree to receive gold—it is necessary to place funds here in the former coin.

Besides the natural products above mentioned, Panay produces a large quantity of manufactured goods, both for export and home consumption. Of these the greater and more valuable portions, included under the native term *sinamay*, are made of the delicate fibres of the leaf of the pine-apple (*piña*), either pure or mixed with silk imported from China, and a proportion of the finer sorts of British manufactured cotton thread. The process of separating the piña fibres and sorting them in hanks previous to manufacture, and the manufacture itself, requiring a great deal of time and care, the pure piña textures are proportionally dear. Some of the finest sorts are of exquisitely delicate texture. Those mixed with silk, though not so durable, are cheaper, and have of late years been gradually superseding the pure piña fabrics, although these latter are still much worn by the more wealthy natives and mestizos. To such an extent, indeed, is silk from China now imported into this province, that, according to the statement of the principal Chinese trader in this article at Manila, fully 400,000 dollars worth is annually sent to Iloilo from the capital. Latterly the price of silk has risen from 40 to 45 dollars per chinanta of ten catties to 80 and 90 dollars, or say from 450 to 900 dollars per pecul.

The greater part of the piña and mixed piña, silk and cotton fabrics is used for shirts for the men, and short jackets or shirts for the women. The price varies considerably, according to the fineness or coarseness of the texture, and the greater or less amount of mixture, some pieces for the men's shirts costing as much as 7 dollars (the value of which, elaborately embroidered at Manila, is sometimes enhanced to 50 or 100 dollars), and the inferior sorts 50 cents to 2 dollars per piece of 4½ varas. The figured work of these fabrics is generally of European cotton sewing thread or coloured German and British yarn, and the stripes of thread, yarn or coloured and white silk. Textures of a cheaper character are also extensively made of hemp and other fibres, costing two to four rials each. There is also an extensive manufacture of coloured silk and cotton goods for "sarongs" (similar to those, principally of Bugis manufacture, used throughout the Malayan Archipelago), cambayas, and silk and cotton kerchiefs for the head. The better class of silk fabrics are excellent both for solidity of texture and finish. Those of cotton are principally made of German and British dyed twist, and of native yarn manufactured from cotton grown in several districts in this province, and also imported from Luzon. The finer sorts are well and closely woven, and the ordinary kinds of a cheap description adapted for more common use. Trouserings, of cotton and mixed silk and cotton, are manufactured to some extent, but the Manchester and Glasgow printed drills and plain grandrills are fast displacing them as articles of general consumption. Among the other manufactures may be enumerated table-cloths, napkins, towels, coverlets, cotton rugs, &c. Of embroidery work, which enters so largely into the industry of the provinces of Bulacan and Manila, there is little done in Iloilo, with the exception of the working of sprigs of flowers on the lace and network mantillas, which are much used by the female population in attendance at church.

In addition to the goods above mentioned, a considerable amount of coarse fabrics is made of the leaf of the sago palm, of hemp, and of other fibres. These are known in the Manila market as *Saguran, Guináras* and *Medrinaque*, and are shipped to the United States and Spain, and in lesser quantity to England. Saguran and guináras are largely used at the government factories in packing the leaf tobacco forwarded to Spain. Price, from 25 to 37½ dollars per pecul of 7½ to 8 varas. Medrinaque has for some years past been exported in increasing quantity to the United States and Europe, where it is chiefly used for stiffening dresses, linings, &c. This article is principally made at Samar, Leyte and Cebú, from whence, in case of direct export, it will be obtainable for shipment. Present prices in the Manila market for Cebú 20 dollars, Samar 18 dollars, per fifty pieces.

Considering that the Philippines are essentially an agricultural rather than a manufacturing region, the textile productions of Iloilo may be said to have reached a remarkable degree of development. Nothing strikes the attention at the weekly fairs held at the different towns more than the abundance of native goods offered for sale; and the number of looms at work in most of the towns and villages also affords matter for surprise. Almost every family possesses one of these primitive-looking machines, with a single apparatus formed of pieces of bamboo, and, in the majority of the houses of the mestizos and the well-to-do Indians, from six to a dozen looms are kept at work. The total number in this province has been computed at 60,000; and though these figures may rather over-represent the actual quantity, they cannot be much beyond it. All the weaving is done by women, whose wages usually amount to from 1 to 1·50 dollar per month. In general—a practice unfortunately too prevalent among the natives in every branch of labour—these wages are received for many months in advance, and the operatives frequently spend years (become, in fact, virtually slaves for a long period) before paying off an originally trifling debt. There are other workwomen employed at intervals to "set up" the pattern in the loom, who are able to earn from 1 to 1·50 dollar per day in this manner. It should be added that Capiz and Antique also produce, in a lesser degree than Iloilo, a proportion of manufactured goods.

Notwithstanding the increasing introduction of European piece goods into Panay, it is gratifying to observe that the quantity of mixed piña stuffs exported rather augments than otherwise with the gradual addition to the general population and the increased means derived by it from the rapidly progressive development of the resources of the islands. Judging from the values of the quantities taken on in almost every vessel leaving for the port of

Manila, the annual export in that direction would not seem to be at all over-estimated if put down at 400,000 dollars. The goods represented by this amount are not, it should be remarked, used in the city and province of Manila alone, but enter also into the consumption of Pampanga, La Laguna, Camarines and other provinces of Luzon. In addition to the export of piña to the capital, about 30,000 dollars worth of cotton and silk sarongs and handkerchiefs are sent yearly to Camarines. Some quantity is also exported to Leyte and Samar, but anything like an approximate value of the goods so shipped cannot be given. In fact the subject of statistics here has received so little attention, either from the authorities or from the local traders themselves, that on terminating his notice of the principal articles exported from Panay, Mr. Loney regrets to find himself unable to supply a reliable account of their united value. The *Estadistica de Filipinas*, issued in 1855, and compiled at Manila by the *Comision Central*, nominated for that purpose, gives, from data probably obtained from the very imperfect custom-house entries, the following as the value of the imports into Manila from Panay in 1854:—

Iloilo—	*Dollars.*	*Dollars.*
Iloilo	264,416	
Guimbal	39,850	
	——— 304,266	
Capiz—		
Capiz	181,681	
Calwo	114,124	
Jbajay	7,095	
Batan	15,147	
	——— 318,047	
Antique—		
Antique	18,866	
San José	2,925	
Cagayancillo	3,061	
Culasi	1,199	
	——— 26,051	
	648,364	

But the most cursory examination of what must be the probable value of the more important articles exported, even adopting the probably understated quantities given in the preceding remarks, leads to the conclusion that the export to Manila from the province of Iloilo alone must equal or exceed the amount given by the *Estadistica* as the total sum for the provinces.

Presuming the quantities and values to be as undernoted, there will result of

					Dollars.
Piña, silk, hempen and other manufactures					400,000
Tobacco, 30,000 quintals, average 3½ dolls.					105,000
Paddy,	30,000	cavans,		1	30,000
Sugar,	20,000	peculs,	,,	3	,, 60,000
Sapanwood,	33,000		,,	1	,, 33,000
Hemp,	5,000	,,	,,	5½	,, 27,500
Hides,	2,050	,,	,, total value	,,	19,800

253

All other articles roughly valued at   45,000
720,300

To which sum if the exports to other islands and provinces be added, it may be fairly inferred that the total value of exports from Iloilo cannot fall short of 800,000 dollars; an amount which does not seem at all out of proportion to the number of its inhabitants. These figures, if Capiz be put down at 700,000 dollars, and the Antique exports be taken at 70,000 dollars, will give to the yearly exports from Panay an aggregate value of upwards of 1,500,000 dollars.

But even the imperfect data of the *Estadistica* would afford some indication of the rapid rate of increase in the exports from the three provinces. For example—

	Dollars.
1852—value of products from Iloilo, Capiz, and Antique	271,335
1853	302,605
,, ,, ,, ,, ,, ,, ,, ,,	
1864	648,369
,, ,, ,, ,, ,, ,, ,, ,,	

Or an augmentation in 1854 of considerably more than double the amount given in 1852. While on this subject, it may be added that the local custom-house has unfortunately registered no complete details of the exports for 1856, though it has commenced doing so for 1857. These details are, however, relatively of much less importance than those of direct foreign shipments, which will demand future attention.

Mr. Loney thus adverts to the present state of the Iloilo import trade:—

"Although perhaps the greater part of the clothing for the population of Panay is furnished by the native looms, still a large amount of European goods is annually imported from Manila. I estimate that on the average (as far as can be judged where anything like positive data are totally wanting) about 30,000 dollars to 40,000 dollars per month are now brought in goods to the port of Iloilo by the mestizo and Chinese traders, and subsequently disposed of at the larger markets of Jaro, Molo, Oton, Mandurriao, &c., from whence a certain portion finds its way into the interior. This branch of the trade is as yet principally conducted by the mestizo dealers of Molo and Jaro, who, on completing their purchases of native-made goods for the Manila market, embark with them (in numbers of from six to ten, fifteen, and sometimes twenty) in the coasting vessels leaving for the capital. The returns for these speculations they generally bring back in foreign (principally British) manufactures, purchased at cheap rates from the large Chinese shopkeepers at Manila. The sale of these goods by retail here is still conducted in the rather primitive way of conveying them from place to place on certain fixed days. In this way goods that appear to-day at the weekly fair or market of Jaro, are subsequently offered for sale at Molo, Mandurriao, Oton, or Arévalo. They are carried to and from the different pueblos in cumbrous, solid-wheeled vehicles, drawn by buffaloes and oxen, a mode of conveyance which, during the wet season, is attended with a good deal of delay and risk. The Chinese dealers at Molo, and a few small traders at Iloilo, have, however, commenced opening permanent shops, and it is probable that the number of these will gradually increase throughout the province, though, as the fairs are also the central point of attraction for all the products within a certain radius of each pueblo, and thus bring together a large concourse of people, the weekly transfer of piece and other goods from one place to another must still continue to a great extent. There are about thirty Chinese permanently established at Molo (mostly connected with others at Manila, either as partners or agents), and two or three at Jaro. A certain number are also employed in voyaging to and from Manila with goods, after realizing which here they return for a fresh parcel, either taking the returns in money or produce. One of the Chinese traders at Molo, who is well supplied from the capital, sells goods to the amount of some 30,000 dollars or 40,000 dollars a-year. Owing, however, to too much competition among themselves and the other traders, I do not, judging from the prices at which they usually sell, think that their profits are in general at all large. The fact that the mestizo dealers look for their principal profit to the piña goods which they take to Manila, and are comparatively less solicitous to obtain an advance on their return goods, has also a tendency to keep prices low, as compared with Manila rates.

"As is the case in most of the provinces where the Chinese have penetrated, there exists a more or less subdued feeling of hostility towards them on the part of the natives, and a tendency, both among the mestizos and Spanish, to regard them as interlopers. But though the government at Manila has been repeatedly urged to withdraw them from the provinces, and confine their trading operations to Manila alone, it does not seem inclined to adopt a measure which would prove injurious to the general trade of the colony. It is true that if a portion of the Chinese were induced to become agriculturists (for which purpose alone they were originally admitted to the provinces), great benefit would accrue in the shape of an increased outturn of produce; but as yet their numbers in the interior are too few to enable them to cultivate the ground on a large scale, and in small isolated bodies they would not have sufficient security from the ill-will of the natives.

"The principal articles of foreign manufacture imported into this province are —handkerchiefs (printed) of bright attractive colours, wove and printed trouserings, ginghams, fancy cambayas, plain grandrills, white shirtings, gray shirtings and gray longcloths, gray twills (29 inches, both American and English), bleached twills, lawns, white jaco-nets, striped muslins, cotton sewing thread, cotton sarongs, cotton twist, or yarn, and woollens (not in much demand). There is also sale for hardware, glassware and earthenware, and for other minor articles.

"Import duties are leviable at Iloilo on a valuation either by tariff, or according to the market rate at time of entry. They are the same as those charged at Manila, viz.:—

	By foreign ships.	By Spanish ships.
On most descriptions of foreign goods	14 per cent.	7 per cent.
With the following exceptions:—	25	15
Cambayas, ginghams, handkerchiefs, &c., entirely of black, purple, and blue, with or without white grounds	,,	,,
Yarn of same colour	,,	,,
	50	40
	,,	,,
	,,	,,
Ditto, red, yellow, rose and green	free	free
Machinery, gold and silver, plants and seeds	free	free
Made-up clothing, boots, &c.	50	40
	,,	,,
	,,	,,
Bottled ale or porter	25	20
	,,	,,

	"	"
Wine, liquors and vinegar	50	40
	"	"
	"	"
Spirits	60	30
	"	"
	"	"

"Tropical productions, similar to those of the Philippines, are not admitted to consumption, nor fire-arms, without a special licence.

"All goods may be bonded on payment of 1 per cent.

"Export duties on produce of every description to foreign ports are, 3 per cent. by foreign, and 1½ per cent. by Spanish ships, with the following exceptions: —Hemp, 2 per cent. by foreign, and 1½ per cent. by Spanish ships; tortoise-shell, mother-o'-pearl shell, 1 per cent. by foreign, and 1 per cent. by Spanish ships; rice, 4½ per cent. by foreign, and 1½ per cent. by Spanish ships.

"No duties are charged on goods arriving or departing coastwise by coasting vessels.

"Port dues.—No special charges are yet fixed for vessels arriving at Iloilo, but they may be stated as about equivalent to those levied at Manila, viz.:—On foreign vessels arriving and leaving in ballast, 18¾ c. per ton; with cargo inwards or outwards, 34¾ c. per ton; with cargo both inward and outward, 37½ c. per ton.

"Wages are moderate at Iloilo:—Labourers, 12½ c. to 18¾ c. per day; carpenters, 18¾ c. to 25 c. per day; caulkers, 25 c. per day.

"Fresh provisions are obtainable at cheap rates.

"The weights and measures in use for produce are—the quintal, of 4 arrobas, or 100 lbs. Spanish, equal to 101¾ lbs. English; pecul of 100 catties, or 140 lbs. English. The cavan of rice (*cavan de provincia*) is equal to one and a half of the Manila cavan, or *cavan del rey*; it weighs about 190 lbs. English, and measures 8,997 cubic inches. The pesada, by which sapan-wood is sold, weighs 13 arrobas 13 lbs., or nearly 2½ peculs.

"The currency is nominally the same as in Manila, but silver dollars have to be paid for nearly all purchases, gold being of difficult circulation.

"From the preceding outline of the trade of this port, you will gather that at present, with an annual export of about 1,600 tons of sugar, upwards of 2,000 tons of sapan-wood, and 350 to 400 tons of hemp, it is (considering the quantity which the foreign shippers would be able to secure) capable of furnishing cargoes for two foreign vessels of moderate tonnage; and next year, as regards sugar, which will form the bulk of the cargoes of foreign vessels loading here, the supply will probably be doubled. The more important question, however, as regards the foreign trade of Iloilo, is not as to the actual quantity of produce (still so very limited) which this island may furnish, but whether the concentration of produce from the neighbouring islands and provinces will in reality be brought about.

"A review of the facts regarding the southern Philippines would seem to lead to a conclusion in the affirmative. With Leyte and Samar giving a combined annual export of 4,000 tons of hemp, Cebú upwards of 5,000 tons of sugar, Negros a (rapidly expanding) product of about 900 tons of sugar and 800 tons of hemp, and without taking into account the possible supply of hemp which may be drawn from South Camerines and from Albay (which produce by far the largest part of the existing export of hemp from the Philippines, and are, during the north-east monsoon, within a shorter distance of Iloilo than Manila), it seems in no way hazardous to assume that, on relatively equal prices being obtainable here, Iloilo will attract in the course of time a gradually augmenting proportion of the products which now go on to Manila. It may be further conjectured that Misamis (which yields a considerable quantity of remarkably good hemp), Caraga, and the other provinces of Mindanao, may also in time contribute their share to the products obtainable at a port which their traders must pass on their way to Manila, though the full development of the intercourse of the neighbouring islands with Iloilo will greatly depend on the amount of European imports with which this latter port should gradually be able to supply its new customers. The opinion of the natives themselves, though not to be taken as a guide, may still serve in some measure as an index of what may be looked for. In talking on the subject to the owners of the small craft whose cargoes of hemp have been brought to Iloilo, they have frequently said, 'If foreign vessels come here and give higher prices, much more hemp from Leyte and Camarines will come to Iloilo.'

"Cebú producing rice and manufactures for its own consumption, there is at present little communication between it and Iloilo; but it is encouraging to learn that one of the partners of the most enterprising Spanish firm at this place intends proceeding both to Cebú and Leyte, to establish, if practicable, a commercial connection, with the ulterior view of getting both sugar and hemp sent to this quarter.

"It is also a favourable symptom that the trade of the contiguous islands is more and more attracting the attention of some of the foreign firms in Manila. The American houses (generally the first in enterprises of this kind) have already, through Spanish intermedia, established agencies at Negros, Leyte and Cebú, for the purchase of hemp and sugar, and it is stated from Manila, on apparently good authority, that one of them has lately advanced a sum of 170,000 dollars for this purpose, the distribution of which should have a stimulating effect on production, and thus give a collateral aid to the future exports from Iloilo.

"Considering the great advantages which would accrue from the establishment of lines of small merchant steamers between the islands, the fact that the government have lately given orders to commence working the extensive coal districts existing at Cebú is not without importance. The subject of steam communication for the archipelago is attracting attention at Manila, and it is not improbable that in a few years the islands will be connected in this way in a manner which will greatly tend to their advantage.

"It should have been previously mentioned that the voyage from Iloilo to Manila during the north-easterly monsoon (from November to March) usually occupies the better class of square-rigged vessels in the trade from ten to fifteen days, and from four to six days on the return voyage. Owing to the protection afforded by the group of islands forming the Silanga, and by other harbours on the route, vessels do not (as is usually the case between the ports on the northern part of the more exposed coast of Luzon and the capital) lay up during the stormy months from September to November; and communication, though less frequent during these months, is seldom altogether suspended for any length of time with Manila. On the average, a vessel leaves for the capital every eight to twelve days."

I add a few further extracts from a report on the trade of 1858, with which Mr. Loney has favoured me, and which strongly exhibits the growing importance of Iloilo.

"The import trade, in direct connection with British and foreign houses, has increased during the past year to a degree which could not have been anticipated. Formerly it did not exceed 7,000 dollars in amount; but now, during a period of two years, it has reached fully 140,000 dollars, and is likely to increase much more in future as the capabilities of the market for taking off an important quantity of manufactures become more fully known.

"Owing to the existence of a stock of foreign articles at Iloilo, obtainable by the native dealers as a general rule (and as a consequence of the more direct manner in which they reach their hands) at cheaper prices than from the Chinese shops at Manila, many of the native, and even some of the Chinese traders, find the advantage of making their purchases on the spot instead of in Manila, and some of the former have ceased altogether to undergo the expense and loss of time they formerly incurred in proceeding to Manila to lay in their stocks, while others make voyages to the capital less frequently than before, and send on their piña goods under the care of friends or agents; consequently, the trade is beginning to be conducted in a less primitive manner than in previous years, when each small trader brought on his goods himself, purchased at high rates from the Manila shopkeepers. Dealers from Antique, from the island of Negros and from Leyte now also find at Iloilo a stock of goods sufficient to supply their wants. Another beneficial effect is, that those who buy wholesale at Iloilo are enabled to dispose of their goods to the small dealers, or to their agents, who distribute them over the interior, at lower prices than formerly. Goods are thus saleable, owing to this greater cheapness, at places in the interior of the island, where they were formerly rarely bought, and the natural consequence is, a considerable increase of consumption. The concurrent testimony of all the older residents in the province is, that during the last few years a very marked change has taken place in the dress and general exterior appearance of the inhabitants of the larger pueblos, owing in great measure to the comparative facility with which they obtain articles which were formerly either not imported, or the price of which placed them beyond their reach. In the interior of the houses the same change is also observable in the furniture and other arrangements, and the evident wish to add ornamental to the more necessary articles of household uses; and those who are aware how desirable it is, from the peculiarly apathetic nature of the natives, to create in them an ambition for bettering the condition of themselves and their families, or emulating that of others, by placing within their reach the more attractive and useful articles of European production, will at once recognize in these facts the beneficial tendency of increased and cheaper imports.

"With regard to duties derivable from imports, we must consider the more or less remote probability of direct imports from Europe or China to Iloilo. It needs very little acquaintance with the gradual and hesitative processes of trade to be aware of the slowness with which they adapt themselves to new channels of communication. Especially is this the case in reference to these southern islands, from the previous commercial seclusion in which they had been kept—a seclusion so great that it may be safely asserted that the island of Panay, with its 750,000 inhabitants, is scarcely known, by name even, in any of the commercial marts of Europe, America, or even of Asia. Consequently, it affords no ground for surprise that no direct transactions in imports have taken place. It must be recollected that the years 1857–58 have been eminently unfavourable for new commercial enterprises of any kind, owing to the depressed state of trade in all the markets of the world. This state of depression, though still felt, is, however, drawing to a close, and the Iloilo market, among others, will doubtless attract the attention of European manufacturers and capitalists, though some time must necessarily elapse before a sufficient number of shippers can be found to send consignments of such a varied nature and assortment as would be required to make up a cargo to suit the wants of Panay and the neighbouring islands. Already consignments have arrived by way of Manila, which were made up specially for the Iloilo market; and this circumstance, and the fact that the Manchester manufacturers are beginning to take an interest in the Iloilo demand, fully warrant the belief that before long consignments from Europe, by the way of Manila, will take place on an important scale, and pave the way to direct shipments to Iloilo. Though it is almost useless to prognosticate in cases of this kind, where so many circumstances may occur to retard or accelerate the development of a new market, still I have no hesitation in affirming it to be much more than probable, that in the course of two years from this time Spanish vessels will arrive from Liverpool direct, or touching and discharging part of their cargoes at Manila, more particularly as by that time direct exports will have taken place, and the sugar crop be raised to a point which will render it easy for the vessels arriving with piece goods to obtain return cargoes of sugar, sapan-wood and hides, all of which products, it is unnecessary to say, can be obtained at Iloilo much more cheaply than in Manila.

"It is also probable that direct imports from China will take place sooner than from Europe. The employment of raw Shanghai silk is much greater at Iloilo than in any of the other Philippine provinces, and the consumption amounts to fully 30 peculs per month, worth, on an average, 600 dollars, silver, per pecul, or say 18,000 dollars per month.

"The export trade from Iloilo direct to foreign markets is, in fact, evidently the primary event on which the commercial fate, so to speak, of the Bisaya Islands depends. The chief obstacle, in addition to those mentioned above, which has retarded its commencement has been the extreme smallness of the yield of sugar. In 1855–56, the Iloilo crop, including some quantity received from the island of Negros, scarcely reached 12,000 peculs, and, instead of increasing, it had been declining in consequence of the discouraging effect of the miserable price of 1·875 to 2 dollars per pecul of 140 lbs.; all that could be obtained for it after incurring the expense of sending it to Manila. In 1856–57, under the stimulus of higher prices, the yield amounted to 35,000 to 37,000 peculs. In 1857–58, these high prices had a still more stimulating effect on the planting of cane, and it was calculated that the crop would yield at least 50,000 peculs; but an excess of rainy weather reduced the actual outturn to about 30,000. The present crop, however, of 1858–59 has escaped the danger of rain, and it is computed that it will yield about 80,000 peculs from January to July next. Some estimates place it as high as 100,000 peculs, but in this I think there must be exaggeration.

"The yield of sugar at Iloilo (leaving out of the question the crop of Isla de Negros, which is now computed to produce 30,000 peculs, and that of Antique, 20,000, both available for the Iloilo market) having fortunately reached the above amount, direct sugar exports have now become possible, and preparations are made for shipments to Australia direct, during the first months of the ensuing year.

"'To reach the consuming markets by the most direct line, to avoid transshipments and save double freights are objects, commercially, of the highest importance.'[4] And there is an aspect of the matter which renders it still more necessary, as regards the Philippine trade, that these objects should be kept in view. Australia is now, after Great Britain, the most important market for the Philippine sugars, and particularly for the reclayed Bisayan sugars of Iloilo and Cebú, which are there used for refining purposes, and it will most undoubtedly be before long the largest consumer of the sugar of these islands. In 1857 the exports of Iloilo and Cebú sugar from Manila to Australia were 18,178 and 51,519 peculs respectively, while to all the other markets, including Great Britain, they were only 11,519 and 41,699 peculs; and the same year the total export of all kinds of sugar to Australia was even more than to Great Britain, being 17,847 tons, or 285,552 peculs, to the former, against 16,675 tons, or 266,800 peculs, to the latter market. In the present year (1858), the total export from Manila to Australia, owing to a deficiency in the Pampanga crop, and the discouragement caused to the Australian importers by the high prices of 1857, have only reached 9,038 tons, or 145,028 peculs.

"In the meantime Mauritius, Java and Bengal all supply large and increasing quantities of sugar to Australia, and Mauritius in particular, possessing the great advantages of greater proximity (as to time) and of machinery and other appliances far superior to those in use in the Philippines, furnishesthe

Australian market with a large quantity of crystallized and yellow sugars, which are much sought for in Sydney and Melbourne, where the steady increase of population and general wealth augment the demand for high-classed sugars. In 1857 the Australian colonies took 24,000 tons, or 384,000 peculs, of sugar from Mauritius; and the latest accounts anticipate that the shipments this year to the same quarter will be 30,000 tons, or 480,000 peculs. To quote the words of the *Port Louis Commercial Gazette* of August 10th, 1858:—'There is no doubt that the present crop will reach the figures of 240,000,000 lbs., say 120,000 tons' (nearly 2,000,000 peculs); 'but as the Australian colonies took 24,000 of the last crop, we must expect they will take at least 30,000 of this, our crystallized and yellow sugars gaining in estimation there.' The same journal, of the 27th of October, adds, 'This facility of realizing produce at fair prices has given animation to business and has improved the prospects of the colony. There are now 150 vessels in our harbour, loading and discharging for and from different parts of the world. Our marine establishments are busily engaged in repairing vessels of different nations that have been happy to seek refuge here; our vast quays are too small for our commerce; the capacious new stores lately erected, and which embellish our port, are filled with goods and produce; 25,000 immigrants have been added to our population this year, whilst only 6,500 have left. Our public revenue has largely increased—companies are prosperous—cultivation has been extended, sugar machinery and works improved and increased, and private buildings throughout the principal part of the town enlarged and improved in appearance.'

"Fortunately for the Philippines, with respect to their better-appointed rivals —Mauritius, Java and Bengal—the low-graded unclayed sugars of Iloilo, Capiz and Antique, Isla de Negros and Cebú, are, in ordinary times, cheaper than those of either of the latter colonies, and consequently more adapted for refining purposes; but nothing can place in a stronger light than the above facts regarding the export from Mauritius the very great importance of *keeping the way open* for exporting the unclayed Philippine sugars to Australia at the cheapest possible cost to the importers.

"The much greater extent and more than equal fertility of the Philippines, as compared with Mauritius, must, in the end, if no artificial obstacles are again imposed on the production of the former, lead to the development of larger sugar crops than those of the latter colony.

"The results of the opening of the ports of Soerabaya, Samarang, Cheribon, and others in the island of Java are encouraging circumstances, as showing, among other similar examples, of what importance Iloilo, as the central port of the Bisayan Islands, may become. Soerabaya and Samarang (and especially the former), which enjoy a favourable proximity to the chief points of production, now export an immense quantity of produce, and orders for the direct shipment to Europe of rice, sugar, coffee, tobacco and other Javan products are transmitted by electric telegraph by the Batavian houses to their agents at these ports over a distance exceeding 350 miles. I cannot at present do more than briefly allude to the approaching commencement of an export of timber and furniture woods from Iloilo and Antique to China. The Spanish ship *Santa Justa* loaded a large cargo of wood this year for Hong Kong, which has lately been sold at 63½ cents per foot. Since then, in anticipation of the demand for the rebuilding of Canton, the price has risen in Hong Kong, and arrangements are being made for the charter of a large vessel, either Spanish or foreign, to convey other cargoes to China; and there is every prospect of there being, before long, an active traffic in this article, which, as before noticed, is of excellent quality, abundant, cheap, and easily accessible near Iloilo, and at the adjoining province of Antique.

"It is recommended that vessels making the voyage to Iloilo from Australia, or any place to the south of the Philippines, should, during the S.W. monsoon, enter the archipelago between the islands of Basilan and Zamboanga, and, on passing Point Batalampon, keep well up to Point Gorda, and make the Murcielagos Island, so as to avoid being driven to the westward by the strong currents setting from off the Mindanao coast during both monsoons.

"Pending the N.E. monsoon, the best course is to make a *détour* to the east of the Philippines, and enter the archipelago by the Straits of San Bernardino. The straits should be entered by Samar and Masbate. Vessels bound from Manila or northern ports may proceed through the Mindoro passage, but they should consult Don Claudio Montero's charts. After passing Tablas and Romblon (an excellent harbour there), make for the Silanga Islands, a good mark for which is the high conical island called Sugar Loaf (Pan de Azucar). During the N.E. monsoon vessels should keep between the islands of Jintotolo and the larger Zapato (Shoe Island), but during the S.W. pass between Oliuaya and the smaller Zapato. The best channel is between Sicogon and Calaguan, but the outer and broader passage between the groups of islands and that of Negros is preferable for large ships. There is safe anchorage through the inner route. At Bacuan and Apiton supplies are to be found.

"The tide through the Silanga Islands and Seven Sins flows at the rate of three to four miles an hour—from the Seven Sins to Iloilo often at six to seven miles an hour."

Commercial prosperity is so intimately connected with general improvement and the increase of human happiness, that one cannot but look with interest upon the results of any legislation which removes the trammels from trade and gives encouragement to industry, and the island of Panay may be considered a promising field for the future. The latest accounts report that the planting of cane has been extended very rapidly in this province, owing to the continuance of high prices for sugar, and also to the fact of the direct export trade to Australia having commenced. Planters now see that the arrival of foreign vessels will lead to a permanent demand for their sugars at prices which will pay them better than those formerly obtainable for the Manila market, from whence, before the opening of the port of Iloilo to foreign trade, all the sugar of this and the neighbouring provinces had to be shipped at a great additional expense in heavy coasting freight, landing and reshipping charges, sea risk, commission, brokerage, &c., all of which are now avoided by direct shipment at the place of production.

"The stimulus given to planting has resulted this year in an increase in the yield to 60,000 peculs (3,750 tons), and, judging from the amount of cane planted for next season's crop, it is fully anticipated that in 1860 about 140,000 peculs (7,500 tons) will be produced, without counting on the quantity yielded by the neighbouring provinces of Antique (30,000 peculs) and the island of Negros (35,000 to 40,000 peculs), from both of which places sugar is brought and exported.

"The difference in the cost of sugar at Iloilo and at Manila is at present 2*l.* 16*s.* 5*d.* per ton, free on board; as will be seen from the following:—

COMPARATIVE COST.

		Dollars.
At Manila, 23rd April, 1859.		
1 ton = 16 peculs, at 3·87½ dollars		62·00
Export duty, at 3 per cent.	1·86	
Receiving, rebagging and shipping, 27 cents per pecul	4·32	
	——	6·18
		68·18
Commission (if in Funds), 2½ per cent.		1·70
Cost free on board at Manila		69·88
" " " " Iloilo		55·71
" " " " "		
Difference		14·17

265

1 ton = 16 peculs, at 2·75 dollars		44·00
Export duty, 3 per cent.	1·32	
Receiving, bagging and shipping, 20 cents per pecul (no boat hire is incurred at Iloilo)	3·20	
	——4·52	
	48·52	
Commission, 2½ per cent.	1·21	
	49·73	
12 per cent., cost of silver	5·98	
Cost at Iloilo, free on board	55·71	
Difference, 14·17 dolls., equal at exchange 4s. d. to	£3 1 5	
Less for additional freight payable per ton, in engaging a vessel at Manila to load at Iloilo, say	0 5 0	
Costs per ton, less at Iloilo	£2 16 5	

"The island of Panay, of which Iloilo is the chief port, is divided into the three provinces of Iloilo, Capiz, and Antique, which contain respectively 527,970, 143,713, and 77,639 inhabitants, or a total of 749,322, according to the official returns of 1858.

    "British Vice-Consulate for Panay,
       "*Iloilo, 2nd May, 1859.* "N. LONEY."

Notwithstanding the favourable prospects for commerce at Iloilo, little or nothing has been done for the improvement of the port or for facilitating the extension of its trade. There is no buoy, no light, no indication of dangerous places, though the Oton shoal is extending itself, and it is of the greatest importance that the safe channel should be pointed out to navigators. The latest Admiralty instructions (1859) are as follow:—

"Port Iloilo, situated on the southern shore of Panay Island, though well protected and naturally good, is not without certain inconveniences, capable, however, of being easily obviated; provided with a good chart, and if approaching from the northward with a pilot, large vessels may enter with safety.

"The depth of water on the bar at the entrance to the creek or river Iloilo is about five fathoms at low water, but at a short distance within it decreases to fifteen feet, and then deepens again. The rise of tide being six feet, a vessel drawing sixteen to eighteen feet can easily enter or leave; and when, as is proposed, a dredging-machine is employed to clear away the mud which has been allowed to accumulate at the shallower parts near the entrance, vessels of almost any burden will be able to complete their cargoes inside. A Spanish ship of 700 tons, in 1857, loaded part of a cargo of tobacco inside the creek, and finished the lading outside.

"The banks of the creek being of soft mud, there is little or no risk to be apprehended from grounding. Proceeding about a mile and a half up the creek, which varies in breadth from one-half to three-quarters of a mile, the coasting craft bring up at the jetties of their respective owners, and have the great advantage of discharging and loading at the stores without employing boats. Beyond this point the creek reaches as far as Molo, to which place coasting vessels formerly could proceed by passing through a drawbridge. This got out of repair, and the present bridge affording no means of passage, they remain at Iloilo, where the Molo traders have had to transfer their storehouses. The works of a new moveable bridge, to allow vessels to pass, have, however, already been commenced.

"The island of Guimaras forms, in front of Iloilo, a sheltered passage, running nearly north and south, of a breadth varying from two miles and a half to six miles, with deep water and good anchorage. The southern entrance to this passage is much narrowed by the Oton Bank, which extends a considerable distance from the Panay shore, and contracts for about a mile the available channel at this port to the breadth of about two miles. This shoal is fast becoming an island. There is, however, no obstacle to large vessels during the north-west monsoon (especially as the channel is to be buoyed), the passage being quite clear, and in the north-east monsoon they can work or drop through with the tide, keeping well over towards Guimaras (the coast of which is clear, with deep waters quite close in), anchoring, if necessary, on the edge of the shoal, which affords good holding-ground and may be safely approached. The whole of this part of the coast is, in fact, safe anchorage during the north-east monsoon.

"If blowing hard in the southern channel to Iloilo, a vessel may proceed to the port of Bulnagar, or Santa Ana, on the south-west side of Guimaras, which is of easy access, and capable of admitting vessels of the largest tonnage, and it affords good shelter under almost any circumstances.

"The approach from the northward to the northern entrance to Iloilo is generally made by the coasting craft through the small, richly wooded islands Gigantes, Sicogon, Pan de Azucar, Apiton, &c., called collectively the Silanga, which lie off the north-east coast of Panay, and afford an admirable refuge for a considerable distance to the vessels engaged in the trade with Manila and the southernmost Bisangas. Though, however, there is excellent anchorage among these islands, particularly at Pan de Azucar and Tagal, it would be most prudent for large ships, in cases where there is no practical acquaintance with the set of the tides, currents, &c., to take the outside channel between the Silanga and the island of Negros.

"After passing the Calabazos rocks and Papitas shoal, and sighting the block-house of Banate" (erected, like many others along the Philippine coasts, for defence against the pirates of the Sulu Sea), "the course is due south, until sighting a group of seven remarkable rocks, called the Seven Sins, which lie between the north end of Guimaras and the Panay shore; a direct course for them should then be made, taking care to keep the lead going to avoid the Iguana Bank. Vessels of proper draught may enter the creek, or, if too large, should bring up on the east side of the fort, where they are protected from the wind and strength of the tide.

"A lighthouse, for exhibiting a fixed light, is to be erected on the Seven Sins, and another on Dumangas Point. Buoys are also to be laid down along the channel near the Iguana and Oton shoals."[5]

The latest report on the navigation of the port of Iloilo is given in the note below.[6]

Iloilo has great facilities for the introduction of wharves, piers and landing-places, but none have been constructed. The entrance to the river, and, indeed, the whole of its course, might be easily dredged, hut little or nothing is done for the removal of the accumulating mud.

1

Archbishop Hilarion says:—"There are multitudes of pueblos, such as Argao, Dalaguete, Boljoon in Zebu, and many in the province of Iloilo, where it would be difficult to find either a boy or girl unable to read or write, which is more than can be said for many of the cities of the Peninsula."—(Answer to Manila Deputation.)

2

Among the arts by which pernicious legislation is defeated, a curious example is presented in the Philippine Islands. White cotton twist being prohibited in the interest of certain home producers, it is found to be more economical to import yellow and green twist, which is allowed to enter, and it is afterwards converted to white by extracting the colour, which is easily accomplished by steeping the thread in a strong infusion of lime.

3

In 1859 it is likely to amount to from 3,000 to 3,500 tons.

4

Quoted from Sir J. Bowring's letter to N. Loney of Aug. 3, 1858.

5

The track of the Spanish discovery ships *Atrevida* and *Descubierta* passes over it. See Admiralty chart of St. Bernardino Strait and parts adjacent, No. 2,577; scale, degree = 6 inches.

6

Vessels bound to Iloilo by the southern passage, if in the N.E. monsoon, should, when to the northward of Point Guinad, beat up along the coast of Guimaras. In April, 1859, in the barque *Camilla*, from Manila to Iloilo, I had soundings much farther to the S.W. than are laid down on the Spanish charts. With Point Guinad bearing south, and Point Balingasag bearing east, I had from seven to nine fathoms water, with soft ground. Stood to the N.W., had regular soundings seven fathoms.

When five or six miles off shore, had four fathoms, tacked inshore, and brought up for the night, Point Cabalig bearing N.E. two miles, eight fathoms water; good holding-ground, soundings deepening to twenty fathoms when one mile off shore.

Point Cabalig and Point Bondulan, when bearing N.E., form two very prominent headlands, which are not shown on the Spanish charts I had. With common precaution there is no danger whatever in approaching the port of Iloilo by keeping the coast of Guimaras close inboard from Point Cabalig until nearly abreast the fort, which will clear the Oton Bank. Even should a vessel ground, she will receive no damage, and can be easily got off, as the bottom is quite soft. When the fort bears S.W. by W. one mile, the channel to Iloilo is then open, and with a flood-tide keep the N.E. point close on board. When past it, keep more over to the other shore, where there are from three and a half to three fathoms water close to the shore, and two fathoms at low water. The port of Iloilo is a perfect dock formed by nature. Vessels lay alongside the wharf, where there are two and a half fathoms at high water, and two fathoms at low water, and every facility for discharging and loading. I discharged 200 tons of ballast and took in 300 tons of sugar within nine days. Labour and fresh provisions are very moderate.

Iloilo, 4th May, 1859. (Signed) J. H. PRITCHARD.

Barque *Camilla.*

CHAPTER XXVI.

SUAL.

The province of Pangasinan consists principally of an extensive plain, or, rather, of a very gradual descent from the mountains where the Igorrote Indians dwell, and extending to those of Zambales. The roads are generally good and have trees planted by their sides, and the lands are rich and fruitful. Many rivers descend from the hills and are used for the conveyance of timber, rattans, and other forest productions. The Igorrotes collect gold in the mountain streams, especially in the neighbourhood of Asingan. Large herds of wild buffaloes, oxen, deer and pigs, are found on the hills, but little attended to by the natives. The fertility of the lands will give a crop of sugar and of rice in the same year. The coast and lakes abound with fish, of which, as of salt, cocoa-nut oil and sugar, there is a considerable exportation. Hides are tanned for the Manila market. Ship-building is an important branch of industry, especially on the Agno River. Multitudes of the women are employed in making straw hats, cigar-cases and other articles, of the fibres of various vegetables, some of great fineness and selling for high prices—a cigar-case is sometimes valued at an ounce of gold. Mats, plain and ornamented, are also manufactured for use and for sale. It is said that the Indian, with no other instrument than his knife for all his domestic needs, and his plough for his field labours, supplies himself with every object of desire.

Women are proud of having woven and embroidered the garments worn by their husbands and their children, and they present a gay appearance on days of festivity. In the year 1755 there was a serious insurrection against Spanish rule, and again in the year 1762, when the English took Manila; but both were subdued, though the population was diminished to the extent of 20,000 by these outbreaks. Two distinct idioms are spoken in the province, the aboriginal Pangasinan people being distinct from the races which penetrated from Ilocos. The Dominican friars exercise the principal ecclesiastical authority in the province.

On our leaving Iloilo, after three days' steaming, and sighting Nasog and the Isla Verde, which had been recommended to us as a preferable course to that of the outer passage by which we had come down, we returned to Manila again to enjoy the hospitalities of the palace of the Governor and the attentions of my friend Colonel Trasierra, in whose hands I had been so kindly placed. We arrived on the *Dia de los Reyes* (day of the kings), one of formal reception at court. In the evening we took a long ride into the country as far as the province of Bulacan, which is divided from that of Tondo by a handsome stone bridge over a branch of the Pampanga River. The question of going by land to Lingayen, which can in favourable circumstances be accomplished in a day, the distance being thirty leagues, was discussed, but the state of the roads not being satisfactory, and the delay consequently uncertain, I determined again to take ship, and on the second day of our voyage we anchored at Sual. The captain of the port came out to pilot us into the harbour, in the middle of which is a dangerous rock not laid down in many of the charts. The narrowness of the passage requires much precaution, but once anchored, it is a very safe and well-sheltered, though small harbour. The appearance of Sual disappointed us; a few scattered dwellings, the church and the custom-house, did not look very promising. On landing, however, the musicians of the pueblo came to escort us with their band, and we learnt that all the authorities were at Lingayen, a few miles off; but a courier was immediately despatched to announce our arrival, and, as a specimen of the language, I give a copy of the receipt he brought back to show that his mission had been properly fulfilled:—

"Recibido del Conductor de S. Idro (San Isidro) alioncio (á las once?) Castilio so sagay agangan cá Sogenti amar som pal ed Señor Aldi (Alcalde) màior sin mabidia pasodo à lacho (à las ocho) ed Labi Martes ed pitcha 11 de Eniro de 1859.

"JUAN GABRIL."

Meaning, that having started at eight o'clock from San Isidro, the despatch was delivered at eleven o'clock to the alcalde.

Carriages having been provided for our conveyance to the seat of government (Lingayen), we started at early day for the convent at San Isidro, which is on the left bank of the Agno, a fine river, affording great facilities for navigation, and presenting charming points of scenery on its banks, with the beauties of which we amused ourselves until preparations for a procession were seen, and the sound of music was heard from the opposite shore; upon which we embarked, and found our Indian escorts, with comfortable carriages and sprightly horses, and their accustomed display, waiting to receive us, the roads and houses adorned as usual, and everything bearing marks of gaiety and good-will. Tropical fruit-trees are seen all along the line of the road, through which the Indian cabanas prettily peep; the women and children in their gay dress giving a picturesque and varied character to the scene. The windows and platforms before the houses were crowded with spectators, who seemed greatly delighted as from time to time we recognized their courtesies or admired some flag more demonstrative or more decorated than the rest. We entered one or two of the ship-building yards, and our naval officials expressed their satisfaction with the state of naval architecture among the natives. One vessel on the stocks was of 350 tons. An Indian ship-builder, who was introduced to us as being remarkable for mechanical genius, came from some distance to ask permission from Captain Vansittart to visit the *Magicienne*, and to instruct himself in matters connected with the application of steam-engines to navigation, and to discover any other improvements of which he expected a British ship of war to bear about the evidence. The leave, which was very humbly asked, was very courteously given; on obtaining which the Indian was trotted off in his carriage without losing a moment. The abundance, adjacency, excellence and cheapness of the materials on the banks of the Agno give it great advantages for the construction of vessels, but the bar is a great obstacle against their getting to sea.

We were met on the road by the alcalde mayor, and I entered his carriage. The superior Spanish officials carry a cane with a gold head and a silk tassel as a mark of their authority; and we galloped away to Lingayen, the cabazera of the province. It has a population of 23,000 souls. The roads were good, except in one part where the Agno had made itself a new channel, and there the horses had some difficulty in dragging the carriage through the sand. We came upon the coast, and the waves were dashing with foaming impetuosity, as if tempest-vexed, upon the shore; but joining again the principal causeway, we pursued our journey without interruption. We had been accompanied by the excellent Vice-Consul Don José de Bosch and Friar Gabriel, who was everywhere our guardian and guide. The vice-consul was thoroughly cognizant of all commercial matters, and furnished me with the information I sought. The friar was delighted to pour out his stores of local knowledge, and they were great, while the alcalde, Señor Combas, was in all things kind, considerate and communicative. In fact, it was impossible not to feel at home when everybody was contributing to amuse, interest and instruct. We visited several of the pueblos in the neighbourhood, and at Calasiao, which has 18,000 inhabitants, the gobernadorcillo brought us specimens of the manufactures of the place, and pressed a fine straw hat on my acceptance, while the good Friar Gabriel insisted on every one of our party carrying away a cigar-case. What we had seen elsewhere was repeated in the pueblos through which we passed, in each of which the friars and the principalia were on the *qui vive*, not only for our comfort and accommodation, but to do us all honour. We returned to Lingayen at sunset, and the good father summoned us to dine with him the following day, on which occasion he said he would do his best to show us what his convent could produce. And certainly nothing was wanting. The tables were crowded with numerous guests, and covered with abundant supplies of substantial and decorative dishes. I imagine the father must have drawn on all the resources of the community, for the meats and drinks, the plate and the porcelain, decanters and glasses, and all the paraphernalia of a handsome public dinner, were there, and there was no small amount of fun and jollity, the padre taking the lead.

Father Gabriel boasted of the immense capabilities of the river Agno. It flows through a large portion of the province of Pangasinan, and was navigable for a great distance in its wanderings. He sketched its course upon paper, and pointed out the many pueblos which it visited. The misfortune was, it had a terrible bar, and could not be navigated from or into the sea. The river is certainly one of considerable depth, and of great beauty, having its source in the Cordillera of Caraballes in the province of Abra, amidst wild mountains, and receiving, in its flowing course, many confluent streams. Between San Isidro and Lingayen there was much ship-building on its banks, and a busy Indian population. On the shores were fine forest trees ready for the hand of the woodman, materials for cordage, bamboos and canes, which are brought down by the wild tribes of Igorrotes. It is said that much gold is found in the sand and mud of the river. Many attempts have been made by the Spaniards, and especially by the friars, to conquer, civilize and christianize the wild tenants of the rough and craggy regions, but with little success. Their numbers are increased by criminals escaping from justice, and who seek and find refuge in the least accessible parts of Luzon.

Father Gabriel, who has greatly interested himself in developing the commercial resources of Sual, which he called his "port," expressed a confident expectation that the establishment of foreign trade and the visits of shipping for cargoes, would induce the natives to bring down their produce and open the way to the influences of improvement.

We found it necessary to prepare for our departure, but our good friends had determined, as we had come by land, we should return by water, and an aquatic procession, with flags and music, was put in motion. The sky lowered, the rain fell in tropical torrents, and the musicians and other actors and spectators dispersed; nothing discouraged, however, after a delay of two hours, sunshine brought them out again. The boats were put in requisition, the bands of music reassembled, and we embarked on the river Agno. All went on pleasantly and perfectly for an hour, when a drenching storm compelled me to leave the open barge in which I was, and to seek the shelter of one of the covered boats. Many of our companions were as thoroughly wetted as if they had been dragged through the water, and we reached San Isidro as if escaped from wreck. There we sought dry garments, and the friars' wardrobes were largely drawn on for our comforts. Grotesque, indeed, were the figures and drapery of many, and a humorous sketcher might have made excellent capital out of the laughing groups. Some got carriages, some horses, and some disappointment, to help us to Sual, where a handsome dinner was provided at the custom-house by the vice-consul. The harbour-master broke out into poetry in honour of the British flag, and *gloria* and *Victoria* rhymed in to the delectation of the guests, and to the echoes of the walls. Our captain was inspired, and harangued our hospitable hosts in answer to the warm *brindis* of the company. The Indians had been studying our national song, and for the first time the noble air of "God save the Queen" was heard in the pueblo of Sual. It was late when we got on board the *Magicienne*, but before our departure on the following day, the authorities, the vice-consul and the friar, with many attendants, were on board to give us a *despedida* as kind as our welcome had been cordial. They brought various presents as souvenirs, and a lilliputian midshipman, who had excited the interest and admiration of the visitors, was specially summoned that he might receive a cigar-case from the hands of Padre Gabriel. As soon as they left, our anchor was raised and we steamed away from Pangasinan and the Philippines. It would be strange, indeed, if we took not with us a grateful memory of what we had seen.

Comintang de la Conquista.

INDIAN SONG OF THE PHILIPPINES.

(FROM MALLAT).

[MIDI | MusiScore]

Si-nor a un Cay-a   sa san-da-ig   di   gan

ang may du sa ni tong a guing ca hi ra

pan

Di mo na ni li ñgot

pi na lu ñgai lu ñgai   pag sin ta sa i yong va tang ca li lo

han   di mo na ni lin ñgot

pi na lu ñgai lu ñgai pag sin ta sa - i yong va

lang ca li lo han,

II.

Signos at planetas nañga saan cayo
Yoao cametayan ñgaioy sumaclodo
Anhin coi ang huhay sa pamahong ito
Valaring halaga oong ang sintay lito.

III.